THE OUTRIDER CHRONICLES

The Ring of Halcyon

PATRICIA REAMY

Carpenter's Son Publishing

Published by Carpenter's Son Publishing, Franklin, Tennessee.

Published in association with Larry Carpenter of Christian Book Services, LLC.
www.christianbookservices.com

Cover and Interior Design by Suzanne Lawing

Edited by Tammy Kling

Printed in the United States of America

978-1-942587-01-9

ACKNOWLEDGEMENTS

First and foremost, to my Lord and Savior Jesus Christ. Without You, Lord, my life would have no purpose or light. To You I give all the honor and glory.

To my dear friend Diane, who is dancing and praising at our maker's right hand. This book that you never got to see finished is for you.

To Carolyn—thank you for being a wonderful mentor and leader to me. I am forever grateful for the support and advice you have given me from the first day we have known each other.

To Pastors Mike and Vicki Hankins and my CitC friends and family — I thank you for keeping the Bible real for me. Your support and love is more than words can express.

And finally, to my husband, Mark, who has given me the love, laughter, joy, and encouragement that has kept me going, I love you so much.

"I remember my affliction and my wandering,
the bitterness and the gall.
I well remember them,
and my soul is downcast within me.
Yet this I call to mind
and therefore I have hope:

Because of the Lord's great love we are not consumed,
for his compassions never fail.
They are new every morning;
great is your faithfulness."

—LAMENTATIONS 3:20-23

PROLOGUE

Many generations ago from the times of Joshua in the Old Testament, God raised up an army of men devoted to serving Him. As the Bible recounts, His army increased God's territory and struck fear among the enemies. Most importantly, they protected His children from harm.

Over the years, God continued to use this army to protect His people. Chosen to serve, the Outriders evolved into an elite group of warriors that are guided by the Holy Spirit to escort and protect individuals from attacks from demons.

But as human nature would dictate, not all that serve in the organization do so humbly. A group within believed that their protection should come with a cost, paid by the recipient of their service. Those that remained faithful to the original calling soon found themselves persecuted by those who now allowed greed and money to become their god.

The leader of the organization, chief overseer Isaac Rosenthal, tried to restore the organization, only to have one of his trusted overseers usurp him. At one point in the struggle, Isaac disappeared, and with him, the great powers that God had bestowed on the chosen leader of his warriors: powers to impart gifts from God to aid the Outriders in their battles.

Two factions arose from the original organization: the Old Guard, who continue to stay true to God's calling in their lives; and the Tempest, who have decided to allow money and greed rule their lives. Despite the modern-day setting, the supernatural battles between God's warriors and the dominion of the devil happen with little of the contemporary world taking notice.

This is the continuing story of the Old Guard, and of one particular warrior named Ariana and her friends.

CHAPTER ONE

The streetlights cast shadows around Ari. She gripped her gun at the ready, flexing her fingers as she slowly peered from behind a corner. Dressed in a worn black leather jacket, she briefly looked back at one of the targets her teammate had just subdued.

A willowy blonde Outrider named Christina picked up the person by the shoulders and dragged them into the privacy of a door jam. Ari turned around and focused on her assigned task. She observed a third floor window of a building across the street. She noted the silhouette of an armed figure when the person occasionally peeked out the window.

Ari backed up and looked around for options to get closer. She scanned for a location for a good vantage point to kill their intended target. Her dark brown hair stood tossed haphazardly into a chaotic mass that swept to long bangs. A stark white streak of hair fell from the top of her head and into Ari's eyes. She blew at her silver bangs, moving them to a less bothersome location. Ari yawned and shook her head trying to wake up. *Sleep. After all this, I need sleep.*

Her eyes followed a series of pipes running up the side of a two-story building to the roof. A one-story building stood between this structure and the target's apartment, but it wouldn't obstruct her view. The shot would be a long one, and without the slightest breeze in the air, she knew she could do it. Ari smiled to herself.

Silently she signaled to her Outrider partners Christina and Mike that she would climb the side of the building. Mike knelt over another one of their deceased targets, shot in the chest. Muscular and sporting dark, wavy spiked hair and a gray t-shirt, he nodded. Ari glanced around the corner before she ran across the street to the building.

Ari put her gun back into the holster, firmly grasped one of the pipes, and breathed in deep. She shimmied up the pipes, stretching her legs out, giving her hands leverage. She hoisted herself over the top of the flat roof and briefly caught her breath before signaling to Christina the okay sign. Hunched over, Ari ran to the far side of the roof and spied on the occupants of the third floor in the building across the street. She peeked over the short, decorative wall of her roof observation point and could clearly see the room and its occupants: three armed guards and her main target, who sat at a table.

Quickly ducking back down, Ari moved away to the side and leaned against the short wall. *Lord, Your will, not mine . . . For Your kingdom . . .* She prepped her weapon and moved back to the wall, once again peering over the edge. Ari saw her opportunity. She breathed out and held her breath, and then briefly aimed . . .

Before her target knew what happened, the shot hit his torso over his heart. He clutched his chest at the point of pain and doubled over. He opened his hand slowly, and a look of shock overtook his face when he saw blue paint on his hand and the same color paint spot on his shirt, right over where his heart was located. He looked around to see where it came from and frowned. The others in the room looked around, and Ari could hear them scramble and yell at each other. She chuckled to herself.

Chaos ensued from the room. From the street, Mike added three orange-colored paint splatters to one of the other targets. Ari peered over the wall again and aimed at her next victim. One of the guards of the now deceased target caught sight of her. In the brief moment that it took that bodyguard to reach for his weapon, Ari quickly changed her aim to a more immediate threat. She shot another guard in another window, square on her chest. Quickly returning her gun back to its original target, Ari squeezed out a shot but missed. Her blue paint ball made a solid swack noise as it hit the window frame. She frowned as she huddled behind a wall. Paint balls whizzed over her head and splattered on a billboard behind her.

From the ground, Mike caught the elusive shooter's shoulder with another orange paint ball. As the opponent checked his shoulder, he briefly stepped out from the cover of the wall. Ari's paint ball caught him between the eyes of his goggles. Christina shot the last armed man as he fled out to the alley.

Ari paused briefly and closed her eyes. *Thank you, Jesus for another victory. I give You all the honor and glory.* Ari signaled to her team the targets were "killed" and slid down the pipes. She met up with Mike and Christina on the street. The trio fist-bumped as they walked back to the entrance of the training room.

As the exercise came to an end, a bell sounded and the utility lights came up, flooding the entire cavernous room with bright floodlights. The trio placed their paint guns and face guards on a table along with their holsters. Their targets—students in Outrider training—walked into view. Mike and Ari smiled. Every one of the six students had what would be considered clean kill shots splattered on their bodies. They all walked up to the table and threw their gear on the table, seemingly frustrated and sulking in their defeat.

As Mike feigned a cough to cover his smirk, Ari unzipped her leather jacket and sat back in her chair. Her fingers ran casually through her spiked, short dark brown hair, being careful to pull strands of her graying bangs down over one eye.

Like her peers, Ari never had an expectation to be recognized for her work. However, her exceptional skills were noticed by her coworkers. As her mentor Sam had told her many times, respect has to be earned. The students gave Ari a wide berth, respecting her like employees around the CEO of their company.

They all sat down at a long table by the entrance of the room to be debriefed. Ari glanced back at the simulated city street where they just finished their exercise. The buildings and streets seemed real enough for the scenario. They were just cinderblock buildings, but they were painted to seem to be brick and stone. The cavernous four-story training room became an engineering feat underground, deep inside the mountain of the Old Guard's headquarters.

Nicknamed "Hollywood" by her peers, Ari's former safe house in the hills of the greater Los Angeles area had been transformed into a multi-functional and multi-level facility. The view of the distant city lights flickered unobstructed below the ridge and hill where the house stood; no other houses were within view. No one would ever guess that a small working community with offices and living quarters thrived inside of the mountainside underneath the original home.

Everyone's heads turned as Ari's friend and the class's instructor Dave walked into the room. Blonde and trim like his wife Christina, Dave carried a clipboard with the notes he took about the training exercise. Another man named Isaac accompanied him and also positioned himself at the head of the table. Toward the older end of what would be considered middle-aged, Isaac liked his graying sideburns and peppered hair short. He looked every bit of the role that he currently filled: the chief overseer and the man who ran the Old Guard organization.

Dave cleared his throat, snapping everyone's thoughts back to the training exercise. "Not bad, class, considering this was your first time running this exercise against three of the best Outriders we have," Dave said as he sat down.

He looked at Ari's team. "I think this is your personal best. You killed all the students in less than fifteen minutes and without as much as a drop of paint on you." Dave looked expectantly at his class. "What do you think you did right, and what do you think you did wrong?"

A moment of awkward silence hung in the room as the students looked at each other, shaking their heads. One of the students named Tim cleared his throat and began to speak "I think our communication has improved since the last time. We didn't have confusion like we had before, that is, at least until you shot our client." Tim paused.

"I thought our strategy was good. I'm not sure how we could have done any better than what we just did."

Isaac spoke up. "Pretty good assessment, Tim."

He looked at Ari. "Ari, you've taught this class before. What's your take on what the students did that worked and didn't work?"

Ari looked at Dave and then at Isaac and shook her head slowly. "Oh, no, you don't. My position here is merely as a participant in the exercise. I'm no longer the instructor, and I really don't want to overstep my role this morning."

"Actually, I'm pretty curious myself to see if you assessed the students the same way," Dave said.

Ari sighed. *I hate when they put me on the spot like this. Okay, Ari . . . Be constructive in your criticism . . .*

She cleared her throat and then smiled at the students. "Overall, not bad. I agree that your ability to communicate with each other and carry out your instructions improved until the end. Your strategy would have worked except you were thinking two-dimensionally. And any semblance of order and strategy you had disintegrated after we killed your client. Your skills will improve with experience."

Sarah looked at Ari. The fiery twenty-five-year-old had straight auburn hair pulled back into a ponytail and intensely focused hazel eyes. "This exercise became an exercise in futility. What in the world do you mean 'two-dimensionally'? I mean you pit students against three of the best Outriders and expect us to win?"

Ari glanced at Dave. He subtly nodded, giving her permission to continue the assessment. Ari tempered her usual sharp witty comeback with a deep breath followed by a more constructive response. "No, we expect you to use this and other exercises to hone your skills and teamwork. We expect you to use these to work on your ability to think clearly on your feet as the situation changes. Not once did you or your teammates look around at the rooftops or other buildings until it was too late. You need to start to think outside the box. You need to start thinking like the attacker. If you were the attacker, where would you position yourself in order to get to your target? You were always expecting the attack to come from the street and up the stairs, never from above, like the rooftop or other building. Remember that our enemies will use every weakness you have to their advantage."

"That's easy for you to say," Sarah protested, smirking as she made a dig into Ari. "I mean, after all, you are the best."

Ari closed her eyes. She hated being referred to as "the best." For Ari, the words were like fingernails on a chalkboard. Admittedly, Ari could be considered the best. From a very young age she had been blessed with gifts that would only become stronger once imparted with the gifts given to the Outriders. God blessed Ari with an ability to discern the thoughts of those around her or that came into contact with her.

A slightly vicious tone and intent laced Sarah's comment. Ari chose to ignore it and focus on the issue. She didn't even have to think of a diplomatic answer. "Just remember, Sarah, when you are on top of that pedestal looking down, there is always someone below you that thinks they can knock you out of the top position, and they are usually right. We are among the best because we train like there is always someone better than us who wants to kill us. We always train ourselves thinking that we will always have room for improvement. Personally, just finishing a training exercise or an assignment isn't satisfactory for me. I want to be able to finish it without any mistakes."

Dave looked at Ari. "So did you make any mistakes during this exercise?"

Ari laughed. "Of course. I probably would have performed better except I came straight into this exercise from an assignment without any rest. I should have not only killed the target with my first volley but also at least one of the others in the room. By not shooting one of the others in the room, that little bit of grace allowed them time to duck and defend themselves from us. I also missed one shot. The round hit the outside wall next to the window instead of the gunman," she told him.

"You beat yourself up over missing one shot?" Sarah asked her.

"Yes. When your ammo clip only has six blades, you have to make every shot count, especially if you have more than one adversary," she said as she looked at the students.

"Blades?" one of the students asked.

"Uh, yes. This," Dave said as he unsheathed a hand blade from his leg. "Of course, the ones in a blade gun don't have a hilt or hand guards, and are a bit more aerodynamically shaped, but the general idea is the same."

"You mean to tell me we are shooting knives at our adversaries? Why not bullets?" asked Tim.

Isaac explained, "Because a bullet doesn't stop a demon, or even necessarily an Outrider. Our bodies have been transformed by Christ. Not just spiritually, but literally as well. When you were imparted with gifts, you were given the supernatural gift of healing not only yourself but also others. We're still mortal, and given the wound is big enough, you can still bleed to death. A bullet does damage, but not nearly as much as a blade."

"Dave, hand me your blade," Ari said as she produced the apple she saved to eat later. "The similarities to a knife end at its appearance. Sure, the blade will slice into the apple just like a knife."

She stabbed the apple with the blade so that part of its tip protruded out the other end. "The lethality of this ancient weapon lies in the retractable barbs."

She yanked the blade out by the handle. The backward motion of the blade activated the barbs to open up, shredding the apple as each barb gripped into the inside flesh of the apple. The fruit appeared unrecognizable once she removed the blade. Several small chunks of apple still held protrusions, bent and twisted metal tines that had broken off from the blade. Ari tossed the mangled hand blade on the table. The eyes of the students followed the blade as it stopped at the other end of the table in front of Dave.

"Right now, the only thing that separates you from us is the experience and the attention to details," Ari said as she sat back.

Dave addressed his class, saying, "Good work, everyone. Before I let you go, I want you to observe one other exercise we give. Ari, if you could help again, I need for you to be the spider. Silas, Mike, Christina, and Brad need to climb. You're up for your evaluations."

Tim leaned over to Sarah, "Spider? What kind of exercise is this?"

Mike and the other Outriders groaned. "Man, this is going to be painful."

He turned and grinned at Ari. "But I'm prepared for you this time, Black Widow!" The other climbers laughed.

"It just figures. I just got a manicure yesterday," Christina balked. "Be gentle with me, Ari."

Sarah spoke up. "Excuse me, sir. What is this examination? Spider? Black Widow?"

Dave explained, "We call it the spider web. It's an exercise/ examination we give our experienced Outriders every once in a while to test their physical skills. The name of the test started off as a joke, but as you'll see, it's aptly named."

As the participants and Ari were finishing getting into their climbing harnesses, Dave spoke to them. "You all know what to do, but for the purpose of the students, I'll explain the objectives. Ari—as the spider, your objective is to stop the climbers from reaching the top. Climbers— your objective is to try to reach the top without being pulled off the wall by the attacker. No weapons other than yourself may be used in order to achieve your objectives, and you can't use the harness or safety ropes to pull your opponent off."

Some of the observers from the earlier exam stayed to help spot the climbers' safety ropes. The four Outriders stood by the rock wall facade, waiting for the start of the exercise. Ari stood slightly back, chalking her hands. She approached Mike and bumped shoulders with him. "Be prepared to be spider food!"

Several in the room laughed at the good-humored banter between the friends. Dave blew his whistle, and Ari intently watched her friends climb the wall as quickly as they could. She approached the rock wall and flexed her hands a few times. Dave turned to his students, "Now you will see why she is considered one of the best Outriders."

A minute later Dave blew his whistle again, and Ari began up the wall quickly. She purposely aimed herself at the slowest of the climbers, Brad.

Just a few handholds up from the bottom, Brad felt a tug on his left foot as he tried to raise it from its lower foothold. Ari had caught his ankle and held fast onto it. He tried to shake her hand off, all the while trying not to lose his own grip. Ari gave his leg one good yank and Brad's other foot slipped. He held fast onto the wall with his two finger-holds, growling, trying to not lose contact with the wall. Ari worked her way up slightly below him and grabbed his waist and yanked hard. Brad fell backwards and swung freely on the rope. She checked briefly over her shoulder to make sure he was okay before she continued to her next target.

Methodically, Ari worked her way to both Silas and Christina. Both Outriders easily pulled off the wall when they were about half way up. By the time Ari reached Mike, her muscles were burning. Given a harder route to climb, he struggled with the last few moves under the overhang. She reached out for Mike's leg, only to have her arm kicked away. The action momentarily made Ari lose her footing, making her hang by only one finger hold. She regained her holds and held her body out slightly from the wall, scanning the terrain above her.

Ari knew Mike would be hard to stop. Gifted with strength and agility, Mike would take more than a typical attack from below to get him off the wall. She broke off her attack and moved off to Mike's side, climbing quickly up an easy route and soon appearing slightly above and to the side of him. Mike tried to move further away, but Ari cut him off. She began to move down towards him, and for a while it seemed the victim became the spider.

Mike tried his best to rip Ari's footholds away from her. Before Mike could break away, Ari did something that no one expected her to do: she let go of the rock face and leapt toward Mike, grabbing on to the back of him. The two combatants grunted and hollered as Mike tried to get her off him. With her arms wrapped securely around his shoulder and waist, Ari took her legs and, with all of her might, pushed against the wall. She could feel Mike's powerful grip hang on. She tugged and twisted several times to see if she could shake him off. Mike gave a guttural scream in a last-ditch effort to hang on. Ari pulled at one of his arms, and his grip finally gave out. Before he could try to regain it, his other hand slipped, and soon the two friends were swinging in the air, suspended only by their twisted safety lines. Both spider and victim had lost their grip of the rock wall.

Looking up, Ari slowly swung herself around Mike, untangling her safety line from his. Lowered to the ground, Ari laid on her back, trying to catch her breath. Her arms and legs felt like rubber.

Dave clapped. "I didn't think you would have caught him that time, Ari. I thought he would have beat you. Congratulations."

Sarah chimed in. "That doesn't make sense. Technically, she killed herself in order to peel Mike away from the wall. What does that accomplish?"

Dave smiled. "The objective. She accomplished her only objective: to stop the climbers from reaching the top."

"But she killed herself in the process . . . "

"Sometimes a sacrifice has to be made in order for the objective to be achieved." Everyone looked at the speaker. Isaac, the chief overseer, continued, "And that, everyone, is the mark of a dedicated Outrider. When faced with no other alternative, they are willing to sacrifice their own lives in order to make sure the objective is achieved."

As the spectators began to break up, Ari got up, stretched her muscles, and then helped her friend Christina out of her harness. On the other side of the room, Sarah walked up to Jim, and the two began to talk. Sarah rocked back and forth from heel to toe, holding her hands behind her back. Sarah's giggle drifted across the room, where Christina and Ari watched the flirtation.

Christina's jaw just dropped. "Oh-oh. Tell me he is ignoring her come-on. She's young enough to be his daughter."

"Good thing I'm not the jealous type." Ari took a drink of water before continuing to remove her harness and pack her small workout bag.

"Yes, but I am." Christina stepped over Ari and marched over to the flirty student. She pushed Jim aside and tapped Sarah firmly on her shoulder. The student's seductive expression immediately vaporized into a look of surprised horror, realizing she may have gotten caught. "Sorry, Sarah. Jim is wanted by his wife, Ari."

"Perhaps next time, sir?" Sarah asked. Jim looked back and nodded.

Looking at Sarah with reproving glance, Christina continued, "I think your instructor is giving the students last-minute information. You better go see if you missed anything." Sarah nodded and walked away.

Christina rolled her eyes and shook her head as she walked back to Ari. She caught the tail end of the discussion between the husband and wife.

"Honestly, I didn't call you over here." Ari said with a sarcastic laugh.

"Then why did you laugh that way?" Jim asked.

"Because this discussion is senseless."

"Sorry, Jim. I called you over," Christina sheepishly admitted as she glanced over her shoulder at Sarah. "That girl is up to something, and I don't like it."

"It was harmless, Christina." Jim brushed off the incident.

"Her flirtation seemed purposeful and manipulative, for whatever reason. It's the first step toward something that will drag you further down the wrong path. Just watch it. Once the snake bites, you can't take it back."

Jim looked at his wife, who had remained silent during all of this exchange. At that moment a caretaker carried their daughter in and handed her to Ari. Ari cracked a huge grin as she kissed and held the tiny girl. "Alexa!"

Jim smiled. "Ari, what do you think?"

Ari cradled their daughter in her arms. "I'm trying not to. For me, it's past now. But like I told Christina earlier, good thing I'm not the jealous type." Ari shook the brief encounter off. Still holding Alexa, she walked over and grabbed her bag.

Her husband Jim threw her a towel. "I thought you could use this."

"Thanks, but I'm not sweating anymore."

"That's good news, because Isaac wants to send you as the observer for the soon-to-be graduates. Due to the large class size, we had to break up the practical assignments into two. Dave will be with the other group. At least you'll have a day to rest."

Ari smirked at her husband. "Yeah, maybe this time I won't nod off observing like I did the last time."

Jim rubbed his hand through his brown wavy hair. His medium frame hunched over his wife as he rested his chin on her shoulder, softly speaking to her. "It was that boring?"

"Watching your students snooze when they should have been protecting? Yes. I let it play out since there didn't seem to be any apparent danger. And when they least expected it, I surprised them." Ari began to laugh under her breath.

"I read the report. You actually snuck up on them and hog-tied them?"

Ari nodded. "I even had time to go to the corner market and buy apples for their mouths. When they realized the error of their ways, I released them. I think Nick thought briefly about filing a formal complaint against me but realized he'd be in as much hot water falling asleep as me, so he dropped it."

"You gave them a bit of senior intimidation?" Christina asked.

Ari shook her head. "Oh, not at all. Like every other class, I just try to make their slip up as memorable as possible so they never repeat it. Although I think to this day Nick feels a bit traumatized by the event and tries not to make eye contact with me, even after I tried to make it up to him."

Christina laughed. "He's acting like a low-ranked dog to the alpha dog in the pack."

Jim joined in, grasping Alexa from Ari and handing her over to Christina. "Don't make eye contact . . ." His piercingly blue eyes stared down into Ari's dark brown orbs. Neither of the silent combatants blinked. Seconds passed . . .

A moment later Ari turned away, blinking and laughing. "Ooooh, Mr. Sommers! Your blue eyes win again!"

Jim stood up and held his arms up in victory. "Yes! I am still alpha dog!" The remnants of the class looked at him as his outburst echoed. A few clapped. Ari buried her head behind her hands, embarrassed.

"Here, alpha dog. Your alpha child needs her diaper changed." Christina handed over a giggly Alexa.

CHAPTER TWO

The sky held nothing back. Ari stood in the shadow of a darkened doorway across the street from where her newly graduated students worked at their assignment. She spied the light in the window as best as she could in the heavy rain.

A bit slower than I would like or feel comfortable, but they are new at this, Ari. Patience . . . 'Better a patient person than a warrior, one with self-control than one who takes a city." She looked up at the dark sky. "Lord, a little favor in the area of less rain would be much appreciated . . ."

Unanswered, but not dismayed, the seasoned Outrider drew her leather collar up closer around her neck, hoping that it would keep some of the torrential downpour from seeping into her already chilled bones. She looked at her watch and sighed. *Time's up . . .* Silently, she slid a metal-lined glove on her left hand and cautiously worked her way across the street and into the building.

Ari walked up to the door and loud heard voices on the other side. She unzipped her leather jacket, holding on to her gun as she opened the door. The talking immediately ceased as all eyes gazed upon the new arrival. The occupants of the room gawked at Ari as she entered the room. Feeling like a half-drowned cat in leather, Ari ignored their stares as her boots made a subtle squish noise as she stepped in.

Gritting her teeth and somehow mustering a smile, she addressed the client. "Hello ma'am. Excuse us for a minute."

She wrapped her arms around the shoulders of the younger Outriders and took a few steps away from the client. "Gentlemen, is there a problem? This should have been done an hour ago."

Jacob cleared his throat. "Uh, ma'am, she doesn't want to go out in this weather."

Ari frisked her wet hair with her hands, shaking the moisture out like the half-drowned cat she envisioned herself being. Her short hair ended up in a fanatical, wild style that mirrored her frustration inside. "Gee, I can't imagine why. Seriously?"

The stylish client stood in her stilettos, tapping her toe stubbornly. Dan cleared his throat, "She doesn't want her Jimmy Choos to get wet."

Ari nodded in agreement as her eyebrow raised. "I don't blame you ma'am. Not for what they cost. Of course you could put on another pair until you get to the destination and then change."

The two new Outriders both shook their heads. "We tried that, but she doesn't have anything else that goes with this outfit." Jacob sighed. "A true dilemma. We went through most of her shoe collection trying to find something." He pointed at a walk-in closet that had hundreds of pairs of shoes lining the walls.

Ari stared at the collection, dumbfounded. "Seriously?" The trio nodded. Ari walked into the closet. She briefly studied what the client wore and then glanced through the seemingly endless racks, where she found a pair of black leather pumps and grabbed them. She handed them to the client, who stared at Ari, amazed. Ari shrugged and said, "I find that black leather goes with just about everything."

The client slipped out of her expensive pair and into the less flashy pumps. A vision suddenly flashed in Ari's mind. She listened intently as the lights flickered and then went black.

The client sighed. "Another blackout? It seems every time it rains, the lights go off. Honestly, I don't know why I pay the luxury prices when they can't even guarantee I'll have power."

Ari grabbed the arms of the two Outriders and their reluctant client. "Ma'am, we need to move you out of here now. Your life is in great danger right now." Ari looked over her back as she withdrew her gun from her holster. "They're here. Take her now."

Ari turned her back to the trio to face the shadows. The two young Outriders seemed frozen, not knowing what to do. Ari spoke sternly to them. "Men. Do as I say—NOW!" Before she could help them, she shot into the dark corner. The room filled with an eerie screech of pain. She shot at another shadow and then quickly turned around. She grabbed hold of the client and quickly screamed to the men, "Grab hold now!" As soon as she felt them grab her arms, she left the apartment, self-transporting back to the back patio of Hollywood.

The client stood frozen in shock. She looked hesitantly around her surroundings. ". . . how? . . . where?"

Ari continued to take charge of the situation. "Jacob, take Ms. Hollander into the house until we can assess what to do now."

The large athletic silhouette of Jacob stood still and silent, holding his abdomen. Ari approached him, seeing blood behind his hand. "Dan, take Ms. Hollander inside and get Jesse, stat." Dan did as he was told as Ari eased Jacob down into a prone position on the patio cement. "You're going to be fine, Jacob. Let me see . . ." She eased his bloody hand away from his abdomen and saw the point of the blade protrude slightly. She gently rolled him over to his side and saw the tiny shaft of the deadly weapon.

Ari returned Jacob to rest on his back. Holding his hand, she said, "Jacob, this might sting a little. Hang in there . . ." She gripped the slender tip of the embedded blade with the tip of her gloved hand and pulled firmly. Jacob gripped Ari's other hand hard as he screamed. Before he finished screaming, Ari had removed the blade and placed her hand onto his wound. By that time, Jesse and several others took over Jacob's medical needs. She watched Jesse and Christina as they both expertly worked on stabilizing Jacob, inserting a saline IV and quickly wrapping his wounds with a pressure bandage before moving him inside to the med ward. After Ari helped to gently settle him onto one the gurneys, she stepped back, allowing Christina and Jesse room to work.

As part of the impartation of gifts, Outriders are given a supernatural gift of healing. Their gift is so powerful that the injuries inflicted by virtually any object that passes through the body—even through the heart—would be healed to the extent that the Outrider would not bleed to death. There were limits to even this power; in order for complete healing to occur, the object has to pass completely through.

Ari stood numbed by the events that just happened. As a former instructor, and many times as the lead on an assignment, she already assessed what went wrong and how all of this could have been avoided. She looked at her hands. They were covered with blood along with her jacket and jeans. She walked over to the sink and threw her bloodied glove into a red trash bin. As she finished washing her hands, several oversseers on the council approached Ari. She followed them silently to their chamber, knowing that she had to officially answer the very questions that ran through her mind. The sound of her heels and those of others walking with her echoed in the stone and cinderblock hallway as they made their way to the council's chamber.

Still damp and dripping from the nightmare assignment, she took her wet jacket off to minimize the amount of blood the overseers would see on her. Ari sat in a chair facing six overseers, including the unemotional Petra and a somewhat concerned-looking Isaac. Jim handed her a towel as he too sat down. She could feel the entire group's displeasure at being awakened in the middle of the night. A furrow dug into Ari's forehead as she thought through the scenario. She buried her face in the towel, noticing Jacob's blood had smeared on her cheek and jawline. Isaac looked at his top Outrider from the top of his reading glasses. "Ari, is everything okay? What happened?"

"I don't know, sir. It just doesn't make sense. By all accounts of the assignment summary, this shouldn't have happened."

Petra laughed under her breath. Isaac shot a stern glance at his overseer before turning his attention back at Ari. "Explain if you can."

Ari cleared her throat. "The first assignment of the newly graduated students is supposed to be easy, on purpose. The assessment in the client summary stated the likelihood of attack was minimal to none, and would happen well after three in the morning if any attack occurred. Also, the assessment also stated that there shouldn't have been more than one entity attacking, if even that."

"And wasn't it like that, Ms. Sommers?" Petra's voice seemed to shrill in Ari's ear.

"No, Madam Overseer. The attack happened hours before the predicted time." She looked at her watch. "It's not even close to three in the morning. Also more than just one demon attacked."

A concerned whisper grew among the overseers. "Can you estimate how many, Ari?" Isaac asked.

Ari thought a moment. "At least four." The overseers broke out in disbelief.

Petra laughed. "I'm sure your mind is playing games, trying to cover up the gross negligence on your part."

"No, Madam Overseer. I distinctly saw four. Perhaps there were more, but I shot two, and as we transported, two more were attacking. That's when they injured Jacob."

Petra huffed and leaned forward in her leather chair. "I know your kind, Ms. Sommers. You would do just about anything to keep your status within the organization."

Ari's jaw clenched. "My kind? Madam Overseer, are you implying that I'm lying to the council? I have nothing to hide, and Madam, I have no motive to keep my status. My only goal is to do His will . . ."

Petra laughed under her breath again and looked at the rest of the council. "Listen to her. She's manipulating your emotions." She stared at Ari. "Your noble response sounds canned. Where did you pick that up? The latest movie? Admit it, Ariana: Your take on the events that happened last night never happened. You panicked when you shot at what you thought was a demon. Instead, you shot Jacob."

Ari's frustration funneled into her clenched fist. "How can you accuse me of lying and then trying to cover it up? I have been dealing with these types of attacks for a long time. I have been trained to assess the situation in an instant."

"Perhaps, Ms. Sommers, your aging Outrider mind is not as quick or sharp as it used to be." Petra finished her dig into Ari. "And I'm not implying, Ms. Sommers. I am stating that you are lying before the council inquiry to cover up your negligence. You could rot in confinement for a very long time for this . . ."

Ari stared Petra down. "Then, perhaps, Madam Overseer, you should see if your fantasy scenario holds up to what the others have witnessed." Petra's thin smile vaporized.

Isaac interrupted the tense exchange between the two women. "Ari, we will question the others. You're excused for now. You understand that as part of the inquiry, you are grounded from future assignments until you have been cleared of any wrongdoing?"

"Yes, sir."

"Thank you, Ari. That will be all. Please have Dan meet us in here immediately."

Ari nodded as she got up. Tearing her soggy jacket from the back of the seat, she felt the daggers from Petra's stare pierce her confidence as she walked out.

The morning meeting concluded and both Jim and Isaac noted Ari's absence. As the people left, Jim went back up to their bedroom. He looked around and the bed and bathroom were empty. He walked down to the med ward, where Josh lay on a gurney, resting. Despite his terrible wound, he would make a full recovery. He saw the silhouette of his wife sitting on the edge of a chair on the other side of the gurney. Her head was buried in her hands; she was immersed in deep prayer.

"You missed the meeting," Jim said. Ari didn't move. He bent over and gently removed one of her earbuds. "You missed the meeting," he repeated.

Ari turned her music off and took her other earbud out. "I didn't think it would matter since I wouldn't get assigned anything anyway."

"You know that your presence is always required if you are in the building." Jim looked at his wife's unusually disheveled appearance. She still wore the clothes from the assignment. "You're still wearing the clothes from last night? Didn't you get any sleep?"

"No, and apparently, neither did you."

"Isaac met with a few of us after we had interviewed the rest of the team, as well as Ms. Hollander. At first most of us thought that maybe you were getting a bit soft in your assignments. Isaac had a hard time convincing Petra and the council, but you're cleared for now."

"Both Jacob and Dan didn't see any demons, but then again, it's hard to see something in almost complete darkness. Other than that, everyone's recollection of the events matched your assessment. I had my doubts."

Ari looked at her husband. "You doubted me? Did you think I lied and made all that up?"

"I never doubted you for a minute, Ari. But there were those on the council that thought . . ."

"Thought that I lied to cover up a mistake?" Ari sounded hurt at the possible accusation.

Jim paused before giving her the answer. "Yes. They thought that you're getting too cautious, too hesitant, with your decision-making now that you're older and have a family."

Ari sat back on the chair. "They think I'm getting too old."

Jim shrugged his shoulders. "Besides Silas, you are the oldest Outrider, Ari."

As if in pain, she stared into Jim's blue eyes. "You know better than anyone that I'm not in charge of my life. All that I am is through Him."

Jim pulled up another chair next to Ari's. "Yes, I know. Age shouldn't have anything to do with it."

The room settled into an awkward silence. Ari glanced sideways at her husband. "You're holding something back. It. What is this 'it'?"

Jim bit his lip. His expression made it obvious that he struggled as he tried to put the words together. "Ari, maybe you should think about giving up Outrider work. Apart from your age, you are also a mom. You have a family who loves you, and Alexa needs you."

Ari buried her face in her hands again. Jim held her hand as he continued his argument. "Ari, you're never home. You're always on assignment. And when you are home, you are either in bed catching up on sleep or in the med ward recovering. In either case, you're in no condition to interact, let alone play with your daughter. I don't want her to grow up not knowing what a wonderful mother you are. Ari, at the very least, if you could talk to Isaac about giving you more time off between assignments . . ."

"I tried. He makes it work for a few days, then my schedule reverts back to its chaotic self." Ari shook her head. I would stop doing Outrider work in a heartbeat except . . ."

"Except what?"

"God. I've prayed about His will and whether I should still be an Outrider. At least for now, He still wants me where I am. I can't deny where God wants me to be."

"I just don't want you to wake up one morning and realize that your daughter is all grown up and you don't know who she is." Jim bent over and kissed his wife on the cheek as he got up.

Ari buried her head in her hands again and groaned in frustration. "By the way, Isaac wants to see you. They want to send you out on another assignment." Jim walked out, leaving Ari alone with her injured pupil.

After a minute, Ari straightened up and walked down the hall. Ari would rather be in bed catching up on much-needed rest or even playing with her daughter. After cleaning up, Ari stepped into Isaac's office. She sat next to Mike in front of Isaac's desk.

"Petra just handed this to me. I have an assignment for you two. You need to leave as soon as possible," the overseer explained as he handed her a slip of paper. "It shouldn't be that difficult. Ari, I know this may not seem like your type of assignment, but this has more importance than what you see on paper. Try not to screw this one up. I know you can handle the client."

"Handle the client? Don't you mean the assignment?" Ari asked.

"Well, of course. That too, Ari. I have the utmost confidence in you two." The two Outriders looked at the information on the paper, looked at each other, and shrugged.

CHAPTER THREE

Ari and Mike arrived across the street from the address that Petra gave them. Ari dressed a little differently than normal. She wore a fitted black leather jacket and matching leather pants, and both her gun and hand blade holsters were strapped to the outside of her leg like a gunslinger. Rechecking the address against the piece of paper, both Outriders looked up. They were staring at a trendy nightclub. The faint *thump, thump, thump* of the music drifted across the street to the bewildered Outriders. A line of hopeful attendees stood behind a rope, patiently waiting to get in. Mike's brow wrinkled, "You have got to be kidding. I thought this guy has some sort of a life-threatening injury he is recovering from?"

"I guess some like to continue to live on the edge," Ari said. "I somehow feel like I've fallen out of grace with the overseers. This assignment borders humiliation."

"Rebecca complained that she feels like she's an overpaid babysitter."

Ari nodded and then nudged Mike with her elbow. "You and Rebecca have been hanging out a lot lately."

Mike shrugged. "I guess. I like the way she smiles at me. And she said she likes my jokes."

Ari sighed as she checked her hair and makeup in the side mirror of a car parked on the street. She quickly ran her fingers in her bangs. "That's not what I heard." She winked at her friend and smacked her lips together, redistributing her lipstick. Ari eyed the bouncer and host at the entrance. Both had wireless headsets in their ears. "This might get dicey. Follow my lead and just play along." Ari confidently crossed the street and tried to walk past the bouncer.

"Whoa, missy. Where do you think you're going?" the bouncer asked.

"I'm running in to get a guy and take him into custody," Ari answered. "I'll be right out." She patted Mike on the back. "My friend will even stay here with you." She began to walk in, but a large arm stopped her when the bouncer grabbed her shoulder.

"No one gets in unless your name is on the list." The bouncer held Ari's shoulder firmly.

"Are you touching me?" Ari asked the much larger man, glancing down at his hand, feigning offense at the act.

"Oooh, you shouldn't have done that. Do you have any idea who she is?" Mike asked the bouncer.

"Uh, no," the bouncer responded. "Like I really care."

With one quick and smooth move, Ari grabbed the offending hand and twisted it, causing enough pain forcing the man effortlessly against the host's podium. Mike removed the headset from the cowering host and pain-paralyzed bodyguard. Ari spoke to both of them again. "Like I said before, I need to go in there for a brief moment, take someone into custody, and I'll be right out. Mike will remain out here with you. Do we have an understanding of the situation?" Both men nodded quickly. She let Mike take over her grip on the man's arm and walked into the nightclub.

Ari stood at the top of the stairs and surveyed the crowd. The dark room sparkled with spots of colored light and the occasional distraction of green and blue laser beam pictures on the walls and ceiling. She walked around the room, staring at the faces. After a few minutes, she walked over to a large sofa. A young man with blonde wavy hair sat with his arms along the back of the couch, casually holding on to the women on both sides of him. He wore a black leather jacket and black t-shirt. He whispered into one of his companion's ears. She sat back smiling at him. He seemed to be enjoying the attention. Ari rolled her eyes and shook her head. Gritting her teeth, she smiled coyly as she bent over and asked the man loudly, "Josh?" Ari batted her eyelashes.

The young man eyed Ari clad in the tight-fitting leather from head to toe, smiling, "Yeah, that's me. So you want a piece of me too?" He patted the sofa's seat next to him.

Ari smiled a superficial smile, gritting her teeth and hiding her disbelief that the Old Guard council actually showed interest in this man. She walked up to him, and bent over again to whisper in his ear, playing along with his advances. "Actually, I really want all of you." Josh broke out in a huge grin. Ari stood up, smiling at the ladies next to her soon-to-be client. "Excuse me, ladies," she told the group as she reached over and grabbed Josh's jacket by the collar. She held his arm firmly as she escorted him out of the club. When she got to the front, she handed the earpieces to the host and bouncer. "Thank you two for your cooperation." The trio left and walked around the corner to a sports car.

"Wait, what are you doing? Who are you?" Josh asked the Outriders.

"After this assignment I'm not sure anymore. But apparently we're here to protect you. We'll be escorting you to Los Angeles," Mike answered. "I'm Mike and this is Ari." We'll be driving you . . ."

"In this a Porsche? Sweet!" Josh bobbed his head as he swept his hand over the shiny black coupe. His head suddenly stopped moving. "Wait, it's a two-seater and there are three of us."

"Mike will drive you and I'll be escorting you," Ari said as she began to put a helmet on as she climbed onto a deep blue-colored sport bike.

Josh eyed Ari again, smiling. "I'd rather have you in the car with me. And you can even sit on my lap."

Mike muttered under his breath to Josh, "Oh, boy. You shouldn't have done that."

Ari got off her bike and approached Josh threateningly, pushing Josh up against the car. "Trust me, you don't." Mike grabbed Ari and pulled her back from Josh.

Josh stood up straight and laughed at Ari, "Feisty, aren't you?"

Ari looked at Mike and muttered, "Remind me to thank Petra and Isaac for this wonderful assignment." She stepped back and held up a cell phone. "Is this your cell phone?" Josh nodded. Ari removed the back of Josh's cell phone.

"Hey, that's mine. How did you get it?" Josh started after Ari. Mike stopped Josh as Ari removed the battery, replaced the back to the cell phone, and then gave it back to Josh.

"What did you do? Give that back to me!" Josh tried to get the battery from Ari.

"Your phone has a built-in GPS," Ari calmly explained as she pocketed his battery in an inner pocket of her jacket. "Unless you want the ones that are trying to kill you to find you easily, the battery stays out."

She zipped up her jacket, put her helmet on, and climbed back onto the bike. As she put on her gloves, Ari spoke to Josh. "In order for us to keep you alive, you need to follow one simple rule: do what we tell you to do, when we tell you to do it. Don't think about it. Don't debate it. Just do it, okay?" Josh nodded.

Ari and Mike put their headsets on. Ari's voice crackled to life over the headset. "For right now, I'll follow you. Stay on the route and I'll catch up. First I need to divert attention away from you guys."

Mike and Josh leapt into the car, and Ari took off to the front of the club again, where she stopped in front and flipped her helmet visor up. She burned rubber, making the back tire screech. As the bouncer and host pointed and began to run after her, she flipped her visor down and peeled away in the opposite direction, making sure all eyes turned towards her as she sped down the street. Mike quietly sped away in the opposite direction, with almost no witnesses. Only one set of eyes watched the car depart, and then they too disappeared into the shadows of the alley.

A couple of hours later, after making sure that no one followed her, Ari carefully worked her way back to the agreed route and began to weave her way up to the back of the Porsche. With a flip of a switch, she turned her headset on. "Mike, do you copy?"

"Yeah, where are you?" he answered.

"Look in your rearview mirror," Ari said as she flicked her wrist in a brief wave. "I'm going to hang further back. Let's go ahead and stop at where we discussed."

"Copy," Mike said.

"Who is that you're talking to?" Josh asked.

Mike turned the microphone to mute. "Ari. You don't realize how lucky you are to say what you did to her and come out intact," Mike warned Josh.

"Hey, you guys are supposed to protect me, not kill me. I could probably do whatever I want to that piece of meat, and she wouldn't be able to do anything back," Josh bragged.

Mike laughed under his breath, shaking his head. "Don't think you are the first to think of trying something. Remember that we're only to make sure you're still alive when you get to your destination. Whether you're missing body parts or are unconscious when we deliver you doesn't matter."

"Seriously?" Josh asked.

"Seriously," Mike said.

"You're joking," Josh laughed nervously.

Mike was, but he wanted to make sure that Ari had nothing to worry about. "Let me put it this way, the last guy that tried to make a move on Ari without her permission is still eating all his meals through a tube." Mike shook his head. "Just behave yourself and you'll be fine." Josh nodded.

Josh sat back against the seat, resigned. "Man, this trip is going to—"

"—be boring," Mike interrupted him.

"Yeah. So what exactly are you protecting me from?"

"A terrible fate. We believe that demons are going to try to attack you."

"Why would they want me?"

"Good question, considering what type of lifestyle you seem to lead.

Perhaps your life will turn around and you become influential in God's kingdom, doing His good works? The devil definitely doesn't want any of his people to have a personal relationship with Jesus and will stop you, given the chance."

"How so?" Josh asked.

"He will kill, steal, and destroy. Many times he will just try to kill our client so that they can't fulfill their purpose. In your case, it's hard to tell."

"My case? What do you mean?"

"All the enemy has to do is convince you that nothing is wrong with your life right now. You continue to live a life void of God and His righteousness; he has you exactly where he wants you."

"Why would I want to change? I get all the women I want, I feel good . . ." Josh stretched his arms behind his head.

"Even with all those stitches?" Mike asked.

"Oh, uh . . . these?" Josh lifted his shirt. Mike saw a large gauze pad held in place by white medical tape. "This wound is nothing."

Mike shrugged. Josh settled back and closed his eyes. The next couple of hours were uneventful. The late night and remote location between cities gave Ari and Mike an easier time to assess possible hazards to their trip.

Ari shivered. The night air had enough of a chill that Ari felt it. Despite the uncomfortable strain of being in such a position for hours, she leaned forward and down behind the tiny windshield to try to stay warmer. Thankfully, there were only a few miles more before they reached their agreed stop. "Mike, do you copy?"

"How are you holding out?" He asked.

"Fine. I hope they have good coffee where we're stopping," Ari responded. "I'm going to go ahead of you and make sure the rest stop is secure. Stay on com. I'll let you know if it's clear." Ari sped up, and as she passed Mike, she looked inside the car, nodded, and then took off.

Ari pulled up to the diner and parked her bike. Another car sat in the parking lot. She took her helmet off and briefly looked in the side mirror and sighed. *Helmet hair . . .* She ran her fingers through her short hair and managed to make it look passable. Blowing her breath into her chilled hands, she walked up into the diner and scanned the few people who were in there.

To the right, a young couple flirted with each other. On the other end, two couples at the same table quietly sipped their coffee. Ari unzipped her jacket and took her gloves off as she walked up to the counter. A blonde waitress chatted with the cook and turned around and smiled, saying, "You can sit anywhere you want."

Ari nodded and briefly walked outside, put her helmet on the bike, and gave Mike the all clear. She walked back in and sat in a booth to the left of the door, a couple of booths down from the young couple. Ari took the seat facing the doorway and the other group in the far corner.

Mike and Josh joined Ari, sitting facing Ari. The waitress came up with a full pot of coffee. "Freshly made coffee. Anyone want any?" Ari nodded, as did Mike.

"I thought you don't drink the stuff," Mike looked at Ari.

"I normally don't, but since I'm kind of feeling like a frozen novelty in leather armor right now, I just need something warm," Ari said as she closed her eyes and wrapped her hands around the steaming mug.

"I can help . . ." Josh started and then stopped abruptly with a grunt as Mike elbowed him hard. Ari looked up and stared at the two men who were smiling suspiciously at her.

"You can help what?" She asked Josh.

"Uh . . . Can I help by offering you sugar and creamer?" the young man nervously asked her.

Ari smiled, still a bit suspicious. "Thanks, but I can reach it from here." She began to prep her coffee, "Are you hungry? We'll probably drive for another four or so hours before stopping again."

Josh grabbed a laminated menu and began to look at it. "In that case I think I will eat." The two Outriders also grabbed menus and perused them.

The waitress came back to their table. She looked out the window and smiled. "Nice bike."

Ari looked at her. "Hmmm?"

"Your bike. Nice motorcycle. What is it?" she asked.

"Uh, Triumph," Ari said simply.

The waitress nodded. "It looks a bit cold outside to be riding. How is it?"

"Um, okay, I guess. But your coffee helps a lot." Ari smiled.

"My husband, the cook, and I used to ride our bikes all over the country. We gave that up to settle down and start this business. Our house is just around back. Now the only time we leave is to stock up, and then we need a truck. We never have time to ride anymore, so we ended up selling our bikes. Are you ready to order?" the waitress asked.

The group ordered, but as they did so, Ari kept an eye on one of the men in the group in the far corner. She discreetly asked the waitress, "Do you know those people in the corner? Are they regulars?"

"Oh no, most people here travel from point A to point B. I have a few regulars, but they usually come in during the hours of the living. The exception is Katy and her boyfriend, Shaun." She jerked her head subtly towards the young couple in the corner. "She sneaks out of her window after her parents go to bed, and they meet up here. Let me get your order in." The waitress walked back behind the counter. The young couple got up and left, saying goodbye to the waitress and cook. They drove off in the sole car that sat in the parking lot.

Ari's adrenaline kicked in. She whispered to Mike, "Escort Josh to the men's bathroom right now." We're in the middle of nowhere, and that group behind you doesn't have a car."

Mike got up, making sure to stand between the occupied table and Josh. As the two men were about to turn the corner to the hallway to the restrooms, the lights began to flicker as the people at the table got up. Before Ari or Mike could react, one man began to shoot at Mike and Josh. One blade caught Mike in the back shoulder, and he fell, pushing Josh behind the protection of the bathroom's door.

Ari yelled at the waitress, "Get down!" The flustered waitress disappeared behind the counter.

Ari bent over in her seat when one blade passed through the back of the booth seat in front of her and sank into the upholstery an inch from her head. Blades whizzed over her, imbedding into the red vinyl booth seat behind her. *Dear Lord, protect us . . . I draw the bloodline around us.*

She grabbed the salt-shaker and squeezed under the table and pulled her gun out of the holster. Unscrewing the top to the shaker, she quickly flicked the open shaker down the aisle. The vial spun as it slid, spreading the fine grains all over the floor. She listened for the barely audible crunch as the grains of salt were crushed under the shoes of the approaching attacker, but didn't hear anything.

Lord, I can't do this without you. You are my rock and shelter . . . Ari crawled out from underneath, and as she peeked, she didn't see the man. Suddenly the man leapt in the air from ten feet away, about to land on Ari. As her left arm cleared the booth, she shot the attacker. The man let out an unearthly screech as he fell back: a noise that only those possessed by a demon would make. The other man kicked Ari as he too leapt into the air, and landing with his feet on her, knocked her back into the aisle. As he knelt over her, she knocked the side of his head with her arm and used her legs to flip him over herself. He lay on the floor, motionless. Ari stood over him and kicked his gun across the room.

One of the women leapt into the air and hit Ari square in the back, knocking her off her feet. Ari turned over and the lady knelt over her, pinning her down. Ari saw the strange red-tinge in her attacker's eyes of the demon-possessed and felt the near-unhuman strength that held her down. The strange lady had an evil hiss to her breathing. The female hit Ari's face hard, momentarily stunning the Outrider. She grabbed Ari's hand blade from her holster. The Outrider struggled with the attacker, desperately holding the attacker's hand to prevent the strange woman from stabbing her. Ari knocked her hand against the side of the booth, sending the blade flying to the ground. With all of her strength, Ari kicked the attacker to the wall and then scrambled to her knees.

The last female demon tackled Ari down and grabbed her throat, trying to strangle her. Ari desperately grasped at the hands around her throat, trying to keep her from crushing her windpipe. She eyed the other female attacker working her way toward Mike and Josh. Ari stretched her hand out to her gun, but couldn't reach it. *Please, Lord, help me.*

As she held Ari's throat even tighter, the demon-lady grinned. Ari desperately tried to take a breath, but her throat wouldn't allow the air in. As she began to lose consciousness, a tear fell from Ari's eye. *I'm so sorry, Alexa . . . Jim . . . I love you.*

Her eyes rolled and the struggling stopped; the Outrider's body went limp. Satisfied that she no longer posed a threat, the lady let go and walked over to where Josh hid. The two women opened the bathroom door and saw Josh cornered against the far wall. As one of them aimed a gun at Josh, she suddenly let out an unearthly howl and dropped her gun. The attacker's body slumped to the floor. Ari held the gun shakily as she rubbed her throat with her free hand. The other attacker hissed at Ari and leapt at her. The demon-possessed woman let out an unearthly howl shot midair; her body fell to the ground. The lights stopped flickering and came back on.

Ari looked around, confused. She didn't shoot the last attacker. She smiled when she saw Josh, still holding Mike's gun tight in both hands. Ari came around the corner before collapsing to her knees. She loosened her jacket's collar and held her bruised throat and sore rib cage, trying to catch her breath.

Ari got up and pried the weapon from Josh's hands before aiding Mike. Mike breathed, but just barely. She skillfully pulled out the blade from his chest and applied clean bar mop towels to his wound. As Ari held the towels against Mike's wounds, she closed her eyes and prayed in the Holy Spirit for help and quick healing. Mike groaned. She glanced over to a shell-shocked Josh and spoke with a raspy whisper, "I need to get you out of here." She cupped her hand on Mike's face before getting up.

"What about Mike? You can't leave him here to die!" Josh protested, partly out of confusion and partly out of the adrenaline coursing through his blood.

"Friends will come to help him, but more are going to come, and they will kill you. We need to leave now," Ari said firmly. She looked behind the counter at an equally shell-shocked waitress. "Apologies for the mess," Ari began as she placed a wad of large bills on the counter. "People are on the way to help this injured man, but there are also more attackers coming. I suggest you and your husband leave now for your own safety."

Ari pushed Josh out the door and into the car. She fumbled for the keys, and started the coupe up, and quickly drove off. The manual shifting caused her pain. After about fifteen minutes, Ari pulled off onto a side road and then onto gravel drive hidden by bushes and trees. Ari turned the car off and opened the door. The surroundings began to telescope away as Ari continued to struggle breathing. Ari glanced at her charge. "Stay in the car. I need a few minutes. If for some reason something happens to me, this is the address you need to get to."

She handed him a business card. "The people there will help you and keep you safe. Just get back on the highway, and it pretty much will take you all the way to Los Angeles." Ari closed her eyes, in pain, dizzy, and exhausted. She collapsed to her knees onto the gravel road.

Josh's face showed fear. "Ari, ma'am, please you can't . . ."

"Just remember that Jesus loves you, no matter what." Ari lay on the road, unconscious.

The early morning still clung onto the darkness. Ari felt pain. She felt shaky, not so much because of her injuries, but from her lack of sleep. Ari made a mental note to herself: *I need to tell Isaac I need time off.*

Ari tried to sit up but ended up groaning in pain. Josh looked over to Ari. "I hope you don't mind. You scared me when you collapsed on the road, but you seemed to be breathing. I thought I'd take you to the nearest hospital in the next city we get to."

"What time is it? Where are we?" Ari asked, looking around.

"It's around 4:30 a.m. I tried to wake you up, but you looked pretty rough, so I let you sleep," the young man told her. "We're on the highway, headed west."

"No hospitals for me, Josh. Pull up to the next gas station." Ari sat up, rubbed her throat, and felt her rib cage. They felt better. The bruising on her side of her face and throat had all but vanished. Josh looked at her. "How'd you do that?"

"Do what?" Ari replied.

"Heal that quickly. I've never seen anyone heal like that before," Josh shook his head.

"Our abilities are a gift from God." Ari looked at Josh, who sarcastically rolled his eyes in disbelief. She questioned him, "You don't believe that God healed me?"

Josh laughed under his breath. "Yeah, right. Whatever."

"Do you believe in heaven?"

Josh nodded.

"Do you believe in Jesus?"

"Well, yeah, I guess."

Ari shook her head. "No. Do you believe in Jesus? Do you proclaim Him as your Lord and Savior?"

Josh shrugged his shoulders. "I used to," Josh explained, "I used to join my mom every Sunday at church. I felt so close to Him, I could swear I could hear his voice when I prayed."

"What happened?"

Josh paused as he fought back emotions that he hadn't felt in years. "I heard Him ask me if I trusted Him. I told Him yes. He told me to keep looking at His light, no matter what. The next day a cop knocked on our door telling me that my mom got into an accident. The nurses told my older brother that she kept asking God to watch over us before she died." Josh feigned a laugh. "What kind of merciful God kills the mom of a seven-year-old? My brother tried to hold our family together, but we got separated into different foster families. I kept praying for the abuse to stop, and for my brother to find me, but it went unanswered. I was angry, and I guess the rest is history. So here I am."

"I'm sorry to hear that, Josh. But God isn't the source of the pain and suffering."

"Then why did He allow my mom to die? Why did he allow me to get separated from my brother?"

The Outrider shook her head. "I don't know, Josh. God has a plan and a purpose for each and every one of us. He knew us and what we were going to do even before we were born."

Ari paused. She realized that Josh's situation was similar to her own. All of a sudden she too experienced emotions that she never came to terms with when her mother and father were killed. "When I was young, both my parents were taken from me too. I remember being angry at my mom for leaving me and my dad alone. I was only four when she didn't return home, and my dad received the bad news. And I also questioned God, why me? The only answer I received was that I can only see things as they happen, but God sees things down the road. His plan is for us continue, and someday it would all make sense."

"So did it ever?"

"You mean make sense?" Ari asked back. Josh nodded. "No," Ari answered, "at least not yet. That's how I know His plan for me is still in action."

Ari continued. "Josh, Jesus said 'I am the way, the truth, and the life. No one comes to the Father except through Me.' I pray that your heart will lead you back to a true relationship with Him. Ask Him to forgive you of your sins, and allow Him into your heart and into your life."

"What if I don't want to give up my sins? I kind of like going to the bars, not to mention the women."

Ari nodded, not so much to agree with him, but to acknowledge the Holy Spirit that spoke to her. "Your injury that you're recovering from— how did you get it?"

"I had one too many drinks, and I made my moves on someone else's girl." He lifted the corner of his shirt and showed her a large gash most of it still under a bandage. "Eighty-three stitches, and a few days in the hospital."

"So you like getting beat up for your bar habits?"

"Well, uh, no. But hey, you get shot at and beat up for a living," Josh pointed out.

Ari raised her eyebrows. *Touché, Josh.* "Yes, but what I do is a calling. We protect people, more than what you can say for how you got your wounds." Ari could feel the prompting from the Holy Spirit. She eyed a gas station coming up. "Josh, pull in there—we need to fill up. I need to wash up, too."

Josh pulled off the highway and into the station. The large gas stop allowed both trucks and cars to park near a convenience store. Ari grabbed his arm before he got out of the car. She continued to talk to her young charge. "Josh, 'God so loved the world that He gave His only son, so that whoever believes in Him shall not perish but have eternal life.' God's gift to us is His son, Jesus. And Jesus died on the cross, taking the sins of the world with Him. All we have to do is believe and proclaim that Jesus is our Lord and Savior, allow Him into our hearts and into our lives, and ask for forgiveness for our sins. He loves us Josh. He loves you. That's why we were prompted to find you."

Josh's eyes were getting watery. "Jesus wouldn't want anything to do with me. I can't forgive myself for some of the things I've done. How can someone else forgive me?"

"Your sins are in your past, Josh. The devil doesn't want you to forget them so you stay chained to those memories. The blood that Jesus shed on the cross cleanses us from all sin. When we commit our lives to Christ, our hearts, minds, and spirit yield to God. We are new creatures in Christ. If you truly repent, He has forgiven you. He loves you more than any person here on earth could." Ari shrugged.

"The enemy will always try to test your resolve to remain in Christ. I'm not going to sugarcoat this: there will be days that you will ask yourself why you chose salvation. But as long as you do His will—God's will, you will never feel regret, remorse, or guilt about your actions or of your past." Josh nodded, still trying to take what Ari just said to him.

"Josh—you can be just like Mike and me. You can beat the devil and his followers back to where they belong. You can do God's work here on earth. Just open your heart and accept Jesus as your Lord and Savior."

Josh hesitated and then broke free of Ari's gentle grasp. He cleared his throat and stared straight ahead. "The car needs gas." He stepped out of the car. Ari sat back hard and closed her eyes. *Now I know why Isaac wanted me on this assignment. Lord, help me say the right thing.* She craned her neck. "Don't harden your heart, not now."

Ari got out of the car. She could see Josh had tears in his eyes. The Holy Spirit stopped the ministering Outrider. *Patience, Ariana.* She hung her head and backed off. Ari looked at her hands, still covered in Mike's blood. Giving a big sigh, she said, "I need to get cleaned up. I'll pay when I get out."

Ari walked unnoticed to the restroom. She looked in the mirror and perked up, surprised she didn't look too bad. She washed the dried blood off her hands. After Ari finished, she walked up to the counter to pay for the gas. "Pump number five . . ."

The young lady looked at her. "The young man already paid." Ari looked out and saw that Josh and the Porsche had left already. She rolled her eyes and shook her head. *When are they going to learn?* Ari walked over and grabbed a bottle of water, paid for it, and walked out the door. She walked behind the building, took a long drink of water from her bottle, looked around, and then self-transported.

Ari showed up near the diner where she and Mike were ambushed. She walked behind a grove of trees and bushes and saw the police cars and other city vehicles parked haphazardly in the parking lot. She frowned as she saw her bike being loaded onto the back of an open trailer.

Suddenly, she felt a hand on her shoulder. Gasping, a familiar face held a finger to his mouth. "Dave!" Ari whispered. "Were you able to get Mike?"

"We got here too late," Christina chimed in quietly. "They took him to the hospital. Isn't that your bike?"

"Yeah. I need it too. Our client took off with the Porsche," Ari admitted.

"You lost the client, the bike, and the Porsche, and your team member Mike is hurt badly?" Dave asked.

"Yeah . . . It sounds a lot worse when you put it that way." Ari scratched the side of her neck.

Dave smirked at Ari. "It sounds like our top Outrider needs to get retrained." He and his wife Christina began to quietly laugh. "How did you lose control over everything? What happened?"

"There were four demons in the diner, but we didn't realize it until it was too late. After fighting the attackers and finally stopping them, I pulled the blade out of Mike but had to get Josh out of the place in case more attackers arrived. We took the car, and we had just stopped at a gas station off the side of the highway to fill up. He took off when I went to the restroom to clean up."

"You're hurt?" Christina asked.

"Yes, but I'm fine," Ari said. "Do you know what hospital they took Mike to?"

"I heard them say City General," Christina answered.

"I hate to ask this of you, but can the two of you get Mike while I find Josh?" Ari asked.

"You owe us," Dave said.

"Yeah, I know. I really appreciate this. Do you think you can cause a distraction so I can get my bike off the trailer?

Christina winked. "I thought you'd never ask." She and her husband walked quickly to the diner.

Christina began to wail, "My brother! I heard he got shot, where is he?" The men gathered around her, trying to calm her down.

Ari snuck up to the back of the trailer. Mounting the flatbed, she had just removed the ties to it when the truck began to pull out of the parking lot. Jokingly, she looked up. *Lord, honestly, do you have to make it challenging every time?*

Ari put her helmet on and unsecured her bike. She turned it around and then started it up. Psyching herself up, Ari talked to herself. "I've never done this but how hard can it be? I mean they do this all the time in the movies, right?" She launched herself off the moving trailer and landed roughly onto the pavement, and miraculously she and the bike were still upright and intact. The Outrider faced the oncoming traffic and quickly swerved off to the side of the road and stopped.

Ari not only caught the attention of the tow driver but some of the officers in the diner parking lot. She sped off on the side of the road and worked her way across into the westbound traffic lanes. She could hear sirens behind her, but they had no way to catch her with the speed and maneuverability of the bike. Ari leaned down and shifted, pulling away from the police.

As she began to approach an entrance ramp, a motorcycle cop pulled up behind her. The siren blared and then she heard shots. *Is he crazy? We're going one hundred miles an hour and they're trying to shoot me?*

Suddenly a bullet ripped into her front tire, and she lost control of the bike. The bike careened over to the inside lane and then hit the barrier separating the oncoming traffic. The bike came to an abrupt stop, disintegrating upon impact. Ari went airborne over the top of the handlebars. She flipped, and at the moment an oncoming car bore down on her, she closed her eyes and prayed, *In You I trust, Lord.* Ari disappeared as she self-transported. The driver slammed on the brakes, causing an accident as other vehicles piled up around them. The officers stopped and tried to see where the body of the biker got thrown.

As Christina and Dave were being questioned and consoled by an officer, they heard over the police radio about the accident further down the road. The officer also stopped talking to hear some of the details on the radio before turning it down. "What happened to the motorcycle driver?" Dave asked.

"It doesn't sound like they're going to make it. After crashing, their body got thrown over the barrier into the oncoming traffic. They were speeding well over eighty miles an hour before the bike hit the retaining wall. They think the bike driver slammed into one of the vehicles. Even if they didn't, well, with that kind of speed, no one survives hitting the ground." The officer closed his notepad. "I think I have enough information from you. Thanks, and I hope your brother is okay." He walked away and into the diner.

Christina and Dave were numb. Dave smiled and gave Christina a hug. "She's still alive. It's Ari. You know: the Outrider that has nine lives." A tearful Christina hugged back.

◆

In the air for only a split second, Ari reappeared in the back of Hollywood midair, upside down. In a fraction of a second, she somehow righted herself. She came in almost horizontally at the near end of the pool and ended up feet first in the deep end. The enormous splash caught the attention of everyone on the main floor. Jesse and Jim ran outside and saw an unconscious body floating in the middle of the pool. Jim jumped in and retrieved the person. Jesse carefully removed the helmet, and both men were shocked to see Ari.

Unzipping her leather jacket, Jesse listened for any sign of life. Her hearbeat barely audible, Ari had stopped breathing. The impact had knocked the wind out of her. Jesse gave her mouth-to-mouth until she spit up water and began to breathe. Ari's eyes opened. After she caught her breath, she looked around and smiled, then, as if she lost her mind, began to laugh. "Thank you, Jesus, for your grace! Totally insane! What an adrenaline rush! But I don't recommend trying again." She tried to get up, but pain and Jesse stopped her.

"What happened? Where on earth did you come from?" Jim asked.

"You wouldn't believe it even if I told you." Ari winced as she tried to get up again, "I thought water would be a softer landing than that."

"Where do you think you're going?" the physician asked her. Jesse examined her.

With the help of Jim and Jesse, Ari stood. Jim saw her suck in, trying to hide the pain she felt. "Are you okay?"

"Yeah, I'm fine except for a bruised ego. This assignment has been a nightmare. Where are the extra keys to the Porsche?" Ari asked as she walked inside.

"Hanging with the rest of the keys. Why, where's the Porsche?" Jim asked, his brow furrowed.

"With Josh. Somewhere between here and New York, I imagine," Ari said matter-of-factly as she walked upstairs. She began to peel her wet jacket off.

Jim followed her, "Where's the bike?"

"Um, it disintegrated when it hit the retaining wall. As I flew uncontrolled over the wall and into the oncoming traffic, I decided a landing in the pool made for a better chance of survival than hitting the oncoming car's windshield. I really thought water would be softer than that." Ari took her boots off and dumped the water into the tub.

Jim scratched his head. "You mean you trashed the bike and lost the client and the Porsche? Where was Mike during all of this?"

"Um, he got shot. We were attacked in a diner along our route." She struggled to get her wet shirt over her head, feeling the pain of not only her most recent impact with the water but also her earlier injuries while fighting the demons.

Jim helped her extract herself from her shirt. "Is he okay? Where is he?"

Ari grabbed a towel and dried herself. "Um, I'm pretty sure he's fine, but EMS got there before help from here arrived. He's in a hospital right now. I have Dave and Christina rescuing him while I get Josh and the car back."

"Why didn't you stay with Mike?" Jim asked his wife.

"Because of the attack. I had to clear Josh out of there in case we ran into more demons."

Jim had an incredulous look, trying to understand what had happened. "So how did you lose Josh and the car?"

"I drove the car for several minutes and pulled off to a side street hidden by trees and bushes. I must have passed out, so Josh drove to a gas station. I woke up before then and went inside the store to wash up while he filled up the car. When I got out, Josh had left." Ari began to remove the rest of her wet clothes off and dried herself with a towel.

Jim shook his head, his hand holding the growing pain in his forehead. "You were injured? Let me get this straight: you got injured, Mike got shot, you crashed the bike, flipped yourself mid-crash into our pool, lost the client and the Porsche, and now Mike is in the hands of regular people in a hospital that don't understand our supernatural healing."

"Yeah." Ari smiled sheepishly. "Like I told Dave and Christina, it sounds a lot worse when you put it that way. Where's Alexa?" Ari finished getting her wet clothes off and began to dress in dry clothes.

She put on another holster and gun and then grabbed a dry pair of boots and a jacket.

"She's with Liz in daycare like usual. Where do you think you're going?" Jim asked.

"I have to find Josh. And I think I know where I can find him," Ari said as she zipped her jacket up.

———————◆———————

Ari could feel the *thump, thump, thump* of the bass rhythm against her chest as she walked up to the same nightclub she and Mike entered a few nights earlier. The same bouncer and host were at the door. Ari approached the bouncer. He stepped to the side, giving the Outrider a wide berth, and allowed her to enter. She smiled. "It will only be a minute."

She scanned the crowd again and fixed her eyes on her target. Sitting on the same couch as when Ari first saw him, Josh had his arms around a young lady. "Excuse me," Ari told the lady as she grabbed Josh by the shoulder. Not even giving him time to stand on his own, she dragged him up the stairs and past the bouncer. "Where are my car keys?"

"Nice to see you too, Ari. What car keys? And how did you get here?" Josh asked, teasing her.

Ari suddenly shoved Josh's face up against a brick wall, twisting his arm behind him. "I'm not in any mood for games, Josh. My friend is badly injured, and my status as an exceptional Outrider is now in question, all because of you." Josh pulled out her car keys with his other hand. "Now, where is the Porsche?"

"Around the corner." Ari walked Josh to the car. After she made sure they were alone, she self-transported with Josh in tow back to Hollywood.

Josh couldn't believe the instant change in scenery. "How did you do that? Where are we?" he asked, amazed. He took a step, and then his knees gave out.

Ari caught his arm and helped him stand up again. "Self-transport,

Josh," Ari said. "The practice of self-transporting to a specified location allows us to be discreet. We usually materialize close to the coordinates out of view like the alley across the street and walk the rest of the distance. There are several reasons for doing so: The organization doesn't want to raise questions or suspicion of our existence. We have learned over the millennia that they work most effectively without being hindered by limitations of governments, borders, and stereotypes."

"Your self-transportation is something on the scale of being straight out of a science fiction movie," Josh said. "How do you do that?"

Ari explained, "The ability is imparted to us. Our deliberate and concentrated thought can take us anywhere in the world in the mere instant it takes to blink an eye. The physical ability to do so doesn't make sense in the natural world, but as a chosen warrior of God, I realized that there were many gifts that were given to the Outriders that normal people don't have. It is not that the average person couldn't have these abilities—they could, if only their unbelief didn't exist and an unshakable faith in God did."

Ari gave him a look that quieted him instantly and quashed any other questions he might have. Still upset that Isaac gave her this assignment, and upset that Josh couldn't be trusted, Ari had little patience at this point in the assignment. Still holding his shoulder, she led him inside and then down to the med ward.

"Josh, I want Jesse, our doctor, to take a look at that wound you have before we go any further," Ari told him.

Josh could see his escort's anger. "Ari, ma'am . . . I'm sorry." Josh stuttered, afraid of the Outrider's reaction. "I filled the car and the next thing I knew, I flew at one hundred twenty miles per hour down the highway with a joyride. I stopped at a gas station several hours down the road, and as I thought about it more, the more I felt bad about abandoning you. But then I got back into the car, and it didn't seem to matter anymore again. I never meant to hurt anyone, but it always seems to end that way. I decided to come clean with you."

"You have to trust the Holy Spirit to guide you again." She put her hand over his heart. "From now on, let your heart lead you. Your head might be saying one thing, but as long as you've given your life to Jesus, your heart will never lead you wrong. I know that feeling, Josh: you feel vulnerable because you are not in control anymore. Just let Him guide you." She boldly stared at Josh's face. "Josh, repeat after me." The young man nodded. He repeated the words Ari said. "Lord . . . I ask you to come into my heart . . . forgive me of my sins . . . today . . . I am a new creation in Christ . . . Old things have passed away . . . and today all things have become new . . . I will never be the same . . . In Jesus' name, amen."

As Josh repeated her words, Ari could see a physical transformation overtake her charge. Josh grinned. "I feel as if weights were taken off from around my neck. I can't stop smiling."

"Congrats, Josh." Ari smiled back.

Jesse stepped forward and smiled at his patient. "Congratulations." He examined Josh and patched up some of his recent injuries. He released the young man back into Ari's hands. She guided him down the hall to the elevators.

Josh tapped Ari on her shoulder, stopping them in the hall. "Ma'am, what just happened to me?"

Ari smiled. "You just let Jesus into your heart. You are a new creation. There is no old, no past, anymore. All you have done before now has been forgiven."

"I don't want to disappoint you. What if I backslide?"

"Don't worry about me. If I see you doing something contrary to being Christ-like, I will let you know. I would worry more about disappointing yourself. Don't allow the devil to tell you lies about who you have become. Read the Bible. The truth is in the word. His word."

Ari escorted him down to the training level and into a separate bunkroom from the other students. "For reasons unknown, God wants you to become an Outrider like me. You have to be trained, among other things. You're free to wander around this level for the next few days or so while you get acclimated, but you're restricted to here for now. If you want to go to the rest of the building, you will need to be escorted by an Outrider or overseer. In the morning, Isaac and Jesse will be down here to assess whether you're ready to have your Outrider gifts imparted to you.

"Once you've been given your gifts, you will be able to join the rest of the class and wander through most of rest of the complex. Your meals will be served down here. It's not that we don't like you with the main group, but we find that those that you train with will inevitably be the Outriders that you work the best with, and you'll build a very strong friendship. We'll have clothes for you to wear by tomorrow morning. Oh, and I recommend reading a little of this every morning." Ari handed him a Bible as she finished talking to him. "Just let us know if you need anything else."

Josh nodded, "Ari, you risked your life to get me, even after I dumped you at that gas station. Why?"

"If it were my choice, I'd let you continue living the way you had been up to now. But it isn't my choice. Like I said before, my life is not led by my will every day. I endeavor to live by God's will. Many times the two are in conflict, but I've never regretted following God's plan for me. It may not be what I expect to do, but I know I'm walking in His blessing if I allow Him to lead me. It's going to be a long day for you tomorrow. Try to get some rest. I'll check on you in a few days." Ari turned and walked up to the elevator.

"Thanks. I owe you." Josh said.

"I'd reserve that comment until after your impartation experience. You might want to take it back." Ari winked as she got onto the elevator.

CHAPTER FOUR

In rough shape, Ari made her way down to the morning meeting a few minutes early. She wandered into the kitchen and made herself a smoothie. After adding blueberries, pomegranate juice, and some ground flax seed, she added a scoop of protein powder and a spoonful of spirulina. She added coconut milk into the blender and let it mix for a minute before pouring the thick, gray/green beverage into a glass and drinking it.

Hiding her yawn behind her hand, Ari leaned up against the breakfast counter as the room began to fill with Outriders and overseers. As the meeting started, Mike and Jim leaned up against the counter as well. Mike grabbed a chocolate doughnut from a box in the dining room and took a big bite. Jim did the same with a powdered doughnut. Ari looked at both of them and shook her head as she whispered, "It's so unfair. Guys seem to be able to eat anything and not gain an ounce. If I ate that, it would go straight to my hips."

"What is that stuff you're drinking?" Mike asked as he finished his first doughnut.

"Breakfast," Ari answered after taking a gulp.

"Mmmm . . ." Jim said as he took a big bite out of his doughnut. He emerged with a ring of white powder around his lips.

Ari shook her head. "How appropriate. You're foaming at the mouth . . ."

"Is there a problem back there?" Isaac asked the trio. The three shook their heads. Isaac looked at Ari. "Ari, we need for you to do reconnaissance," Isaac began. "We normally could have one of the other Outriders do this, but given the nature of this and the fact that you speak both fluent Spanish as well as a little Portuguese, we thought it best to give it to you. We will have Dave fill in for you as instructor until you return."

"What am I investigating?" Ari asked and then took a drink.

"There's been unusually heavy demonic activity that has manifested in a remote area of jungle north of La Paz, Bolivia, just south of the Brazilian border. The closest village is not even named on the map. There have been reports coming out from the jungle of madness and strange murders, along with a giant man wielding a sword," Isaac explained.

"Sounds like someone caught some sort of jungle fever and just went a little crazy with a machete," Mike joked.

"I would think the same except the murders reported have all been devout Christians," Isaac told Ari. "Entire families and villages have been wiped out. This man that has been wielding the sword has been killing every person in his path. If this story is true, he needs to be found and has to be stopped. But I sense that there is more to this than what we know."

Ari's expression turned to a frown. "Sword-wielding giants in the jungles of Bolivia? Why can't the manifestation occur on a street in a clean metropolitan city, or better yet, on a sandy beach in the Pacific?" Ari sighed and straightened up. "When do you need for me to go?"

"By tomorrow morning. At least you'll be able to plan and rest a little before going," Isaac said.

"Whom do I get on my team?"

"Whoever you need and is available," Isaac said.

Ari looked around the room. "Silas and Brad, and if she's available, I'd like to take Essie too," Ari said.

Isaac looked at her. "That seems like a lot of Outriders for reconnaissance of one madman, Ari."

"This man has wiped out entire families and villages in frontier towns. Normally people that live on the fringes of completely untouched wilderness are prepared for the worst and armed to the hilt, and they haven't been able to stop this guy. With all that and its remote location we don't have much of a backup. I feel better to err on the side of caution, especially if you're alarmed about this being more than what meets the eye," Ari explained.

Isaac nodded and handed her the file. "Very well. Get your team together and brief them. Then I suggest you get some sleep." He paused for a moment. "Ari, I have a bad feeling about this. I'm praying the blood of Jesus over you and your team. Be careful." Ari nodded.

Immediately after the meeting, Ari gathered her team at the dining room table. She filled them in on the details of the situation. "We each need to make sure to take our travel bags, water, and food for at least a few days. We also need to have at least two loaded guns and an extra ammo clip, along with your hand blades."

"And bug repellant. Don't forget about that," Essie added, her tightly curled auburn hair bouncing as she nodded. Once again, her nose crinkled at the thought of all the insects. Shorter than most of the Outriders, Essie's boldness and young spunky personality, along with her immaculately manicured fingers and toes, betrayed her urban upbringing when she spoke up.

"Why all of the gear and our travel bags, Ari?" Brad asked. His shaved head betrayed a faint shadow of where his hair used to grow. His dark complexion and serious expression contrasted to his usual jovial antics that he would pull off with the help of his friend and fellow Outrider Mike.

"We may not run into this man for a few days, depending on how fast he's moving and how far into the jungle he decides to hide. I hope that by us being there, it will draw him out. Trust me when I say the faster we get out of there, the better I'll feel," Ari said. She looked at her watch. "We'll leave at 6:00 a.m. tomorrow morning. Get some rest, everyone."

Ari climbed up the stairs and into her bedroom. After taking her shoes off, she set her alarm and slipped under the covers. The exhausted Outrider briefly prayed thanksgiving before falling asleep.

Ari's dreams were wild. Brilliant sunlight blinded her as she heard a voice telling her, *You have come to the kingdom for such a time as this.* She saw the momentary glint of sunlight off the blade of a sword. She felt herself flinch as the blade came close to her. Then, after a bright flash of light, she saw a shadow stand over her and hold a sword above her with both hands. With savage force, the swordsman stabbed her deep, to the hilt of his sword.

Ari woke up, her arms instinctively up trying to protect herself from an imaginary weapon. Beads of sweat clung to her upper lip and neck. Out of breath, she briefly examined her chest for wounds. Relieved, Ari plopped back onto the bed, staring at the ceiling as she rubbed her face. Rolling onto her side, she looked at the clock. *I still have a few minutes before the alarm goes off.* Ari looked at her hands; they were uncharacteristically trembling. She clenched her fists a few times, breathing deeply, trying to shake the memory of her unnerving vision. She closed her eyes and spoke Scripture over herself: *For who is God besides the LORD? And who is the Rock except our God? It is God who arms me with strength and keeps my way secure.*

Finally stepping out of bed, she shuffled to the bathroom. Looking in the mirror, Ari shook her head. She looked almost as rough as she felt. Her short, dark hair streaked with silvery gray stood in a wild mess. A quick shower made her feel better, but still not quite back to normal. Ari got dressed and then fixed her hair and makeup. She stood stooped over the sink, feeling queasy, when Jim walked in. "Well hello, stranger," Jim joked with his wife. Alexa held out her hands from Jim's hold of her. Ari kissed her daughter and then Jim.

"How long is this assignment?" Jim asked her.

Ari shrugged as she turned around, finished with her touch-ups. "I'm hoping only a day or so, but it may end up being a week or two. It just depends on how quick we can find this guy."

Jim frowned. "And when do you have to leave?"

"Not until tomorrow morning," Ari answered.

"It doesn't give us much time to reacquaint ourselves with each other," he told her. "Christina said she would watch Alexa this evening so you could get a good night's sleep." Jim looked at his watch.

Ari looked at her watch and sighed. "Less time getting reacquainted, if you consider its dinner time." Jim leaned over and passionately kissed his wife. Ari closed her eyes, taking in the emotions of the moment. It seemed like it has been too long since she had seen her husband, let alone felt his touch. He stopped and her eyes took a few seconds before they fluttered open. She remembered to breathe in again as she quietly spoke, "I guess we can be a few minutes late."

Jim gently kissed her again, making her close her eyes again. "Okay, we'll miss the first course and be late for the entrée," she said dreamily as she looked at him. Ari held his face in her hands and she kissed him again. Her eyes closed and didn't open again as she smiled. "Well, maybe we can just grab a couple of sandwiches later . . ."

As the diners were finishing up their dessert, Ari and Jim emerged from their bedroom. Brad smirked watching them as he elbowed Silas. He cleared his throat loudly and made Ari blush as she walked down the stairs. Alexa waved her fork. Their friends cleared their throats and quietly snickered. They sat down with their friends and quickly blessed their food and ate. Ari bent over and kissed Alexa, then leaned over and whispered to Brad and Silas, "You're just like a couple of obnoxious schoolboys."

Isaac looked at the couple, "Nice of you two to finally join us."

Ari playfully glared at her mentor. "It just occurred to why so few Outriders get married. It's near to impossible to have a decent relationship or family time with the work we do."

"Faith, if it is not accompanied by action, is dead," Isaac quoted the Bible, teasing her.

"Yeah, but He also commanded us to be fruitful and multiply," Ari pointed out, taking a bite from her fork. "The only one able to do that without a spouse was Mary, the Virgin Mother."

"I promise to give you time off when you return, Ari," Isaac told her.

Ari shook her head and her fork at Isaac as she swallowed a bite of food. "Oh, no. You say that every time, but you never specify how much time, and for some reason, my time off never seems to materialize. I want you to say it with witnesses."

Isaac looked at the group and then at Ari. "Okay, how about a couple of weeks?"

"Three," Ari countered back, "and with Jim."

"Two with Jim and one additional week for yourself," Isaac counter-offered.

Ari thought about it for a moment and then smiled. "Deal," Ari said.

They finished their meals and went back up to the room. Ari rechecked her travel bag and then the gear bag. Satisfied her bags were in order, she went out onto the patio into the rose and lavender sunset and began to pray.

Midway through her prayer she saw the brilliant sunlight and heard the voice again tell her, *You have come to the kingdom for such a time as this.* She saw the glint of metal again, and then had visions of the large man with the sword. He barely looked human. Shiny, dark green scales covered parts of his pale green-gray skin. He stood on two snake-like appendages that allowed him to tower over Ari. His teeth were pointed, with long fangs like a wild animal. The last moments of the vision, he looked down at Ari. With both hands on the hilt of a longsword, he plunged the sword into her.

Ari bolted up from her vision and sat on the balcony chair trying to compose herself. *Come on Ari. Shake it off. Just because this is the second time you've had this vision doesn't mean it is going to happen. Perfect love casts out fear . . .* She prayed for a bit more and went inside. She kissed Alexa on the forehead and pulled the blanket onto her sleeping daughter, who was already in her crib. Ari got ready for bed and set her alarm for 3:30. She lay in bed still exhausted from her last assignment. Her fatigue finally caught up with her. Unable to think about the vision or anything else, her mind slowly fell into a deep sleep.

Ari awoke as the alarm went off. Jim's arm gently held her in an embrace. She stretched over and hit the snooze, and curled back up into Jim's arms. *Really. I have to get up right now? Unreal. . . .* The dark room enveloped the young family as Ari lay in bed, staring at the ceiling. She closed her eyes. *Thank you, Jesus, for your peace and love. I need to enjoy this moment one last time before I disappear in the mountains of Bolivia.* After a few minutes she gently moved Jim's arm to the side and turned the alarm off. She got up and gently kissed her daughter and tucked the covers around her.

Ari quietly showered and got ready, praying to herself. After dressing, she slipped her leg holster on and slipped two hand blades into the holster. She strapped an additional leg holster for an extra gun onto her right leg. Ari made some adjustments to her arm holster before slipping her other gun into it.

Silently walking out to the balcony one last time, she prayed before she had to leave. "My help comes from the Lord who made heaven and earth . . . The Lord shall preserve you from all evil; He shall preserve your soul. The Lord shall preserve your going out and your coming in from this time forth, and even forevermore." She put her earbuds in and played her praise and worship music, exalting God. Ari then prayed for protection of herself and her team and for His knowledge and wisdom on how to deal with this strange man.

Finished praying, Ari went back inside, kissed Alexa again, and then gently caressed her husband's face. He awoke, looked at her with a smile, and whispered, "Are you leaving now?"

"I'm afraid so. I'll be back as soon as I can. I love you so much, Mr. Sommers," Ari said as she kissed him.

"I love you too, Mrs. Sommers. Stay safe."

She grabbed her bags and walked out the door, quietly closing it behind her. The others on her team were already down at the dining table, eating. Ari dropped her bags on the floor and went into the kitchen. She grabbed an apple and a muffin and several bottles of water, and then went into the pantry and grabbed several of boxes of protein bars and granola bars along with a box of freeze-dried meals. She stashed some of the boxes into her travel bag along with the extra water and gave the rest to the team for them to store in their own bags. Ari normally wouldn't worry about bringing extra food, but since they would be in a remote location, she wanted to make sure they had enough calories for at least a couple of days.

As she ate the muffin and apple, she dug into the gear bag and tossed extra ammo clips to her team. "Clip these to the back side of your belt," she instructed them, as she did the same. She felt over armed and about ten pounds heavier with all of her weapons. After they were done eating, Silas led the team in prayer.

The team got up, grabbed their gear, and walked out onto the patio and a lightening sky. They disappeared, self-transporting to the other hemisphere.

They reappeared just outside of the village Isaac reported the mysterious sword-wielding man had last been seen. While it was still very early in the morning, the surviving villagers began to stir. The overcast morning blanketed the mountains; the low clouds obscured the tops of the hills around them. The air hung thick with moisture, and Ari felt almost sticky from all of the fog and mist. An old lady appeared from the mist, walking down the road when she spotted the group. She stopped and began to walk back. Ari quickly spoke in Spanish to her: "Please ma'am, we're here to help. We have heard of the large man that had killed some people here, and we are trying to track him down and stop him. Can you help us?"

"Where did you come from?" The lady asked Ari. "You don't have a car."

Ari told her, "We've walked quite a way, searching for the man. Is there a place here in the village we can drop our things off?"

"Yes," the old lady said in Spanish. "You are welcome to leave them in my home."

"Have you seen this man? The large man with the sword?" Ari asked, still speaking Spanish.

"Yes," the old lady said again. "He came here again last night." She began to cry.

Ari dropped her bags and walked up to the lady and hugged her. The team looked at Ari. "She said the man came back again last night."

They escorted the old lady back to her home. Ari asked what had happened last night. The old lady shook her head as she described how she heard screams in the night and gunfire. She looked at Ari and said, "But the guns don't hurt the man. He can't be killed. The elders had prayed the night before for God's help, and then last night they were killed by this man. So much for God's help," she spit out.

Ari spoke to the lady, "Ma'am, I believe we're the answer to their prayers. I'm sorry we didn't get here sooner to help them."

The old lady laughed skeptically. "There are just four of you. How are you going to stop him when ten armed men in the village couldn't stop him?"

"Our God is the God of the impossible. He moves mountains and parts the seas," Ari answered. "Can you tell us which way the man went?"

The old lady pointed up the slope into densely wooded forest on the far side of the village. "He walked into there somewhere."

As the team stared into the thick jungle, Ari thanked the old lady. She went into her bag and pulled out bottles of water and tossed each of her team members a bottle. She also gave them each a couple of protein bars. "I don't want to venture too far from the village for this trip. I want to get an idea of the terrain we're dealing with and whether we will be able to safely engage him in there."

They walked outside and stared at the mist-obscured hillside. Ari turned and addressed her team, "Our priority is to keep this village out of harm. If for some reason we can't find this man and subdue him, or if something happens to me, your orders are to return to the village before dark and evacuate the villagers until the man can be apprehended or stopped." The group nodded.

They continued to walk through the village and saw families weeping, as covered bodies were carried inside homes. Ari hung her head and closed her eyes as they continued to walk. She prayed a short prayer for the Comforter to come and bring peace to the survivors.

The Outriders stopped at the edge of the forest. Ari brushed her bangs out of her eyes as she looked at freshly broken leaves and matted grass along what appeared to be a rough path into the forest.

While the group tried to peer into the seemingly impenetrable forest, Ari softly quoted from the Bible. *"I will say of the LORD, He is my refuge and my fortress; my God, in Him I will trust. Surely He shall deliver you from the snare of the fowler and from the perilous pestilence. He shall cover you with His feathers, and under His wings you shall take refuge; His truth shall be your shield and buckler. You shall not be afraid of the terror by night, nor of the arrow that flies by day, nor of the pestilence that walks in darkness, nor of the destruction that lays waste at noonday."*

She withdrew her gun from her shoulder holster and took the safety off. "If this thing is as big as they say it is, it has to leave a pretty easy trail for us to follow. Stay alert and make sure to stay out of range of its sword," she told the group. They followed Ari's lead and also pulled out their guns as they walked single file into the forest behind Ari.

Silently they hiked for several hours as Ari followed a path of broken branches and disturbed greenery. They walked into a clearing next to a wide, shallow stream. Ari stopped, looked around, and then slipped her gun back into its holster as she took her backpack off. "Let's take a rest before continuing." The others followed suit, sitting on logs and boulders.

In any other situation, the surrounding landscape would have had Ari speechless with its beauty. The deep green trees stretched their endless arms and fingers to the heavens. The mist obscured the tops of the trees and whatever animals were in them. Strange calls and sounds came from every direction. The stream ran wide but shallow. The sound of the water would normally calm her down, but she couldn't shake the vision she had. Ari reached into her pack and grabbed a bottle of water and a granola bar. She munched on the bar silently as she looked around.

Silas noticed the furrows in her brow. As she scanned the area surrounding them, she seemed more jumpy than normal. "Ari, you need to rest too. Relax." He took a long draw of water from his bottle. He watched Essie frantically wave off some invisible insect near her face. He laughed. "I guess some folks are better in urban warfare than in the middle of some jungle."

Ari smiled, hung her head down, and shook it. She could hear Essie hold back a scream. Ari got up and stepped over to Essie. The young Outrider cracked a smile and shrugged her shoulders at her leader. Without a word or breaking eye contact with Essie, Ari's hand shot out into the air in one swift move and snatched the pesky bug midair. Essie cleared her throat. "Thanks, Ari." Without a word, Ari returned to her boulder and sat down and continued to eat her snack.

Silas laughed. "Who needs bug spray when we have Ari's quick hand? It might mean we now have an environmentally friendly pesticide." The two men began to laugh, making Ari and Essie laugh too.

As she was laughing, a glint of something on the other side of the stream caught Ari's attention. She waded a dozen yards across the knee-deep stream to where she saw the glint. Just under the water, Ari saw a golden arrow. She picked it up and held it up, mesmerized by the flawless metal and how light it felt. *Now how on earth did you get here?* Curious, Silas stood up and yelled, "What did you find?" Ari handed him the arrow. Silas whistled. "I've never seen anything like this before."

Ari suddenly stopped and held her hand up, telling the group to be silent. She looked around and noticed the forest suddenly became eerily silent. The cacophony of animal sounds that surrounded them disappeared; her own heartbeat and the stream around her feet were the only noise she could hear. She moved to a position closer to Silas.

"What's wrong, Ari? Silas asked in a hushed voice.

"The forest just got too quiet. This can't be a good sign," she answered as she looked around. She silently signaled to her team to spread out and hold their position. She removed her gun from its holster and signaled to Silas to follow her. They had stepped partway into the stream when suddenly they both heard a noise and looked ahead to a large tree directly in front of them.

A very large human-like creature moved out from behind the tree and stood immediately in front of Ari. He stood at least five or six feet taller than Ari. His arms seemed longer in proportion to his body than a human's, and his color ranged from an ashen grayish green to dark green. His upper torso, shoulders, and waist areas were covered in scales. He didn't have legs, but in their place were appendages like a snake or serpent's body, covered with scales. A third appendage of what seemed to be a tail helped the creature hoist itself well above Silas and Ari.

He appeared just as startled as Ari. Taken aback by his sheer height Ari mumbled, "My dear Jesu . . ." when the man's serpentine leg back-swiped and hit Ari and Silas. They both flew through the air off to the side. Silas hit a large tree trunk hard and fell to the ground unconscious. Ari landed a dozen yards away in the stream, stunned, and struggled to get her breath back after having the wind knocked out of her. She rolled over onto her hands and knees and got up just as she saw Brad shooting at the creature at almost point-blank range. Their normally lethal blades didn't seem to stop the man at all. Before she could come to his aid, Ari saw Brad take the full force of the creature's sword slash across his chest. Brad fell to the ground.

Ari yelled at Essie, "Get out of there! Essie, don't try to fight it. Get out!"

Essie also tried shooting blades at the being as she began to back up. Her foot caught a tree root, and she tripped and fell backwards. Ari ran when she saw Essie in trouble. Pushing off a nearby tree trunk, she managed to jump onto the back and shoulder of the attacker. She held her blade gun against the base of the man's skull and shot several blades. The man didn't even flinch. None of the blades penetrated his tough skin and scales.

Ari dropped her gun, grabbed her hand blade, and tried to sink it between two scaly plates as far as she could between two of his vertebrae in his neck. That action caught the large man's attention, but the creature acted like he was bitten by a pesky mosquito. He briefly stopped his advance toward Essie and reached up with one of his snake-like appendages and grabbed Ari by the shoulder and threw her over his head. The Outrider flew another dozen or so yards across the clearing before her back slammed into a tree trunk.

Ari grunted in pain as she fell to the ground. Stunned and in agony, Ari didn't stay on the ground very long. Despite hurting, Ari tried to get back up. She heard Essie scream. Still on her hands and knees, Ari could see over the tall, leafy ground cover as the giant's sword swung down hard. Suddenly, Essie's screams became silent.

The strange giant looked up and began to move toward Ari. She could clearly hear the scales of its legs rubbing up against rocks and ground, and against itself. Holding her ribs in pain, Ari slowly got up and drew her other gun from her leg holster as she backed up. *Guide my hand, Lord. Flash forth lightning and scatter them; shoot out Your arrows and destroy them. Stretch out Your hand from above; rescue me and deliver me out of great waters, from the hand of foreigners . . .*

Ari briefly aimed and shot the man in one of his eyes. The man stopped for a moment and staggered, then he continued pursuing her. Ari shot again, aiming for his other eye, but missed. The man slashed down with his sword, catching her in her left arm and side, and then deeply through her right leg. She cried out in pain as she fell onto her back, grabbing her leg.

The creature moved forward and stood over Ari, his appendages pinning her down. Holding his sword over his head, he began to swing it down towards her. She grasped her last hand blade with her injured left arm. Despite her pain and the tiny size of her blade, she managed to stop the sword from hitting her. The giant repositioned his serpentine leg to hold her arm down, then changed his grip to bring the sword straight down into Ari. As the sword's tip came down, Ari wiggled and moved slightly out of the way of the sword, but not nearly enough. Ari cried out in pain as the man drove the sword deep into her, just below the right collarbone.

Gritting her teeth, Ari freed her arm and quickly raised her gun. With strength and aim that wasn't her own, Ari shot the giant man in his other eye, blinding him. The creature staggered away and slumped down, hunched over in pain.

Lord, I need you. This can't be happening. Ari dropped her gun and clenched the hilt of sword. The creature had sunk the sword so deeply, it pinned Ari to the ground. The sword had passed completely through her and was embedded into the soft earth beneath her. Each breath she drew shot pain through her chest. She pulled at the hilt with her left hand, but it only moved it a few inches before numbness began to overtake her body. Ari felt cold and shivered. She tasted blood in her mouth. Desperately she fumbled with the hilt and drew it out a few more inches before her hand went limp.

Ari closed her eyes as she felt herself begin to slip into shock. *Please forgive me, Lord. I couldn't stop this creature. Please send someone to finish the task.* She heard a noise and opened her eyes and smiled weakly. Silas stood over her.

"Hang in there, Ari," he told her as he pulled the longsword's blade out of her. Ari barely felt it. He pulled out a large handkerchief from his pocket and used it as a tourniquet above Ari's leg wound. He unzipped the front of Ari's leather jacket and removed a couple of cloths from her inside pocket. He folded them and gently pressed them against her chest and back wounds. Ari fought to keep conscious.

"That creature is injured. It needs to be stopped," Ari whispered, her words slurred from her shivering. "The sword. Use its sword."

Silas left Ari momentarily, picked up the sword, and walked over to the giant who caused all of this. The creature held his face and eyes in his enormous hands. It heard Silas' footsteps and swiped his arms and serpent-like legs at the air blindly. Silas lifted the heavy sword, stepped forward, and swung it, cleanly decapitating the monster and stopping its killing rampage.

Silas ran back to Ari. She looked at him and barely talked above a whisper. "Check on the others. If they're alive, they need to be tended to first."

"Ari, you're injured pretty badly. I need to get you back to Hollywood," Silas argued.

Ari mustered enough strength to correct Silas. "Assist Brad and Essie first. That's an order, Mr. Monroe. Do it."

He nodded and walked quickly into the forest. As he walked, he began to pray for his missing friends. He came across Essie's decapitated body. He continued to walk and stumbled across Brad. He had a large deep slash across his chest, and gasped for breath. Silas removed his own jacket and t-shirt. He ripped his t-shirt to lengthen the fabric and then carefully tied it firmly against the wounds on Brad's chest. Silas put his jacket back on and gently lifted Brad, holding him in his arms as he self-transported back to Hollywood.

Silas walked in as the morning meeting broke up. He looked at Isaac and Jim briefly as he quickly walked down to the med ward. The meeting immediately broke up as Christina and Petra rushed after Silas. Silas laid Brad gently onto one of the gurneys. He walked out immediately and strode up to Jim and Dave. "Ari's hurt badly. If you can help, I can use the extra hands." Jim nodded and left with Dave and Silas.

In the med ward, Jesse walked in, washed his hands, and put on a pair of surgical gloves. Christina returned from the other room with a saline IV, hooked it up, and inserted its needle into a vein in Brad's hand. Jesse cut his jacket and makeshift bandage open and placed a pressure bandage over the side with the shallower cut while he worked on the other half. Christina pulled out a mask and fed Brad oxygen to aid in his struggle to get enough air. They worked intensely on Brad, refusing to let him die.

Silas returned back to the forest floor where he left Ari and Essie. He and Jim knelt stopped near Ari's unconscious body. Silas told Jim, "Take Ari back to the med ward. I need Dave so we can get our bags and retrieve Essie's body."

Jim gently cradled Ari in his arms and self-transported back to Hollywood. Christina saw Jim as he entered the med ward with Ari. He gently laid her on the other gurney. She regained consciousness, but just barely. She began to slip into shock. Jesse looked over and said, "I'll be there as soon as I can stabilize Brad's chest bleeding."

Christina placed a rolled up blanket under Ari's feet so that they were higher than her head. She grabbed three pressure bandages and tossed one of them at Jim. Christina applied the one to her backside and shoulder while Jim took care of her leg. She grabbed another saline IV and began to set it up. Christina struggled to find a usable vein in Ari's left hand. She switched to her right hand. "Jesse, I can't seem to find a viable vein in Ari's hands," Christina yelled.

"Try further up in her arm," Jesse responded.

Christina looked into Ari's eyes as the Outrider briefly regained consciousness. "I'm sorry, girlfriend, but we have to cut your beautiful leather jacket off."

Ari just blinked at her friend. "Brad . . . Ssssilas . . ."

"Don't worry. We're all here."

"I'm cold . . ."

"We'll wrap you up in some warm blankets. Don't worry," Christina said as she winked at her friend. Christina carefully cut off and removed panels of Ari's jacket as well as her jeans. She finally found a vein, swabbed the insertion site with iodine, and then inserted the IV needle. Jim adjusted the IV as Christina carefully covered Ari in a blanket. "Does that feel better?" Ari blinked. Christina looked at Jim. "Make sure she doesn't fall asleep until we can get her stabilized."

A couple of hours later, while Jesse worked on Ari, Silas walked back into the med ward. With the gurneys taken, he sat down on a chair by Ari. Silas' somber face spoke volumes to the physician. He had just finished retrieving the last of the items from their chaotic assignment in Bolivia, including the remains of Essie's body.

Jim held Ari's hand, still by her side. Ari worked on a third pint of blood, which seemed to have stopped her from going into shock. Jesse finished stitching up her leg. He put the last few stitches in before he cut the suture and bandaged her leg loosely with a padding of breathable gauze.

As Jesse washed his hands and put on another pair of gloves, he shook his head. "I stopped counting at two hundred fifty stitches. The cut went clear down to her bone. It's a miracle that he missed her femoral artery. I normally wouldn't even worry about stitches with you guys, but like with Brad's chest, the cut is so long and deep, I just wanted to make sure it wouldn't try to shift and open while it healed."

The physician looked back at Jim. "You realize she's blessed to be alive. The sword punctured her lung, and she suffered some cracked vertebrae and ribs in her upper back. I have her on a mild sedative to keep her from moving too much, so she might seem out of sorts."

Jesse examined and cleaned Silas' head wound and then examined his bruised side. Silas winced when Jesse gently pressed. He looked at Silas. "You have a minor concussion and some broken and cracked ribs. Are you having any problems breathing or coughing up blood?"

"No, other than it hurts if I breathe in too deep," Silas admitted.

Jesse spoke to Christina, "Can you go into the top drawer and get the medical tape and scissors for me?" Christina nodded and got the supplies Jesse asked for. Jesse asked Silas, "Can you stand for me?" He took a clamp and grabbed a cotton ball and pressed it down on an alcohol dispenser. He rubbed the cotton over Silas' side.

"Hey, that feels kind of good, Doc," Silas said as the cool alcohol rubbed onto his skin. When it dried, Jesse began to apply a thick layer of white medical tape tightly over his tender side. "Is this going to help my ribs heal?"

"Kind of. In itself it doesn't really hold your bones in place like a cast. More than anything, it will help remind you of your injured side. You'll be less apt to bang it up or use those muscles when you feel the tape there. It will protect you a little bit, but just don't go starting any wrestling matches for a few days." Jesse smiled.

Ari saw Silas standing. "You're hurt," she said, noting the tape being applied to his side.

Silas smiled at her. "Not anything worse than what we got during training. I'll be fine. Nice to see you awake."

"How do you feel?" Jim asked Ari.

"I've felt better." She tried to look around the room then looked at Silas. "Where's Brad and Essie?"

Silas looked at Ari. "Brad is on the bed right next to you. And I'm afraid that Essie didn't make it. Her injuries were too severe."

As Ari tried to look over to Brad's bed, his respirator's alarm went off.

Jesse walked over to the machine. He looked at the monitor readings and turned the alarm off and allowed the respirator to continue. He looked at Ari. "Other than prayer there isn't anything more I can do. His lungs aren't able to get enough oxygen into his bloodstream. We have the respirator set at the maximum volume of oxygen without burning his lungs out. There's just too much damage."

Jesse stepped forward and began to pray over Brad. He placed his hands over his chest. After a few moments, Brad's breathing seemed less distressed and his eyes opened. He looked up at the physician and smiled.

Petra stepped in the med ward and looked around, shaking her head. Furious that the assignment had gone so badly, she approached Ari. "You should have gotten everyone out of there sooner. You realize that someone has to answer to this mess, and it's not going to be me."

Ari cried when she saw Brad's condition, and now she continued to sob while Petra rebuked her. "It happened so quickly. I got thrown too far to help Brad. And then when I saw that creature go for Essie, I tried to stop him and save her. No matter what I tried I couldn't get that thing to stop his attack. I couldn't kill it." Tears rolled down her face uncontrollably as she instinctively tried to get up.

"She needs our help," Ari said, confused. She struggled to get up, while Jim and Silas held her on the gurney.

Jesse walked over to Ari. "Ari, calm down. You're beginning to bleed more," he said as he checked under her pressure bandage. He looked at Jim. "Hold her down and make sure she doesn't pull out her IV." Ari's struggles became almost frantic.

He walked over to a cabinet and pulled out a small vial and syringe. He filled the needle partially with the contents of the vial and then slowly injected it into Ari's IV stent. Ari's muscles relaxed as she slumped back onto the gurney. Her crying stopped and she fell asleep.

Jesse shot a look at Petra. "She just lost one of her friends under her lead. She's feeling responsible and is distressed. She doesn't need the bad news and reprimands at the moment when she's fighting to stay alive herself. Try and give her a break for now, at least until she's stronger,"

Jesse warned the overseer.

"I'm just trying to find out what went wrong so I can report back to the council." Petra shot back.

"And I'm trying to make sure you don't lose another Outrider. The council can wait until Ari is stronger," Jesse retorted. With that comment, Petra growled to herself in frustration and stormed out.

CHAPTER FIVE

A ri walked further into the council room, glancing to the sides to see some of her fellow Outriders lined up against the wooden paneling. Ari felt like she had walked into a school principal's office. Even the smells within the room reminded her of grade school; the large chamber smelled of rosewood oil and stale brewed coffee. The dark wood floors and beams enveloped the space, and the small council table at the far end seemed lost in the vast space. The conference room table had been turned on purpose, making her and anyone else that walked in feel small as they faced the somber faces of the council.

A panel of windows backlit the figures behind the table; the contrast between the darkness of the room and the bright sunlight coming in made it hard for Ari to see which silhouette belonged to which overseer. She could see a single chair facing the long table, and several chairs off to the side with more of her peers sitting in. She saw Silas smile at her and nod his head.

Despite being an exceptional Outrider for decades, Ari knew she had to answer for the death of Essie. A week had passed as she recovered.

Now that she had regained some of her strength, both she and Silas spent the last few days in debriefing meetings. Ari felt the weight of the death of her friend as she sat in a chair facing the panel of overseers.

As strict as it sounded, the inquiry usually became nothing more than a formality. Ari sat, trying to find a comfortable position on the hard wood chair. Her mending body still felt pain and tenderness, despite her expedited healing.

The length of the debriefing began to uncover a truth, one of which Isaac also had sensed: Petra had an ulterior motive for the proceedings. Towards the end of the previous day's proceedings, Ari walked out in the middle, upset at the belittling Petra had continued to throw at her. Ordered to return today, Ari sat, facing the very council she left, angered and frustrated. During the uncomfortable silence, Ari quickly prayed. *Vindicate me, Lord, for I have led a blameless life; I have trusted in the Lord and have not faltered.*

Ari looked at the council and noticed Isaac at the far end of the table; her husband and Sam were not present. "Excuse me, but where are Jim and Sam?"

"They are unable to attend the debriefing," Petra answered. Ari's brow furrowed. "They have been asked not to attend as their emotional attachment to you might impede a fair and equitable assessment."

"Ari," Isaac spoke softly from the end of the council's table, "we had research done on the creatures you and Silas described. We believe you had run into an ancient enemy called the Nephilim."

"*Nephilim?* You mean the giants from the Bible?" Ari asked.

"One and the same. We thought that they were eradicated back in the Old Testament days, but apparently that isn't the case. We hope that you and Silas killed the last of them. If not, that means a significant shift in our roles as Outriders."

"How are you feeling, Ariana?" Petra began her questioning.

"Fine, ma'am," Ari answered.

"Do you know why you have been called back into this inquiry?" Petra asked.

"I'm assuming why I'm here has to do with your questions not getting answered yesterday, Madam Overseer," Ari answered as she shifted her weight.

"We have your report of what happened. What is your assessment of the mission?" Petra shuffled some papers, not looking at Ari.

Ari paused, trying to make sure her statements could not be misinterpreted. "I don't think we could have avoided a confrontation with this creature that would have ended any better."

The overseers murmured. Ari continued. "I knew going into the mission that we were at a disadvantage: we didn't even know what we were looking for and that we were dealing with something really nasty. There were so many unknowns that we took all the precautions and it didn't even seem to matter."

"But you seem to have known the situation to have requested three other Outriders on your team," the overseer pointed out.

"Yes. From the report I knew we were dealing with someone able to wipe out entire frontier towns."

"Is there a reason why you didn't ask for more team members?"

Ari shrugged and shook her head, shifting her weight on the chair trying to get comfortable. "The assignment required only reconnaissance. As it stood, Isaac had questioned why I even needed three others. The number seemed more than what we needed, given we didn't know what we were going into. That would give us two pairs that could surround the man if we needed to. Isaac thought that four seemed excessive, and I knew I pushed it even then. I probably wouldn't have been able to request any more on the team even if I did ask."

Petra looked at Ari over her reading glasses. "Ariana, you seem to be uneasy about answering these questions."

"Not at all, Madam Overseer. I am still in quite a bit of pain from my injuries. I begin to hurt if I sit in one position for any length of time."

Petra picked up a paper and adjusted her reading glasses as she glanced at its contents. "Ariana, I understand that your assignment before this, you also were the lead?"

"Yes."

"And this is the assignment when Mike got seriously injured?"

"Yes."

"And yet, despite his injuries, you abandoned him?"

"Not exactly," Ari answered.

"A simple yes or no will suffice. According to your report you left him in the diner while you and Josh continued, is that correct?"

"Yes."

"And you managed to destroy a $30,000 motorcycle, cause a major accident on a highway, lose your client, and a $100,000 sports car?"

"I only temporarily lost Josh . . ."

"A simple yes or no to the question, please." Petra cut Ari off.

Ari shook her head. "Yes."

"And did you not lie to the council on your account of the initial assignment for Daniel Long and Jacob Martin?"

"No, ma'am."

Petra looked sternly at Ari over her reading glasses and pulled out another sheet of paper. "According to your report there were 'at least four demons, probably more'. And you stated that the attack occurred hours before the time stated in the initial report assessment."

"Yes, Madam. That is correct."

Petra put her papers down on the table. Without even looking at Ari, she spoke. "So what you are telling us, Ariana Sommers, is that the council who put that assignment case together lied to you? What possible purpose would that serve to lie to one of the very people we are trying to keep safe?"

Ariana didn't answer. Her head bowed as she started to laugh. Petra asked, "Is something funny? Do you have a problem with the question, Ariana?"

"I'm sorry Madam, but I thought this was supposed to be a debriefing, not a trial."

"There is nothing funny about this, Ariana. For the last three assignments, you had team members that have gotten severely injured and killed."

Ari became defensive. "Did you ever think that my track record might be a bit rougher because of the advanced level of skills needed for the assignments that have been given to me?"

Petra's shrill answered back. "There shouldn't have been anything difficult about Mr. Long's and Mr. Martin's first assignment."

"There was nothing 'simple' about that assignment. Any other Outrider in my position would have had the same outcome, or worse," Ari explained.

"Are you saying that you are better than your counterparts?" Petra asked.

"Not at all, Madam Overseer. I'm merely stating that . . ."

"A simple yes or no will suffice." Petra cut Ari's statement short.

After a noticeable pause to control her emotions, Ari said "No." After another brief pause, Ari continued. "Madam, if this is a debriefing about my last assignment, why are you focusing on my other assignments?"

"Perspective, Mrs. Sommers. Personally I think you are trying to remove anyone that is in direct competition for your position in the organization," Petra said.

"What?" Ari asked. "Are you accusing me of trying to kill my friends?"

"Perhaps it's just coincidence that the two Outriders that are right on your tail were involved in your last two incidents. You abandoned one, and if the giant man didn't take you out first, I'm sure you would have seen to it that Silas became its next victim," Petra said.

"I can't believe you would even think that, Madam Overseer." Ari sat dumbfounded.

"I agree. And such accusations do not have a place in a debriefing, Petra," Isaac said.

"Sir, I tried to get to point out . . ." Petra tried to explain.

"Ari, I think this debriefing is finished. I believe you can make a final statement to the council," Isaac said.

"The past three days have been an insult and degrading to me as an Outrider and to this organization. Madam Overseer—you've dragged this process down to where the mere thought of making a mistake would make an Outrider not want to take on any future difficult assignments."

"That is enough, Mrs. Sommers," Petra tried to take control of the crumbling demeanor of the room.

Ari stood up and looked at her counterpart spectators and asked them, "Who in this room would like to be put in the hot seat at all, let alone for days?" Ari returned her focus back to the council. "Yes, I'm deeply saddened at the death of my friend Essie. I would do anything to have her back with us."

Ari continued, "Your debriefing and interrogations didn't even touch on the most important aspect of the last assignment: the threat is still out there. We may have killed one, but I believe that there are more and that they are testing our strength and resolve right now.

"It is bad enough that we are split from our parent organization, but now to be splintered yet again by this circus atmosphere? God's people have an enemy that we can barely hurt, let alone kill. If we don't get our act together and act as one, we don't stand a chance." Ari paused to make sure she got the attention of the council. "Thank you."

"Thank you, Ariana. That will be all for now," Isaac said.

Ari stepped out of the room. She leaned against the hallway wall. The last few weeks had taken their toll on her; beyond the pain of her injuries, Ari felt singled out and emotionally drained.

———————◆———————

Days passed since the debriefing. Ari worked her way to the chief overseer's office. She paused in front of the door to Isaac's office, hesitating to knock on it. She bit her lip as her hand froze, and debated whether to knock, when she heard his voice. "Come in, Ari." Ari poked her head in. "Please, come in and have a seat."

Ari closed the door and slid herself into one of the chairs. Isaac took his glasses off and looked at the disheveled Outrider. "How are you doing, Ari?"

Ari shrugged as she answered. "I should ask you that. If Petra had her way, she would have had me incarcerated, locked away until Jesus' second coming. I haven't heard anything come from the debriefing, which is starting to worry me." Isaac paused as he looked at Ari. Ari felt awkward and shifted in her seat, uncomfortable to be the subject of Isaac's silent, visual contact. Ari closed her eyes. "Just spit it out, sir."

The chief overseer looked at his friend and sighed. "The effort of keeping Petra from throwing you onto the security block and throwing away the key has taken a lot of effort. After talking to Jesse and reading the reports, I realize that you need time to heal before anything else. But unfortunately, we are a bit short-handed. I need to get this class trained and up to speed as quickly as possible. Ari, I need for you to take over the training class this time around and have Dave go back out into the field as an Outrider."

Ari coughed. "Excuse me, sir, did I just hear you right? You want me to teach again?"

"Yes. Petra didn't want to assign you to anything, let alone allow you to teach the next generation. The class instructor assignment gives you time to recover. Besides, Josh is a special case that needs a little more attention. He needs a role model."

Ari looked at her mentor. "Sir, shouldn't the role model be one of the guys?"

"You already have a rapport with him, and he seems to trust you."

Ari leaned forward in her chair. "Isaac, I don't know if you read that report closely, but he left me in the dust on the side of the road while he decided to steal my Porsche for a joyride. He has little respect for me. I'm beginning to wonder why he's even here to train as an Outrider." Ari sat back, crossing her arms.

"Ari, you of all people know God's plan for us sometimes doesn't make much sense. During my prayer time I have been told that Josh will be vitally important to our organization. He needs a good role model— one that will make sure his path is not only straight, but will also be there for him in case he needs help."

"Sir, with all due respect, I don't know if I could be . . . unbiased with Josh, given his history," Ari said.

"Ari, if you can't fulfill your duty as an instructor, I will have to concede to the wish of the council majority," Isaac said as he sat forward in his chair.

"Which is what?" Ari asked.

Isaac sighed, then said, "They want to have you tried for murder, falsifying testimony and insubordination. Even if you were able to be acquitted for murder and falsifying testimony, Petra has a pretty airtight case against you for insubordination. You walked out in the middle of your debriefing with most of the council as witnesses. She wants you to spend a very long time on the security block."

After an awkward pause, Ari saw the concerned look on Isaac's face. Her shoulders slumped in resignation. "Fine, but I'm not even prepared for this."

"I'm sure you will have no problems getting up to speed. Dave will spend the next few days transitioning things over to you." He got up and patted Ari's back. "That's it for now. Ari, let's go down and meet your class."

Ari and Isaac got on the elevator. Dave met them and began to fill Ari in on where the class left off. "The training will start next week. There are a couple of students that are still getting acclimated to their imparted gifts. Jesse is down there already prepping Josh. I'll get you the folders on all of the students so you can get up to speed."

The elevator door opened and the trio began to walk down the hall. Ari grabbed Isaac's shoulder and stopped. Concern crossed her face. "Isaac, Josh just renewed his personal relationship with Christ just recently. He's barely born again. I don't see how he can receive imparted gifts as well as go through training as an Outrider. He has more than just Outrider issues to learn. Aren't you taking a huge risk that he won't backslide?"

Isaac nodded. "Yes, I am. But I completely trust the Holy Spirit in this matter. And I know you will keep a close eye on him and make sure his training is complete." He turned and continued to walk down the hall. He turned into a room and Ari followed him.

Josh sat on a gurney, a bit bewildered. Isaac smiled. "Good morning. Just relax."

Ari looked at Jesse. "Is he going to be okay going through this right now?"

Jesse nodded. "I don't see any problems. His injury might give him more discomfort during the process, but once his impartation is complete, his healing should speed up significantly."

Ari looked at Josh. "I should probably warn you that what you're about to experience is, uh, intense, for the lack of a better description. It won't be a pleasant experience by any means, but you will be a better person after it's all said and done."

"What are you going to do?" Josh asked.

Ari pointed to herself. "Me? Nothing. However, Isaac will assist you in receiving your imparted gifts. I'm here for you. I won't leave your side until I know you're okay. You do, of course, have the right to refuse the impartation. If that's the case, I will be more than happy to take you back to the nightclub, where you can continue to live without a purpose."

After a minute, Josh shrugged and lay down. Jesse and Ari began to restrain him.

Josh began to panic. "What are you doing? What's going to happen?"

Jesse spoke in his ever-present calm demeanor. "Like Ari mentioned, the impartation of gifts is pretty intense. It's just a precaution so that you won't fall off the gurney. Don't worry. None of us will leave you. We're all here for you." Josh settled back down and closed his eyes.

Ari held his arm and squeezed. "Don't worry, Josh. Your mind and body are going to be supersized. It's kind of cool and freaky all at the same time."

Jesse and Isaac walked over to Josh. Isaac looked at the young man. "Josh, if you're not comfortable doing this, you are by no means being forced into doing this."

Josh looked at Ari. "Did you go through this?" Ari nodded. Josh pursed his lips and feigned a brave face. "I guess if she can go through this, I can do it too."

Ari let go of his arm and stepped back. "Just relax. I'll still be here." She smiled.

Josh tried to smile back and closed his eyes. Isaac began to speak in a different language and suddenly Josh realized what Ari meant. His body twisted and arched; he felt as if fire consumed him. He screamed before collapsing against the gurney, awake but not sure what just happened to him.

Ari cautiously approached him. She stepped closer to Josh so he could see her, but she didn't touch him. She knew the Holy Spirit surrounded him. After a few minutes the exhausted student fell asleep.

"That's it?" Ari asked.

Jesse nodded. "Some seem to handle the impartation better than others."

"What is that supposed to mean?" Ari asked. "It took me days to recover over what I went through."

"Well, uh, yes. Yours was pretty rough, from what I recall," Isaac said as he scratched his chin.

"A little? From what I remember, it almost killed me." Ari said.

"Oh, no. That part of your impartation just felt like it," Jesse corrected her. "He's just sleeping now. Josh should be ready to go in the morning."

Ari sat on a chair against the wall. She picked up the top folder in the pile and began to read its contents.

Later that afternoon, Jesse assisted Josh off his gurney. Ari grabbed the folders and walked the newest student down to the barracks. She walked Josh to the barracks' door. There were a couple of guys in the room. They turned around when Ari entered. "Nathan and Tom, I presume. I'm Ari. The class schedules changed and I'll be teaching you guys this year. You have a new classmate. Meet Josh."

The three students shook hands and seemed to warm up to each other fairly quickly. Ari left the room and met two other students named Abby and Ruth in the hall. They all walked down to the end of the hall by the elevator. The three male students met up with them as Ari introduced Josh to the other students. When all seemed to be settling in well, Ari spoke to her new class. "We'll begin classes tomorrow at 8:00 a.m. We'll meet in the training room at the end of the hall. Be dressed in your sweats and t-shirts as we'll test everyone to see what you're capable of both physically and mentally." Everyone nodded and Ari left them for the tiny instructor office. She dropped the folders off on the desk and locked the door. As she passed the students again, she waved. "See you tomorrow."

The next morning the elevator door opened. Ari and Dave stepped off, both speaking softly to each other as they made their way to the office. Neither acknowledged any of the students eating their breakfasts. Ari finished up a granola bar and carried a travel mug of what appeared to be coffee. Once inside the office, the door closed.

The students looked at each other, puzzled, and then ate the remainder of their breakfast in silence. When the students finally made their way to the training room, Ari and Dave were already there. Ari was dressed in a fitted t-shirt and jeans with a black tailored jacket on top. She held a clipboard, and a whistle and stopwatch hung from around her neck. The five students lined up in a makeshift line along the back wall.

Ari spoke to the group. "Step closer. I don't bite, at least not on the first day." Ari maintained a straight face so the students didn't know if she told a joke or not. "My name is Ari but you will address me as ma'am, instructor, teacher, or Mrs. Sommers. I will be your instructor this year unless there is another change in schedules. This is Dave, and once again, you will address him properly as sir, instructor, teacher, or Mr. Baker. He will be transitioning the class to me, and will fill in for me if I'm not available." She paused to let the information sink in.

"I wouldn't expect you to do anything that I can't do. Given that, I expect only the best effort from you every time. Don't think you can slide through your classes with minimal effort. I know what you are capable of and expect nothing less."

Ari stepped to the side and began to pace between the students, taking mental note of each of their potential attributes. "My job is not to be your friend or pal. My job is to make sure you know what you are doing and don't get killed on your first assignment, or for that matter, on any assignment. Your muscles and brain will be put to the test, and I guarantee both will feel like chewed-up gum that has been sitting on hot asphalt. Outrider training is not going to be easy. When you finish your year, I guarantee you will be prepared for just about anything the enemy can throw at you."

As Ari continued to address the class, Josh's smile slowly melted away. The sexy, tough Outrider that brought him safely to Hollywood had transformed into a female dictator in skinny jeans and heels.

The first training day continued as Ari tested the students' physical and mental abilities. The final test of the day required teamwork while they worked under stress and changing conditions. The students were given the task to keep one of their own alive while under attack. Normally Ari would be one of the experienced Outriders trying to attack the students, but as the instructor, she had the daunting task of evaluating the scenario as it played out. The teams were outfitted with paint ball guns and protective gear. The students huddled in a quiet circle, planned their positions and roles, and then disappeared in the vast underground room as they scurried behind the corner of a mock building.

From the control booth above the training room floor, Ari blew her whistle, signaling that the attackers were released into the scenario. She watched the monitors and screens in front of her, seeing the positions of everyone. Occasionally she jotted notes down onto her clipboard. Within seconds, chaos seemed to erupt among the students. In less than ten minutes, the students' exercise ended. Ari held back a smile as she saw a dejected target student covered in paint ball splatters. Soon she saw that all of the other students had suffered equal demises. Ari sounded the bell and switched the floodlights on, ending the exercise. What a change from the group that had just graduated. She walked down from the booth to debrief the group.

She cleared her throat and then looked at her students. "Believe it or not, you didn't do too badly on your first run through the gauntlet."

Josh shook his head, rubbing a particularly sore spot on his arm where a circle of paint marked a hit. "How do you expect us to protect someone when we're not even familiar with the surroundings or layout?"

Ari sternly stared at him. "Our setup down here is as close to any real life situation you will face. Most likely you won't know the streets, buildings, or even the interior layout of the buildings when you are escorting clients. You have to be constantly thinking ahead, looking three scenes ahead of the one you're currently in, to make sure you don't fall into a trap."

By the looks of the faces of her students, she could tell they weren't grasping what she just said. "When you ski, or drive a car or ride a bike, you don't look at where you are at the moment. You're looking ahead in your path to see where you need to go next or if you have an obstacle like another car or person, right?" They all nodded their heads. "Protecting someone is the same way. You are constantly looking for other options or routes to make sure you can get out of the situation. Always have a plan B, and preferably, a plan C and D too."

Ari paused for a moment as she saw the proverbial light bulbs go off in their heads. Her students nodded. "My comments to you: given that this is your first time, your choice in rooms to hold out in was acceptable. I see the strategic advantage to only having the one door at the end of a hall and no windows to the room. However, if you had to leave, you didn't have any alternate way to get out of the room. You would have had to go down the same hall and a hail of weapons from both sides in order to get out."

Ari's constructive comments to her students continued with the occasional rebuttal from the students. At the end of class, Ari gave the students one of their long-term assignments. "I want to see what you would consider your typical outfit that you would wear on an assignment. I'll give you time to think about it and shop for what you need. I want everyone to come to class with their outfits at the end of next month."

"Why would you want to see what we would wear?" Josh asked.

"Because if there are any issues now, I want to nip it in the bud before it causes problems," Ari explained. "It will also give you the entire year to reconsider what to wear and how to refine it."

The room slowly emptied out. Ari trailed, turning the lights off and closing the door.

◆

Weeks passed and the morning of the big outfit reveal came. Ari walked out of the elevator with Isaac and Dave. Ari dressed as if on assignment. As if to add weight to the seriousness of her calling, she even wore her holster and hand blades. The early morning echoed Isaac's voice. He brought up concerns as they made their way to Ari's office. "I don't understand the purpose of this exercise, Ari. The whole thing seems to be a waste of time and energy," Isaac said.

"After the first couple of years teaching, I found it necessary to play this out. Trust me, Isaac. This will not only save face for the Old Guard but also will save the students from a humiliating introduction to the rest of the Old Guard, and to our clients. I feel strongly that the person should be allowed to show a little bit of personality in their wardrobe, but to a limit." Ari continued, "You're more than welcome to stay and observe."

"Perhaps for a few minutes." The chief overseer looked at Dave. "Did you teach the students what to wear as well?"

"Yes, sir, but not the extent that Ari demonstrates. I don't think my method is as effective as what you are about to experience." Dave scratched the back of his neck.

As always, Ari's stride down the hall to the training room had purpose in its gait. Before they reached the door, she spun on her heel and stopped her two associates. "I must remind the both of you that it is imperative that you keep your reactions neutral, no matter what the students are wearing. If you have any comments, please make sure they are constructive in nature."

The comment came to a shock to Isaac. "I always do, Ari."

Ari eyed the two men before continuing into the training room. The sight of the students in their costumes made Dave crack a laugh, only to quickly cover it up with a coughing fit. Isaac's eyebrow went so high up on his forehead it disappeared behind his bangs, something Ari never saw happen before. Ari craned her neck with her hand and closed her eyes. She turned around and spoke softly to Isaac. "This is the reason why I have the students dress for me while they are still students."

Ari cleared her throat and stepped toward the students. They were standing in a loose line in the middle of the room. As Ari walked by each of them, they turned and faced her. The first female student was dressed head to toe in tight-fitting black leather and stiletto heels. The next student wore baggy Bahama shorts, a bright orange t-shirt, and high top gym shoes.

Next, Josh sported almost identical dress as when Ari first met him, with a black leather jacket and a charcoal grey button-down shirt. His black jeans and cowboy boots finished his attire.

The next student made Ari and Dave do a double take. She wore a black latex body suit with a belt and stiletto shoes. Ari bit her tongue. *What is the deal with women thinking they need to wear stilettos?* The next student wore jeans and a white t-shirt and gym shoes.

Ari turned away from the students and cleared her throat again. "Okay . . ." She turned around and faced them again. "We're Outriders, not superheroes." She looked at Josh and the other male student who were dressed in the white shirt and jeans. "You two. Tell me why you chose this as your assignment outfits."

Josh cleared his throat. "Um, I guess because it's comfortable for me, and I'm used to wearing this." The other student nodded.

"Congratulations, you two. Your dress is the closest to what I would consider both appropriate and functional. As Outriders you need to blend in with your environment. If you stick out too much, you draw attention to not only yourself but also to the person who you are trying to protect or hide. Dan, my suggestion is to make sure to have a jacket with your t-shirt so you can dress up your ensemble if needed, but more importantly to hide your weapon."

Ari turned her attention to the leather-clad female student. "Definitely doable, Bethany, in some situations, but leather is warm and you might draw attention. Are you comfortable in stilettos?"

The student nodded. "Yes, ma'am. I love to shop in them."

Ari nodded. She moved her attention to the casually dressed male student. "Nathan, you look like you're ready to hit the beach."

"I wish."

"Unfortunately, it's a bit too casual, especially if our client requires you to enter upscale establishments. You need to blend in as well as offer the illusion of being able to protect those whom we are assigned to. I don't feel that with you."

Ari moved on to the last student dressed in latex and stilettos. "Believe it or not Abbey I tried this my first year. I didn't even make it out of the building before I changed. Are you comfortable?"

"Surprisingly, yes. I feel like I'm not wearing anything."

"Hmm." Ari pointed to what she wore. "It took me years to figure out what was comfortable for me and still appropriate. Ladies, note that I am wearing ankle boots with a fashionably high but wider heel for stability. I also had special pads attached to the soles to deaden the noise as well as add extra grip when I need it. I wear at least a leather jacket, because you never know what the weather will be where you are going. My preference is a patterned fitted t-shirts or button-down shirts in maroon or black. Mostly because t-shirts usually don't need to be ironed, can be laundered easily, and if they can't be cleaned up, they are cheap to replace."

The look on the students faces convinced Ari the information had not sunk in yet. She eyed the rock wall and looked at Dave. He nodded. "Okay students. Get into your climbing harnesses. You're going to do the wall with your garb on. We're going to do the spider web. The object is for you to try to make it to the top. Dave's objective will be to try to keep you from making it to the top."

Ari looked back at Isaac. "Sir—if you can find a few folks to spot the class." Dave got into his harness. "While you are doing this exercise, I want you to make note of your outfit choices, particularly what works and what doesn't. Remember that you will have to work and be comfortable in what you are wearing, sometimes for days, before you will be able to change."

"Madam, I doubt we will ever have to climb a rock face with a client," Josh pointed out.

"We train you to be prepared for every situation. Granted, the rock wall is extreme, but if you can get through this without any problems, you can get through just about any other situation."

Several Outriders came in and spotted the class. Ari blew the whistle and the students began to climb up the rock face. The two female students started to run into problems with their heels, as did Josh with his cowboy boots; the soles of their shoes were too stiff and slick to hold onto the tiny wall perches. The women's shoes fell one by one from the wall. Ari couldn't tell if the shoes were shed intentionally.

Soon the second whistle sounded, and Dave began to clamor up the rock face. He went for the student that struggled the most—the female student in the latex named Abbey. She seemed to overheat in the impermeable material. Dave didn't try very hard to yank her off the rock wall. Dave methodically made his way to each of the students and picked them off. As if to emphasize their hopelessness, Ari kept them suspended in the air on their safety lines until Dave made his way off the wall.

Ari stood as the students were lowered to the floor. "I think that will be all for today's class." She threw an oversized towel at Abbey. Puzzled, the student asked, "Am I sweating that bad?"

"Yes, but that's not why I threw the towel at you. I highly recommend you reconsider wearing latex if only for this reason." With one swift move, Ari slipped her hand blade from her holster and slashed across the student's thigh. She did it with such precision that she nicked the latex layer with a scratch without cutting completely through and cutting into Abbey's flesh. The student gasped, startled at such a bold and dangerous move by her teacher. Ari slipped the hand blade back into her holster. She instructed the student. "Now kneel."

Still confused, the student knelt to the floor. Abbey's skin-tight body suit suddenly began to split at the scratch mark and began to spread up along the side of her thigh and up onto her hip. Quickly covering herself with the towel, the student ran away, back to her barracks.

"Unconventional to say the least. Crude . . . but effective. I imagine the students won't forget this exercise," Isaac noted. "I thought the reports were exaggerated, but you are tough on your students."

"I'm in charge to make sure they know how to keep from getting themselves or the client killed. I take that assignment very seriously."

"Good work. I am looking forward to seeing how well they do on their first assignment." Isaac patted Ari's shoulder and walked out.

Dave feigned a punch on Ari's arm. "Good going. You managed to impress the boss and kill every ego in your class in one fell swoop. I feel sorry for your class already."

"Yeah, thanks. No sympathy for me, eh?"

"Not if you can get all of your female students to dress in latex. In fact, I think all of our female Outriders should look like that. We might be able to drum up more business for the Old Guard."

"Tell you what—you convince your wife Christina to dress like that, and I'll recommend it to Isaac for the rest of us," Ari said with a smirk.

Dave winced and laughed. "I can feel her punch my arm already. So much for us looking like superheroes."

"Personally, I'm counting my blessings. I would seriously have to reconsider working elsewhere if the guys started wearing tights and knee-high boots. The picture in my mind is not a very pretty one."

She and Dave laughed as they left the training room.

CHAPTER SIX

Months passed. Ari sat in the instructor's office working on the student assessments. Someone quietly knocked on the door. "Come in," she said, her voice carrying through the thick metal door.

Jim poked his head in before he walked through. "Alexa and I missed you at dinner."

Ari twisted her arm to look at her watch. "Is it that late already?" Ari squinted her face apologetically as she sat heavily back in her chair. "I'm sorry, Jim. I didn't realize the time. You should have gotten me."

"I know you're under the gun to get the student assessments in before tomorrow, so I thought I'd leave you to your work. I brought you something to eat." Jim revealed a small dish with a grilled cheese sandwich.

Ari smiled, "Thanks. Did you make this?"

Jim rocked on his feet. "One of the few things I do know how to cook without setting the building on fire. You would think with all the time you spend away working on your assignments that I would be a gourmet chef by now."

"What is that supposed to mean?" Ari asked, a little on the defensive side.

"Nothing. Well, except you are missing out on your daughter's daily life."

"I always think the work load is going to get lighter and easier, but it never does. I've requested time off, but we're understaffed right now. Isaac is trying to get as many students trained as possible." Ari tossed her pen onto her desk. She briefly prayed before taking a huge bite of her sandwich.

"You do realize that you can say no if you need time off."

Ari shook her head, speaking while trying to swallow. "I tried that. They always come back at me asking if I can go out just one more time before I take time off." Ari swallowed and took another large bite.

"Take it easy, Ari. I know I didn't burn it, but it can't be that good," Jim laughed as he wiped a string of melted cheese off her chin.

Ari shook her head as she tried to swallow. "No, it's great, Jim. I haven't eaten since breakfast. Thank you so much for doing this."

"Just try to finish up early enough so you can see Alexa before she goes to bed. I love you, Mrs. Sommers." Jim bent over and kissed his wife.

"I love you too, Mr. Sommers. I'll be up in a while." Ari watched her husband close the door behind him.

Ari finished eating her sandwich and dug deep inside of herself to find the mindset to finish the assessments. *Lord, thank you for everything. I know I would be nothing without You. I can use some of Your wisdom to finish these assessments . . .*

Hours later she closed the last of the folders. She had just stood up when someone knocked at her door. She looked at the clock, wondering who would be seeing her at such a late hour. "Come in."

The moment the shrill of the voice began, Ari knew Petra's voice even before she stepped through the door. "I knew you would be up finishing up your paperwork." Petra stepped in, keeping the door open behind her.

"What can I do for you, Madam Overseer? I was just about to head upstairs."

"I received a complaint from one of the students." Petra sat down and crossed her legs, her one leg bouncing annoyingly from the knee.

Ari frowned and settled back in her chair. Apparently this was not going to be a quick discussion. "About me, or the class in general?"

"About your . . . how should I put it? Your less than professional approach in teaching?"

"Less than professional? In what way?"

"You are brutal on the students."

"Madam, I hate to break the news to you, but what I do to them during class is nothing compared to what they will face out there. What I do will keep them alive longer once they start Outrider work."

"Your hands-on teaching method sent a student to the med ward."

"The student goofed off on the climbing wall. Her line ended up tangled. She panicked and unattached her harness from the safety line and fell off the wall before I could help her. I personally brought her to Jesse in the med ward. Ruth will be fine. She has a bruised shoulder and sprained wrist from her fall."

"I beg to differ, Ariana. Disaster seems to follow in your wake. Your records are being reassessed by the council." Petra uncrossed her legs and leaned forward, placing her hand on Ari's desk. "You are reckless, with no regard to the lives around you. You need to be relieved from all duties and rot in a cell somewhere on the security block."

"Gee, thanks for the constructive criticism to help me work to improve my weaknesses, Madam. I always enjoy our talks. They make me feel so wanted around here."

"Your attitude is bordering insubordination, Ariana," Petra threatened the Outrider. "Isaac will hear of this." Petra got up. Ari didn't acknowledge the overseer leaving. The overseer left, slamming the door.

Ari buried her head in her hands. Exhausted and feeling cornered, Ari growled in frustration. She got up and left the tiny office, closing the door behind her.

Ari stepped into her apartment, and the light from a single table lamp lit the room, signaling to her that she missed both Jim and Alexa before they went to bed. Ari quietly closed the door and locked it before placing a pile of folders on the table. "You're late." Jim's curt voice came from the dark shadows in the kitchenette.

"Thank you for reminding me. I tried, but as I walked out, Petra invited herself in and sat down," Ari said.

"You have an excuse for everything."

"It's not an excuse, Jim. It's the truth." Ari replied, her voice becoming defensive.

"What would she possibly want to talk to you about so late at night?"

Ari answered with a sarcastic tone in her voice. "We had a very pleasant exchange. Petra also thought my memory faulty. She had to remind me of all of my friends who have gotten hurt or killed under my lead. She called me reckless and is threatening to throw me down in security for insubordination."

"Great. That's all we need now," Jim mumbled under his breath.

"What, you think I'm reckless too?" Ari asked defensively.

Jim pointed a finger and responded. "You take chances other Outriders would never dream of doing. And, your sassy tongue is what is going to get you in trouble."

"Did you ever think that perhaps the reason why they kept sending me out on hard assignments is because they know no one else could accomplish what I can do because I'm willing to risk a little more?" Ari threw up her hands and said, "I can't believe you don't even support me for what I do in this organization."

"We all do things for this organization, Ari. It's just not you. This organization doesn't revolve around your needs. Your priorities are screwed up. I support you, but I also have to keep the best interest of the organization in mind, but most importantly I make sure our daughter is put ahead of the work I do for the organization."

Ari's eyes showed the emotional wound Jim just inflicted. Her voice faltered as she spoke. "That's where we differ. No one is more important to me than you and Alexa. That is, no one except Jesus. Even before I knew you, I have always put God first. I would never go on an assignment if God told me otherwise. Maybe you think my priorities are messed up, but I think otherwise."

Jim waited before he responded. "I need to go to bed. I have an early meeting tomorrow. We can discuss this after that tomorrow morning. Turn the light off when you're finished." Jim shuffled back to the bedroom and closed the door.

Ari stood in place, not knowing what to do. *My husband just prioritized that morning meeting before our marriage. How can he possibly go to sleep without having this settled, or at least to come to an understanding?* Ari grabbed the folders, opened the door, and walked out of the apartment, turning the light off before she closed the door.

More months passed as the grind of training began to take its toll on both students and teacher. The sun had just broken over the ridgeline when Christina hopped up the stairs to the dining area. A solitary figure of her friend sat hunched over a bowl and coffee mug. "Good morning, Ari," Christina said as she disappeared into the kitchen. Re-emerging from the kitchen with a coffee cup and a couple of pieces of buttered toast, Christina stooped over Ari and repeated her greeting. "Good morning, Ari."

Ari's left elbow rested heavily on the table; her left hand and arm supported the weight of her head. She raised her right hand slightly over her head and a spoon waved a silent, sleepy response back to Christina.

Christina sat down and crunched into a toast point. After swallowing, she asked, "Where's Jim?"

"He's upstairs asleep, I think. Alexa too, so I thought I'd let her sleep a little more before I hand her over to the sitter."

Christina chewed another bite as she observed her friend. "Something seems different with you and Jim." Silence met her comment. "Is everything okay between you two?"

"Just peachy, Christina," Ari said as she poked absently at her oatmeal.

"Now why don't I believe you?" Christina asked. "I rarely see you two together anymore, and when I do, I don't see that spark in your eyes like I used to."

"Five years of marriage and a kid later . . . I guess we've sort of settled into our routine," Ari said.

"Ari, I'm your best friend, and all these years I've known you, I have never seen you or Jim settle for anything," Christina said.

"Admittedly we don't have time alone anymore. We had another argument last night over why I'm never around for him or Alexa. I told him that I try, but it has been so busy with the reviews and grading." Ari said, then took a bite of oatmeal.

"Maybe you need to dedicate one evening as a family or date night?"

Ari's eyebrows raised. "Not a bad idea. I'll have to propose it to Jim and see what he says. I see Dave has returned to Outrider work. Is he home?"

"No, he's supposed to come back today or tomorrow. Hopefully he'll come back before I have to leave this afternoon," Christina said. "I haven't seen him in weeks."

"Welcome to the new reality. Welcome to my world," Ari said with a smirk.

"I enjoyed Outrider work a lot more when I stayed behind and helped Jesse. I guess we're so short-handed they have me on assignments too."

"Don't feel bad. I think Isaac felt a bit disappointed when you said you wanted to study more under Jesse. I think he knew how good you were and knew losing you as an active Outrider would make a pretty big dent in the case load."

"Really?" Christina asked, surprised.

"I know I missed having you as a backup." Ari said this and took a last bite of her oatmeal. She quickly washed it down with coffee before getting up. "Sorry to abandon you, but I have to finish grading papers. See you at lunch?"

Christina smiled and answered, "It's a date!"

When Ari walked into the training room, the sound of grunts and slams onto the mat greeted her. This particular day, the students began working on their hand-to-hand combat skills. The students' skills were at various levels, but to Ari they all seemed hesitant as if unsure and lacking confidence. She blew the whistle and all the students stopped, exhausted, and stared at her. "Grab your waters and have a seat on the floor around me." The students did as she told them, and stared up expectantly. "All of you look as if you are afraid to hit the other person."

She didn't get a reaction other than some looked at the floor. "Josh, come here." Josh stood up and sauntered over to Ari. "Josh, I want you to try to hit me. Remember to use the movements and skills that I just taught you the past few days."

The young man nodded and held his hands up. His first attempt was weak; Ari blocked his slow-moving arm easily. Ari taunted him. "C'mon, Josh. You just slapped me. I know girls that can hit harder than you." Josh's second volley struck harder, but still, Ari easily blocked him. "Better, but I know you're capable of more. Imagine you're fighting for your life. Try again." He attempted a few hits. Ari still blocked his blows, but she noted an improvement. "Try to block me. Remember all the different ways I taught you to not only block but to use the attack as a way to counterattack."

Josh tensed up and nodded. "Relax, Josh," Ari said.

The young Outrider in training nodded again, and Ari saw his shoulders relax. Ari attacked, throwing punches quickly. Either through a miracle or by just sheer luck, Josh blocked or redirected most of her advances, albeit awkwardly and with uncertainty. A few blows escaped and hit Josh on the arm and abdomen. As he bent over with the wind knocked out of him, Ari swept her leg under Josh's, and he fell flat on his back on the mat.

Before he knew what just happened, Ari continued her attack. Once again Josh awkwardly but successful redirected Ari's blows away from himself. He took his feet and kicked Ari, making her stumble backwards and onto one of her knees. The kick landed on Ari's healed injuries from the Nephilim.

She bent over, in pain and winded. Her retreat gave Josh enough time to get to his feet and try to attack her again, knowing that he may well have the advantage over his teacher. Just when he ran towards her, about to give her a body slam, Ari gave her student a full frontal kick to the chest, sending him backwards again. This time the force propelled the student's body. Josh hit the wall before he slid down to the ground into a sitting position.

Still holding her sore side and shoulder, Ari walked over and held her hand out to the dazed student. Josh grabbed her hand and stood up. "Good job blocking. Are you okay?" Josh nodded and got up with Ari's help. Ari looked at the clock on the wall. "Why don't we break now for lunch and meet back here in the afternoon?" The students filed out quietly.

As Ari finished cleaning up after the class, she noted a lone figure of a former student standing at the doorway. "Hi, Jacob. Do you need me for something?"

"Um, yes. Well, uh, no. Actually I came here to tell you that Isaac wants to see you as soon as possible."

"Thanks. You can tell him I'll be there in a few minutes," Ari responded. Jacob nodded and walked out the doors. Ari wondered if Petra's constant complaints finally wore out Isaac. Ari grabbed a towel and proceeded to Isaac's office. As she walked in, Ari instinctively gritted her teeth when she saw Petra sitting in one of the chairs.

"We're pulling you from being the instructor," Isaac stated.

"And the reason?" Ari asked.

"We need the students to survive long enough to be assigned at least one assignment," Petra said as she smirked.

"What is that supposed to mean, Madam Overseer?" Ari asked defensively.

Petra feigned being surprised at her reaction. "My, we are a bit protective of our egos, are we?"

"Ego? You think that being an instructor is an ego trip for me?" Ari asked, raising her voice.

"See, Isaac, this is just one more example that the great Ariana can do no wrong," Petra spit out sarcastically.

Ari stood up out of her chair when Isaac put a calming hand on her shoulder. "Enough, Petra. You too, Ari." Isaac paused to make sure both women were listening before he continued. "Ari, as you may have heard, Mike and Beth were injured in unrelated assignments and will be out of commission for a few days. We are desperately understaffed considering the workload, and it is my understanding from your latest assessment that it is still too early for the students to graduate to their first assignment."

"Yes, sir. Sending them out right now would be more of a hindrance to our organization than help," Ari said.

Isaac handed his Outrider a folder as he spoke. "Try to get rested. You go out tonight. I'm sorry I couldn't give you more time beforehand, but this came up at the last minute."

"Who will teach the class?" Ari asked

Isaac glanced over to Petra. "Since both you and Dave are going to be away on assignments and I can't afford to spare any Outriders, Petra has decided to step up to the challenge."

Ari's laughter died down as she studied her mentor's dead-serious expression. "Sirs, permission to speak freely?" she asked.

"Of course, Ari." Isaac answered.

Ari cleared her throat. "With all due respect, the students need someone with a mentoring spirit, sirs. They don't always pick things up the first time and if you continue without making sure they understand or can do the work, they will begin to tune you out. The whole experience will snowball since one lesson taught depends on retention and the skills from the previous lessons. Also, the personalities in this class are touchy. They will surge forward when provoked to a point, but belittling them will be counterproductive and most of them will begin to tune out."

"Noted," Petra interrupted.

"The files on the students are—" Ari said before being cut off.

"Thank you for the concern, Ari, but I think I can handle this. I think that will be all, Ariana."

"Uh, sure." Ari said as she got up and walked out.

———————◆———————

"Ari, what a pleasant surprise. I haven't seen much of you the past few weeks," Petra said, greeting the exhausted Outrider as Ari entered the house.

Ari dropped her travel bag off to the side. "Hello, Madam." She passed Petra on her way to the kitchen. Ari took a deep breath. Every time she had to interact with Petra, Ari felt as if her skin crawled. She always tried to find something positive about everyone and focused on that one thing. That attitude made her and her teams more effective. But for some reason, Ari struggled to find anything positive about Petra. *Forgive me, Lord. Help me not to judge someone. Please give me Your patience and kingdom knowledge . . .*

Ari grabbed a bottle of water from the fridge then retrieved her bag.

"You will be at the morning meeting in a couple of hours, right, Ari?" Petra asked.

Ari stopped in her tracks. "Probably not, Madam Overseer. I haven't slept in days."

"That wasn't a question or invite, Ari," Petra corrected her.

"Yeah, thanks, Madam Overseer," Ari said as she continued up the stairs. Ari disappeared behind her bedroom door.

Ari closed the door quietly. She stayed in place until her eyes adjusted to the darkened suite. Jim still slept. She peeked behind a cracked door to see Alexa sleeping as well. Ari closed the bathroom door behind her. She glanced at herself in the mirror before stepping into the shower. *Thank you, Jesus, that I made it back safely.* The soap and water seemed to wash the exhaustion from her aching muscles. Ari lingered under the showerhead; her neck felt the gentle massage of the water.

"You made it home."

Ari opened her eyes and wiped water and hair out of her face. Jim stood by the door. He squinted from the light. Still feeling exhausted, she could only come up with one word. "Hi."

"You're back early. You said until tomorrow," Jim said.

Ari turned the water off and grabbed her towel, drying herself as she spoke. "I got done with the assignment early. I'm just glad to be home."

"Why don't you get some sleep?"

Ari shook her head. "I ran into Petra a few minutes ago. She expects to see me at the morning meeting. I may as well just stay up until then. Less than two hours of sleep is not going to feel good."

"Just be sure to see Alexa before you go to bed."

"Of course. Thanks," Ari said before she dressed.

Jim hopped into the bathroom for a quick shower. When he stepped out and got dressed, Ari giggled with her four-year-old daughter. Alexa's wild bed-head hair hinted that she had just woken up from her sleep. Despite her size, Ari held the heavy toddler on her hip. Alexa mumbled to Ari what she missed the past few days. "Do you want some breakfast, Al?" Alexa nodded. "Well, let's go grab some as soon as daddy is ready."

"Let's go!" Jim bubbled as he grabbed Alexa and held her upside down. The young girl squealed a giggle before being flipped upright. The trio left the suite for the dining room. Jim sat Alexa down, and then proceeded to the kitchen. He grabbed a bowl and a colorful cereal box from the cabinet. Ari poured two cups of coffee and added a generous amount of sugar and coconut milk into one. She handed the undoc-tored coffee to her husband as she sat next to Alexa. Both Jim and Ari watched their daughter eat her cereal.

Alexa picked out a round, pink piece of cereal and handed it to Ari. "Is that for me?" Ari asked her daughter. Alexa grinned and nodded enthusiastically. "Thank you, Alexa." Ari opened her mouth and her daughter put it in her mouth. Ari crunched on the sweet cereal bit. "Mmmm. Yummy."

Before Alexa could fish out another piece of cereal, another Outrider approached Ari. He whispered into her ear before leaving. By the frown on Ari's face, Jim knew the news was bad. "What's going on?" he asked.

"Nothing. I'll be right back." Ari took a big sip of coffee before leaving for the elevator.

"Wait, you just got back. What about us?" Jim asked.

Ari turned around and replied, "I know. I'll be right back. I promise."

Jim sat back in his chair. Alexa looked around and asked, "Where did Mommy go?"

"I don't know. But she'll be right back, sweetie," Jim said as he watched

Ari disappear in the elevator.

Over an hour later, Ari reappeared back at the dining room. Jim picked up Alexa. "Jim, I'm so sorry. Petra wanted me to . . ."

He stopped briefly next to Ari. "I have to drop her off to the sitter before I get to work."

"I can drop her off for you," Ari said, offering to make up for the lost time.

"We're okay. The sitter is on the way to my office. See you at the meeting," Jim replied as he walked away. Alexa turned around and waved at Ari. Ari waved back.

Ari went back into the kitchen and prepped another coffee in a travel mug and made her way down to the training level. The students sat huddled around a table, eating their breakfast. Josh's head perked up at the sight of the exhausted Outrider. "Ari! Ma'am! Are you back?"

Ari laughed as she answered. "Yeah, you wish. How is your training going?"

The students looked at each other before Josh answered her. "Uh, fine I guess."

"Fine, you guess? What is that supposed to mean?" Ari asked.

"Well, we do the assignments and exercises, but Madam Overseer doesn't tell us if we did it right or not unless we really screw up. I mean, don't get me wrong—it's not like we enjoyed you yelling at us and breathing down our necks, but we kind of appreciated you trying to push us beyond our comfort zone."

"So Petra doesn't push you?" Ari asked as she sipped coffee.

"No, not really." Ruth spoke up.

Ari frowned as she asked, "So when do you guys finish your training?"

Josh spoke up again, saying, "We graduated yesterday. We're just waiting for our room assignments."

Ari hid her shock. She knew the class should still have at least another three or four months of exercises and training. She masked her emotions behind a grin. "Congratulations. I guess I'll see you upstairs pretty soon." She waved as she made her way back to Isaac's office.

Ari stopped in front of his door, and hesitated to knock. She turned to leave and heard his voice. "Ari, please come in."

She opened the door and walked in. Isaac closed a folder and took his reading glasses off. His face beamed a warm smile while she closed the door behind her and sat down. "How do you always know it's me before I even knock?"

"Your walk is very distinctive. When I hear it stop in front of my door, I know you want to talk to me." Isaac laughed. "I don't know why you hesitate to knock every time."

Ari shrugged and said, "I guess I always think you're busy and I don't want to bother you with something that I shouldn't even worry about."

"Well, if you're worried about it, it must be pretty important."

Ari asked, "I heard the class graduated yesterday. Are they ready? How did their final exercise go?"

"I understand from Petra that they haven't had one yet. She decided their final exercise would be their first assignment."

Ari looked confused. "If it will be their first assignment, how will Petra grade them? She hasn't been on an assignment in decades."

"I believe she is going to pair them up with Outriders and have them assess how the assignment is going."

Ari sat back in the chair, still confused, and after a silent moment, she shrugged her shoulders. "I don't know who to feel sorry for—the poor Outrider that will get stuck with the student rookies, or the student rookies."

"Mmm," Isaac replied simply before looking at the clock. "We better head up to the meeting." Isaac escorted Ari back to the common area for the meeting. Isaac made his way to the head of the table while Ari squeezed in toward the back by the kitchen, leaning on a counter next to Jim and Mike. A sling cradled Mike's arm while his shoulder healed. Ari noticed Silas' absence from the group. *He must still be on that assignment. Angels, watch over him, please.*

The meeting began and the assignments were handed out to the Outriders. Isaac cleared his throat. "The last set of assignments will require the Outrider to work with our newest training graduates. You will also be responsible for an assessment since this assignment will be considered their final exercise." Isaac opened a folder, and not even looking up, he said, "Ari, you will be assessing Dan and Ruth. Here's the file." One of the Outriders walked the file back to Ari. She opened it and began to read the details while Isaac continued to speak. "You will be going out this evening after dinner."

"Isaac, sir . . . I just got back this morning. I need some serious sleep," Ari pleaded as she passed the folder back to him.

"How much time to you need to rest?" Isaac asked.

"In all honesty, sir, a week. I haven't had a full twenty-four hours off in months. I can't even remember the last time I've been home resting for more than two days in a row."

"We can't afford to have you take that much time off right now," Isaac explained. He looked at the folder and wrote something as he spoke, "How about if we give this assignment to Christina, and then you can take the one that was assigned to her. I believe that assignment goes out tomorrow afternoon. You will assess Josh and Abbey. It's the best I can do for now."

"Isaac, I don't think it's wise to switch assignments. We spent a great deal of time pairing the tasks with the optimum people," Petra reminded her boss.

"Yes, I understand, but given these are only student assignments, there shouldn't be much of an issue," Isaac said.

"Thank you, sir." Ari said.

Isaac closed the other folder and passed it to Ari. "That's it for now, everyone. I command angels to watch over you, and may the blood of Jesus cover and protect you completely. Godspeed, everyone."

The meeting broke up and the people began to disperse. Jim asked, "You do realize tomorrow is our anniversary?"

"I'll be home way before dinner," Ari said reassuringly.

Jim huffed sarcastically and rolled his eyes. "I've heard that one before."

"I always try. It's not like I'm lying or doing this on purpose. You know what it's like. Things take an unexpected turn and you're stuck."

Jim shrugged his shoulders and quietly said, "Perhaps we should take a break from each other."

There was a long pause. Ari fumbled as she tried to find the words. She gathered her shattered thoughts. "Um, so that's it? You want to end our relationship?" Tears welled up in her eyes.

"I'm tired of this. You're never here, and when you are, you are too exhausted or hurt. You don't have time for anything except sleep, let alone time to reconnect with us. I'm tired of raising our daughter alone. I feel like we have to take a back seat to your other priorities."

"We need to talk about this, but at this moment, I'm too tired to think straight. When I get back tomorrow afternoon, can we talk? I want to know that we tried everything we could to reconcile before breaking our covenant. I'm so sorry, Jim. I know we can work this through," Ari said, almost pleading. "I'll get a sitter so we can talk alone over dinner in our room."

"If you aren't there, I'll assume you aren't interested." Jim said emotionlessly.

"I'll be there." Ari said before glancing at her new team walking away. "Sorry—I have to catch them before they disappear. I know you find this hard to believe, but I love you, Jim." Ari peddled backwards a few steps before running after Josh and Abbey.

She caught up and tapped her new teammates on their shoulders and said, "Meet me here armed and ready to go at 10:00 a.m. sharp tomorrow morning. Here's a copy of the assignment. Have the information memorized by tomorrow. Let me know if you have any questions."

Ari pulled a couple of sheets of paper out of the folder and handed them to Abbey. "Abbey, you tested higher in your skills, so you will be the lead on this assignment. See you tomorrow."

The students nodded and walked away. Ari turned around and saw Jim step into the elevator, headed to his office. Too tired to even frown, Ari headed back to the suite to sleep.

CHAPTER SEVEN

The next morning Ari stood leaning against the table, sipping coffee. She wore a black leather jacket and jeans, and a maroon and blue fitted t-shirt. The Outrider barely got enough sleep. Ari's disposition sunk the air around her: even her hair seemed unhappy. When she awoke, their quarters were empty. Ari went to the balcony to pray before getting ready and heading down to the kitchen and dining room to meet her team. She hoped to see Jim in the living area, but he wasn't present. Ari took another sip of coffee before she looked at the clock. Finally, the two recently graduated students appeared. Ari stood up straight and didn't even look at Josh or Abbey as she spoke. "You're fifteen minutes late."

"I blame him," Abbey said as she pointed at Josh. "Honestly, I've never seen a guy take so long in the bathroom before." She giggled as she adjusted her holster.

Josh straightened out his collar and said, "I wanted to make sure I looked perfect for my first assignment."

Ari continued, "When you are late like this, it shows me that you don't have respect for me or the assignment. Not a very good first impression for your final grade's assessment. Your tardiness shows me that you're sloppy and can't follow even the simplest of instructions. And when you are sloppy, that is when Outriders get hurt or killed. And if you are just one minute late for an assignment ever again, you won't have any future assignments to look "perfect" for, is that understood?" Ari said as she glared at her charge.

"Yes ma'am," Josh answered.

"Do you have your blade guns and hand blades?" Ari asked. Both students nodded. "Let's go," Ari said as she led her team out to the patio.

The team reappeared in a forest clearing by a shallow river. Ari stared upstream, and several miles away stood a white-capped mountain ridge. The sun warmed what would be considered a brisk day. The sky sparkled an unbelievably blue color. Ari knew their location was remote, but didn't realize just how much until they arrived. She noticed no airplane contrails crossed in the sky. The bright green flora and the scent of fresh pine sap around them announced late spring. Ari briefly glanced at her students. They stood a few yards from her, gawking at the change in scenery. "So this is Alaska," Josh said, bobbing his head in approval.

"After you two," Ari said as she bowed. "I'm just here to observe. Just act like I'm not even here. Lead the way."

Abbey took the lead. "C'mon, Mr. Perfect. Follow me." She began to follow the gravel river bed and turned up a path through the forest, toward a village where their target client lived. Their roughly hewn path overlooked a steep wooded slope, thickly covered with brush and trees. An occasional bare spot revealed itself between the greenery, where rocks and boulders slid down in a small avalanche. The forest interior became dark; very little direct sunlight made it to the forest floor. The other side of the path sloped downward at less of an angle, also covered thickly with trees and bushes.

After half an hour of hiking on the path, Ari stopped them. "Guys, stop. Quiet." She held her hand up as she stared into the trees and thicket to her side. Ari instinctively drew her gun from her holster.

"What is it? Is it a bear?" Josh asked.

Ari clenched her teeth and took a deep breath as she spoke. "I've had this feeling before. And if it's what I think it is, we're in serious trouble. Go back to the river. Hug the waterline—get as far from the trees as you can. And spread out. I'll take up the rear. Move it. Quickly."

The two students hustled past Ari on the narrow path and stopped in their tracks when several stones and pebbles fell from the slope above and tumbled into the chaos of greenery next to them. Before Josh could take another step, he briefly cried out in pain as a large arrow pierced his abdomen. The force of the shot threw him backwards off the path and into the brush below.

Both Ari and Abbey dove for cover: Abbey behind a large tree and Ari behind a large boulder. "STAY DOWN!" Ari yelled as she tried to see who shot the arrow. She caught a glimpse as the large human-like creature moved between the trees.

Not again . . . Ari aimed her blade gun at the creature as it moved toward Josh. "Hey, you there! Look this way!" The creature faced Ari long enough for her shoot its eyes to blind it. The creature howled an unearthly howl of pain as it clutched its face, dropping its bow in the process. The yellow metallic weapon slid down the steep embankment onto the path. Ari grabbed the bow and rushed past, toward Josh.

"Josh! Are you okay?" Ari asked, noticing him grimace in pain, clutching the part of the golden-hued shaft where it penetrated his side. "Don't pull at it. It needs to come out the other way." Ari knelt next to him and gently pulled the arrow through his back. Abbey held pressure against his exit wound as Josh continued to press his entry wound.

Ari grabbed the bow again and the newly released bloody arrow and walked back up the path. The Nephilim knelt on the ground as it clutched its face.

Nearly at point-blank range, Ari raised the bow and aimed the arrow at the creature. *Lord, please forgive me for what I'm about to do, but I know this creature should not be allowed to terrorize God's children.* Ari released the bowstring. The arrow sunk deeply into the center of the creature's chest, and it slumped heavily to the ground. Its snake-like leg appendages coiled tightly, then loosened. The creature lay unmoving, dead from Ari's shot.

Ari climbed the slope and grabbed the quiver of arrows from the dead Nephilim before returning to Abbey and Josh. His bleeding had slowed down significantly. Ari said, "Josh, we're going to get you back to Hollywood. Abbey, do you think you can carry him?"

"Uh, yeah, I think. Can you help?" the young female student asked.

"I would," Ari answered, "but I can sense there are others near and are approaching. We need to get to the clearing right now. Quickly."

Abbey hefted Josh to his feet, and the two hobbled back to the riverbed. Ari took the rear again, looking up the hill as she walked backwards just as quickly. She kept an arrow ready in position in the bow, just in case. As they reached the gravel, both Abbey and Ari breathed out a sigh of relief.

They were almost home. Ari took one last glance into the brush. She saw several arrows fly from the cover of the forest towards them. Moving instinctively to protect her charges, she used her gun and hand blade to bat the first two arrows off course and to the side. Ari realized she couldn't stop the others fast enough, so she shoved Josh and Abbey a step to the side and turned around, grasping Abbey and Josh's arms tightly. She hoped to self-transport before the other arrows got to them. At the moment she self-transported her team back to Hollywood, Ari felt a searing pain hit between her shoulder blades, and she lost her grip on her students as they arrived.

Thrown slightly, Abbey and Josh ended up safely tumbling on the green lawn of Hollywood. Abbey got up immediately and checked on Josh. In a lot of pain and still breathing but alive, she picked him up and dragged him back into the living area of Hollywood's main floor.

Just after lunch, there were a few Outriders who helped her carry him back toward the med ward. Abbey stopped in her tracks and looked out at the lawn. "Ari . . ." The young student grabbed one of the other Outriders. "Ari should be with us, but she let go right as we materialized." Several others were waved over to help with the search.

"Over here!" someone shouted. The group converged on the gulley at the edge of the lawn. A couple of men clambered down next to Ari. The shaft of a long golden-hued arrow had sunk deeply into Ari's upper back. Luckily it had missed her heart, but the gravity of the situation became worse: Ari bled heavily from the wound, and she gasped desperately for air.

Both her and Josh's injuries were made worse by transporting while still injured, but Ari knew at the time they had little choice. The men carefully pushed the arrow through to remove the projectile from her body. As they did so, Ari grimaced silently in pain; her teeth and mouth were covered in blood. Once they removed the projectile, they pressed her wounds to try to control the bleeding.

Ari could sense the activity around her, but didn't know she was the focus of all the fuss. Ari knew she had to stay awake, but her eyelids kept drooping. Finally exhausted, she closed her eyes and felt someone slap her. She saw Jesse's face and heard his muted voice talk to her.

"Ari! Stay awake! Don't you leave me, not yet," the physician said as he vigorously but gently slapped Ari's cheeks to keep his patient from slipping into shock. His brow furrowed with concern. Ari's lips were blue and her skin pale. He packed her wounds and started an IV. Ari's eyes began to roll upward. Jesse pinched Ari's cheeks, and he gently slapped her face again, over and over. "Ari, stay with us. Please, Lord, we still need her. Talk to me, Ari. Tell me about your family. How old is Alexa?"

Ari opened her eyes. She tried to focus on the figure bent over her, but she couldn't. The room went black as the Outrider slipped into shock.

◆

Jim sat slumped in his chair, unemotional. He stared almost vacantly at the small table set elegantly for a romantic dinner for two. The tapered candles were down to the last few inches; the drips left trails of intricate, waxy stalactites down the edges of the glass candlesticks. The food remained untouched and cold, except for the empty glass of water that Jim had been nursing for hours. He looked at his watch and finally blew out the candles. He began to throw the food out when someone knocked on the door. "Come in."

Mike poked his head in. "We've been looking for you all over the place," he said.

"I've been out getting provisions for tonight," Jim said, still unemotional. "Do you need me for something?"

"It's Ari, Jim. She's hurt really bad. She's in the med ward." Mike stepped aside, expecting Jim to rush out the door. Jim continued to clear the table. Puzzled, Mike looked at Jim. "Jim, didn't you hear me? Ari's in the med ward."

Jim closed his eyes trying to contain the emotions rolling around in his head. Anger and frustration brewed just below the surface. "Our last chance at reconciliation, and now this. I bet she did this on purpose so I would have to spend time at her bedside. She doesn't realize that more time at her bedside means less time with Alexa." Resentment and bitterness had been growing in Jim's heart for years and had hardened it to the point he didn't care what happened to Ari. "She's always in the med ward, Mike. She's everywhere except where she should be."

"Uh, okay. I just thought you would want to know since you are her husband, and your wife is in critical condition." An awkward silence followed Mike's confused look and explanation. "Maybe I should just leave you right now. Let me know if you need anything." Mike quietly closed the door.

After Jim cleaned up, he went into the bedroom and packed Ari's travel bag with her belongings, including several picture frames. He zipped it up and left the suite. Jim poked his head into the med ward. Behind a curtain, Jesse adjusted the drip on Ari's IV.

Jim's heart softened momentarily, seeing her helpless and frail. Ari's unconscious body depended on a tangle of tubes and monitor leads from a respirator. "What happened?" he asked the physician.

"I'm not exactly sure of the details, but from what I gathered, she and her team ran into the Nephilim. Josh also received an injury and is in the gurney behind the other curtain.

"By the time I started administering aid to her, she had already slipped into shock. She didn't have enough blood to keep functioning and stopped breathing. She's unresponsive, and at least for the moment, is dependent on life support. I've been testing her to see if there is any sign of brain function, but so far I haven't gotten anything definitive. She needs to know you're there, Jim. She needs someone to offer encouraging words to her; she needs prayer and a miracle."

Jim stood staring at Ari for a minute. She had so many tubes and wires in and around her, she didn't even look like a human. "I actually only came to drop her stuff off for her, Jesse. The council can probably find quarters for her when she wakes up."

The physician looked confused at Jim. "I don't understand . . ."

"I can't handle this anymore," Jim said simply. "Just tell her if she's missing anything to let me know."

Jesse ushered Jim out of earshot of Ari and said, "Jim, this really isn't the best time to drop that bomb on Ari. I don't think you quite understand. She's beyond critical. And I believe Ari can hear us. She needs to know she has something to fight and live for. She needs your ability to bring her back."

"I don't think I'm the right person anymore, Jesse," Jim admitted.

"What happened to you two? You were the model couple that everyone aspired to be."

"Life. In fact, too much life and not enough living. She never spent more than a few moments for quality family time before she had to run off for some other assignment. One day she walked in and felt as if I stared at a stranger."

Jesse shook his head and said, "I'm sorry to hear that, Jim. Of course I can't tell you what to do. I just ask you to make sure you have prayed about this and have peace about it." Jim started to speak, but stopped himself. Jesse asked, "What?"

"Nothing. It's bad enough thinking bad thoughts about someone. I don't want to speak ill over her too," Jim said.

Jesse decided to change the subject. "I should let you know that she saved her team. Abbey said that she would have been dead if Ari didn't put herself between them and the oncoming arrow."

"That's the problem, Jesse. She saves everyone else except us, her own family." Jim placed the bag on the floor against the wall and walked out.

CHAPTER EIGHT

The Nephilim came down the ridge like a dam that had just burst, flooding the valley. They were so numerous that they covered the landscape like a carpet. The Outriders stood their ground, holding swords and shields like in ancient times. As the first swords were about to touch in combat, their blades began to glow red-hot and burst into flames. Ari heard a familiar voice command to her, "ARI, WAKE UP."

Ari's eyes snapped open. Her heart pounded from the nightmarish dream she just envisioned. Her eyes tried to focus.

For the past few weeks she heard the voices around her, but could not respond. Ari's mind played tricks on her; she couldn't tell if the voices came from people or dreams. The voices seemed distant and garbled. She pleaded silently to God: *Please, Lord, You said 'for those who hope in the Lord will renew their strength, and they will soar on wings like eagles; they will run and not grow weary, they will walk and not be faint.'*

Ari looked around; an empty blood bag hung next to a saline bag next to her head. A cement wall guarded her perimeter. A heavy metal grating and door separated her from the common area. Ari groaned: she lay in a cell on the security block.

The injured Outrider tried to get up, but her chest injury sent shooting pains and spasms through her body. Ari had settled back onto the bed when the realization of her confined limitations sunk in. She closed her eyes and drifted to sleep.

"Ari . . ."

Ari's eyes opened and she saw Jesse hovering over her. "Hmmm?" Momentarily confused, she regained her thought. "Jesse, what happened? Why am I down here?"

A shrill voice answered. "You purposely led the students into harm's way. You changed the location of their assignment so that it would be more challenging. You violated our code of conduct and lied not only to the students, but to the council," Petra said from the far side of the block. "You tried to kill both of the students with the bow and arrows you found and blame it on those giant Nephilim. This time, Ariana, you committed multiple infractions that cannot be ignored, including attempted murder."

"Changed the location? Code of Conduct? Lied to . . . Attempted murder? What are you talking about, Madam Overseer?" Ari asked.

Petra walked into Ari's cell and gently pushed Jesse to the side. He disconnected the spent blood bag and checked her vitals when he abruptly had to stop. Petra yanked the remaining needle out of Ari's hand and tossed it to the side. "She won't need this anymore. Your services are no longer needed down here, doctor. Thank you."

"But, Madam . . ." Jesse said as he began to argue.

"That will be all, Mr. McCaffey," Petra said curtly.

"I'll check on you later, Ari," Jesse said as he picked up the spent equipment and left the security block.

Petra continued and said, "Both of your students gave separate accounts of what happened, and their stories corroborate with each other's. You have been found to be a danger and have been sentenced to the security block. How long you stay here will depend on how your rehabilitation goes."

"Rehabilitation?" Ari asked as one of Petra's men grabbed her arm and jerked her to her feet. They dragged Ari out into the central area and leaned her against a wall. Ari held her wound as the man raised a billy club over his head. She tried her best to protect herself with her arms but collapsed to the floor, trying to get away from the attacker. The man purposely beat her wounds before stopping at Petra's command.

"No one upstairs cares about you anymore, Ariana. Your own family even abandoned you. Everyone thinks you're the scum of the earth, trying to keep yourself at the top at the expense of other Outriders. I have you where I always thought you should have been. And I've taken it upon myself to get you to back to a respectful individual; one that is humble and admits to their mistakes and wants to repent of their sin." Petra paused before continuing. "Do you admit that you tried to kill Abbey and Josh?"

Ari's weak voice wracked with pain as she spoke, "Madam, please believe me: I didn't try to kill anyone other than the Nephilim."

The two men dragged Ari's battered and bloodied body into the darkness of the isolation chamber and locked the door. She could hear footsteps walking away until she heard the gate lock. Ari rolled over onto her back and nursed her wounds. She tasted blood in her mouth, and the bandage felt wet. Her wounds reopened and bled heavily again. She felt cold, especially against the hard cement floor.

Ari rolled over onto her side, facing the far wall, and curled her legs as tight as she could. The semi-fetal position didn't offer much comfort or additional warmth, but at least it would protect her a little more if they decided to return to give her more "incentives" to admit to wrongdoing. Tears began to silently fall from her face. Ari didn't know if what Petra told her about Jim and her friends was true. No doubt lies were being spread about the last assignment. *And what about Josh and Abbey? How could they lie about what had happened?*

Ari knew the dangers if she closed her eyes, but the darkness seemed to beckon her to sleep. *Jesus . . . I have no one else to turn to. I need Your healing and comfort. Please . . .* Ari drifted into unconsciousness. She felt as if a warm hug and a blanket gently wrapped around her and stopped shivering.

Several hundred feet above Ari's head, an impromptu meeting broke up. Petra and some of the council informed the Outriders of the egregious actions that Ari allegedly committed. Christina, Dave, and Mike sat at the table, in shock.

After a few moments of silence, Mike pulled his hand through his thick wavy hair, his stare wide and vacant. "That might explain how she's been able to keep at the top for such a long time. I mean, think of it. The last few assignments she's had with others, someone on her team got hurt. And usually it was the person who was the biggest threat to her."

Christina looked at Mike with disbelief before reaching over the table and punching his arm. "Listen to you: Ari never had any feelings of being threatened by anyone. You should know better than anyone that Ari isn't like that."

Mike pointed his thumb at himself as he spoke. "Yeah, but I'm the one that not only got shot but also abandoned at the diner."

"Yes, but she made sure that your wounds were packed, the attackers were subdued, and help was on the way before she left you. She could have just as easily left you on the floor to bleed to death," Christina said, correcting his abbreviated account of what happened.

Jesse appeared from the kitchen with a bottle of water and slid into a seat next to Mike. He spoke softly, saying, "I don't know what Petra and the other council members are up to. Ari's wound doesn't corroborate Abbey's story. She said she shot Ari before Ari could shoot her. Ari's entry wound is the back. How can Ari be in a position to shoot Abbey if she wasn't even facing her? There are other things that don't make sense. If Abbey did shoot Ari, where is the bow that she used? And why be so concerned about Ari's welfare when they first materialized at Hollywood? Abby grabbed several of us to help look for Ari. I'm worried that both Ari and Abbey may have been subjected to less-than-stellar treatment by Petra and her men."

"How is Ari?" Christina asked.

Jesse took a large gulp of water before answering. "Rough. She had just gained consciousness when Petra asked me to leave. Ari is far from stable. She should be recovering up here in the med ward, where she can be monitored."

Christina slumped back on her chair. Her eyes looked watery. Her husband rubbed her shoulder and asked, "What's wrong?"

"I just realized that Ari's assignment should have been mine. If there were Nephilim, I'm sure the outcome would have been much worse," Christina said. "Jesse, is she allowed visitors?"

Jesse shrugged. "I don't know. I somehow doubt it. I left her down in her cell before Petra and her men were done talking to her. They won't allow me to return to check on her. I've had to appeal to Isaac, but I haven't heard back yet."

Dave added his thoughts and asked, "Speaking of Isaac . . . where has he been during all of this? Has anyone seen him today?"

◆

Ari groaned when she awoke. She shivered, and as she breathed, she heard a raspy noise from her lungs. A quiet voice came from outside her dark cell. A familiar male voice waivered. "Ari . . . Are you awake?"

Ari replied, "Yes. Is that you, Isaac? Where are you?"

Isaac was taken aback at how Ari responded. Ari's sluggish voice wavered from shivering. He could barely hear her because her speech sounded so weak and breathless. He kept his voice tone optimistic. "I'm a couple of cells away from you. They brought me down here a day after you were placed in the isolation cell. I received an appeal from Jesse to continue to monitor your condition. I questioned Petra as to why she had you moved to the security block prematurely when I lost consciousness.

"I think they slipped something in my Earl Grey tea. The next thing I knew, I awoke down here. I can hear your struggles to breathe, Ari. I'm so sorry that you have had to deal with all of this. I refused to believe any sort of treachery existed within the Old Guard. How are you doing? Are you in pain?"

Ari's raspy voice simply said, "Fine, sir. Blessed."

"Well, that's a canned faith-filled Christian statement if I ever heard one. Why do I find that hard to believe? The truth, Ari. What is your real situation?"

Ari paused. "I don't know if I will make it, sir. I want to believe I will, but the bleeding won't stop. I have a hard time catching my breath. I'm shivering from being cold. I want to sleep so badly, but I know I would not wake up if I did."

"Would it help you if we talked?"

"Yes, sir."

"Tell me of your happiest day," Isaac asked her, trying to take her mind off her dire situation.

"Before Alexa's birth, my life had always been filled with sadness and death until I married Jim. He became the first promise of life I had received. After Alexa's birth, she didn't cry like other babies. She smiled at me as if to say, 'Everything will be okay.'"

Isaac smiled at her recollection and added, "One of the happiest days of my life was when you and Jim made me an honorary grandfather. Even today, I love watching over her while you two worked. And admittedly I had no qualms handing Alexa back over to Jim when that peculiar odor came from her diaper," Isaac chuckled. "Ari, do you remember your mother?" The room remained silent. "Ari, talk to me."

Ari's words slurred. "Sir . . . please . . . I didn't . . . try to kill . . . them. I'm innocent."

"I know, Ari."

"There are more . . ."

"More what, Ari?"

"Nephilim."

Isaac asked, "Are you sure?" Again, silence answered his question. "Ari, are you still with me?"

Isaac strained to hear Ari's weak voice. "And gobs loves you too. My mom would say that to me when I said 'I love you gobs.'"

"Ari, tell me more about your parents," he asked.

The isolation cell remained quiet. Ari barely remained awake. Tears escaped from the corner of her eyes. *Lord, I never expected to die locked up here. I always thought if I did die young, I would be killed on assignment doing Your will. I never thought my friends and family would scorn me like this. Please Lord, forgive me of any sin or wrongdoing I may have done. I hope my friends and family will someday know the truth and forgive me.* Ari slowly closed her eyes.

Ari tried to think of a happy moment, but her memories began to fail her. She decided to concentrate on God and His scriptures. *My heart pounds, my strength fails me; even the light has gone from my eyes. My friends and companions avoid me because of my wounds; my neighbors stay far away . . . Lord, I wait for You; you will answer, Lord, my God . . .*

Ari fully expected to take her last breath in the darkness of the isolation cell. She felt surrounded by warmth, as if God had wrapped his arms around her. The warmth turned into extreme heat, as if her insides were aglow like fiery coals. She sucked air in deeply, hoping that the colder air would cool her off. After what seemed like an eternity, Ari finally opened her eyes. A pair of hands that gently held her glowed enough that she could make out the man's face. "Isaac? How did you get in here?"

"With a lot of experience, and a little bit of grace," he answered. "I admit that moving so freely did come with a price: materializing in a three-dimensional world definitely takes practice. Although rare, I had heard stories where an Outrider would not materialize where they should have and ended up in walls or sides of mountains. More common is that they would materialize slightly above ground level and fall, which sometimes makes for some comical entrances."

Isaac continued, "And as you may also know the ability to accurately land is also greatly hindered by certain substances, namely metal or stone, which is why you rarely see us do transports inside buildings. Only one or two Outriders I know can do this even today."

Ari spoke. "But the security block design intentionally placed the floors several stories underground in the side of the mountain. They even lined the cell walls with layers of concrete and steel plating. Even for a highly experienced Outrider, trying to transport out of a security block would likely end up in disaster."

"I couldn't be sure if I could still self-transport through metal. It's been decades since I've had to do that. Are you feeling better?" Isaac asked.

Ari breathed in deep and tentatively pressed her finger at her wound. The scar didn't hurt or feel like a recent wound. In the darkness, she said, "You still have your touch, old man. I almost feel like my old self."

"It's not me, Ari. I'm merely a vessel for God. Are you well enough to transport?"

"Hmmm. Let me think: the residual pain from self-transporting while still healing, or possibly ending up a dark spot inside the side of this mountain, or certain death by beating and torture if I stay behind. You made this a very hard decision, Isaac."

"Hold my hand tight. I have one stop to make before we leave Hollywood," Isaac said. Before Ari stood completely upright, the scenery changed to the inside of his office. "Good. It looks as if she hasn't called a locksmith yet." Isaac stepped behind his desk and retrieved a couple of files and a small silver-colored box. He stepped around and grabbed Ari's hand when he realized she still wore a bloody hospital gown. "I think you may want to grab that bag over there in the corner."

Ari inspected the contents and looked at her mentor, perplexed. "Why do you have my travel bag?"

"Jim handed it to Jesse when you were in the med ward. After you moved to the security block, Jesse dropped it off here for safekeeping. We better go. You will be able to change at our destination."

Once again, before Ari could blink, the scenery changed again. Self-transporting while wounded usually caused problems, aggravating the wound. Ari took a step and collapsed to her knees. Even though her wound had been healed, she still required time to recover. Isaac picked up the battered Outrider and her bag and proceeded to carry her. With her arms around Isaac's neck, Ari winced, still in considerable pain.

She looked around and tried to figure out where they were. The air felt thick with heat and humidity. The tradewind clouds hung low at the horizon as the early morning sun seemed to set the haze of moisture in the air on fire with an orange and golden blaze. *This is too beautiful to be hell. But wherever we are it looks like the entire place is on fire.* Across the muddy and pothole-ridden road were flooded rice paddies and a scattering of simple, small houses.

Looking across the road again, most of the property they were heading toward hid behind an overgrowth of vines and foliage covering a stonewall. The chief overseer carried her through a gate and then kicked it closed behind them. He walked down a stone path to the house. The scent of jasmine hung heavy in the air. Ari couldn't help but notice that the vividly green garden, lush, and bursting with vibrant color. As they approached the house, she noticed the structure—single story except for a small pergola on the second floor that copied the look of a traditional A-frame Thai house.

Isaac opened the door and walked into the foyer. The panoramic view blew Ari away. The property perched on a low cliff overlooking the Andaman Sea. Further out on a small peninsula than the neighbors, homes on either side or along the beach couldn't be seen. The green yard and garden edge ended abruptly at a small overlook with a small private beach and the sea below.

The property consisted of a complex of buildings; the main building contained a spacious living area and kitchen with a master bedroom suite on either side of the main living area. Two smaller buildings skirted both sides of the backyard. Each was set at a lower level than the main house and led to the cliff and beach below. Each of these bungalows was designed as a master bedroom suite with a small private living area, patio, and full bathroom. Mirroring the main house, each smaller building sported floor-to-ceiling glass on three of its four walls, with gossamer layers of white chiffon and organza tied back from both the glass walls and bed, affording the guest privacy when needed.

Ari stared at the back of the main house's living area. A large patio with an infinity pool overlooked the sea and the islands beyond. Isaac gently slid the back patio door partially open and carefully laid his charge onto one of the lounge chairs by the pool. "Welcome to Thailand, Ari," the chief overseer grinned.

Ari's pale face glowed in salmon-hued sunlight. She tried to sit up towards the rising sun and whispered, "Wow."

Isaac sat on a lounge chair next to Ari, staring at his injured Outrider. The mentor raised a finger and smiled. "I have another surprise for you, if you can wait a minute." He disappeared through a doorway and reappeared with familiar faces.

Ari's face lit up; she beamed a smile. "Silas! Sam!" Isaac helped her up to her feet, and she struggled to take a few steps to hug her long-time friend. Tears came to her eyes as she clung to Silas tightly; her voice cracked as she softly spoke. "You're a sight for sore eyes."

"Petra can't get rid of me that easily," Silas said. He laughed and then winced, still in pain, hugging her as tight as he could. "I remember getting back to Hollywood really late. I ran into one of Petra's goons on the edge of the lawn. He shot me from the other end of the yard. I remembered the thought, what an awesome shot, and then realized I was the one hit. I felt intense pain and then woozy from the blood loss. The next thing I knew, I woke up to Isaac and Sam in this place."

Isaac held Silas' shoulder. "I got Silas out before they could figure out whether he was dead or not. I brought him here and began to declare life and healing over him. To bring Silas all this way and not have him enjoy the beautiful scenery would have been a shame."

"Who knows about us?" Silas asked.

Isaac pointed as he spoke. "Just those of us in this room and Jesse. And Jesse is sworn to secrecy."

"Where are we?" Ari asked.

Sam held his arms out. "We're just a few minutes from the outskirts of Phuket City. Actually, Ari—your parents used to use this home as a safe house. They saw how much I liked it, and they blessed me with it. I've had the house renovated, but since then I haven't had much time to be able to come out this way. I don't think anyone in the organization other than Isaac knew about this house. We are on our own small peninsula on a small island. The neighbors can't see anywhere inside the property line. It is totally private, but it's only a short boat ride or drive into the town. Make yourselves at home." Silas followed Sam inside.

Isaac slid the back window panels completely to the side. The living area and kitchen now opened up completely to the backyard. He walked back onto the patio and stared at the spectacular sea view. He rubbed his neck as he slowly sank into a lounge chair. Ari looked over at her mentor. *Isaac looks like he has aged a couple of decades since before my last assignment.*

Isaac spoke, not looking at Ari. "The realization of what happened at the cost of dedicated Outriders like you and your friends sank in. At first the events were small, and seemed part of everyday Outrider life at Hollywood. All has culminated into this one action; I see now that the council will blame you and your friends for your actions. Up to then I was numb from the events. For the first time I didn't know what to do." He closed his eyes, finding sanctuary in the one place that never failed to give him peace. "Lord, please give me your kingdom wisdom and discernment to know what You want for me to do."

Ari slowly sank into a lounge chair next to him. Despite her pain, she tried not to make noise. She settled back, admiring the view of the sea. The water sparkled in the morning sun. The humidity clung to the air, still backlit by the rising sun. The air looked as if it were smoldering. The last remnants of the morning haze began to lift; the thinning veil rose into the low-hanging clouds. Silhouettes of junkets and small fishing vessels dotted the water. After a few minutes, Ari asked her mentor, "Isaac? I don't understand why Abbey and Josh lied about the assignment. I mean, what purpose or gain would they get from bearing false witness against me?"

Isaac sighed and said, "They are young, and their minds are very much influenced by those who have the power to shape their careers. Apparently integrity is not as high of a priority with the younger generation as it should be. My only hope is that the guilt of your death will weigh heavily on them." Isaac looked at Ari. "I'm sorry, Ari," he said, "perhaps I kept you away from your family too long . . ."

"Don't start double-guessing what you cannot change. What is done is done, Isaac." Ari struggled to get up. Her grimace of pain erupted into a small scream.

After struggling for a bit more, Ari slumped back into the lounge chair. Her eyes stared at the scenery. A few tears escaped down Ari's cheek as she quietly asked, "So now what?"

"You and Silas need to remain here for now. Everyone thinks that both of you are dead and we need to keep it that way, at least for now. Besides you have a much more important role now." Isaac sat up, facing Ari. "Ari, I'm not getting any younger. It appears that Petra is attempting to unseat my position. She has many loyal followers, at least on the council. I hoped this wouldn't happen for a while longer, but it is what it is. Sam and I need to take care of something, and Sam will return tomorrow evening if he can. And I will return to the security block."

"Won't they miss me?" Ari asked.

Isaac shrugged and said, "I imagine they will, but there are so many men helping Petra with her plans that I suspect if I tell one that someone already took your body away earlier to be disposed of, they will believe that it had been done. I have to make sure to stop by Jesse's to make sure his story corroborates."

"Does this mean I won't be able to return to Hollywood? Or will we be able to return to Hollywood? Will someone let us know?"

Ari's questions were met with silence. She looked at Isaac. Isaac's eyes were glassy. He knew more, but hid the truth from Ari. "Isaac? When will we be able to go back?"

"I don't know, Ari. The situation is too dangerous for you right now. It will be a while. A change in their hearts has to happen first. Or maybe someone will step up to assume control. Only the Lord knows when the right time will be." He looked at Ari. "Perhaps a few months, or it could end up longer, maybe years."

"Years?" Ari sat up in the chair and looked at the chief overseer. "Isaac, I have a family. I can't be away for that long."

"I wish I had a better explanation for you Ari, but we have to allow the events to unfold. I had long suspected that we have those who are sympathetic to the Tempest within the Old Guard.

"You mean we may have a Tempest mole inside the Old Guard?" Ari asked.

Isaac nodded and continued, "I knew as soon as this person or persons felt comfortable that they would begin to act on Amon's behalf. I now believe that the assignment they gave you and the newly graduated students was no accident. The profile specs of the assignment were altered to make it appear less threatening. That assignment should have never been given to rookies."

Isaac paused, bowing his head. "We suspect that one of the moles is Petra, but she has such a large and loyal following, it is almost as risky to confront her. Doing so may disband the Old Guard to the point I fear we may never be able to pull it back together. I hope you can forgive me Ari. I sensed you were in grave danger. I should have never allowed the events to play out, but I am compelled to allow the scene to unfold as it is meant to do."

Ari sat, speechless. She finally spoke up. "So you led me like cattle to the slaughter?"

Isaac shook his head. "I never envisioned that the deception and deceit would be so bold. It is very apparent that the person or persons embedded in Hollywood have seen you as the threat to whatever they are plotting. I had arranged your schedule to give you more time off, but it would always be altered by Petra. She claimed that the assignments she gave you and Silas had to be handled by someone with enough experience. She always seemed surprised when you came back. I didn't put the pieces together until just now." Isaac sat back, sorrowful at what had become of the Old Guard. "I wonder how many more Outriders she has done this to before you. I hope you can see why you can't return at least for now."

"All I see now is that Hollywood and the Old Guard are wide open and vulnerable. And now who will protect you?" Ari asked.

Isaac shrugged. "Someone who is led by the Holy Spirit will step up. Perhaps Dave or Mike, or even Christina. God will provide, Ari. You know that better than anyone."

The two sat staring at the sunset. Ari stared vacantly at the spectacular scene, numb and unsure of what to make of what Isaac just told her.

As if on cue, Sam came out and sat at the bottom of Ari's chair. "I'm so glad to see you. They weren't expecting you to make it."

Ari tried to laugh but ended up holding her abdomen. "Yeah, like a cat, I keep landing on my feet."

Sam continued, "I just changed the linens in one of the masters in the main house. I want you to sleep in there. Silas will be in the other master. And when I return, I will be in the little house right there." He pointed down a few steps to where one of the guest bungalows stood. "There's an intercom system, so if anyone needs anything, just give a call."

Sam held his hand out to Ari and helped her up. Ari stumbled. After he realized her frailty, Sam picked her up and carried her. Ari looked toward the patio doors, mesmerized. Bewitched by the unbelievable view from the patio doors of the master suite, Ari couldn't help but stare at the scenery. Sam sat Ari on the edge of the bed and threw an oversized robe over her shoulders. He continued to talk to his slightly distracted charge. "You still have your bloody clothes on."

Ari pointed to her travel bag. "Isaac had my bag."

"You'll be uncomfortable wearing your Outrider garb here in this heat and humidity. And you'll stick out as a foreigner. At least for tonight, you can wear one of Silas' linen shirts to bed," Sam offered. "And we need to make sure you can protect yourself."

Sam walked into the closet and grabbed a small chest and put it on the bench at the foot of the bed. He pulled out several cases and a couple of holsters. He loaded two guns and handed a holster and gun to Ari. He cleared his throat. "As much as I think this place isn't known to the rest of the Old Guard, someone may get wind that you're alive."

Ari stared at the weapons in her hands. Her eyes began to get glassy. Sam cupped her cheek with his hand and wiped an errant tear. "Ari, are you all right?"

"I'm fine. It's just that I see the beauty outside, and then I feel this heaviness in my heart for my friends and family. I miss Alexa and Jim. I have a hard time grasping that we're fugitives in such a beautiful place." Ari breathed in deep, still just staring at the weapon in her hand.

"Why don't you get some rest? Isaac and I will stick around until tonight." Ari nodded to Sam's suggestion. "You truly are blessed, Ari. God has something planned for you." Sam kissed Ari's forehead and closed the door behind him.

◆

Ari awoke as the sun set. She seemed to drown in the oversized oxford shirt, curled under an airy white comforter. Stiffness had settled into Ari's healing body; she took longer to get up than she'd like. She closed her eyes again and prayed briefly. *I love you, Mr. Sommers, and miss you so much. Please forgive me for my actions against you. Please give Alexa a kiss for me. Lord, please protect my family from harm. Ease any sadness they may feel and give them peace over the events that happened. Please give them Your joy and allow laughter to come back into their hearts.*

Ari finally rolled out of bed. *Definitely stiffer than I am used to, but I'm catching my healing in Christ Jesus . . .* She saw airy, tropical clothes hung in the closet. *Sam had gone shopping and came back and somehow didn't wake me. I wonder if he got my size right?*

The healing Outrider stepped into the shower and outlined the remnants of her wounds with her fingers. They were all healed over but left deep scars. *So many . . . how did I live as long as I did? Your mercy, Jesus . . .*

Her tears began to flow freely, indistinguishable to the shower water. Ari had been alone before, but this felt different. The dynamics and politics of the close-knit Outrider group had shifted again. Although Isaac still held respect, Ari now realized that he no longer possessed the commanding presence he used to have. The younger Outriders were of a different breed. They were eager to please in order to get ahead. She held herself in her arms. She knew that they would not have the support of the Old Guard if they got into trouble. They were alone.

Ari slipped into her new clothes. Her fingers ran across several of the airy shirts hanging in the closet. *Thank you for Your grace and mercy, Jesus.* She refocused her attention to slipping a cotton tank top on, and then studied the buttons on her blouse and marveled at how her new clothes fit. The soft, airy white linen shirt would keep her cool in the hot tropical sun. The pants were some sort of cotton/khaki material, also very light and breathable.

Ari looked down and frowned at the shoes. Similar to the China doll shoes she used to wear when she was a girl, the shoes barely sported a heel or sole. *Not my style, but at least they fit until I can find something I like.* She armed herself and then walked into the living room.

The smell of curry and grilling chicken immediately attacked Ari's senses. Isaac got up from the living room and helped Ari manage the two steps down into the main part of the common area. Sam bustled in the kitchen, carrying pots and utensils. Silas carefully chopped vegetables. "Mmmm. What's cooking?" she asked.

"Dinner. We were going to wake you in a few minutes. I hope you like red coconut curry," Sam said.

"Love it! I can't believe how hungry I am. Thanks for the clothes, Sam. How did you get my size right?"

"Well, young lady, I did practically raise you since you were born," Sam boasted.

Ari sat next to Isaac at the dining room table. "Nice to see you up and about, Ariana," her mentor said, beaming. The two other men brought bowls and platters of food over from the kitchen and joined the group. The food displayed itself as colorfully as the garden in the back: the deep red/pink hue of the red coconut curry bathed grilled chicken and sliced banana and slivers of light green lemongrass. The cool-looking green papaya salad enticed Ari to try a little of the fiery side dish, but she opted to pass. Steam rose from a serving bowl of fragrant jasmine rice as it was passed to Ari.

The fragrant rice invited her to take a larger-than-normal scoop. Sam laughed, "I guess you are hungry! I made some Tom Ka Gai for you. It's probably a little easier for your stomach, considering you haven't eaten anything for a few days." Sam passed a steaming bowl her way. Isaac said a brief prayer to bless the food and the friends surrounding the table before they began to eat.

Ari inhaled as deeply as she could. The broth hinted of lemon grass and ginger. "Thanks, Sam." Ari sipped the delicate broth. Again she inhaled the broth, which was slightly sweetened with coconut milk. Savory notes of chicken broth and straw mushrooms danced around a subtle tang of lemongrass. "Where did you learn to cook like this?"

"Our neighbor to the right. They're expats who have been here for decades. They were nice enough to come over and teach me a few years ago."

The small group enjoyed their late afternoon meal. As they finished up, Isaac spoke up. "Ari and Silas, I need to speak to you for a minute." Sam began to gather the plates and bowls to bring back to the kitchen.

The trio walked outside and sat down around a glass table. Isaac slid an envelope over to Ari. She felt lumps through the thick cardstock paper as she ripped the one end open. Her necklace with her father's cross and key slid into her hand, along with her wedding ring. Tears came to her eyes. "I thought I lost these forever." She clipped the necklace around her neck, and fingered the ring. Deciding to believe her marriage could still be reconciled, she slipped her wedding band onto her finger.

Isaac opened the battered silver box and retrieved a ring. He handed it to Ari. "I have a favor to ask of both of you. I believe that this ring will fit you, Ari."

Ari looked at the ring. Crudely forged with a small raised cross on the surface, the ring looked old and battered. A simple geometric design surrounded the cross, which protruded from the metal. Ari turned the tarnished ring over and over. The understated workmanship left Ari with an unremarkable impression. Puzzled, she looked at her mentor. "What's this?"

"A very old ring handed down for generations and generations. It's called the ring of Halcyon. Legend has it that whatever the key unlocks will be vital in fighting God's ancient enemies like the Nephilim. But unfortunately, that's all conjecture. We aren't even sure if the legend is true anymore."

Confused, Ari looked at the battered ring again. "This? Why are you giving this to me? It sounds like it belongs with you, Isaac." She tried to hand it back to her mentor. "What is it made of? Silver?"

"I believe it is bronze." Isaac leaned forward towards Ari, pushing the ring back at her. "It is yours, Ari. But whatever you do, Ari, keep that ring safe. Try it on your right index finger. It should fit."

Ari laughed. "What did Sam slip into your curry?" She looked at her mentor again. "Your finger must be at least four sizes bigger than mine." She slipped it on her right index finger, and it fit perfectly. Perplexed, she looked at Isaac in amazement.

"I have been praying about this for a very long time. There is much more at stake than just you or me, Ari." Isaac then looked at both of his charges. "I believe that Ari is to be the next chief overseer, but you have much to learn, and unfortunately, we don't have much time."

Isaac looked at the other Outrider. "Silas, since you are here you need to protect Ari, at any cost. And when both of you are stronger, perhaps you can find out a little more about the ring."

Silas shot a puzzled look at the chief overseer, and then looked at Ari before returning his gaze back to Isaac. "I think you have that backwards, sir. If anything, Ari needs to protect the rest of us." Silas laughed, but when he saw Isaac's serious expression, his laughter dissolved into a disguised cough. "Sir, Ari is more than capable of protecting herself and those around us. I don't think I understand."

Isaac saw Ari studying the mysterious ring and leaned forward. "I believe that the ring knows who the next wearer will be. In this case, Ari, you will have the rights and responsibilities of a chief overseer, and your abilities will grow over time, as God sees fit."

He looked at Silas. "Remember what I told you, Silas. You need to make sure Ari remains safe until such a time that she is to return to the Old Guard. I fear there will be no hope in the future of the Outriders without her."

"Isaac, what you're saying . . . it's beginning to scare me." Ari looked at her mentor with deep furrows in her brow. "You make it sound like you don't expect to be around much longer." Ari laughed nervously.

"Ariana, I believe you are to be the next chief overseer, but the time is too early to reveal it to the Old Guard, especially now with all this drama. Normally I would gradually work the person into the position over a period of a year or so. But now it is much too dangerous for you. You would be vulnerable until the ascension and transition is complete."

"Ascension? Transition? What, is it like training and a ceremony?" Silas asked.

"Um, sort of. The gifts of the chief overseer are imparted to the person, similar to what the new students go through. The transformation will occur in stages, usually three, sometimes four over a period of a year or so."

"I don't think I like the sound of that, Isaac." Ari shook her head and backed off. "There is no way you would be able to talk me into going through another impartation. Besides, I can think of others that have been overseers that are way more qualified than me to fill your position."

"You won't have a choice. The impartation will happen to you, whether you want it to or not. I recall a while back hearing someone say that God doesn't call the qualified: He qualifies the called. You of all people, Ari, should know that. To Him you have all the qualifications to lead the Outriders. He will provide to you exactly what you need when you need it the most." Isaac straightened up and looked at Sam in the kitchen. "It's time for us to get back, Sam."

"What do you mean?" Ari got up and blocked Isaac's path.

"It means that if I'm right, when the time comes, the Holy Spirit will begin to impart the gifts upon you. I don't think you have anything to worry about. The timeframe is months, even years from now, unless something happens to speed up the process."

"Like what?" Ari asked. "What would speed up the process?"

Isaac shrugged. "I'm not sure exactly. Circumstances in which the Holy Spirit senses that you are needed sooner than later. Perhaps my death?" Ari's eyes became glossy as she hung her head. Isaac held her shoulders with his hands. "Ours is not to know, Ari. We just have to have faith in God that His timing is perfect, no matter what the situation or the circumstances."

"When will we know when we can return?" Silas asked.

Isaac smirked. "If someone doesn't come to retrieve you, the Holy

Spirit will tell you when the time is right." He looked at Ari again. "In the meantime, once you are well enough, I hope you will try to find out more about the ring and its origins. I had tried when the organization was still unified, but after the split it became much too dangerous for me to wander off on a quest like this. Unfortunately, I didn't get very far."

"How far did you get?" Ari asked.

Isaac scratched his five-o'clock shadow on his jaw. "Well, uh, not as far as I'd like. And actually, nowhere. You have as much information as I had."

Ari smirked in disbelief at her mentor. "You're joking, right? Where are we supposed to start to find anything on this ring? I assume that Outriders have been looking for the answer for a millennia, and you think we'll be able to do it?"

"Yes, I do. And I know you will be able to do it before the Nephilim overpower us in the next few years."

"Overpower?" Ari asked.

"Mmm," Isaac said, nodding his head. "I think the last couple of run-ins were mere rehearsals for them. They are testing the waters, so to speak. They are testing the strength and resolve of the Outriders. I fear that without whatever secret that ring will uncover, we won't be able to defeat them."

Silas sighed and crossed his arms. "Great. No pressure at all, is there?"

Isaac looked at Sam and nodded. Sam dried his hands and walked over to his charge. As Sam hugged Ari, she quietly confided, "I'm afraid I won't see you again." A tear escaped and fell from her chin.

Sam looked at Isaac. "Can you give us a moment?" Isaac nodded. Sam held his hand out to Ari. "Walk with me, Ariana." Ari grasped his hand as she struggled to her feet. Sam hugged Ari as the two walked to the back garden and down the path toward the beach. In the setting sun, Sam looked at Ari, whose head looked downward, her sadness apparent in her body. She didn't want to make eye contact. Ari's tears flowed more freely as she occasionally sniffed. She hoped that if she didn't look at him that maybe he wouldn't have to leave her.

Sam held her face in his hands, forcing her to look him in the eyes. Ari whispered, "Please stay. Don't go."

"I have to. I promise to return tomorrow, or as soon as I can."

Ari hugged Sam and cried. "For the first time in my life, I'm scared, Sam. I've never been without my Old Guard family, or for that matter, you."

"Silas will be with you."

"It's not the same."

"Ariana, you have Jesus with you and a battalion of angels standing around you, watching over you. No harm will come to you." Sam held her tight.

"Apart from Jim and Alexa, you are the only family I have." Ari kept hugging Sam. Ari didn't want to let go. She had never felt as vulnerable as she did right now. She knew she had to let her mentor go. Ari squeezed Sam. "Please give Alexa a big hug for me." She buried her face in Sam's arms.

"I'll see you before you even miss me." With those words, he kissed her forehead as he had done a thousand times, then walked up the slope to the main house. Isaac met him on the patio. Ari watched from the short distance as the two men disappeared.

Ari collapsed on the beach and buried her face in her hands, sobbing. "Lord, You promised life and not death. You promised me joy, Lord . . . Your joy . . . You who are my Comforter in sorrow, my heart is faint within me . . . Praise be to the God and Father of our Lord Jesus Christ, the Father of compassion and the God of all comfort . . . Please, Lord, I need you now more than ever."

CHAPTER NINE

S everal weeks passed. Petra berated her men for not knowing Ari's true status, just as Isaac had predicted. No one missed him for the few hours he left the security block. Jesse played along with Isaac's ploy. He confirmed Ari's death; her body was sent to be cremated as per her final wish. Petra informed Jim of his wife's death. After he left her office, she was taken aback at the lack of emotion from Jim.

Early in the morning, as the sky turned rosy from the pre-dawn sun, Jim prayed deeply. Rebuked by the Holy Spirit during his quiet time with the Lord, he finally stopped for a moment. Half-jokingly, he looked up at the lightening sky and asked, "What do you want me to do?"

A voice quietly answered him: *The right thing. Forgive her. She only did what I told her to do.*

The Lord revealed how Jim had hardened his heart against Ari. He slid to his knees and asked for forgiveness.

Later that morning, he packed a bag. Alexa climbed into Jim's arms and straddled her legs around him. Her arms wrapped around his neck, and her sleepy head rested against his shoulder. He held her close and clutched a duffel bag with his other hand. The last thing he wanted to do was lose Alexa during a self-transport. "She's all I have now, Lord. Alexa reminds me so much of Ari, and she brings such happiness to my heart." The father and daughter appeared on the bottom of a familiar long gravel driveway. Jim sighed as he put Alexa down on the ground. She began to run up the driveway.

The cool of the morning caused a layer of ground fog to hover at the bottom of the field by the road. Jim inhaled deeply; the scent of sweet mown grass, the deep fragrance of wisteria mixed with the faint earthy undertone of a cattle farm a couple of miles down the road, made Jim pause to reflect and appreciate the beauty of the Virginia countryside. *Ari, I can see why this area grew on you.* Alexa's quick footsteps got louder as she ran back to Jim.

"DADDY!!! Hurry up!" She grabbed his hand and tugged, dragging him up the sloped gravel path like an anxious dog on a leash.

Jim dreaded this moment, but he felt obligated to tell their good friends Leigh and Bob what had happened to Ari. Jim took a deep breath as he neared the farmhouse. *Lord, You've given me the strength to continue so far. Please give me the wisdom to know what to say to them.*

As they stepped onto the long front walkway, a very large golden retriever approached them with her tail wagging. "Bunch!" Jim grinned and bent down to vigorously rub the dog's face. Bunch approached Alexa and the friendly dog began to lick Alexa's face. The toddler fell backward onto the edge of the lawn and began to giggle uncontrollably.

"Bunch! Get off her right now!" the owner of the overly friendly dog growled as she ran out of the house in her bare feet. Leigh was dressed in an oversized t-shirt and cropped khaki pants, her long peppered hair was pulled into a loose bun held in place with a couple of cherrywood chopsticks. "Sorry about that. Are you all right?" She helped Alexa up and brushed her off. "Oh my word . . . Is that you, Alexa?"

The toddler nodded her head enthusiastically. "Hi, Aunt Leigh!" Alexa wiped the dog slobber off her cheek and then hugged Leigh.

"You have grown up so much since last year!" Leigh looked up and saw Jim. She stepped over and gave him a big hug. "Jim! It's great to see you."

"Hi, Leigh. It's great to see you too. Is Bob home?" Jim reached down and scratched Bunch's shaggy neck. He used the friendly dog as a distraction to keep any awkwardness he felt at bay.

"Yeah, I think he's finishing up his shower. I'm glad you came for a visit. How long can you stay?"

"If it isn't too inconvenient, I'd hoped we could spend a night or two here."

Leigh looked at her friend's vacant but slightly distressed look. "Uh, sure. Stay however long you need to. Are you hungry?"

"I am!" Alexa bounced up and down, holding her hand up.

Leigh shuffled back towards the house as she spoke to Alexa. "I was making eggs, bacon, and cornbread. Do you like cornbread?" Alexa looked at her dad. She looked at Leigh and shrugged. "You mean to tell me that you never had cornbread before?" Leigh pretended to be shocked. "Well, we will have to fix that, won't we, Alexa?" The toddler nodded in agreement.

Leigh ushered the visitors inside. They stepped into the farmhouse. A couple of cats of the same color decorated the black and white checkered floor. The low ceiling and open living space hinted to the post-war farmhouse's age.

Alexa's attention transfixed onto one of the sleeping cats in the other room. She gently petted the tuxedo cat, who squinted and purred at the attention. Jim walked over to the kitchen window and fingered one of several deep blue glass flasks on the sill. He spoke out loud, "I remember Ari picked this up at a flea market. She knew the flask's antique age, but didn't want to pay the price the seller asked. She talked him down to a price that almost embarrassed me. She could haggle the feathers off a bird." He smiled as he pictured Ari. "We must have walked for hours just looking at stuff, and I couldn't believe that's all she wanted to buy. How long have you known Ari?"

Leigh twisted her mouth and looked up as she tried to think. "I think we've known Ari for decades." Leigh chuckled at her recollection of her first meeting. "The cabin that had been in Ari's family for decades that sits in the next valley from our farm? We met Ari when she tried to fix it up. You know Ari: she had always grown up in the urban sophistication of cities. She defined the phrase 'urban chick.'"

Leigh continued with a smile. "We saw her floundering in a dry goods store in town. Ari tried to buy provisions and looked very much like a fish out of water. We helped her with her renovations, and before we knew it, we became close friends."

Jim knew how special Leigh and Bob were in Ari's heart. The couple became one of only a handful of non-Outrider people that Ari trusted with the knowledge of her true and dangerous calling.

"Jim?" Leigh asked again.

"Hmmm?" Jim came out of his memory and looked at Leigh. "I'm sorry, what did you ask?"

"Coffee . . . would you like a cup of coffee?" Leigh asked, holding up the glass carafe.

"Uh, sure."

"You sure do seem distracted. Is everything okay? Where's Ari?"

As if to save Jim from the question, Bob bounded down the wood stairs. He wore a heather gray t-shirt and an old, well-worn pair of jeans. "Did I hear you mention Ari? And did I hear a vaguely familiar voice?" He peeked down the stairs. "Hey, Jim, how are you?" They shook hands and patted each other on the back.

"Hey, Bob. How's it going?"

"Great seeing you and that little girl there. Hey, babe." Bob winked at the toddler.

"UNCLE BOB!" Alexa squealed as she ran into his arms.

"Oof!" Bob pretended to be tackled by the little girl. "That's Mister Uncle Bob to you, missy." Bob held her upside down for a few seconds before flipping her upright again.

Jim helped Leigh get breakfast made while Bob and Alexa set the table. They all sat down. Alexa blessed the food and they began to feast on a homemade country breakfast. Jim crunched into a thick slice of bacon. "Mmmm. This is great. It doesn't taste like store-bought bacon. Where did you get it?"

"Our neighbor smokes his own bacon. We got a couple of slabs for helping him fix his fence. He cures the pork belly with sugar and a bunch of spices before he cold smokes it," Bob explained. They continued to eat in relative silence. Bob and Leigh exchanged glances. They knew Jim wanted to say something, but didn't disclose anything. Leigh and Bob kept quiet. They knew he would talk when he was ready.

Leigh turned her attention to Alexa, who bit into one of her cornbread muffins. "Well, missy, do you like it?"

Alexa's small shoulders shrugged when she answered, "It's all right."

"Try it with this," Leigh suggested as she spread a small pat of butter onto the corner and then poured some sorghum syrup onto the same corner. Alexa nibbled at it and her eyes got big. "Do you want some more syrup?"

Alexa answered with a very enthusiastic nod. "Please, Aunt Leigh!" Leigh poured more syrup on her cornbread, and the girl eagerly ate it.

Alexa then picked up a yellow blob of scrambled eggs with her fingers. "Alexa, fork or spoon, please," Jim corrected his daughter. Shyly, she put the eggs back on her plate and picked up a fork and showed her father. "Thank you, ma'am." He combed her light brown hair with a couple of fingers, flipping it behind her ear.

The toddler shoved a couple of forkfuls of breakfast into her mouth and then asked, "Daddy, can I be excused? I want to swing with Buttercup."

"Only if Buttercup will let you. If she doesn't like it, you have to let her go, okay?" Jim told his daughter as he wiped her sticky hands with a moist paper towel.

"Okay. Thanks, daddy!" Alexa disappeared upstairs to spend time with her favorite cat.

Jim turned his attention to the war zone around Alexa's plate. He brushed the crumbs and food bits into his hand and then onto an empty corner of her abandoned plate. Jim grabbed the untouched bacon off her plate and bit into it.

"She doesn't like bacon?" Leigh asked.

"She's just like Ari. She doesn't like to eat meat."

"Speaking of Ari, where is she? Is she on an assignment again? I feel like it's been ages since I've seen her. The last couple of times you came alone with Alexa," Leigh said, taking another sip of coffee. Awkward silence followed her question. Jim stopped chewing and swallowed. His eyes betrayed the situation and became glassy. "Jim, what happened to Ari? Is she okay?" Leigh stared at Jim with a protective mother-eye gaze. "Did you get into a fight and break up with that sweet lady?"

Jim shook his head and managed a painful smile at Leigh's question. Now that he had to explain it to their friends, the reality of the situation began to sink in. *Ari really is gone, isn't she?*

He couldn't look his friends in the eyes as he began to speak. He stared at his dark reflection in his coffee mug. "They accused Ari of attempting to kill a couple of young Outriders on their first assignment. Ari was injured badly and placed in confinement. While there she apparently died from her injuries."

His friends remained silent, shocked at the news. Leigh put a comforting arm around her friend as he struggled to continue his explanation.

Jim sighed. "She had been working so much, Alexa and I barely saw her. After years of putting up with her not being there, I told her just the day before that I wanted to get a divorce."

Bob's head dropped, looking down. Leigh looked at Jim, unable to say anything as she cried for her friend. "Jim," Leigh's voice finally cracked as she reached over and held his hand. "I'm so sorry."

"That evening when she didn't show up for dinner, I packed her belongings. They told me she remained critical in the infirmary. I guess all those years of Ari recovering in the infirmary numbed me. I dropped her things off. I looked at her briefly, with all the tubes and wires around her, keeping her alive, and I didn't see Ari. I saw a stranger on that gurney," Jim said. "I was so repulsed by her that I couldn't even talk to her, to let her know that I was there for her. I actually thought to myself we would be better off without her. I never saw her alive again after that." A single tear fell from his eye.

"You can't blame yourself for her death, Jim. I think she will forgive you if you forgive yourself first," Leigh pointed out. Jim nodded.

After a moment, Jim straightened up and tried to brighten his expression. "I wanted to tell you in person. I know you were close to her."

"What are your plans? Are you going to bury her at the cabin?" Bob asked.

"I told them to do whatever they wanted with her body. Now I regret saying that. I'm in uncharted waters. I don't know what to do. If we're not imposing on you, I hoped to stay here until the morning before her funeral and see if I can make some sense of my life. I planned on not attending, but I thought it would be good for Alexa. I would spend the night at the cabin, but my mind isn't in the right place to watch over Alexa too."

"Of course, Jim." Leigh responded without hesitation. "You and Alexa stay as long as you need to."

"I thought I'd come by to tell you and invite you to the funeral if you wish. We won't have a body to bury; it's just a ceremony. You aren't obligated at all. Ari won't mind. Funerals are for the rest of us that are still living. They're supposed to make us feel better and give us closure, but I'm not sure so about that."

"I wish we could, but we have a contractor coming out to begin building our greenhouse for us. They're pouring the foundation for it. I gotta keep an eye on these guys like a hawk. The last time they worked on our land they took out a hundred year old tree because they thought the roots might be too close to the stone wall they were building." Leigh frowned and then gave Jim a hug. "We'll come out and visit her later this week, and make sure the property is tended to. After the funeral, will you be staying in the area for a while?"

Jim shook his head. "Probably not. I know I need to take time off, but part of me knows that I would be slapped by Ari if I grieved over her death. She always fought for life and believed in enjoying every minute." Jim cleared the table. "Let me help you with the dishes."

Jim rolled up his sleeves and washed and rinsed the dishes. No words were spoken between the old friends. Leigh observed the grieving man silently as she dried the dishes and put them away. Occasionally his eyes would look at the windowsill and the cobalt blue glass vial that Ari bought for her friend. He stared beyond through the window and saw Alexa playing with the dogs and Bob. Leigh peeked over his shoulder as Alexa ran by and asked, "Does Alexa know?"

"I told her, but I don't think she understands. She knew that her mom went away for long periods of time so Ari's absence didn't seem strange to her. Even when Alexa saw Ari gravely injured, that didn't faze her," Jim sighed as he rinsed a drinking glass and dried his hands. "I'll try to explain it to her later."

Later that afternoon, Leigh sat on the porch and read Alexa a story. The young girl's eyes followed Jim as he walked with one of Leigh's dogs towards the woods on the side of the property. Alexa fidgeted in Leigh's lap. "Aunt Leigh, can I get down? I want to go with daddy."

"No honey, I think your daddy wants some alone time," Leigh explained as she kissed the top of the toddler's forehead. "Let's finish reading this book together, feed the dogs and cats, and if your dad isn't back by then we'll go looking for him, okay?"

The girl nodded. "Is daddy okay?"

"He's fine, sweetheart. A lot has happened the past few days and he's trying to sort it all out in his head."

For the rest of the day Jim seemed absent from his normal state. He barely talked. He spent hours at a time sitting on the grass, staring straight ahead. He barely slept that night. Early the next morning Jim prayed for hours. He prayed for Alexa and for the Old Guard. He prayed for the strength to be able to move beyond the emotions he seemed mired in. When he finished, Jim got up and walked into the house, and as Leigh, Bob, and Alexa finished breakfast, he walked back out with their duffel bag. For the first time since he stepped on the property, Jim's eyes showed purpose and life again. He hugged his friends; he didn't want to let go. "Thank you for helping me find purpose again."

"And what is that?" Leigh asked.

"Alexa. My purpose is to make sure she grows up knowing her calling, whatever it may be."

Tears came to Leigh's eyes as she hugged Jim. "You know we love you guys, and you are welcome back anytime. We'll keep watching the cabin for you, and we'll make sure Ari's grave has fresh flowers. Don't be a stranger." Leigh gave Alexa a big bear hug; Bob did the same. Jim wrapped his arm tightly around his daughter as she held hers around his neck and tucked her chin on his shoulder. She waved at their friends and then disappeared.

◆

The cabin's interior seemed lifeless. Even the air seemed stale and motionless. Years earlier, shortly after the attack, Leigh and Bob spent their free time making the cabin's restoration returned it back to its original condition. Most of the interior of the first floor had to be replaced. Walls, windows, and cabinets once splintered and damaged by dozens of blades were changed out with near replicas. The hard maplewood flooring was painstakingly sanded and refinished to remove all traces of the bloodstains.

Jim stared at the wooden staircase and saw Leigh and Bob had done a great job. He could not see any evidence of the attack.

His memory flashed back to the day that Ari disbanded the remaining Old Guard, and knew the Tempest were about to attack. That night the Tempest shot Ari in the back with a blade, and she died. Jim refused to believe that the woman that he had always loved just died. He spoke life over her body, and with faith that could raise Lazarus, Ari began to breathe again. Jim realized he missed the opportunity to miraculously save Ari this time because he had become so self-absorbed. A fresh tear fell from his face.

Jim sat dazed on the staircase and rubbed the wooden riser. Years before, Ari's blood nearly completely stained the wooden staircase. Even with its complete restoration, Ari's cabin seemed to have lost something. The warmth, love, and fellowship that Jim always associated with the cabin seemed to have died with Ari. He now saw why the cabin seemed so lifeless to Ari after the death of her first husband, John. The place just didn't seem the same without her. Everything seemed so empty now.

His heart almost buried itself in sadness. "Lord, please forgive me for hardening my heart against Ari. I miss her so much . . ."

"DADDY!!" Alexa ran up to Jim and hugged him. Jim snapped out of his stupor again.

"Hi, sweetie. What do you have there?" He hugged her as she crawled up on his lap. He looked at what she grasped tightly in her hand. The wooden picture frame cradled an old picture of his Outrider training class. Four familiar faces grinned back at him: John—Ari's first husband—Ari, himself, and Silas.

Jim couldn't help but smile. He recalled what he and his friends thought that moment when they had just graduated and the photographer snapped the picture: *with God we are invincible. No one can stop us.* The photograph caught a moment in time—our friends with their arms joined, carefree and laughing. He stared at his friends. John was the first to be killed, and now Ari and Silas. His eyes became glassy when he realized he was the sole survivor amongst his friends and former classmates. Jim snapped out of his guilt and asked, "Do you know who all these people are in this picture?"

Alexa pointed a tiny finger at Jim. "That's you, Daddy."

"Yes, that's right, Alexa." He kissed the top of her head.

"And that's Mommy. Her hair is different."

"Mmm. That's Mommy."

"That looks like Uncle Silas. His hair is so long." The toddler giggled.

"Yes, that was Uncle Silas."

Alexa pointed at the last person, puzzled. "Who is that, Daddy?"

Jim hugged his daughter. "That was my best friend, John. He was Mommy's first husband."

"Do I know him? Where is he?"

"He died years ago. John is in heaven."

Jim stared at his young daughter, thinking *I can't believe how much she looks like Ari.* He watched her swing her legs as she studied the picture. The corner of his mouth smiled, seeing Ari's joy fulfilled in their daughter. "Alexa, remember what I told you what Mommy did?"

"Uh huh. She helps people who are in trouble."

"That's right, sweetie. Mommy and Uncle Silas were hurt really badly." Jim shifted his position, pausing to try to think of how to tell his young daughter so she would understand. "Mommy's injuries were too much for her to handle. She stopped breathing. Mommy died." He could see with her reaction that she didn't understand. "Mommy is no longer with us."

"Have her come back, Daddy."

"I can't, Alexa." He tried to explain. "Remember that butterfly you had last summer? Remember how after a few weeks it stopped moving?"

"Yes. It went to sleep."

"Yes, but it's a different kind of sleep called death. When someone dies, they don't wake up. Mommy is the same. Her body stopped moving. She is sleeping and won't ever be able to wake up. It is all part of life. It's all part of God's plan for us, and when we die, our bodies stop moving, and our souls leave our bodies and go to heaven."

"So I can't see Mommy again?"

"Not for a while, honey. Her soul is in heaven right now, with Jesus and the angels. Someday you'll be able to see her again."

"What's a soul?" The little girl asked.

Jim scratched his jaw, trying to think of the best way to explain it to his young daughter. He put his hand on his chest and mirrored his other hand on hers. "You and I and everyone have a soul inside our body. It's the life within us. It's what makes you different than Aunt Leigh, or even me. Your soul is the heart of who you are. When we die our bodies stay here, but our souls go up to heaven."

"So can Mommy see me now?"

"I don't know, honey. I want to say that she can. I know she is happy. And I know she loves you very much, Alexa." Jim hugged his daughter.

The little girl looked confused. "How can Mommy be happy without us? Doesn't she miss us?"

Jim sighed. *Lord,* he thought, *these are difficult questions to answer, even when it's not a young child. Help me answer her so she will understand.* "The Bible —God's word and promises to us—says that in heaven, *'Jesus will wipe every tear from their eyes. There will be no more death or mourning or crying or pain, for the old order of things has passed away.' He who was seated on the throne said, 'I am making everything new!'"*

"Mommy is with Jesus now. She is no longer in pain or suffering. And she knows without a doubt that He won't let anything bad happen to us. She is happy knowing that we are in good hands." Jim held his daughter's tiny hand in his. "To her now, the time we will be apart is a blink of an eye. Mommy is not suffering anymore."

"What about Uncle Silas? Is he with Jesus too?"

"Yes, honey."

Alexa paused in her questions and then nodded. "I'm happy for them."

"You are?" Jim looked shocked.

"Uh huh. Because I know Uncle Silas and your friend John will keep Mommy company, and she won't be so lonely."

"For a four-year-old, you have become quite the grown-up young lady." He kissed his daughter. "Aunt Leigh worried that you didn't eat much breakfast, so she packed a small snack for you. Are you hungry?" The young girl nodded.

"Well then, I guess we both better eat something." Jim picked Alexa up and they walked to a sack on the dining room table, where he grabbed a banana and peeled it for her. He broke it up in smaller pieces. He sat his daughter down in a chair and then went into the kitchen and got some coffee going. He briefly sat and took a bite out of an apple before getting up and tugging off sheets covering the furniture in the living room. He opened up the blinds, allowing the bright sunlight to pour in.

A few minutes later, the chief overseer and Sam materialized a few yards from the front of the cabin. The early morning dew burdened the late summer grasses with even more weight; their tips were already bowing low with ripe seeds. Sam made a path through the tall grass, up to the cabin door, and knocked. Jim answered. He could see Jim's eyes had lost their depth and fire he had from love and life. "Come on in," Jim spoke softly.

Sam hugged Jim. "I'm so sorry, Jim." He saw Alexa, and the little girl ran up to the overseer. "Papa!" She jumped into Sam's arms.

Sam wrapped his arms around the toddler. "Oooh, Alexa! I missed you. I'm glad you decided to come. All of Hollywood sends their condolences, Jim."

Jim closed the door behind them. "Thanks. I decided to come. I wanted to get here early and meet up with some old friends and then open up and air out the cabin. Make yourself at home."

"Dave and Christina should be arriving here soon," Sam said.

Sam worked his way to the kitchen. In the silence, he poured a cup of coffee. "Jim, would you like a cup?"

"No, thank you."

The men sat at the table. Alexa crawled up onto Jim's lap. She turned her focus onto her half-eaten banana. Jim tucked a lock of hair behind Alexa's ear. "I can't believe what they said she did. Your mom never lost it, even in the worst situations. Something made her snap like that. I know the possibility always existed that she wouldn't come back, but I never thought it would happen. Mommy always had been like a cat, landing on her feet."

"Jim, you can't go and second-guess everything now. It's always easier to see the situation in retrospect. We can't change what has already happened," Sam said.

Someone knocked on the door, and Christina, Jesse, and Conrad walked in. Christina's red and puffy eyes and nose revealed her already emotional day. Conrad removed his tweed newsboy cap and twisted it in his hands. Christina hugged Jim and whispered in his ear, "I'm so sorry, Jim." Jesse also hugged his friend before retreating to a comfortable chair. Soon afterward, Dave and Mike walked in.

For what seemed like awkward minutes, the friends stood silently, sipping coffee. Occasionally the friends would talk about their last assignment or the meetings. Jim helped Alexa finish her banana before he got up and talked with each of his friends and then addressed the room, "Thank you for coming. I know Ari would be telling all of us not to make such a big fuss over her. I know that this is as awkward for you as it is for me, so why don't we go ahead and put her to rest right now?" The group filtered out the door. Alexa ran to join her father.

The solemn group followed Jim and Alexa into the meadow and up the hill. Alexa wandered off collecting wild flowers as she wove up the hill behind the group.

Jim approached the gravesite and stone marker. His emotions churned inside. He loved Ari, but couldn't reconcile in his mind what she had tried to do. Jim felt a tug on his arm. Alexa held up a bouquet of wildflowers. The lacy Queen Anne's lace, blue astors, and black-eyed Susans lifted the spirits of those at the somber occasion. Alexa pulled out a single delicate red bloom of cardinal flower and handed it to Jim. He smiled and brushed her face with his hand. "Thanks, sweetie." Alexa began to hand a flower to all the friends. "Do you want us to give these flowers to Mommy?"

Alexa nodded. "I want Mommy to have flowers in heaven."

"That's very thoughtful of you, Alexa." They both stepped forward. Jim knelt next to Alexa, and they both placed the flowers next to the gravestone. Their friends followed suit.

"Do you think she likes the flowers I picked?" Alexa asked.

"I think Mommy loves the flowers you picked for her." Still kneeling, Jim hugged his daughter and kissed her. He stood up, holding Alexa's hand, and turned around to his friends. No words were spoken, no ceremony. Everyone knew Ari would want it that way.

The group returned to Hollywood. The council had ruled that no ceremony or service was to be held for Ari. Jim resigned himeself to the ruling and retreated to his bedroom apartment. He sunk into a wing chair and began to read from his Bible. *"'We were therefore buried with Him through baptism into death in order that, just as Christ was raised from the dead through the glory of the Father, we too may live a new life. For if we have been united with Him in a death like His, we will certainly also be united with Him in a resurrection like His.'"*

Isaac stared at a photograph on his bookshelf. "Silas and Ari knew the dangers of what we all do. Their passion wasn't just about living their life. Their passion was about living life through His death. They are faithful servants of God, never questioning or complaining about the tasks assigned to them. Please keep them under Your wing, Lord."

In the living room, Sam sat on the fireplace mantle, facing the activity of the dining room and kitchen. Sam paused, gathering his thoughts, and making sure to quell any emotions that would try to bubble up from his heart and give away the truth about Ari and Silas. He had known Ari since her birth. After her parents' deaths, he felt partly responsible to raise her.

Jim came in and sat next to him. Sam pulled out a small photograph of a young Ari and showed it to Jim. Jim gawked at the photograph, amazed at Ari's likeness to Alexa. Sam cleared his throat and spoke fondly, from memory. "From a very early age, Ari was fearless. If she had any fear, Ari never let it show. She trusted God completely. She truly had a servant's heart. Ari understood from a very early age that she was only a vessel that God would use at His bidding."

He recalled an awkward moment from his memory. "One afternoon I caught Ari in one of the bathrooms shared by a few of the Outriders. At first I thought she snooped in their quarters. I rebuked her, but I quickly realized she had cleaned their bathroom on her day off.

"I questioned her why she didn't leave that for the Outriders to clean themselves, and her answer floored me. She said she appreciated working with them and their fellowship. She explained that this task became one of the few ways she could honor and serve them.

"She made me swear to secrecy. Even today I didn't think anyone ever knew she did this for the very men and women she worked with. Ari always put others' needs before her own. How could they think she tried to kill the students? I hope that this isn't a precursor of things to come for the Old Guard," Sam voiced quietly.

Several stories below them, Isaac had returned to his cell in time before being missed. He knew they would search the corners of the earth to find him. And he knew the politics behind what Petra did. She would not let anything bad happen to him, at least for now. He muttered as he sat down, "I pray that Ari and Silas will be able to find the secrets the ring has locked away."

◆

Christina bit her lip, holding back emotions. Petra's curt announcement of Sam's involvement with the attempted murder of the students made her blood boil. The story continued that he had somehow persuaded and practically brainwashed Ari to perform the vicious act. Petra and the council went on to speculate that he also had to do with Silas' untimely death, and now of the disappearance of their chief overseer.

None of it seemed to make any sense. Everyone respected and loved Sam. They detained and dragged him down to the security block for interrogation. "It is quite apparent," Petra continued, "that Sam didn't work alone. I'm sure he had others doing his work." The Outriders stood in the silence, looking at each other, not expecting such accusations against one of the pillars of the Old Guard.

Christina whispered to her husband, "I can't believe that Sam would have done that, especially to Ari. She was like a daughter to him. What about all the decades of faithful service to the Lord and this organization? I can't believe he could have been such a different man."

Mike nudged his friends with his elbow. "Speaking of a different man, look at Jim." The group looked at Jim, who had his arm around Sarah. He whispered something in her ear, and she giggled. Holding hands, the two of them got up and walked to the living room.

Rebecca and Christina both rolled her eyes. Christina let go of her husband's hand. "Excuse me, sweetie." She walked up to Jim. "Excuse me, sir. If you have a moment, I need to speak with you."

"Sure, Christina. I am headed to my office anyway." The two walked down the hall. Jim sat down on a small leather sofa on the far end of the room and invited Christina in. She sat on an overstuffed chair, facing her friend. "What's on your mind, Christina?"

Christina whispered, "It's Sarah, sir . . ."

Just as Christina gave voice to her grievance, a firm knock persisted on his office door. Petra stepped in, along with Sarah. "Hello, Christina."

"Hello, Madam Overseer."

"I'm sorry to interrupt your meeting, but I need to speak to Jim," Petra explained.

"Uh, sure ma'am." Christina got up and began to walk out.

"Sorry, Christina, we'll talk later," Jim said. Christina nodded and walked out. The door closed behind her, and she continued down the hall.

CHAPTER TEN

D ays passed while Ari and Silas healed. The shortened sunbeams on the floor meant the morning was late; Ari lay in bed staring at the mysterious ring Isaac had given her. For several nights she had been awakened by violent dreams; the latest nightmare vision was of attacking Nephilim, towering over her and the others as they struck everything and everyone in their path with each swing of their swords.

Ever since she placed the ring on her finger, her nights recalled vivid images of Outrider battles. Ari had no idea if the images were just dreams, or if they were a prophecy of their future, or if the visions were recounting the past.

As she twisted the ring slowly around her finger, she found the ring and its rough design beautiful in a rustic way. *Halcyon . . . That's Greek or Roman in origin. If that's the case, that narrows our search to most of Europe, western Asia, and northern Africa . . . that is if you can consider nearly an entire continent narrowing the search . . . Assuming that it is Greek or Roman in origin and not just using the name because of name or meaning of the name . . . I wonder what Halcyon means? Are they a person?*

Ari decided to sit up and get moving. She felt strong enough to try to spend the entire day out of bed. She wandered over to the other side of the house to see if Silas had stirred to life. She spied him in the bathroom, fresh from his shower. He stood in front of the mirror with a towel wrapped around his waist. He leaned into the bathroom mirror, staring at the scar on his chest. He saw Ari in the mirror looking at the same scar. He chuckled under his breath. "Another inch over I'd be in a compost pile."

Ari gently outlined a large healed gash near his heart. "Don't be silly. You can't compost humans. The fat causes problems with the breakdown by helpful microorganisms." Ari playfully slapped the scar.

Still sensitive, Silas flinched at her slap. "Hey, ow!"

"Sorry. I just wanted to make sure you knew you were alive and how blessed you are."

"So what are we supposed to do for the next two to seventy-two months?" Silas asked sarcastically, buttoning his linen shirt up.

"Lay low. Try to blend in." Ari looked at Silas' hair, then at hers. "This isn't going to be easy to do. Your hair screams displaced tourist, and my skunk-striped hair sticks out like a sore thumb." Ari ran her fingers through her silver streak. "I may have just the solution for both of us, literally." Ari walked back to her bathroom and came back with a small box.

Silas looked at his box. He couldn't read the Thai text, but he knew what the box contained from the picture. "Are you serious? Do you know how bad I look with dark hair?"

"When in Rome . . ." Ari patted Silas on the shoulder.

"Wait. What do I do? How do you do this?"

"Mix the packets together in the bottle, put the gloves on, and work it into your hair. Leave it in for twenty-five minutes and rinse until the water runs clear. Try not to get it on your skin." Ari pushed her panicked friend closer to the sink and then stepped back, closing the bathroom door behind her.

Silas looked in the mirror again, combing his fingers through his long blonde hair. "Here goes nothing . . . "

An hour later, Silas stepped out of the bathroom, his hair transformed to a shiny medium brown. Ari met up with him. He looked at her, "Your hair? How did you get yours done so fast?"

"I have a bathroom too, you know. And my hair is mostly black to begin with. I only had to worry about the silver streak." She ran her fingers through Silas' newly dyed hair. "I think it looks good on you. I had to do a double-take. I almost didn't recognize you."

"That's the idea, isn't it?" Silas smirked, a little shy with his new image. "I think we should try it out. Do you want to go into town for lunch?"

Ari looked at Silas. "What do you think? Personally, I wouldn't mind staying home and getting some rest."

"We'll be quick. I promise. Besides, we need to pick up groceries for the next few days."

Ari rolled her eyes. "Fine. Let me get dressed and put some shoes on."

The two Outriders rode into town on a scooter. After a couple of turns, the bike came to an area dense with stalls and people. "I think we can walk from here," said Silas. He pulled the scooter up to an impromptu parking area where several other scooters were haphazardly placed. He pushed it next to a wall. Ari winced in pain as she struggled to swing her leg over. Silas offered his hand. Accepting his offer, she bit her lip, hiding the pain she felt in her ribs. "Thanks."

"I think there's a shop Sam told me about not too far from here," Silas encouraged Ari as he held her hand.

Ari nodded and they wove themselves into the morning crowd. Ari's eyes couldn't focus on the frenzy of action and explosion of color. Fruits and vegetables of every color and shape surrounded them. Heaps of green, leafy vegetables formed pyramids on tables and in baskets. Many she recognized; quite a few, she didn't have a clue. Exotic scents attacked her as they walked down the narrow sidewalk. Voices championed each stall's produce to entice them to stop and buy.

An old man shoved a knife blade in front of Ari. Silas was about to react, but Ari held his hand at his holster. The man just offered Ari a slice of papaya. Ari nodded and smiled, graciously accepting the sample. She bit into it; the sweet flavor surpassed anything they could find in the States. She offered Silas the other half and he devoured it, closing his eyes at the full flavor.

Every once in a while, Ari stopped at a stall and made small purchases. She kept passing the bags back to Silas to carry. Silas moved on while Ari lingered further back, admiring the scene before them. Then Ari stopped in front of a stall. The hawker ran up to Ari, trying to bargain with her to buy one of his many handmade metal works. He held up a brass bowl, then an ornate platter. Ari's gaze fixated on a gleaming object on the wall.

Silas backpedaled down the sidewalk after he realized Ari had stopped. He followed her gaze with his own eyes to see what stopped her. A brass sword, the length and shape roughly that of the longsword that impaled her, hung on the wall. The hawker smiled and brought the sword down for Ari to handle.

Ari couldn't keep her eyes from its cutting edge. Purely ornamental in nature, heavy and almost awkward, the sword in her hand reminded her of the sword in her visions. The only difference—the one in her vision sliced through bone as easily as flesh. "Ari, are you all right?" Silas asked.

"Yeah, I'm fine. This sword reminded me of the one that skewered me, and of a vision I had recently." She handed the weapon back to the hawker. He tried to bargain with Ari, but she politely shook her head and walked away.

"Vision? Of what?" Silas asked.

"These creatures. They were huge. And they carried swords that looked like that. And so did we. We had swords as well."

"The creatures—were they friend or foe?" he asked.

"Definitely foe," Ari muttered with a small laugh, trying to shake the imagery off.

"How often do you get these visions?" Silas asked as he tried to weave around the people passing by.

Ari shrugged. "I don't know. It seems a lot more since I've gotten this ring from Isaac."

Silas walked up to a stall and showed the hawker two fingers. The lady smiled and bowed and quickly assembled contents into bowls. Her hands expertly tossed translucent rice noodles at the bottom of each bowl and then tossed ingredients on top. The lady ladled an aromatic broth from a very large kettle into the bowls.

The two Outriders sat at a plastic table and stools as the lady offered them a heaping plate of fresh basil and cilantro. Hidden underneath were thinly sliced Thai peppers and wedges of lime. Ari and Silas silently garnished their dishes. Ari plucked off leaves and squeezed a wedge of lime into her broth.

Ari gave their food a short blessing before dipping her spoon into the magic elixir. She inhaled, trying to guess the ingredients of the broth. More than one animal was used—beef and pork for sure. She sensed the subtle but distinct spices of star anise and possibly clove. Ari sipped the broth and closed her eyes.

"Amazing, isn't it?" Silas asked.

"Wow. It reminds me a bit of pho, but the broth is unbelievable. Why can't soup taste like that in the States?"

"Probably because most people don't like to eat dog."

Ari looked at her bowl and then at Silas. "You're joking, I hope."

"Of course. I'm sure she has been cooking and perfecting this since she was a kid." He slurped some noodles down.

Ari picked the meat out and put it in Silas' bowl. She looked around at the people bustling around. No one stared at them for more than a glance. "I think the hair is working. No one is paying any attention to us."

Silas held his fist up at Ari. Ari bumped her fist into his, and their fingers split open as if the hands exploded on impact. All this while both slurped noodles in their mouths, not even looking at each other. They enjoyed their meal in relative comfort. If anyone was searching for them, no one would be able to easily recognize them from a distance.

◆

Several months passed without word from Hollywood. Ari stood and doubled over, trying to catch her breath. She sported a sleeveless blue ribbed t-shirt and biker-style fitness shorts. Her skin glistened with sweat. Usually Ari could run several miles, but she pushed the recovery of her injury ahead of its normal schedule to try to forget about Sam's disappearance. The resistance and give of the loose sand demanded more of a workout than she anticipated.

The time seemed like an eternity since they began their exile. Ari felt as if she had gone stir crazy. She had never had this much time off without working. Even when injured, she only took a few weeks off at most. Ari put her holster back on, grabbed her towel, and stretched her back and legs before she collapsed onto the sand. She sat down and leaned on her elbow.

The sun had just risen above the horizon. The beach became ablaze with amber light. She spent the next couple of hours praying. "Lord, I give you all the praise and the honor. Please protect my friends and family from evil. Your blood was shed so that we could live and live victoriously. Give us Your kingdom knowledge to know what our next move should be. Lord, I wish only to do Your will, but I miss my family. I miss doing Your will as an Outrider . . ."

Ari dropped her head, looking at the ground as tears began to fall. She had never been without her family like this, ever. A feeling of loneliness and isolation suddenly washed over her. Someone like Sam or Jim or even Isaac had always been there for her. Even when the organization had broken apart, she still had her friends with her. She wrapped her arms around herself. *Please Lord . . . I need You now more than ever.*

Silas remained with her, but it wasn't the same. After years of persecution from him, she hadn't completely trusted him to the level of friendship they once had. *Obviously Isaac trusts him, why can't I?* Ari tried to convince herself that things were like they seemed, but her heart told her differently. Silas came down the stairs to the beach to keep watch over Ari. She quickly wiped her tears away.

Tentatively Silas asked, "Ari, are you all right?"

"Yeah, I'm fine. I just need a moment."

"Uh, okay . . . sure. Call if you need anything." Silas rubbed his neck and walked a few steps in the sand towards the stair, then stopped and turned. "You're not alone, Ari. You still have your family. You have me too. I know I screwed up your life. But I have a new heart now. I can't imagine how I made it without Jesus. You led me back to Him, Ari. I am forever grateful, and I'll always be here for you, even if you may not believe me. I hope you can fully trust me some day. I miss your friendship . . . I miss you." Silas turned away and started back toward the stairs.

Ari watched her associate walk away. She bent over, her head and arms between her legs. Silas had just opened an emotional avalanche that Ari tumbled into uncontrollably. She got up and stormed out after Silas.

Silas picked up a seashell and casually tossed it back into the waves. He heard footsteps approach him. He turned, a little confused. "Ari . . ."

Ari marched up to him and punched him on the jaw as hard as she could. Not expecting it, Silas fell back into the sand as he held the side of his face. "What are you doing?"

"You slimy piece of . . ." Ari fumed. "Family? Trust? Friendship? *You miss me?*" Ari straddled the downed Outrider and began to pound his chest with her fists. Silas tried to grab her wrists, but Ari moved too quickly. Before he could stop her, Ari grabbed her blade gun from her holster and pointed it at his temple.

Ari cried as she spoke to Silas. "You sure have a weird way of showing friendship and trust, or don't you remember? You tortured me and tried to kill me . . . Did you miss my friendship then? What about John? He trusted you like a brother and you murdered him. Why shouldn't I kill you like you did him, or for that matter, most of the Old Guard?" She pressed the barrel firmly against his head. She made sure Silas remembered his past transgressions as a Tempest, as he systematically hunted down the Old Guard and killed them.

Silas raised his hands above his head and froze. "You shouldn't kill me; because of you, I have a changed heart. Because both you and I are children of God. Because you have compassion and forgiveness and you saw I could be redeemed. You had enough faith to lead me to salvation after I did all that to you."

Ari stared at the man; tears stained her cheeks. After a few seconds, she lowered her gun. Tears fell as Ari pictured her first husband murdered by the very man that lay in front of her. "He was your best friend, Silas. John trusted you. Why do you think I could ever fully trust you again?"

"I don't, Ari. I have to trust God and allow Him to work on your heart."

Ari rolled off and collapsed in the sand next to Silas. She lay on her back and stared vacantly at the sky as her tears silently fell. "You have no idea how much you messed me up. A part of me died every time your Tempest murdered someone I cared for. I finally got to the point where I didn't want to get close to anyone anymore for fear that they would be killed.

"To this day I still have this invisible brick wall around me. It's a prison. No one can get in and I can't get out." Ari got up and brushed sand from her hands, then put her gun back into her holster. "I used to not be that way, Silas. You changed me into something I don't like." She turned and headed back to the house.

Silas propped himself on his elbow and rubbed his jaw as he watched Ari disappear at the top of the stairs.

Ari stepped into the shower and continued to pray. The late morning sun bathed her in light. Each day she prayed for her friends and family she left behind. She cried as the shower washed sand and tears down the drain. Despite his promise to return, Sam never did come back. They both understood that if he thought someone was watching him or if it became too dangerous, he would lay low. *I just wish I knew what was going on at Hollywood.* She got dressed and grabbed a loose linen blouse and slipped into khaki capri pants.

Silas had just poured his second cup of coffee when Ari emerged and walked into the kitchen. She steered clear of Silas as she reached inside the refrigerator and pulled out a bottle of water. Ari took a long drink of water.

She tried to remain angry when she grabbed a purple fruit and expertly cut the thick outer skin of the mangosteen to expose the creamy white inside. She picked at one of the white sections and placed it in her mouth. As she discreetly spit out the seed into her fist after sucking the white flesh off, the Holy Spirit reminded her, *Like the fruit you are eating, the tough skin on the outside protects the tender sweetness inside. Amon and the Tempest had peeled your tough exterior away and left you vulnerable. Silas' heart has been renewed. Unforgiveness keeps you bound to the things of the world. The situation you are experiencing now is not Silas' fault.*

Ari dropped her head and silently thanked the Lord for reminding her. Ari cleared her throat. "Silas, I owe you an apology. I shouldn't have blown up at you like that. I miss my family and friends. I'm on edge and feel like I'm hiding from the Tempest again. I shouldn't have attacked you like that. I know you've changed, and I treated you unfairly." Ari shook her head as a tear trailed down her cheek.

"I guess I did put you through the wringer."

"You just have no idea, Silas. My parents were killed when I was kid. I barely knew my mom. Sam raised me with a little help from Isaac. But you know how it is: as nice as Sam and Isaac were to me, they still weren't my parents.

"When you killed John, a part of me shut down. When you lose the love of someone you had a covenant relationship with, your entire core is shaken. I thought that maybe God didn't want me to have a family. I hesitated when Jim wanted to marry me. I wondered when the proverbial other shoe would drop and ruin our relationship. For the first time since before my parents died, I felt like things might be normal when I gave birth to Alexa."

Ari closed her eyes and hung her head. "I guess there is no such thing as 'normal' in an Outrider's life, let alone my life. I've worked so much that I barely know my own daughter. I actually asked Isaac for time off and he agreed. He gave me as much time as I needed to take after the last assignment. Just when I thought things were better and my life was normal, all this happens. I keep wondering when I get a break." Ari walked over to the sofa and sat down, unable to look at Silas.

The two sat in silence. Silas finally moved over to a chair facing Ari. He tried to find words during the silence, and finally cleared his throat. He spoke quietly. "Lord knows I have made your already difficult life even more so. Please believe me when I say this: I would never do anything to hurt you now. I believe you're being refined, Ari; you're being hardened and strengthened with all of what you've gone through. He's preparing you for something greater that will take all of your strength and tempered emotional experiences in order to succeed."

Ari looked at Silas. "I can't imagine anything that is going to be more difficult than what you put me through."

"I pray we don't have to deal with anything of that magnitude ever again. But we do live in the endtimes . . ."

"Great . . ." Ari slouched in the sofa. She twirled the ring on her finger, and after a minute, she gave a big sigh. "Enough of this self-wallowing. I need a break. I thought of taking a short excursion this afternoon after lunch. You in?"

"You want to go into town?" Silas sipped at his coffee.

"Actually, I thought of going a little further." Ari spit out another seed.

Silas knew her lack of detail meant she hid something. "Further where?"

"Um, I thought I'd visit a friend."

"Ari . . ."

"I haven't seen him in years. He is not associated with the Outriders and doesn't know about my affiliation with them."

"Ari, where?"

"Greece." The silence that met Ari's answer accentuated Silas' dumbfounded expression. Silas held his cup and stared at her in disbelief. She continued, still with a seed in her mouth. "What? Isaac said that once I felt better, I should try to find out more about the ring."

"Ari, you know that we have to keep a very low profile . . . " Silas reminded her.

"And I will. I just want to see if a friend who happens to be a professor at the university in Athens would know more about this ring. The trip will be quick. Just an hour or so, and I'll be out of there. No one will think of finding me there. Come with me. They're not even looking for us."

"Quick, you promise," Silas added.

"I'll have you home in time for dinner."

"At the first sign of danger . . ."

". . . we're out of there," Ari promised.

"You will listen to me when I tell you that we have to leave, right?" Silas asked.

"Of course."

Silas finally put his coffee cup down. "You're up to something more, Mrs. Sommers."

"Not at all, Silas. Why would you think that?"

"Because I know you almost as well as you know me. We think the same way, Bash."

"Bash . . . I haven't heard that name in a very long time." Ari laughed. She grabbed a tangerine and peeled the rind and began to eat the sections.

"Yeah, you probably haven't heard it since we were in Outrider training together. Matt, our instructor, kept slamming you against stuff, apparently to try to teach you a lesson in humility. I think he had a hard time believing a female could be so good at everything. After he slammed you against the wall for the umpteenth time, I finally started calling you Bash because hard slams is how every class seemed to end for you."

"Yeah, hard way like with a brick wall, a cement floor, a wood beam . . ." Ari rubbed her head. "I think I still have a lump on my head from one of his lessons."

"Just curious, but how did you come up with Greece?" Silas asked, taking another sip of his coffee.

"The design and name both seem to be Roman-Greco, and also the name of the ring. Halcyon is the genus of a bird. A kingfisher, I think. They're all over the world, so I hope between the name of the ring and the design on the ring itself that my friend the professor could narrow our search a little." Ari finished the last of her tangerine. "We can probably leave when you're ready."

"I'd like to say I am ready, but with you Ari, I'm never quite sure." Silas looked at Ari with skepticism. "You really have no idea where to start, do you?"

"Nope. But I'm sure there must be someone at one of the universities who knows more about this ring."

Ari quickly dressed in a light denim jacket, red t-shirt, and khakis. She walked out of her bedroom and joined Silas on the patio. With that, Ari made sure she had ahold of Silas before they disappeared in the afternoon sunlight.

They reappeared in a narrow alley of dingy whitewashed buildings. The early morning sun already heated the stone and plaster walls. Silas thanked God for the shade in the narrow alley as they worked their way down the hill. They entered a small neighborhood square as Ari strolled to an outside café.

An older gentleman sat at one of the tables, sipping on coffee and talking to another man. Both men were in the middle of an animated argument, hands waving and slapping each other on the shoulders.

Ari walked up to the men, and her shadow fell over one of them. The man stopped arguing and looked up at the person that put him in shade. When he finally recognized the figure, his face transformed into a huge grin. "Ariana!" He stood up and gave Ari a huge bear hug.

In broken Greek, Ari spoke. "Good morning, professor. I knew I would find you here. Silas, please meet Professor Dmitri Kyrolos. Professor, this is my friend and associate Silas Monroe."

"What brings you here to our wonderful country? And you came on such a beautiful morning!" The professor waved his arms up to the cloudless sky.

Silas shaded his eyes. "Yeah, this sun is a lot more intense than what we are used to. I should have brought sunscreen."

"Come, come. Please have a seat." The professor spoke in broken

English and gestured for the two Outriders to sit. "Would you like a coffee?"

"No, thank you, sir." Silas politely waved off the offer. Ari shook her head.

"What brings you here and so early, Ariana?" The professor sipped at his coffee.

Ari took off her ring and handed it to the professor. "Sir, I wondered if you knew where this ring would have come from? I think this is Greek or Roman in design. It is known as the ring of Halcyon, but the name confused me. I didn't think that kingfishers were indigenous to this part of Europe."

The professor scratched his salt and pepper beard as he turned the ring over and over. "Curious, Ari. I find it interesting, this particular ring named as such. Where did you get this?"

"It is a friend's ring. It has been passed down from generation to generation for many centuries."

"I believe you have a ring key." The elderly man handed the ring back to Ari.

"I don't think I understand, sir," Ari said as she slipped the ring back on her finger.

Professor Kyrolos continued to stroke his peppered beard. "Ancient Greeks and Romans sometimes used rings as not only jewelry but also as keys to unlock small lockboxes. I believe this ring does the same."

"Does the ring give a clue where we might find the thing that the ring unlocks?" Ari asked.

"Not really, if the object even still exists. But if it does, perhaps the name helps. Like I said, that is an unusual name. Halcyon is the Greek name for kingfishers and is used today for the scientific name for the bird species. There are some kingfishers that nest in the southern islands of Greece—Crete for one. But some colonies have been found as far north as Macedonia." The professor leaned towards Ari. "You know, Ari, there are many ruins and caves dotting the coastlines on many of the islands. There are many places for something small like that to be hidden, provided it hasn't already been moved, or worse, looted or destroyed." The man began to laugh. "I don't envy you, Ari. You have your work cut out for you."

Ari sat back on the chair. Suddenly she felt no closer to the secrets the ring held. The younger gentleman at the table asked in Greek, "May I see the ring?"

Ari looked at the professor. "That's okay, Ari," the professor assured her. "He's an associate director of antiquities at the museum."

Ari handed him the ring. The man held his index finger up and waved it as he looked at the ring. "This is an unusual pattern for the cross. I have seen this before, but where?" His eyebrows knitted together as he thought hard. "I recall that this pattern was associated with another Christian symbol of unknown meaning or origins . . ." The man began to outline a familiar shape onto the café table with his finger.

Ari looked at Silas, then looked at the director. She grabbed a pen from the professor's pocket. "Please?" She handed the pen and a napkin to the director. He drew the Outrider symbol onto a paper napkin.

Ari looked at Silas. The director caught the subtle reaction between the two Outriders. "You know what that symbol is?" He leaned forward in his chair. "What is that symbol?"

Ari skirted the question with another. "Does this new symbol remind you of where you may have seen the first?"

"Yes, yes, it does. There is a photograph of a mosaic. It is fresh in my mind because we were referring to it recently because of some of the unusual designs. If you would like to, I can take you to the museum archives and show the photograph to you."

Ari nodded. "That would be great." Ari looked at the professor. "Would you like to come with?"

The elderly man held his hand up and shook his head. "No, thank you. I have a class this morning. Nicholas, we will continue our discussion tomorrow morning, yes?"

The director smiled. "Of course. You are not going to get out of this argument that easily." Ari and Silas followed the man down the street, and they turned a corner. "The museum is only a few blocks away."

The trio walked into a back doorway and down a quiet hallway lined with unmarked doors. The director stopped at one door and unlocked it. "Let's see . . ." He began to scan a wall lined with horizontal file cabinets. He tugged on one of the thin long drawers, and it finally slid open. He pulled out the contents and placed them on a large table in the middle of the room. The director flipped the stiff protective cover off the photographs and slid the top one over to Ari and Silas.

"We found this mosaic in a building in Crete, but it has been missing now for several years. We never thought someone would steal a mosaic off a wall like that. We think that the building was a temple before they converted it to a church." The director pointed at the two obscure cross symbols. "See the two symbols form an "X." Curious how the two crosses form yet another cross . . ." the director mused as he examined the symbol. "At first we thought that this portrayed part of a myth, but the cross symbols wouldn't be relevant. So as of yet we haven't been able to confirm the mythological story or the creature the man is battling. We believe it may be a giant."

The mosaic in the photograph showed a sword-wielding man attacking a larger creature with a scaly, snake-like upper torso and legs. Both Ari and Silas recognized the symbol on the man's belt as that of the Outriders. The Outrider symbol appeared again in the mosaic inside a circle where that symbol overlapped with the patterned cross of the ring Ari wore. The two Outriders looked at the photograph. "This looks familiar," Ari whispered to Silas. "I've seen this piece before."

"Isn't this the artwork on the wall of Amon's office in the organization's building?" Silas whispered back.

"Director, does Greek mythology have giants?

"Of course, but so do most of the ancient cultures. The Greek myth says that they were all born from one goddess named Gaia. They battled Hercules and the Olympians. The survivors retreated to Palline, the Greek peninsula that is now called Kassandra. Over time they were hunted down by Hercules and killed. According to the legend, only one survived."

"Really? What became of this survivor?"

The director laughed. "The myth says his mother turned him into a dung beetle so he wouldn't be killed."

Ari poured over the details of the photographed artwork. In the mosaic, on the cliff above a cave, a brown, four-legged creature could barely be made out. "What do you suppose that figure is?" Ari pointed.

The director squinted. "We can't tell. It might be a dog or a large cat."

"Are there caves that are named for animals that live in or near them?" Silas asked.

"Well, if you account for the local names as well, they are almost as numerous as the grains of wheat in a field. Fish Cave, Bird Cave, Bear Cave . . . you name it."

"Bear? Are there bears in Greece?" Ari asked.

"Eh, not so much now. Only a few hundred scattered in the more rural areas of the country and islands. They have been hunted down by man and dogs."

Ari shook the director's hand. "Thank you for taking the time and showing us the photograph."

"You are welcome, Ariana. Please come visit us again. Perhaps for lunch or dinner, eh?"

"Yes. We'll be back."

The director watched the two curious people walk down the street until they turned the corner, out of sight.

CHAPTER ELEVEN

Several years passed and Alexa quickly matured into a young girl. She sat at the table with her arms crossed, staring at a plate of food getting cold. Jim had problems keeping up with his daughter.

Mike and Rebecca walked up to the table. "Hi, guys! Do you mind if Rebecca and I join you two?"

Jim stretched his hand at the open chairs. "Help yourselves." He yawned.

"Why the long face, Alexa?" Rebecca asked the young girl. Alexa didn't respond. She pouted as she poked her finger at a slice of chicken.

"Hey, Al, Uncle Mike asked you a question," Jim told his daughter.

"Fine." The girl continued pouting.

Mike's fiancé Rebecca bit her lips trying to keep a straight face. Jim scratched his head and said, "I'm debating in my mind whether this is just a phase all preteen girls go through, or whether Alexa inherited Ari's stubborn streak. Right now I'm just trying to convince Alexa to eat a few more bites off her dinner plate."

Rebecca stooped over to talk more privately to the little girl. "What's wrong, buttercup?"

Still pouting and rolling her eyes, Alexa spouted. "Dad's trying to make me eat this chicken, and I don't want to."

"Why not?" Rebecca whispered back.

"Ew, it's gross," the girl answered as she stuck her tongue out.

"I think she inherited Ari's vegetarianism." Jim rubbed his neck. "I just have problems making sure she eats enough protein."

"Would you like a cheese omelet? I'm making one for Mike," Rebecca offered.

"Sure! Can I help you?" asked Alexa.

"Only if your dad says it's okay. I don't want to override his authority," Rebecca answered. Resigned, Jim nodded.

"Thank you, Daddy. I love you gobs!" Alexa held her hands out to her dad.

Jim smiled and hugged his daughter, "Yeah, right. And gobs loves you too."

"I'll be back in a flash," Alexa said before disappearing into the kitchen with Rebecca.

Sarah walked up to Jim. She appeared to have just finished working out. Her skin glowed with perspiration under her light gray sweat suit. She purposely kept her sweat jacket partially unzipped, showing her black sports bra and oversized half tee. Even covered in sweat, Sarah knew how to look pretty. She laughed. "It looks like you have your work cut out for you."

"Hmmm? Oh, no." Jim laughed. "At this point they pretty much self-feed. It's just a matter of finding the right combination of what is cool and edible against what is gross and old-fashioned."

Sarah laughed again. "May I sit here?"

"Uh, sure . . ." Jim cleared his throat.

"I think I'm going to tell Rebecca that I want some bacon in my omelet." Mike excused himself and disappeared into the kitchen.

Leaning against the kitchen island, the two women watched the innocent flirtation happen.

"There she goes again," Alexa sighed.

"You don't like Sarah?" Rebecca asked.

The grade-schooler shook her head. "She's half my dad's age. And I don't like the way she acts," Alexa said as she finished grating the cheese.

Mike watched the flirtation between Sarah and Jim as the two women returned to making breakfast. He muttered to himself, "Now why don't I ever have that happen to me?"

"Eyes and tongue back in your head, please," Rebecca warned her fiancé Mike as she slapped the back of his head. "I have a right mind to go up to her and remind her that he is still mourning his wife."

"Rebecca, she's been dead for over four years," Mike said. "Ari wanted him to move on and be happy. I'm glad to see him interact again. Besides, I don't think you have anything to worry about," Mike added. "Jim doesn't look too comfortable talking to her."

Rebecca turned the omelet onto a plate, walked back to the table, and leaned over to Mike. "Just in case, I better intervene." She grabbed another small plate and sat herself between Jim and Sarah. "Sorry it took so long. Mike couldn't find the eggs. They were buried in the back of the fridge." She split the omelet in half and gave half to Alexa and the other half to Mike.

Alexa bowed her head and prayed over her food before taking a forkful. "Thanks, Rebecca."

Both women smiled at each other. Rebecca looked at Jim, "Alexa so reminds me of Ari, don't you think?"

Sarah smiled awkwardly and got up. "I better go. I'll talk to you later." She walked away and down the hall.

As Jim watched Sarah saunter away, Mike joined the table. He also observed the attractive Outrider walk away. The look elicited another slap from Rebecca; this time to his arm. "Ow!" he half-jokingly said as he held his upper arm.

Jim looked at Rebecca. "Pretty harsh of you to bring Ari's name up like that."

Rebecca slapped Jim on the forehead. "Jim, she's half your age. She's young enough to be your oldest daughter."

"So what, I'm supposed wither away and die without feeling love again?" Jim paused. "I loved Ari and miss her, but she's gone now. She felt lost when John died, and she didn't want me to go through what she experienced."

"Jim, she's been after you even before Ari died. She is up to something," Rebecca told her friend.

"I don't think so," Jim countered.

"And I do." Rebecca stood firm.

Jim snapped. "You have no idea what I'm going through or how I feel. There isn't a day that goes by that I don't think of Ari." Jim shook his head and rubbed his neck. "But I can't live in the past. Even if I don't feel like it, I need to keep going forward."

"I guess I shouldn't be too harsh on you," Rebecca finally admitted. "I just want to make sure you don't make a mistake that you're going to regret later. Just promise me that you will pray hard about this."

Jim nodded. He smiled at his daughter, who finished her omelet. "Did you finish your homework?

"Almost," Alexa admitted.

"You better get upstairs and finish it. You have school in an hour," Jim reminded her.

"Can I hang out with Mary after school?" Alexa could be heard asking, as she climbed the stairs in front of Jim.

Mike looked at Rebecca. She looked back at him, "What?"

"Cut the poor man some slack. He's trying his best," Mike answered.

"I did. I can tell he's not ready, but Sarah has her sights and claws in Jim and won't let him rest. I just hope he can live with himself if he moves on too quickly and marries another woman before his heart has healed," Rebecca countered.

CHAPTER TWELVE

Time away from their friends and family seemed to be an eternity. Despite the passing of years, Ari and Silas tried their best to keep their agility and Outrider skills. She made sure that neither of them lost their ability to fight the enemy. She converted one of the guest bungalows into a workout room. Thick tatami mats lined the floors to soften the falls.

Despite their continued training and fellowship, her defined confinement led Ari into periods of boredom. She and Silas had made several forays to Greece to see if they could find any other clues to the ring's origin. They never found anything and seemed as far from the answer as Isaac decades earlier.

After dinner, Ari sat on the beach and watched the sunset. Amazed at God's beauty, Ari watched the flame red and deep amber sun contrast against the dark lavender and indigo sky at the far horizon. Ari stared at the ring on her finger. Praying for revelation, she rubbed her thumb over the cross and hoped it would whisper its secrets to her.

With the passage of so much time, she realized something bad had happened to Sam. *If they could have, he or Isaac would have sent word to us by now.* During her prayer time she tried to discern those she used to work with, including Sam and Isaac, but either because of the distance or the length of time being away from everyone, she couldn't seem to focus on those she left behind.

She occasionally felt Jim and Alexa's presence but only long enough to know they were alive and happy. A wave of sadness hit Ari. The holidays were approaching, and she wished she could be with her family and friends. Darkness began to settle on the peninsula. Frustrated, she got up and walked up the path to the house.

Ari passed the jasmine vine at the top of the stairs and deeply inhaled the intoxicating scent. She stepped into the training room to grab a water from the fridge. The hairs on the back of her neck stood up as she turned around and instinctively held her arm up to protect herself. Silas had jumped out from behind the countertop to see if he could catch her off guard. They occasionally provoked each other this way to keep themselves honed. He tried to swing a Japanese bamboo sword called a *shinai* down onto her, but Ari's hands sandwiched the blade and stopped his blow. She grabbed the end of the sparring weapon as Silas tried to yank it up and away from her grasp. She held it firmly as the two combatants vied for the weapon.

"I almost had you, Bash." Silas laughed.

"Not even close, dude." With that, Ari's leg kicked the shinai where Silas held it. He lost his grip. The hilt of the sword flew up and bounced off his face.

"OW!" Silas backed up a step. He held his hand to the side of his face.

"Are you all right?" Ari asked as she dropped the shinai on the floor and offered assistance.

"I'm fine." Silas quickly swept his leg under Ari. His action made her fall backwards onto the tatami mat. He grabbed the shinai again and tried to hit Ari as she scrambled on the floor, trying to get out of the way.

"You were always too trusting, Ari. That is one of your weaknesses," Silas explained as he towered over his unprotected friend.

Ari whispered, *"Vindicate me, Lord, for I have led a blameless life; I have trusted in the Lord and have not faltered."* Before Silas finished grasping what Ari just said, she rolled to her feet and grabbed another shinai resting on a stand. In one swift and effortless move, Silas lost his advantage.

Ari made her first mock attack. Silas defended himself. Ari said, "I may be too trusting, but the Bible says, 'The Lord is my strength and my shield; my heart trusts in him, and he helps me.' Her first volley went for his head and shoulders, and then to his side. Silas effortlessly blocked her advance and then replied with several shots to her side and legs. With practiced moves, Ari stopped his parries.

Apparently getting cocky with his growing confidence, Silas attempted to do a fancy series of parry and thrusts towards Ari. Seeing an easy opportunity to set Silas straight, Ari pinned Silas' shinai blade against the floor and then tripped his awkward stance, forcing him down to the ground. In one continuous move, she knelt next to him and held the tip of her bamboo sword to his throat. She wanted to make sure Silas knew how serious his slip up had become. He held his hands up, crying, "Uncle!"

Ari removed her shinai from his throat and began to get up. As she did so, Silas swept his legs under hers again and caused her to fall backwards. Before Ari knew it, she had to defend herself again, pinned against the ground from his attack. She held her shinai with both hands as the full force of Silas' blows came down on her. He took the rare advantage of her weakened position and unexpectedly hit Ari's upper arm with the tip of his bamboo sword after a fierce volley. Ari cried out but managed to continue to protect herself. She reciprocated with a leg sweep to Silas, but he didn't fall. Silas wobbled, off-balance long enough for Ari to roll away and get back up on her feet.

Both competitors glared at each other with their shinai at the ready. The tips of the bamboo swords rubbed up against each other as they tried to find weakness in the other's hold. Unaccustomed to being winded during a battle, both Ari and Silas panted. Silas grinned as he paced around Ari, saying, "It appears that the student has surpassed the teacher."

"If you think that you're better than me, you have another thing coming, buddy," Ari said as she began her next volley. Several minutes of attack and counterattack occurred. The last of her moves caught Silas off guard, and his step faltered long enough for Silas let his guard down for a split second.

Ari took advantage of the moment, and with one seamless move, took the length of her shinai across his midrift and lifted up and flipped Silas' feet over his head. He landed on his back, and then, with seemingly full force, she sliced the shinai through the air toward his face. About to hit his face with her bamboo sword, Ari stopped just centimeters from his face.

Silas closed his eyes, expecting a blow. When it didn't come, he tentatively opened one eye to see the bamboo blade of her shinai just an inch from his face. She held it there for a second and then backed off, settling back to a more relaxed position. Silas held his abdomen as he rolled to his side and groaned in pain. Ari held her hand out to help him up. "Are you okay?"

"Yeah, considering I deserved that. Where'd you learn to do that move?" He waved her hand off as he still tried to catch his breath.

"I didn't. You're the first time I ever did that. I imagine if it were a real sword, I'd be talking to two halves of you."

Silas grimaced as he got up to his feet. "Touché, Mrs. Sommers. You won that round."

Ari rubbed the welt on her shoulder. "I don't know. I think you got some points. You almost had me." Ari plopped down on the mat and lay down, staring at the native wood ceiling. "I thought about that mosaic again. Other than that giant creature and the human, the picture also contained a kingfisher and that other animal in the background. That animal must have something to do with all of this. Why else would they put it into the mosaic?"

"That thing looked like a shapeless dark brown blob. That could be just about anything, Ari. What kind of animal did the director think it could be?"

Ari sat up and shrugged. "He didn't say. I don't think they knew what it was either." She got up and offered her hand to Silas. Holding his sore abdomen, he accepted her hand and got up too.

"I'm getting too old for this," Silas joked.

"This is as close to retirement I ever want to get," Ari admitted.

Silas walked to the door. "I'm headed back to the house. Are you coming?"

"In a minute. I want to put some ice on my shoulder." Ari rubbed the welt again. Silas nodded and disappeared into the growing darkness.

Ari grabbed a handful of ice from the freezer and wrapped it in a dishtowel. She bit her lip as she applied the pack to her sore arm. She closed up the room and padded back up to the main house. As she passed through the door, Silas slipped past her. He wore his swim trunks and had draped a long towel over his shoulder. "I'm taking a quick swim and a jacuzzi to hopefully loosen up my battered muscles. You want to join me?"

"Thanks, but not tonight." Ari smiled as she watched Silas prepare to dive into the water. Backlit by the pool's underwater lights, he stood at the pool's edge. His shoulders were curled forward, forcing his upper body to be hunched slightly over. The shape of his silhouette reminded Ari of a bear. A bear . . . Then the vision came into her head. "Silas!"

Ari's shout distracted him enough that he pulled back mid-dive. He turned and tried to look at Ari, flopping in the water sideways. "You did that on purpose, didn't you?" Silas surfaced, spitting out the words along with some water.

"I know what that figure in that mosaic is supposed to be. That tiny blob is supposed to be a bear. The animal is raised up on its haunches, which is why it didn't look that familiar."

"Um . . . great. It's a bear. And this helps us get closer to finding where and what your ring is supposed to open how?"

"I'm not sure. Maybe there's an area where bears and kingfishers hang out together?"

Silas folded his arms over the edge of the pool and nested his head in the palm of his hand. "Oh, sure. Perhaps they hit happy hour at the

Parthenon Bar and Grill on Friday nights." He started to laugh. Ari took her bare foot and gently pushed Silas' head under water. He surfaced, squirting water from his mouth. "Hey, I thought that joke was pretty good."

"Define 'good,'" Ari asked.

"Ha, ha. Help me out," Silas asked as he stretched his hand towards her.

Ari grabbed his hand. Before she knew it, he gave her a forceful yank. Ari flew over his head and bellyflopped into the water.

Silas guffawed, he was laughing so hard. He turned around and then panicked. Ari floated face-down in the water, not moving. "Ari?" He swam over to her body. He flipped her over and pulled her body onto the patio. He bent over to see if she was breathing. "C'mon Ari. You couldn't have drowned doing that. Not you . . ."

Just as he bent over to give her mouth to mouth resuscitation, Ari snapped her eyes open and whispered, "Boo!"

Silas fell backwards into a sitting position, startled. "Don't do that to me, Ari."

Ari began to laugh. "Serves you right. Parthenon Bar and Grill?"

"I knew you'd find that funny." Silas looked at Ari and shoved her shoulder like a kid brother shoving his sister. Ari threw him a towel and dried herself with another. Ari turned around, facing away from him. He suddenly became aware of the curves in her back, and how her biceps and shoulder muscles became more defined when her arms went over her head.

Ari sensed a change in his thoughts and heard a change in his breathing. She stopped drying herself and wrapped herself in the towel. Softly, she corrected her friend. "Silas, please, don't go there. I have a hard enough time away from my family, especially with the holidays coming up."

"I'm sorry, Ari. It's just that you are such a remarkable woman. You always have been." Silas covered himself with a towel. An awkward silence settled over them as the two watched the pool water. Silas took a deep breath and coughed. "I think we need a change of scenery."

"What, do you want to go back to Greece and follow that bear lead?"

"No, not that far." Silence met his comment. "The change of scenery might make you forget about spending Thanksgiving so far away from home."

Ari sat up and huffed under her breath. "Home . . . I've never had enough time to call anywhere home. I feel like Job in the Bible. My home and family have been taken away from me. The life that I had been blessed with seems to have been cursed."

"Home is where your heart is," Silas reminded her. "Home is where your family is. You know that Jim and Alexa love you very much."

"You mean 'loved.'" Ari reached into her pocket and rubbed a small river stone and wondered if Alexa even had hers anymore.

"No, I mean love. Besides you know that God is still with you. He will never leave you nor forsake you."

Ari thought about Jim and Alexa, and her heart felt like it broke. She felt uneasy talking about her separation from her family. She sighed and stretched her back, then intentionally forced a change of subject. "Speaking of loved . . . I would love to somehow have a traditional Thanksgiving meal for the holiday. How hard do you think it would be to get a turkey and all the trimmings from the market?"

"The turkey might be hard. It would be easier to get a duck or goose. I wonder what a roast duck would taste like doused in soy and fish sauce and roaring hot chili peppers?"

"It's actually pretty good, especially with a touch of ginger and green onion too. But it's still not roast turkey."

"We'll come up with something. In the meantime, are you up for the trip?"

"Where do you want to go?"

"Chieng Mai. It is in the northern part of the country. They have a small festival, with a few lanterns and open-air food stalls."

Ari stared at Silas with a discerning eye. She sensed he omitted something from her. "I don't know, Silas . . ."

"It's harmless. I promise you'll enjoy it. And I'll have you home before you turn into a pumpkin." Ari pursed her lips. She nodded. Silas' face widened into a grin. "You won't regret it."

"I'm already regretting it. I'm going to bed. Good night, Silas."

"Good night, Ari. See you tomorrow morning."

◆

The next day, as the sun began to draw longer shadows of the late afternoon, Silas grabbed Ari's hesitant hand as they strolled onto the patio and disappeared. They both reappeared in Chieng Mai in a narrow sidewalk alleyway between buildings. Silas followed the sounds and smells of a crowd and grilling meats. They turned the corner and their senses were overwhelmed. Stalls of food and souvenirs crowded the streets and square. Men and women were shouting, holding up lanterns that they were selling.

Ari couldn't help but smile. Festive sounds filled the air, and bright bold colors of saffron and red surrounded them. The smell of grilling meats invited them closer to the stalls. The two wove through the thick crowd of people. She elbowed her cohort and had to yell in order to be heard over the din. "I thought you said this was a small festival."

"Only a few thousand or so. If you see anything that interests you, grab me. Otherwise we'll get separated. If we do get separated from one other, I'll meet you at the stairs of the building over there." He pointed to a whitewashed building with stone stairs. Ari nodded.

The two continued to walk and take in the sights and sounds. Silas worked his way through a skewer of grilled, marinated meat. Ari's skewer had cubes of marinated tofu, also grilled to a slight char. The flavor of sweet, hot, salty, and bitter intensely assaulted her mouth to about the same level as the sights and sounds around her. They tried several other nibbles of street food as they wound their way through the crowded stalls.

The heat of the day began to wear on Ari. She stopped momentarily to look at a street play between what appeared to be an evil spirit against a young girl. Ari's eyes gazed at the sword the evil character held. With several flourishing tines sticking out of the blade by the hand guard, it resembled a very long Outrider blade.

The evil character began to look out towards the audience. Every once in a while, you would hear a child scream, scared by the actor. The actor then jerked his glare towards Ari. Suddenly, Ari stopped laughing. A vision of her and Silas battling one of the Nephilim flashed before her eyes as the people around her began to spin . . .

"Ari? Are you okay? Silas asked as he cradled her head. He looked down at her. A small crowd of concerned patrons circled above her, including the actor who played the evil spirit. He had taken his mask off and knelt next to Silas. Startled and slightly embarrassed, Ari tried to get up, but then everything started to spin again. "Take it easy. Here, drink this." He handed her a bottle of water one of the vendors gave him. "What happened?"

"Nothing. I'm fine. I guess the heat got to me." Ari took a drink and then tried to get up. She leaned heavily on Silas' arm. She didn't want to tell him that they would face the Nephilim again. She smiled and bowed her head to the actor. He smiled and got up, disappearing behind a curtain. The two friends slowly walked, holding each other tight, until they reached some stairs.

Silas sat Ari down and then held his hands out to her. "Stay right there. Don't move. I'll be right back." He wove his way into the crowd and disappeared. Ari craned her neck, trying to see where he went off to. Her eyes wandered off, and she noticed the crowd was bigger than when they had first arrived. The sun had already set, but the sky held on to the light. Amber and lavender clouds gave way to indigo and cobalt blue shadows. Jeweled points of starlight pierced the darkness.

A few minutes later, Silas appeared holding two unlit lanterns. They were cylindrical, delicately made of thin beige silk fabric, and intricately stained with patterns of flowers and vines. A simple spoke of four wires held a small homemade can of lantern oil in place. "Depending on whom you talk to or read," Silas explained, "the lanterns represent anything from dead ancestors to letting past worries go. I say we release these as God's promise to us that we will see our friends and family soon. What do you think?"

"They're almost too beautiful to let go," Ari said as she admired the craftsmanship.

"Just like those we left behind." Silas' eyes glistened. Ari's eyes glistened too as she nodded, unable to respond. "Do you feel well enough to stand?" Ari nodded as she stood on the bottom stair. Silas handed her one of the lanterns. A man with a small makeshift torch lit Ari and Silas' oil. The heated air began to fill the lanterns as the golden glow within grew in strength.

Ari looked around. From her slightly higher vantage point, she could see hundreds of lighted lanterns, and hundreds more being lit. Soon thousands of gossamer lanterns glowed, lighting the night. As if on cue, the people released their lanterns into the sky. Ari and Silas also released theirs. The delicate structures rose above them and joined the thousands that floated above them. Both Ari and Silas laughed and grinned at the amazing spectacle. Tears ran down Ari's cheeks. *Alexa would enjoy this. I wish she was here with me.*

The lanterns floated over the river and shrunk to tiny dots of light as the breeze gently led them away. The crowd thinned out as the people headed back to the food and festivities. Ari stood on the stair, looking at the fading light of the lanterns drifting over the river. The reflections of the light in the river made it look like there were twice as many. "I promised to get you home before you turned into a pumpkin," Silas reminded her as he held his hand out to her. At first she didn't respond. Then, she nodded and joined Silas as they returned to the vacant alley and transported back to their temporary home.

CHAPTER THIRTEEN

"Mr. Carter . . . Mrs. Baker . . ." Petra handed Christina an assignment folder. "You leave this evening. It should be simple for a couple of experienced Outriders like you. It's just a simple escort, something even a rookie would be able to handle. Mr. Carter, I would like to speak to you in private for a minute."

Mike followed Petra. Christina opened the file and poured over the details. A few minutes later, Mike reappeared. He shook his head. "Man, Christina. I can't screw this one up."

"It seems routine. We're supposed to self-transport to these exact coordinates. That seems kind of unusual in itself, but I'm sure there's a legitimate reason. We're to escort a pastor and his wife safely to their next location, where we're to hand them over to the deacons. The protection of the pastor and his wife will be up to the church from that point on. The likelihood of attack is minimal. I imagine we'll only need one blade gun and an extra ammo clip at most. Meet me back here after dinner, around seven."

Mike's brow furrowed when he looked at Christina. His eyes betrayed the conflict raging in his head.

Christina looked at her friend. "Mike, are you okay?"

"Yeah, I'm fine. See you this evening." Mike walked off.

◆

Christina and Mike were as practiced at self-transportation as an Outrider could get. Only Ari and Silas were more accurate; all four could materialize within inches of their intended target and were among the few who were trusted to be able to self-transport to an interior. Despite Mike's accuracy, his lack of concentration occasionally made him drift to the side by several feet.

The file on this assignment made it specific to transport to exact coordinates. Christina knew that they would arrive in town and near their intended client. Normally the team leader would be given the freedom to instruct their team where they should transport. They would choose a discreet location near the coordinates, ensuring that their instantaneous appearance wouldn't startle anyone and raise suspicion. Christina briefly wondered why they were so insistent on them appearing exactly in that position, but she figured there be a good reason why.

The duo reappeared in the middle of a small meadow in the middle of a forest, a couple of yards away from each other. The sun had already set behind the trees, but the sky still held enough light to see they were completely surrounded by dense stands of trees. The crickets sang their late summer chorus. The smell of sweet grass and wildflowers danced with the earthy scent of pine and moss. Christina took a look around. "Great. The coordinates they gave us seem to be off. So much for precision self-transporting." She began to tromp through the tall meadow grass.

The ambush only took a few seconds before it was complete. With no time to take cover and barely able to pull her blade gun out, Christina took blade hits. Her right shoulder and chest were hit first. She faltered as she cried out in pain, only to be pierced by several more blades in her torso. She collapsed to the ground. Christina struggled to breathe and remain alive. Confused, she labored to turn her head to see who shot her.

Mike stood over her with his blade gun pointed at her. "I'm sorry, Christina. May God forgive me. Orders are orders . . ." He leveled his gun at her head, when he suddenly collapsed to his knees and slumped onto the earth next to her. Several inches of a slender blade protruded from the base of his skull; the precision shot severed his spine at the base of his neck, killing him instantly. The shrouded figure bent over the lifeless attacker and removed the blade, and with it, the only evidence of who killed Mike.

Christina never saw who came to her aid. She had stopped breathing just seconds before. The hooded figure felt for a pulse as petite fingers wiped blood from the dead Outrider's face. The mysterious person picked up the lifeless body and disappeared in the growing mist, self-transporting to safety.

◆

Moments before, Ari's lone silhouette sat on a log on the deserted beach; the sun just over the water and still low near the horizon, hidden behind tradewind clouds in the distance. She wore a thin ivory linen hoodie, the hood pulled over her head to ward off the early morning chill. The blazing sunburst behind the clouds announced another glorious morning. The sand and water sparkled as if covered with fire-lit diamonds. Ari's figure barely moved in the hours that she communed with God.

Silas kept a respectable distance from Ari when she prayed. He didn't want to intrude upon her time with God. He too used the time to pray, but he kept his promise to watch over Ari at the same time. He happened to open his eyes to see Ari stand up suddenly. She appeared agitated; her steps in the sand seem to falter as she held her hands to her face in horror.

Silas quickened his gait and began to run toward her when she suddenly disappeared, self-transporting to an unknown location. He stopped just at the top of the stairs at the end of the lawn. Suddenly, Ari reappeared behind him on the patio. She held a motionless Christina in her arms. "Silas! Go grab as many pressure bandages and clean towels as you can, quickly!"

Ari lowered her lifeless friend to the stone and cement patio. Her ivory pullover soaked in her friend's blood as Ari began to pull blades out of her friend. "Christina you are not going to die on me! It is not your time. The devil is NOT going to steal my best friend." Ari placed her hands over the most critical of the wounds and began to speak in a strange tongue.

Silas stopped in his tracks inside the house as he spied Ari commanding life over Christina's body. He closed his eyes and began to pray in agreement. Ari's commands went on for many tense minutes. Suddenly, Christina took a big gasp of air as her eyes popped open. Silas snapped out of his prayer and rushed the supplies to Ari. He started to pack one of Christina's wounds when he realized the only signs of her fatal injuries were the bloody holes in her blouse that the blade had left as it tore through the fabric. Her wounds had completely healed.

Despite what appeared to be a complete, miraculous resurrection and healing, Christina groaned in pain, dazed. "Where am I? What happened?" The injured Outrider did a double take when she realized who knelt next to her. Christina's eyes opened in shock. As she began to comprehend, tears watered her eyes. "Ari! Oh, thank you, Jesus! I thought I'd never see you again." She hugged her friend, her eyes closed as the tears began to flow.

Christina suddenly pulled back, and she stopped crying momentarily. "Wait, um, am I . . .?" She looked up at the sky.

Ari laughed. "No, you're not in heaven, although you came pretty close. Here, take a bite of this banana."

Christina broke a piece off and slowly chewed. She beamed a wide grin and hugged her friend again. "I thought you were dead. I thought I lost my best friend forever. We buried you." Christina's face twisted in confusion.

"Isaac. As soon as I came around, he whisked me here. He brought Silas here already."

Christina struggled to sit up. "How did you know and how did you find me?"

Ari helped her. "I had a vision of the attack. I arrived just moments after you were shot."

Christina's eyes focused on the man behind her friend. At first she didn't recognize him with the dark hair. "Silas?"

Silas waved sheepishly. "Guilty. I'm glad you're okay, Christina." He bent over and gave her a warm hug.

Christina wiped tears away with her fingers. "We thought both of you were dead. Hollywood hasn't been the same since. Sam went missing several months ago, and Isaac before that. And now Mike's betrayal. I can't believe he wanted to kill me."

"Killed. You mean you can't believe he killed you," Ari corrected Christina.

Christina smiled sheepishly, "Yeah, I guess. It just sounds weird that way."

"Let's get you inside and cleaned up," Silas offered as he helped Christina to her feet. He caught her as she stumbled. "Why don't I carry you in?" Christina wrapped her arm around his neck as he lifted her, carefully cradling her.

Ari directed Silas as she pulled her soiled hoodie off, revealing a heather grey ribbed sleeveless t-shirt underneath. "Put her in my bed for now. We'll work out the sleeping arrangements later. For now, missy, you need to rest. Let me get you a clean shirt to sleep in." Ari rushed in ahead of Silas.

Silas eased Christina gently at the edge of the bed. She looked around in Ari's bedroom. Unlike her quarters at Hollywood, where pictures and kid toys surrounded every available open space, her Thai bedroom seemed cold and sparse. Nothing personal adorned the room other than a few pieces of driftwood and seashells. A well-used Bible sat on the nightstand next to the bed, along with a small dark riverstone. The worn leather binding and tattered corners translated to a well-loved companion book. Only the edge of the pages closest to the binding still showed hints of the original delicate gilding.

Christina opened the cover of Bible. Carefully tucked against the binding, a tattered picture of Jim and Alexa held a sole, coveted spot inside the cover. Christina recognized the picture as the one that Ari carried in her leather jacket. The photo had seen better days; tinges of old blood stained the creases and edges. She closed the Bible and ran her fingers across the well-worn leather cover.

"I think this should fit you," Ari said as she held up a loose cotton blouse. "And these leggings might be too loose on you, but that might be a good thing when you're sleeping. There are clean towels in the bathroom, and there should be an extra toothbrush in the middle drawer. Make yourself at home."

Christina showered and slipped into the shirt and leggings. She crawled into Ari's bed and stared at the charcoal gray riverstone and the Bible on the nightstand until she fell asleep. Ari grabbed the soiled clothes and quietly closed the door. Silas stood by the sink, washing his hands. "How did you do that, Ari? I know you have the ability to heal others, but except for Isaac, I've never known anyone else to be able to heal someone so critically injured almost completely."

Ari shook her head as she examined Christina's clothes piece by piece. She tossed each one into the trash after she saw holes and tears in each piece. "I don't know. I do know it was God. I only acted as His vessel to bring Christina back to life. It must be the ring, or something that Isaac gave me before he left."

"Do you know who shot her?"

"Yes." Ari carefully removed the used blade from the cloth wrapping and tossed it onto the counter. Ari's eyes were glassy.

"You killed this person, didn't you?" Silas asked as he examined the bloodied weapon. The tip didn't seem to penetrate very far.

"Mike shot her. He stood over Christina with his gun drawn, about to shoot her point blank in the head. His finger sat on the trigger. I had no choice; otherwise, he may have had an involuntary muscle contraction. I shot him at the base of the skull. My blade shattered the first vertebra.

He died instantly."

"Mike? I can't believe that. Why would he do something like that?" Silas slumped up against the counter.

"I heard him apologize to her, saying 'orders are orders.'" Ari's brow furrowed. "I'm wondering who would give such an order that would convince Mike enough to turn on a friend."

"Perhaps Christina would have a better idea. It sounds like things were pretty chaotic at Hollywood in the days leading up to this."

"I guess we'll have to wait. If she feels anything like what we did, it will be at least another day before she wakes up." Ari broke off another piece of the half-eaten banana and chewed on it thoughtfully.

Days passed and Christina's strength finally allowed her to walk around unassisted. The trio sat at the table eating dinner in relative silence. Ari looked at Christina's face. She could tell her friend held something back. "Christina?"

"Mmm?" her friend answered with a full mouth.

"Is there something you want to tell us?" Ari asked.

"Mm . . ." Christina swallowed her food. "Yes, but I can't think of an easy way to tell you."

Ari laughed, "Chrissy, it's only us. Just spit it out."

Christina bit her lip. She glanced at Silas, who just shrugged his shoulders. Her eyes focused on her friend Ari before she looked down at her plate. She pushed some of her food around before she spoke. "Ari, Jim remarried just a few days before I went on my last assignment. He married Sarah. I'm so sorry, Ari. I didn't even know about it until after it happened. Apparently they kept it quiet and small on purpose. They knew a lot of us had feelings for you and Alexa."

Ari froze mid-bite. She lowered her fork back down to her plate. After a few tense, silent seconds, she quietly asked, "Is he happy?"

Christina felt Ari's heart break as she answered. "He seems so. I haven't seen him this happy since before your last assignment a few years ago. He didn't know you were alive, Ari. We didn't know you were alive."

"Isaac and Sam knew of our situation. And Jesse," Silas clarified.

"Both Isaac and Sam are missing. Sam has been missing for months— Isaac for quite some time."

"And Jesse had been sworn to secrecy. And I doubt he didn't know about the marriage before it happened too," Ari added.

"If Isaac has been missing, who married them?" Silas asked.

"Petra."

Silas rolled his eyes. "Now that's what I called a holy and sanctified marriage . . ."

"I need some air," Ari said as she pushed her plate away. "Excuse me . . ." She got up and walked out the back patio door.

Silas shoved another forkful in his mouth, took a swig of water, and quickly wiped his mouth. He winked at a distressed Christina. "Don't worry: she'll be okay. I think she knew something like this happened, but I think deep in her heart she hoped that it didn't. I'll keep an eye on her." Silas grabbed another mouthful before taking off after Ari.

Silas ran down the stairs towards the beach. He stopped at the bottom step, observing Ari standing ankle-deep in the waves rolling onto the beach. The surf's loose foam softly covered her ankles, then vanished into the sand as the water retreated. She stared out at the encroaching inky blackness of night. A few lights of distant freighters dotted the horizon. Suddenly her back stretched backwards as she buried her face deeply in her hands, her elbows bent high and away from her body in anguish and defiance.

"LORD! WHY??" Ari screamed at the top of her lungs at the darkened sky and ocean. Her steps paced back and forth. "What have I done to offend You? Do you no longer hear my prayers, or do the pains in my heart no longer concern You? For every blessing I have been given, I seem to be dealt a double dose of curses. Please, Lord, I have nowhere else to go." Ari whimpered, "*Hear my cry, O God; listen to my prayer. From the ends of the earth I call to you. I call as my heart grows faint; lead me to the rock that is higher than I. For you have been my refuge, a strong tower against the foe. I long to dwell in Your tent forever and take refuge in the shelter of your wings. Please, Lord. I need You."* Ari paused, crying.

After a few minutes, Ari straightened up; she no longer showed any tears or emotions. *I submit completely to Your will, Lord.* "You win, Lord. I never had a choice, it seems from the beginning, but I kept deciding to fight it . . . to fight You, Lord. If You want me unattached by complicated relationships, so be it. I am Yours to do with as You will. Please forgive me," Ari muttered under her breath. After a few minutes of watching the water, she took a deep breath and turned around.

As she took a step back towards the house, a searing heat suddenly hit her heart, as if being shot. The feeling of intense pain quickly radiated throughout her body, as if fire spread throughout. Her body contorted in pain as she collapsed in the damp sand. Unable to scream, she stretched out her arm as if to grab an unseen hand to help her.

Observing from a distance, Silas thought Ari had been shot. He sprinted out to her, only to realize she wasn't bleeding. She appeared to be experiencing a seizure. Feared that she would drown in the rising tide, Silas struggled with her writhing body and carried Ari back to the main house and to her bed.

"What happened?" Christina asked as she dried her hands on a kitchen towel.

"I'm not sure. One moment Ari was screaming at the top of her lungs asking God what she did wrong, and the next thing she's incapacitated on the sand."

Christina checked Ari's eyes; they were unfocused and began to roll back. Ari's breathing was shallow, and her skin hot to the touch. "I think she's going through an impartation," Christina explained. She held Ari's forehead, brushing her hair out of her face. "Ari, don't do this now. We're not prepared to handle it."

"I don't think she has a choice," Silas argued.

"Ari!" Christina slapped Ari's cheek a few times. "Ari! Focus on me; focus on my voice. Ari!"

Ari's eyes focused on Christina's slate blue eyes. Both Christina and Silas could see the the pain wrapped in her eyes. "What . . .?" The incapacitated Outrider struggled to speak.

"You either got struck by lightning or you're going through part of what Isaac said you would," Silas explained, trying to keep the situation light.

"AHHHHGGHH!" Ari groaned as her back arched again. Her fingers contorted and strained in odd angles. Her friends fought to keep her from falling off the bed.

"Christina, she's burning up!" Silas pointed out.

"That's normal for an impartation. I wonder how long she will have to endure this?" Christina asked.

Once again, Ari's mind and body were being transformed by God and the Holy Spirit. Her mind and body were being cleansed, now receptive to that which God had intended for her to have. What she thought had been dreams she had had for years were now being revealed to her; information and a window to the past gave her insight on the future vision God had for the organization. She heard their voices and understood the wisdom that spoke to her.

No sooner than Christina finished her question, Ari's body began to relax. The work finished, the cleansing fire within Ari began to dissipate. The incapacitated Outrider slept deeply, her mind slowly digesting everything she just received.

For two days Christina and Silas took turns as they watched Ari. At the moment they thought they would have to seek medical help for her, Ari's eyes snapped open and stared at her friend.

Christina sat up and asked, "Ari, how do you feel?"

"Disoriented. And thirsty. What happened?" Ari's whispered question came out raspy and dry.

"We think you experienced an impartation. Do you feel different?" Christina asked.

Ari shook her head. "Not really. I have some interesting visions and memories. And I feel like I could sleep a week."

"Let me get you some ice chips to suck on," Christina said as she disappeared through the doorway. A minute later she reappeared with a bowl and a spoon. She carefully ladled a frozen piece of ice into Ari's waiting mouth.

"How long have I been out?" Ari asked with a partially full mouth. She crunched into the ice chip.

"Slowly, Ari. You need to suck on those pieces of ice slowly so that your stomach doesn't freak out. You were out for two days. We knew not to rush you to wake up, that the Holy Spirit continued to work on you."

"I don't think He's finished with Ari, at least not yet," Silas said. "I distinctly recall Isaac mentioning that this process takes months, sometimes years. It's just however long the Holy Spirit decides it should take. It's all part of growing into the position."

Ari struggled to get up but then settled back down on the bed. Her muscles were too weak. Christina held her hand on her friend's shoulder. "Uh, no. You are ordered to stay in bed until at least tomorrow."

"No, honestly, I feel fine," Ari replied. "Besides, I know where to find the bear." Ari got up and slowly stumbled past a confused Christina.

"What bear? I think you're still having visions, Ari," Christina said as she chased after the recovering Outrider.

"Silas, we need to go back to Greece," Ari said.

Silas glanced up from the book he held. "Right now? You just woke up from a two-day coma just a few moments ago. I don't think this is a very good idea."

"It's a cave. There's a bear inside the cave," Ari tried to explain as she stumbled towards the closet.

Silas shook his head and said, "If there's a bear in the cave, then it definitely isn't a good idea. How do you plan on getting past the bear?"

"It's frozen," Ari explained.

"Frozen bear? In a cave? In Greece? Ari, I don't think your mind is completely done with the impartation. You're not making any sense," Christina said.

"It makes perfect sense," Ari said as she tumbled to her knees.

"You are not going anywhere right now, missy," Silas said as he helped her to her feet. He lifted her and placed her in the bed. "And if you don't stay put, I'll tie you down."

Christina nodded and said, "Your body needs at least twenty-four hours to finish the impartation. Don't rush it. If the bear is truly frozen, he's not going anywhere."

"Besides, whatever that ring uncovered sat there for a millennia. Waiting another day or two is not going to make any difference," Silas said.

Ari laid back as Christina tucked her under the covers. "Perhaps you're right," Ari said, agreeing, before falling asleep.

The next evening Christina grabbed the last of the dinner dishes off the table. "Ari, maybe I should come along?"

Ari shook her head as she spoke. "We talked about this already. I don't even know if we're going to find anything. Silas and I have already tried a few times unsuccessfully. It's been several millennia since the last Outrider saw what this ring holds. For all we know, it may have been destroyed or reduced to dust by now. No sense all of us wasting time on this."

"And explain again why he's going?" Christina asked, pointing at Silas.

Ari rolled her eyes and walked away. Silas locked his blade gun and slid it into his holster. "Because," he said, "I was told to keep her safe, no matter what."

Christina laughed. "Ari? She should be protecting us."

"I know! That's what I told Isaac, but he didn't think that was funny," Silas replied.

Ari looked at the clock. "We better get going. Christina, please consider what we talked about."

Christina pouted and said, "Ari, I look absolutely hideous with dark hair."

"I heard that one before," Ari said, giggling as she play-punched Silas' shoulder.

"I command angels to watch over you two. And try to stay out of trouble!" Christina said as her friends walked out onto the patio and disappeared.

CHAPTER FOURTEEN

Ari and Silas reappeared. The sun already baked the bleached landscape. Hearty brush clung precariously in the cracks between the rocks and boulders.

"Where are we?" Silas asked.

"Crete. I thought we'd start in the south and make our way north." With that, Ari started walking down the deserted beach. Still early, the morning sun beat down relentlessly. "This way," Ari said, pointing to a town that shimmered in the rising heat.

They walked over a hill and followed a road to the nearest town. Ari walked up to what appeared to be a tourist kiosk. In broken Greek she asked about the oldest church or monastery's location. The guide pulled out a paper map and explained the location, then pointed out something else not too far from its location. Ari thanked the guide and walked over to Silas.

Silas looked at Ari. "The bear is here?"

"There's a high probability. There are hundreds of caves dotting the island. I asked the tour guide for the oldest church or monastery's location. He also told me about a cave a few kilometers from the monastery that the monks used. There are many niches and a labyrinth of caves inside. Whatever we're looking for may not even be here on Crete, but it's the only starting point I have."

"What do you expect to find?"

Ari shook her head. "I don't know. I don't think Isaac even knows. He just told me what he knew about the ring. I sensed that he hoped that I would find the significance of this."

The two walked back to the same beach. She looked at the map then folded it and placed it inside her pocket. Grabbing Silas' hand, she suddenly noticed the strength and warmth from his grasp. She looked at him and smiled before they disappeared.

The two reappeared by the edge of the sea several miles from where they were before, on an outrcrop of rocks. Silas looked around. "These rocks look like they've been arranged."

"I think this is an old dock that the monastery used. It doesn't look like it's been used in centuries." Ari began to walk, climbing up a set of stairs. A path wound back and forth up the side of the cliff. A few minutes later they reached the top.

Silas wearily eyed the path as it continued up a slight slope. Inside of a ravine, a path began its perilous climb as it switchbacked to the top of the cliffs still several hundred feet above their heads. He was thankful that the shade from the trees and the cliffs kept them from hiking the entire trip in the relentless Greek sun. They reached a series of buildings, most too small to be considered dwellings. Ari decided to try the largest building. She stopped at the wooden door. About to knock, she stopped herself and briefly prayed for favor. She knocked.

A man in a loose-fitting long black robe answered the door. His full beard almost covered his mouth, making his words seem to come from the air around him.

Ari bowed and asked as best as she could in his language for permission to speak with one of the monks that would have knowledge of the history of the caves and monastery. The monk eyed the two Outriders with suspicion, but then allowed them to enter the courtyard.

"Please wait here," the monk softly told them in Greek. "I ask that you honor our customs and keep your voices down so that you do not break the concentration of any of the monks in prayer and contemplation." Ari nodded and the monk disappeared down a corridor.

"Keep your voice down," Ari instructed Silas. Silas nodded as he surveyed the surroundings.

A few minutes later, the monk came back with another man dressed identically to him. Without words, the new monk held his hand out, ushering Ari and Silas to another section of the monastery. A door opened and the friends walked in with the monk following. They sat down on simple wooden chairs in front of a small wooden table. In broken English, the monk spoke. His soft and gentle voice whispered, "My name is Antony. I understand you want to know the history of the area?"

Ari nodded. "My name is Ariana, and this is Silas. We wondered if this area had been used by Christians before your monastery was built?"

The monk smiled. "Oh, yes. The reason for the monastery's location is because of the holy nature of the ground here. The legend says a great battle between three angels and an army of demon giants occurred in this very spot. The giants were defeated and retreated into the earth." The monk raised his hand and waved it in all directions. "That story is connected to all of the caves we have here in the area. The legend explains that all of the caves were created by the giants when they dug their way up to the surface. Many humans died before the angels came to save them. When the giants retreated, they went back into the caves. The angels asked God for help, and a great earthquake shook the earth and collapsed all of the entrances to the giants' home deep in the earth."

Silas looked at Ari, "I wonder how the angels were able to defeat the giants?"

The monk got up. He waved to Ari and Silas to follow him. They walked down another corridor and entered a large, ornately decorated chamber that appeared to be an altar. Antony stopped, waved his hand in the stations of the cross, and then approached the altar. He carefully removed the silk fabric covering the altar. A stone slab revealed itself, held up by four stone legs. In between the legs and under the slab, a shelf encased in glass protected its precious contents. Ari saw metal objects glinting in the dim light. The monk reached underneath, opened the glass case, and gently laid the objects on the altar.

"May I?" Ari asked the monk.

After hesitating, the monk nodded. "Please be careful. They are very old."

Ari gently picked up a dagger; the length of the weapon was roughly about that of her forearm. A longsword still lay in the case; it looked like the two weapons were a set. Despite their extreme age, the metal looked as if they were made yesterday. Upon closer inspection, neither had any scratches or pits, and the metal shined untarnished. The dagger's design was simple and elegant. The crosshatched handle drew the eye to the center of the hilt, where two very distinct cross patterns had been artfully designed into the metal. Ari knew she had seen those designs before. She held her hand out next to the hilt of the dagger and compared it to Isaac's battered ring on her finger. The patterned cross on her finger matched identically to one of the dagger's crosses.

The monk's eyes grew big. "How can that be? No one has seen these objects in many, many years, and no one outside of our brotherhood has seen them for hundreds of years."

"How did you come across these weapons?" Ari asked.

"As the legend tells, after the last battle, there was one badly wounded angel. The villagers tried to help him but he died. These are his weapons. Who are you that you would have known about this cross?"

Ari looked at Silas. Silas unbuttoned the first two buttons on his shirt and then turned around. He lowered the collar line of his shirt to reveal the distinguished symbol of the Outrider marked into his skin at the base of his neck. The Outrider symbol identically matched the other cross embellishing the hilt of the weapons. The monk fell to his knees in fear and bowed his head. "Please forgive me for not recognizing you. You are the angels . . ."

Silas buttoned his shirt and then helped the man to his feet. "Sir, we are like you, simply servants to the Lord."

Pointing to the weapons, Ari asked, "Are there more like these?"

The monk shook his head. "If there are, no one has ever found any. They could be hidden anywhere, even in the caves, or perhaps they've been lost over time."

Silas picked up the longsword. "This is very similar to the sword the Nephilim used on us in the jungle. The markings are different, but the weight and balance are almost identical."

Ari twirled the dagger in her hand. The light glinted off the shiny metal. Her mind flashed back to a vision she had of the attacking Nephilim. The vision showed her in the heat of a battle; the glint of the metal blade blinding her before it pierced her abdomen. Ari jolted back to reality. The two men stared at her. "Ari, are you all right?" Silas asked as he put the sword down.

"Yeah, I'm fine. I have a feeling that we haven't seen the last of the Nephilim." She looked at the monk. "Sir, may we take a look around? I suspect that there will be more of these weapons somewhere."

"You are welcome to go anywhere you feel you need to. If you wander into the caves, I recommend using these." The monk handed Silas a ball of dyed red string and an oil lantern. Silas looked confused. "Many of the caves are labyrinths, some by design. You could easily get lost. The string is to help you find your way back to the entrance. If you need help, please let me know." Silas nodded and thanked the man.

"One last question, sir." Ari asked. "I wondered if you have seen either of these crosses anywhere else?" She showed him her ring again.

The monk thought for a moment. "Yes. It is in one of the niches in the back of the cave we call *Panagia Arkoudiotissa*. Locals call it the Bear Cave. There is a small church inside the cave dedicated to the Madonna. You will find many icons and relics inside."

"Um, are there bears in that cave?" Ari asked.

The monk smiled. "Oh, no. But when you enter the cave, you will see why it is called as such."

Silas elbowed Ari. "Maybe that mosaic depicts a bear and not a large dog?"

"Thank you, sir." Ari handed the dagger back to the monk.

The monk gave the dagger back to Ari. "Madam, I believe that these belong to you and your friend. They belong to your people."

Ari bowed, humbled by the gesture. "Sir, when we win the battle, these will be returned to you."

"Thank you. I hope that before you leave that you will bless us and join us for a simple meal." Both Ari and Silas nodded. They followed the monk to another section of the main building and into a dining hall. Other monks were filtering into the room, silently sitting at the table. Ari and Silas sat at the far end as another monk placed a bowl of stew and a crusty piece of rustic bread in front of them. Someone at the far end of the table said grace in Greek, and then the monks began to eat in silence.

Ari took a bite and closed her eyes. The delicious flavor of the meat almost overpowered the images of the cute little rabbit's final struggle before its demise. Her heightened gift of discernment was a gift from God, but unfortunately, it didn't distinguish who or what she discerned. When Ari came into contact with the flesh of butchered animals, she experienced the same flashback visions of the animal's well-being as she would experience for a human. After Silas took a bite, he whispered to Ari, "What is this meat?"

"A cute little bunny. I mean, rabbit, I think," Ari whispered back. She struggled to push back the awkward visions as she ate. She silently thanked God for the generous thick slice of rustic bread.

After the meal, Ari and Silas parted ways with the monks and began their search. Ari wrapped the weapons in muslin cloth the monks gave them, and then wrapped it in a length of leather binding. She tied more of the leather binding loosely from near the ends and used it as a sling to carry the precious bundle on her back.

The two hiked the rocky terrain of the ravine for several kilometers before they came across a cave entrance. They passed a small building next to the entrance and stepped into the darkness. Their eyes took a moment to adjust to the dim light. A raised pool with a staircase carved into the limestone stood prominently in the middle of the cavern. On the staircase was a large limestone stalagmite formation that looked like a large bear on all four legs. Silas stared at the stalagmite and said, "Well that's an interestingly shaped rock, isn't it?

Ari walked up a small embankment to the back wall and began to search. She began to walk into a small opening between two rocks. Silas panicked momentarily when she disappeared from sight. Ari squeezed back out into the main chamber. "There is a chamber that opens up a little from this tight squeeze. There are a couple of tunnels that break off behind this wall. Toss me that roll of twine," she said.

Silas tossed her the twine and then followed her. He lit the lantern and held it as Ari tied the end of the twine to a stalagmite. Ari hooked the reel of twine to her belt loop then pulled a small flashlight from her jacket pocket. "Lead the way," she said to Silas. As they moved forward, Ari allowed the twine to unravel. The beam of light from her small flashlight swung to the sides and then up above.

"What are we looking for?" Silas asked.

Ari shrugged and answered, "I haven't the faintest clue. If all we have is a little hole for this ring to fit in somewhere in here, we are searching for the proverbial needle in a haystack."

"Which way?" Silas asked as he stood before two tunnels.

Ari stepped around him and shined her flashlight down each of them. Neither looked very inviting. The corridor to the right, water dripped all around, and the floor of the cavern disappeared under the water. The tunnel to the left, rubble covered the floor from its partially collapsed rooftop. Rocks and boulders littered the floor. Ari pointed her flashlight at the roof of the tunnel. Cracks ran up for as far as her light would reveal. Twenty feet above the tunnel's floor, a very large boulder, wedged as if waiting for someone to walk under it. "Great," Ari muttered under her breath. "So Silas, which way do you wish to go?"

Silas' brow furrowed as he pondered his dismal options. "Hmmm. Walk and possibly swim in frigid water, or possibly get crushed under a two-ton boulder? I guess the water. At least if I drown, you could retrieve my body and try to resuscitate me. I don't think there would be much of me left to resuscitate if that boulder fell on me."

"Wet it is," Ari said with a sigh. Silas led the way, making sure each footstep landed on something solid. Ari followed. The tunnel curved a bit, but for the most part there was very little uneven climbing. Silas noted that for the quarter of an hour they walked, the cave sloped almost imperceptibly downwards. Ari noticed it as well but for a different reason. The wet ground gradually grew in depth. Soon they were slogging through water that was up to Ari's waist.

Silas trembled and tried to shake off the cold as he said, "You would think the water would be warmer since it's about one hundred degrees outside."

"I wish," Ari said as her jaw chattered. "I don't know how much more of this I can take. Besides, we're near the end of the string."

"Why don't we turn around and try that other tunnel?" Silas asked. He followed the trail of red twine, with Ari following as she spooled the string back onto the reel. They returned back to the chamber where the two tunnels split. Silas held the lantern into the partially caved-in path. "Are you up for some climbing?"

Ari handed the spool of twine and her flashlight to Silas and grabbed the lantern from his hand and said, "Why not? We're here, so we may as well make use of the time." Silas shrugged and followed her. They clamored over what used to be part of the ceiling of the tunnel and looked at the chamber before them. "Here goes nothing."

After an hour of carefully surveilling the walls, Ari noticed a large rock with a cross faintly carved into the hidden side. She noticed it had the same pattern as the one on her ring. Above it hid a small crawl space. "Silas, take a look at this."

Silas walked over and lifted his lantern up to the hole. "It looks like it goes back quite a way."

After a few meters the crawl space turned into a taller corridor but was still pretty narrow and claustrophobic. The one side of the wall was lined with niches and holes leading to other corridors. After turning into the other corridors and walking for several minutes, Ari stopped in front of one that had the symbol of the Outriders faintly etched into the back of the niche. She ran her finger along the etched symbol of a sword bisecting a circle representing the earth. "We who promise to protect the people here on earth" . . . She hoped that somehow, by touching it, it would reveal itself to her. As the ring on her finger crossed the center of the etched Outrider symbol, she heard a whisper. "You have come to the kingdom for such a time as this . . ."

She stopped tracing her finger and looked at Silas. "Did you just say something to me?" Silas shook his head. She looked at where her finger had stopped. On the symbol at the point where the tip of the sword intersected the top of the circle, Ari felt a little indentation. She examined it closer. A tiny hole in the stone revealed itself to her. "I wonder . . ." Ari thought out loud.

"What?" Silas asked, taking the lantern from her hands.

"The ring is the key," Ari whispered. "The professor is right. Isaac said it's the key. I thought he meant that metaphorically, but I think he meant it literally." She slipped the ring off her finger and stuck the face of the ring into the hole. It fit perfectly. Slowly she turned the ring and heard a faint click. Ari pushed, and all of a sudden, the niche wall slid back a few inches and then off to the side. Ari and Silas coughed from all the dust and dirt that the sudden movement created. When the dust finally settled, they couldn't believe what they saw.

Silas stepped forward with the lantern, brushing the fine dust off his shoulders as he gawked at the room. Ari ran her hand along a rack holding dozens of swords just like what the monastery had. There were also daggers, short, trident-shaped sais, as well as bows, arrows, slender spears, shields, and breastplates. There were also a stack of vambraces and greaves to protect the forearm and shins. Silas picked up a sword and gripped it in his hands, then twirled it with the grasp of just his right hand. "I can't believe the balance on these, and they aren't that heavy. I wonder what the alloy is that these were made from?"

"I don't know, but apparently it's a pretty strong metal. The Nephilim's sword broke my titanium hand blade," Ari said as she grabbed a piece of each of the armor sections. "Grab one of each weapon. We need to head back now." Ari grabbed an extra set.

After wrapping the items in some leather they found in the corner, they walked out of the room. Ari removed her ring from the niche wall.

The wall moved back into place, sealing the room tight. Once outside, the two Outriders took a better look at their findings. Albeit dusty, the metal gleamed in the sunshine as if brand new. Ari studied each piece. They all had the Outrider symbol on them.

Ari began to wrap up the weapons. She looked at the time and said, "We need to get back. I'm sure Christina is missing us by now."

Silas helped Ari with their special packages and they vanished from the landscape, like two mirages that never existed.

◆

By the time Ari and Silas returned to the house, the sun had already set, and the rosy glow of the sky at the horizon began to darken into deep hues of purple and blue. Ari smiled, glad to see the inviting warm amber glow that came from the home's windows.

"Where have you two been?" Christina asked, like a mother to her overdue children. "I would looked for you except I had no idea where in Greece you two had gone."

Silas gently flipped the bundles onto the coffee table and unbundled them. The glint of the weapons mesmerized Christina. "We found something," Silas said, "I'm not quite sure what we're supposed to do with them, but we have them."

Ari grabbed a couple of water bottles from the fridge and tossed one to Silas. She took a long draw of water and said, "I believe these are the only weapons that can defeat the Nephilim."

"Uh, yeah. These weapons actually take some skill in using," Christina said as she awkwardly twirled a sai in her hand. "I much prefer the weapons that point and shoot."

"But Christina, these weapons are elegant . . . noble in design," Silas explained as he handled the sword as expertly as he handled the shinai.

"So, what, the three of us are supposed to go against one of the giants?" Christina asked.

"Not just one," Ari said, clarifying. "There are hundreds, maybe even thousands."

Silas froze and stared in disbelief at Ari. *"Thousands?"* Silas asked. "Just one took all four of us out. I don't like the odds."

"Look, guys," Ari began, "we didn't know what we were dealing with before, but now we do. God has given us access to these weapons for such a time as this. These are the arms that will work against the Nephilim."

"But there are only the three of us," Silas pointed out.

Ari shook her head. "No. There are dozens of us. The rest of the Outriders just don't realize it . . . yet."

Christina crossed her arms, and in a sarcastic, incredulous tone asked, "So, what, we're supposed to wander into Hollywood and say 'Excuse me, but you were all deceived about our deaths. But we're back and we are going to take over training so that you can learn the proper way to handle these ancient weapons so we can go into face-to-face warfare with a battalion of Nephilim.' That will go over well . . . almost as well as a midnight swim in shark-infested waters."

"Uh, well, I haven't worked out all the kinks in the plan, but yes— that is sort of the plan." Ari sheepishly rubbed the back of her neck.

Silas picked up a pair of sais and began to twirl them in his hands. He froze with his feet spread in a backwards lunge and both sais pointed forward; one of the sais by his face, the other thrust forward. "I feel like a ninja."

Ari and Christina barely cracked a laugh before a sound of glass shattered the light mood. Silas slumped to the ground; an arrow almost identical to those in the bundle from Greece had hit Silas in the chest. Ari grabbed the stash of weapons and slid behind the kitchen island. Christina grabbed Silas by the collar and dragged him behind the island as well. The shaft stuck out just below and to the left of his heart. Christina grabbed clean kitchen towels from the drawer and spoke to Silas, "This is going to hurt a little. Your shoulder blade is in the way, so I'll have to pull it out." She yanked the arrow straight out and quickly packed his wound tightly with a towel. Silas grimaced. Ari closed her eyes and briefly prayed over Silas' wound. At the end, Silas heard her speak, "By His wounds, you are healed."

Ari could see the two giant figures approach the back of the house in the reflection of the glass oven door. Without removing her eyes from the reflection, she grabbed one of the daggers from its tip, readying herself to strike back. As one of the Nephilim raised his sword over his head to break the glass door, Ari sprung up to her feet and threw the dagger as hard as she could. The dagger sliced through the glass cleanly and sank deeply into the chest of the first Nephilim.

The creature gurgled a cry before collapsing to the ground. Ari barely ducked behind the counter again as an arrow broke through the glass and missed her by less than an inch. The tip and shaft sunk deeply into the teakwood cabinet behind the island. As the creature crashed through the glass door, it picked up the sword of its fallen cohort.

Ari grabbed the sai from Silas and the sword with her free right hand. The creature brought the sword down onto the counter where Christina crouched over Silas to protect him. Ari stood between Christina and the sword and stuck the sai out, trapping the blade within its tines. She twisted her weapon, which pinched the sword's blade, and forced it out of the Nephilim's hand.

The creature swiped one of his scaly legs at Ari's back and sent her flying over Christina and against the far wall. Her breath and weapons knocked from her, Ari tried to get up. The creature wrapped one of his serpentine appendages around Ari and began to squeeze. Like a boa constrictor, his grip tightened every time Ari breathed out. Ari heard ribs crack. She desperately clawed at the snake-like grasp around her torso. Ari's sight began to black out as she lost consciousness.

Sensing his victory, the creature tightened his grip, but only for a moment. The first few inches of the length of a spear came through the center of his chest; Christina thrust the lance as hard as she could into the back of the creature. It collapsed forward to the ground, the deadly coil around Ari finally loosening.

Ari gasped for breath, unable to move. Christina rushed over and manhandled the heavy snake-like coils off her friend. Ari held her crushed ribs as she tried to catch her breath. "Thanks," she said in a raspy whisper.

"I would have helped sooner, but he kept wriggling his slimy looking legs and I couldn't get close enough," Christina said.

"They're not slimy. If they were, I probably could have gotten out." Ari coughed, still trying to catch her breath. "How is Silas?"

Christina examined Ari's torso. She was badly bruised and several ribs were obviously in odd angles from where they should have been. "He'll be fine. Don't move. I'll be right back to tape you up." Christina disappeared to her bedroom and emerged with a box and a pair of scissors. She cut strips of the skin-tone athletic tape and one by one, peeled the backing off and laid each one into a pattern that emulated the muscles around Ari's ribs. Ari bit her lip as Christina pressed each piece firmly into place, the warmth of her hand and Ari's skin activating the special adhesive.

After a few minutes, Christina asked, "Can you breathe better?"

"Define better. I have so much tape on me, I feel like an elephant is sitting on me. But at least it doesn't hurt as bad," Ari responded as Christina helped her to her feet.

The injured Outrider looked around. Two door panels were demolished, as well as several pieces of furniture. Ari tilted her head, amazed at the remains of the Nephilim. Their bodies began to melt away and dissipate into a foggy gray mist a few inches off the ground. After a few more minutes, any trace of their bodies disappeared.

"Huh. That explains a lot as to why history hasn't dug up any of their bones," Ari mused. "We probably should move to another location. I'm sure more will come to this location, and we aren't in any condition to be able to sustain another attack like that. Silas, are you well enough to walk?"

"With some assistance," he replied.

"Grab your gear. We need to make our way to the port in the old part of the city," Ari said. Stiffened from pain and the tape, she awkwardly bent over to pick up the weapons. Carefully wrapping them again in the leather and muslin cloth, she rigged the bindings so that the package fit over the shoulder.

As her friends left to their rooms, Ari began to grab provisions for their trip: several bottles of water, dehydrated fruit and fish, and some fresh fruit. She too went to her bedroom and grabbed her travel bag. Even though it had been years since she used it, out of habit she had kept it updated and packed, *just in case.*

The trio hefted their bags onto their backs. Once again, Ari bit her lip, hiding the instant pain she felt with the weight of the bag against her sore back and ribs. Each of them climbed onto their scooter and rode down the road to town.

CHAPTER FIFTEEN

The early morning bustle by the old port made Ari wonder whether some of these people ever went to bed. Barely above the horizon, the sun and tradewind clouds promised a sweltering day ahead. Assigned to sell the scooters at a decent price, Christina and Silas bartered with several men as Ari disappeared in the crowd. She returned a few minutes later, and spoke to one of the men next to a traditional-looking wooden sailboat. Silas could see Ari held her rib cage; she finally handed the man what appeared to be money, and then she nodded.

Silas strutted over to Ari. "You okay?" he asked.

"Yeah. Just starting to feel pain and the lack of sleep."

"What did you pay that guy for?"

"Provisions and passage for the three of us on his sailboat."

"What? Why?"

"We need time to heal. We can't even begin to think about taking on the Nephilim in the condition we're in. The Nephilim will not be able to get to us on the boat when we're in open water."

Silas scratched his head and asked, "Uh, I may be mistaken, but won't they get us when the boat returns back to shore?"

Ari shook her head. "Not right away, at least if we don't return to here."

"So if we're not returning here, where are we going?" Christina asked, joining in mid conversation.

"Kuala Lumpur. The trip in his boat will take about a week. By then we should be able to self-transport," Ari answered.

"Transport to where?" Silas asked.

Ari shrugged. "It depends. I think I know but I need to pray about it."

At this point the captain returned with a several men. They all carried large bundles and crates of what looked like food and water. They walked on to a relatively small wooden boat with sails. Less than two hundred feet in length, a two-story enclosed split level cabin looked inviting, with fresh paint and large windows.

A small wheelhouse sat on top of the structure. The plain decking had bench seating in the center area, with some pillows and tables. To Silas the size of the boat seemed smaller than small. As if to emphasize how small, a super tanker passed the boat on the way to the main port in Phuket.

Silas looked at Ari, concerned. *"This? We're crossing open ocean and into the Straits of Malacca in this?"*

The captain waved at Ari, signaling that she and her friends could come on board. Ari picked up her travel duffel and said simply to Silas, "Yes." She walked past her friend and up the wooden gangplank onto the deck of the boat.

Christina shrugged, then followed suit. Silas picked up his bags and the bundle of weapons and followed Christina, shaking his head. The ancient boat's motor grumbled and spit to life, belching a cloud of smoke. The captain pulled his moorings, and his ancient boat motor sputtered as it slowly moved the sail boat into open water.

One of the deck mates opened a door for Ari and ushered her and her friends into the two far aft quarters. "I hope you don't mind. I have two rooms booked; one for you, Silas, and we should be across the hall from you. We are the only passengers on this boat. They will pick up guests when they get to Kuala Lumpur." The door opened to his room and Silas' jaw dropped.

Modern bedding and light fixtures made the room look like a luxury hotel room. Only the occasional creak of the wood and the slight sway of braided cord curtain tie-backs betrayed the room's location on a boat.

A porter politely passed Silas with a tray of fresh fruit and bottled water. He placed it on a small table in the corner. Silas popped his head into the private bath to see it clean and modern with glass tiles and chrome fixtures. Silas stepped over into Christina and Ari's room. Also lavishly appointed with plush beds and pillows, the richly decorated room credited a staff who paid attention to every minute detail.

Bowing to the man who just put an identical tray of fruit and water on their table and exited, Ari then gingerly sat on the edge of one of the beds. She held her rib cage, in obvious pain. Christina knelt next to her, taking her friend's shoes off. "How are you feeling?"

"Rough. I am having problems breathing," Ari answered as she put her worn Bible on the nightstand. She placed the dark riverstone next to it.

Christina helped Ari down into her bed and covered her. She walked around to the wooden blinds and closed them one by one as she spoke to her friend. "Get some rest. I'll bring you dinner later." Christina turned on a small light in the bathroom and partially closed the door before shooing Silas out of the room. She pushed him into his room and down onto his bed.

"Hey, careful. I had heard from Dave that you're pushy, but I didn't think you were like this!" Silas winced as she tried to look at his chest wound under his bandages.

The wound had healed as expected. Christina re-taped his bandage and then made him lie down. "Try and rest," she told her friend. "If there isn't any sign of movement from you, I'll bring you dinner as well."

"You can wake me, and I'll get up," he offered.

"We'll see. You had a pretty major hit there."

"I know. I don't know what Ari did, but it looks a lot worse than it feels. What are you going to do while we nap?"

"Go on deck and get a little reading done," Christina said as she winked and strutted out, closing his door.

Careful to not wake Ari, Christina quietly grabbed a book from her travel bag. She noticed Ari's Bible and decided to read some Bible passages as well. She carefully grabbed the frayed and worn Bible before exiting the room and quietly closing the door behind her. Christina made her way up to the deck and spied a lounge chair. One of the porters rushed to her side. "May I sit there?" She asked the porter.

"Miss, you may sit anywhere you wish," he politely answered. "Would you like something to drink?"

"Do you have ice water?"

"Of course. I will be right back." The porter disappeared inside.

Christina sat down, facing the water on the starboard side of the boat. The porter returned with her water as she settled back onto the chair. He poured water from a glass bottle into a glass filled with ice. "Thank you, sir." The Outrider bowed her head as the porter bowed before exiting from her view.

Christina carefully opened Ari's Bible. The stained picture of Jim and Alexa still resided just inside of the cover. Christina knew from its telltale bloodstains and creases that Ari kept this photo in her leather jacket's pocket.

She flipped the picture over and studied the next photo. Christina didn't recognize the two people in the photo, but she guessed from the age of the photo and the way they were dressed that they were probably Ari's late parents. She never met them; Ari's parents died a decade before she even became an Outrider.

Christina began to page through the Bible and noticed a particular page that the book opened to. Its words and paper seemed to be particularly worn. The book's spine broke, hinting that this particular page had been referenced many times over the years. Shakily underlined in ink, and later highlighted with a yellow marker, Christina recognized the verses from the passage in Luke as the parable of the persistent widow. *"And will not God bring about justice for His chosen ones, who cry out to Him day and night? Will He keep putting them off? I tell you He will see that they get justice, and quickly."*

Christina's mind drifted, reminded of Ari's statement that she seemed to never be able to catch a break. Christina whispered her prayer, "Lord, if Ari is Your child, would You not protect her and her interests fiercely like a mother bear to her cub? Why do You allow such things to happen?"

His word came back in a whisper in the ocean breeze. *"Ariana is My child, as are you and the one you travel with named Silas. I care for all of you deeply. Her journey has been long and difficult. Her life experiences have brought her closer to Me. Like the desert acacia tree, her roots have been forced to go deep within My word in order to depend on Me in her times of need. Because of this, she will always be able to find My everlasting water and withstand even the heaviest of winds that try to break her boughs. Ariana has been forged and tempered into the warrior leader I need her to be."*

Christina knelt and bowed her head. She buried her face in her hands. She had sensed God's presence many times, but had never heard His voice as clearly as she had heard just now. The voice continued to speak to her. *"Do not fear, Christina, for I am with you too. Keep watch over each other so that no harm may befall you, and so that you do not stray from My calling in each of your lives."*

When she finally opened her eyes, she noticed that those on deck near her were also on their knees. The entire deck lay in the shadow of passing clouds—that is, everywhere on deck sat in the shade except where Christina knelt. A single shaft of sunlight hit the prayerful Outrider as if to emphasize the moment's holiness.

The porter approached Christina with a newfound admiration. "Madam, who is this God that calls you His children and keeps you in His everlasting waters?"

Christina gawked, amazed, "You heard Him speak?" She looked around and the faces nodded in agreement.

"Oh, yes, madam. And we heard Him speak to us in our native language," the porter answered.

Christina sat in the lounge and patted the seat for the porter to sit next to her. He obliged, curious to know more about her God. "His name is Jesus Christ, the son of man. He died so that we may live a life free of sin and shame. *'For God so loved the world that He gave His only son, that whoever believes in Him shall have everlasting life. Everyone who calls on the name of the Lord will be saved.'* No one is left out from this deal. All are invited to join Him."

An hour later Silas woke up. "Ugh," he moaned as his chest muscles twitched their argument against trying to move at that moment. Ignoring the pain, Silas rolled out of bed. The floorboards creaked as he worked his way to the deck. He saw the deck crew standing around Christina. She stood up and the crew dispersed, smiling and laughing. "What happened?"

"Truly amazing." Christina giggled. "They accepted Jesus as their Lord and Savior. I told them some of the teachings and parables of Jesus."

Silas laughed. "I can't leave you alone for one minute." The two friends laughed as the small boat continued to sail east.

◆

"Hey, sleepyhead. How are you feeling?"

Ari felt a tender hand gently shake her shoulder. The healing Outrider groaned and pulled the comforter over her head.

Christina partially removed the comforter and spoke softly to her friend. "Ari, just let me check your ribs, and I'll let you go back to sleep."

Ari peeked from under the cover. "I feel like I've been run over by the Nephilim. Oh, wait. I was."

Christina exposed Ari's taped lower rib cage. She gently soaked a cotton ball in cooking oil and rubbed it gently on a section of the athletic tape. She slowly worked the cotton ball over the strips of tape and then gingerly pulled at the tape, careful not to hurt her friend. After a painful few minutes, the last of the tape peeled off. Christina examined her healing friend. Ari's side appeared to be tender, but her ribs were healing well.

"So?" Ari anxious voice betrayed her need to know the verdict.

"Better," Christina said, trying to keep her observation optimistic.

Ari roughly ran her hands through her hair as she tried to wake up. "Maybe I need something to eat," she said.

"Why don't we get you cleaned up?" Christina offered. "Do you need help?"

"I think I'm good." Ari answered.

Christina cleaned up the wads of used tape and oil as Ari used a washcloth to wipe off the oil. Getting dressed in a ribbed heather gray t-shirt and a loose-fitting linen blouse, Ari stepped out and quickly slipped into a pair of faded jeans. The two ladies made their way to the deck.

Ari couldn't help but look up. The sails had been unfurled, and the sound of the canvas snap from the wind reminded her of when clean, crisp bed linens are first unfolded over the bed. The traditional rectangular-shaped sails billowed out, filled with the strong late morning wind. The boat seemed alive and breathing. The sails filled with air; the wood beams and deck creaked, speaking its satisfaction of finally leaving port and being free in the open sea.

Silas sat at a large padded seating area, his legs crossed under a low table. The feast that the crew had put out for their passengers rivaled any land-locked restaurant. The smells and colors of the dishes were almost enough to feast on in itself. When Silas saw his female counterparts arrive, he jumped as quickly to his feet as he could. He knew he had been called many things in the past, but there existed one thing that no one could fault him for: his impeccable manners.

Both Christina and Silas helped Ari settle onto the padded seating area and cushions. Ari wished for more American-styled seating with chairs and a table. The muscles in her chest and back instinctively tensed up, expecting the full blast of pain as she attempted to achieve her final dining position. Once situated fairly close to the edge of the table, Christina moved piles of pillows to behind her back to support her as much as possible. Christina took a seat next to Ari, and Silas returned to his seat opposite Ari, across the table.

He sipped at his tea and couldn't help but stare at Ari, mesmerized at how locks of her hair seemed perfectly suspended away from her head. They blew in the wind when teased by the ocean breeze, but they always seemed to return to their rightful place. There didn't seem to be a pattern to her soft, spikey hair, but in a strange way, it worked. He studied the strands that fell over her forehead and eyes. He noticed her brown eyes were attentive, yet he couldn't help but notice at times her mind drifted a thousand miles away. Perhaps she thought of Jim and Alexa or maybe the next few places to move to or how best to handle the Nephilim . . .

Christina continued to tell Ari her salvation tale, oblivious to the growing side story. Ari noticed Silas staring at her face. She looked down at the table, unsure of what to do or say, and pushed an overgrown clump of hair behind her ear. Nervously she picked up a bottle of water and poured it into her glass. The heat of her blush began to grow on the back of her neck and ears. Ari looked up again and stared at Silas as she took a long drink of water. She hoped that the glass would hide her from his uncompromising stare.

Still talking, Christina's eyes began to dart between Silas and Ari. Mid-sentence, Christina stopped talking. Her two friends didn't seem to notice. She cleared her throat and Ari's focus quickly switched back to Christina. "I'm sorry, Christina, what were you saying?"

"I feel like maybe you need a little time alone," Christina said.

Ari shook her head, "Oh, no. Why would you think that? Besides the food is here, we should enjoy while we can."

The three friends dined with the captain and crew on dishes of fish and colorful vegetables. As the plates were being cleared, the captain excused himself, and the three friends were left at the table, enjoying coffee and balls of almond flour and sugar that were soaked in honey.

"Such a shame that we had to leave that wonderful home in shambles," Christina said.

Ari licked her fingers, freeing them of the sticky honey. "While we were in town, I sent money and a note to my next door neighbor. They have a key to the property and will hire contractors to fix it. I told her I trust her decisions on everything. I'm sure Kathy will put her own spin on the place, but it will just make it all the more wonderful."

"So now what, chief?" Silas asked.

"Kuala Lumpur, and then from there I think we should head up to Japan. I have an old friend that runs a small Holy Spirit-filled denomination on the northeast side of town. Their church is called "Kyrie." He and his associate pastors are well-versed in hand-to-hand combat with swords and other hand weapons. I'm sure they can give us a few pointers."

Christina added, "I think we can use as much help as we can get."

"Do they know about who you really are?" Silas asked.

Ari huffed a laugh. "Do you mean the Outrider part of me, or the disenfranchised outlaw/ex-con?"

"Either." Silas laughed back.

"Yes. At least the part about the Outrider. One of the associate pastors used to be a physician before Christ led him to help out his neighbors. He still practices medicine, but now helps out at a local clinic. He's done signs, wonders, and miracles. He's returned sight to blind people and even raised dead people from their deathbeds."

Ari grabbed another almond paste ball. "Maybe it's because I don't eat sweets very often, but I'm addicted to these little guys. They remind me of something, but I can't put my finger on it."

Silas tried to talk with his mouth full. "Marzipan," he said stickily. Christina nodded her head in eager agreement. She couldn't talk as she chewed.

The evening wind died down to a light breeze, and the main sail deflated. The golden light of the setting sun bathed the deck in amber and salmon light. At the angle Ari sat, the sail looked like a fiery blade. Suddenly, a vision filled her senses. She saw herself against a wall, trapped. A shadowy figure shot her with a blade. With her hand wrapped around the hilt of a blade in her chest, Ari's legs gave out as she slid down the wall. Still in the shadows, the figure shoots her again. Ari slumps to the side, the pool of her own blood growing underneath her.

"ARI!" Christina snapped her fingers in front of her friend's face. "What happened to you? You look like you've seen a ghost. The blood drained from your face."

"Hmmm? Uh, yeah, I'm fine," Ari answered.

"You just had another vision, didn't you?" Christina asked.

"Hmm," Ari answered simply.

Silas looked at Christina and then at Ari. "So, what, you're not going to tell us what you saw?" he asked.

Ari pursed her lips as she talked to Silas. "Since you've been charged with my safety, I guess I should tell you. The attackers were Outriders. I'm not sure if it's the Old Guard or the Tempest, but I think they're going to find us soon. Er, I should say they find me. I don't think I make it."

Silas sat up from his relaxed, partially reclined position. "Where? When is this happening?"

"I don't know for sure," Ari explained. "The closer the incident is to happening, the more details I get. I couldn't see the face of my attacker, and I couldn't sense the location other than it felt urban, like a lot of buildings close together. Who knows? The attack may not even happen."

"So it isn't going to happen?" he asked.

"No, I didn't say that, but that is a possibility too. I just can't tell, so it probably is a few weeks off, a month or two at most," Ari frowned as she continued. "The closer we get to the event, the more details come to light."

Silas sat back, exasperated. "Great. First the Nephilim, now our former brethren are trying to finish the job."

"Maybe we should go somewhere else?" Christina asked.

Ari shook her head. "No, it's too early. How do we know we don't change our plans so that we walk into that situation? Unless we get something more definitive, we stay the course."

"Well, it's getting dark and I want to try to finish reading the chapter I'm in the middle of right now. Enjoy the evening, you two," Christina said as she winked and made her way down to the room.

Feeling awkward, Ari got up and walked to the starboard side of the boat and looked over the railing. The last glimmer of light reflected on the water. Ari could see a couple of dolphins swimming in the wake of the boat. Her exterior seemed calm and relaxed, but her mind raced a thousand miles a minute. Ari definitely felt an attraction to Silas, but she didn't know what to do. Her heart felt as if she left it with Jim, still back in the States.

"Beautiful sunset," Silas said as he leaned his elbows down onto the railing, staring at the sea.

"Um, yes." Ari answered simply. An awkward silence grew between the two friends. Finally, Ari spoke up again. "I guess I better turn in too. See you in the morning."

"Uh, sure. Good night, Ari."

"Good night, Silas." Ari slid behind the cabin door.

Silas looked at the crew's expectant faces. He shook his head as he also headed inside.

Ari stepped into the cabin and into her room. Christina looked up from her novel. "So?"

"So, what?" Ari asked.

"Did he . . .?" Christina puckered her lips.

Ari looked aghast at her friend. "Christina! Of course not. He has been and is the perfect gentleman."

Christina's head tilted slightly to the side, then she returned to her book. "He's remarried, Ari. Jim has moved on. You need to do the same."

"It's not that easy for me, Christina," Ari said as she roughly unzipped her travel duffel. Her voice held the years of frustration. "I'm beginning to believe there's a curse on me."

"Curse? What are you talking about, girl?"

"My mom . . . my dad . . . John . . . possibly Sam and Isaac, and now Jim and Alexa: Everyone that I have ever cared about . . . that I loved, have been taken suddenly from my life. It's like I'm not supposed to have any heavy relationships."

Christina closed her novel and quoted a verse from memory. "*Consider it pure joy, my brothers and sisters, whenever you face trials of many kinds, because you know that the testing of your faith produces persever-*

ance. Let perseverance finish its work so that you may be mature and complete, not lacking anything."

Ari looked at her friend. Tears welled up in the corner of Christina's eyes. "Christina, forgive me. I keep forgetting about you . . . and Dave . . ."

Christina's half-hearted attempt at a smile made a tear fall. "That's okay. I pray he's moved on with his life. I don't want him to wallow in sadness over me." Her lips cinched to the side as if she contemplated a thought. "Well, maybe he should wallow in sadness for a year or two first, then he can start looking."

Ari burst out in laughter. Christina joined her.

◆

Several days passed on the boat with more of the awkward eye contact and unspoken words. One evening Silas wandered out onto the deck. One of the cabin boys offered him a mug and coffee, poured fresh from a pot. He knew he'd be crazy to turn it down. Ari's crazy hours had him starved for sleep. As he took his first sip, he strained to see in the twilight but noticed Ari sitting on top of a pile of rope toward the bow of the ship, praying. Still in his jeans and oxford shirt, he sat on a lounge chair towards the mid part of the ship and kept an eye on her as he too began to pray.

Ari held her hands tightly. *"Lord, I'm confused. I am beginning to have feelings for Silas, but he killed John and many of my Outrider friends. I've forgiven him, but I don't know if it's appropriate for me to even think of getting into a relationship. Jim is still alive. But he remarried. Does that give me the right to get into another relationship? Please, Lord. Help me make the right decision . . ."*

Ari opened her eyes to see the ghostly white shadows appear in the water as a single dolphin swam at the bow's wake. "Good morning. Where are all of your friends?" she asked. A few seconds later, two others surfaced and swam in the wake briefly, then disappeared again, leaving the lone dolphin to swim. This happened several times over a few minutes.

Ari then heard a voice. *"Alone, the one is a new beginning. When with the others, the one is completed in My perfection."*

Ari took a deep breath. "What is that supposed to mean?" She stood up and walked back to the cabin. As she passed Silas, she said, "Have a good evening, Silas."

"Good night, Ari." After a moment, he followed her in. He watched her enter her cabin, then he entered his own. He decided to take a shower to get rid of some of the sticky feeling from the open ocean breeze he had been in all day. The hot water seemed to wash his achy muscles away. He stepped out and wrapped a towel around his waist. He looked into the fogged-up mirror. He swiped his hand across it and then stared at a large scar near his heart. *"I can't believe I'm still alive. Thank you, Jesus."* He wiped more of the condensation off the mirror and saw Ari. Her eyes became watery as she stared at him. Her brow furrowed in thought. "Are you okay?"

"I saw your scar. I'm so sorry that you've taken such a beating on my account," Ari said, almost in tears. Her skin still glistened with sweat from the muggy night. She walked up to his back and outlined his scar with her finger.

Silas turned towards her and cornered her against the counter. His hand gently cupped her cheek; his thumb caressed beads of sweat from her face. Silas gently kissed her other cheek, then her neck. The saltiness of her sweat reminded him of the ocean that surrounded them.

Ari closed her eyes. *It's been so long. . . .* Her breath became shallow. She could feel the heat of his body against her own. Silently, her tears began to fall.

"Now what's wrong?" Silas whispered.

"I wish . . . I mean I want . . . but I can't. Please Silas. I don't think I can . . ."

"You can't or you won't?" He asked, backing off.

"I won't because I can't. Not while Jim is still alive," Ari answered as she cried.

"Ari, your dear husband remarried," Silas pointed out.

"I know, but he thought I died."

"So, what, that makes it okay for him to pursue other relationships, but not you?"

"No . . . I mean yes." Ari pushed Silas aside and stepped past him. "He doesn't know I'm alive. But I know he's alive. I would be committing adultery if I had a relationship with you."

"But Ari, he's remarried and moved on, leaving you in the dust . . ."

"That doesn't change the marriage covenant we established between the two of us with God. I feel that I would be breaking my covenant relationship with God. I'm sorry, Silas. I can't."

Frustration began to grow in Silas' voice. "So, what, you're going to deny yourself the joy of being in a relationship for the rest of your life? You can't tell me you didn't just feel something."

"I guess so, yes." Ari grabbed her hair with both hands. "I don't know."

Silas shook his head. "Whatever. I hope you're happy being with yourself." He walked past Ari and out of the room. She could sense the deep frustration in her friend. For the first time in her life, she began to question God's word on this subject.

"Silas! Wait," Ari said.

He turned around to see what she wanted. Ari reached up and kissed him. His surprised expression melted to one of love as he embraced her with his arms. A few seconds later, Ari opened her eyes and pulled away. Confused, Silas asked, "Now what?"

"Maybe we're going too fast?"

"Maybe. But we've known each other for over twenty years, Ari."

"Hmm. I think you're right."

Silas looked shocked. "I am?"

Ari lay on his bed as she nodded in agreement. Silas smiled and plopped onto the bed next to her. He bent over and gave her the kiss he had always dreamed he wanted to give her. Ari's hands went around his neck. She had not felt this much at happiness in a very long time.

CHAPTER SIXTEEN

"*You did what?*" Christina asked her friend as she crawled in to the room in the early morning hours. "Ari, you're not even married."

"It just happened."

"*It just happened?* Ari, this type of stuff doesn't just happen to us. We have been set apart. We have our Father's standards to live up to."

"ARRRgggh!" Ari growled as she fell backwards onto her bed. She covered her face with her hands. "I'm so confused, Christina. I want to be with Silas, but the Bible says if I remarry I would be an adulteress. If that's the case, I may as well have relations with a man without marrying him."

Christina shook her head. "Ari, don't go there. We are not in a position to question God's word. It's not up for interpretation. You know in your heart what you did was wrong."

"So remarrying and then having relations with your new husband is considered to be okay according to the Bible?"

"Well, yes, kind of. The Old Testament says that divorce is allowed,"

Christina hung herself on those words.

"Yes, but then Jesus says that anyone that does so and remarries is considered to be an adulteress. Moses made up that law because the people's hearts were hardened. *This was not the way from the beginning*," Ari replied. She took a deep breath and looked at Christina. "The crazy thing is that for the first time in a long time, I felt happy."

"You had happiness, but were you at peace about it? Is this what God told you to do? Did you have His joy?"

"Obviously, not quite. Otherwise I wouldn't be here feeling guilty as all get out. I felt like I'm cheating on Jim. Even though he's moved on, apparently my heart hasn't realized that yet."

Christina sat on the bed next to her friend. "Ari, your marriage is a covenant between you, Jim, and God. Even if you remarry, it doesn't nullify that covenant. That's what Jesus tried to tell us in the Bible. Whatever you decide to do, please pray about this, Ari. I don't want you to fall out of God's will."

"I have. And I will."

That night, Ari didn't sleep. She sat at the bow of the boat watching to see if her dolphin would join her. The wake remained empty. In the early morning twilight, she saw Silas walk towards her. He stopped a few steps in front of her. "Hi," he greeted her simply, seeing how she would respond.

"Hi." Ari couldn't make eye contact. She stared at her feet.

"You disappeared. I woke up and you weren't there." Silas rubbed his neck, knowing that the moment went way beyond uncomfortable. "Uh," he started, "I know this is kind of awkward. If you want to slow down and take a step back, I'm okay with that." Silence met his offer. "Ari?"

Ari looked up into his green eyes. She hoped he would say he hated the evening. He looked at her expectantly as she spoke. "I haven't felt happy like I did last night in a long time. I didn't want it to end. You made me remember how beautiful and precious the love of another is."

Silas backed up and leaned up against a crate. "Uh, oh. I hear a Dear John coming up," he said.

"What I did was wrong, and I knew it. And it's not fair to you." Ari saw she had hurt Silas. "I have been lonely, and this time we've been together, I've grown to love you. Please forgive me. I just don't think I could go into a relationship and feel like it would be okay. It's not the way God wants me to be. If things were different, I would love to be with you, Silas. I'm so sorry."

Silas remained silent. His heart felt like it had been shot with a blade.

"Silas? Please say something," Ari pleaded, tears flowing from her eyes.

Silas sighed. "There's nothing more to really say, is there?" He looked towards the lightened sky at the horizon. "I better go take a shower. I'll see you at breakfast." He turned and quietly walked away; his silhouette disappeared behind the cabin door.

Ari sat back down on the pile of rope and grabbed her knees. She sobbed, wishing her life could be simpler.

CHAPTER SEVENTEEN

Ari lagged behind, getting her bag packed. Her mind scurried between different thoughts, unfocused, as if lost in the waves of emotions that washed inside her head. She stared at the unzipped bag and its neat piles of clothes and personal items stacked near its gaping maw. She began to systematically place items in the duffel, in the same place and order as she had done a thousand times over. She carefully tucked the last items in: her Bible, an extra case of blades, and a spare blade gun. She zipped the bag as Christina stepped out of the bathroom for one last check. "I think that's it, Ari," the bubbly blonde Outrider announced.

"Hmmm."

Silas poked his head in the door. "We need to get going. We don't want the port authority questioning us."

Christina grabbed her bag, along with one of the canvas packages containing the swords. Ari grabbed her travel duffel, threw it over her shoulder, and slung another canvas bundle over her other shoulder before following Christina. Ari bumped into Silas in the hallway. The two friends stared at Ari. "What?" Ari asked.

"You're the one that knows where we are going," Christina refreshed her absentminded friend. "We'll hold on to you, if you don't mind."

"Uh, sure. We need to wait a minute." Ari said.

"Why?" Silas asked.

"I'm trying to find a secluded place for us to self-transport to. Not the easiest thing to do during rush hour in a city where the residents are packed tighter than druplets on a berry." She paused before Silas prodded her to move faster. Ari finally had them reappear in a small dead-end alley.

Silas tried to determine if less humidity clung in the air than in Thailand, but at the moment, he couldn't tell from the torrential downpour. After a little over a week on a tiny boat, Ari felt as if the ground undulated. "Stay quiet and follow me." She took the lead and navigated through narrow alleys and streets before stopping in front of a small wrought iron fence that enclosed a tiny blacktop parking lot.

The three figures appeared in the shadow of a doorway. Ari knocked. A few moments later, the door opened, and an elderly man looked skeptically at the stranger and asked in a foreign language, "Yes, who are you?"

The elderly man stared at Silas as Ari turned around and bent her knees and spoke. "Isaac is a friend and thought you could help us." The old man looked at the base of her neck. He saw the unmistakable mark in her skin of a sword bisecting a circle, the symbol of the Outriders. The elderly man motioned for them to enter. The old man briefly looked around outside, then secured the door.

He shuffled quietly along the wooden floor. After following Ari's lead and taking their shoes off, they made their way to a small room that appeared to be a living room.

A slightly younger man named Kenji walked into the small room in his bathrobe and pointed a blade gun point-blank at Silas. "Who else knows you are here?" The man grilled Silas.

"No one." Silas relaxed as Kenji backed off and holstered his gun.

Kenji bowed and spoke, "My apologies for being suspicious. We had befriended an Outrider a few years ago, and they turned on us and tried to kill all of us for sympathizing with the Old Guard. There are only a handful of us now. Please follow Hide-san and he will show you to our guest quarters."

The elderly man ushered them down the hall and up a flight of stairs. He opened the door. The apartment seemed small with only about five hundred square feet of living space; a tiny space compared to what they had in Hollywood, but it would do nicely. Silas looked around. A tiny kitchenette tucked into one end of a small rectangular room, and a low table on a woven mat floor centered in the space defined the room as the apartment's main dining room. A set of doors led to a couple of small bedrooms and a bathroom. The blonde wooden floors occasionally creaked as the young man waved at Christina and Ari into one of the bedrooms.

Ari bowed to her host. "I didn't realize such spacious accommodations were available in downtown Tokyo."

"This is a guest apartment for visitors. You move in here . . . welcome to use it as long as you need it. Kenji-san will check on you in morning if you need any provisions. Clean towels and toiletries in the bathroom already." The elderly man bowed and excused himself from the apartment.

"Thank you, sir." Silas bowed, grateful for their hospitality. Silas checked out the bedrooms. The larger bedroom contained a full-size bed; the smaller room seemed stuffed with a twin bed and a futon mattress rolled neatly in the corner on the floor.

A familiar face poked through the apartment door. "Someone said there were American Outriders here that are friends with Isaac. I hoped it was you," Sam said as he stepped through the door.

"SAM!!!" Ari ran over and hugged her aging mentor.

Sam wrapped his arms around the closest thing he ever had to a daughter. "You are a sight for sore eyes. I'm so sorry I didn't return, but I feared they monitored my actions. I didn't want to possibly give you away. I returned once, but you two weren't there, and your bags were gone. I thought you moved on." He shook Silas' hand, and then gave him a hug as well. He reached out to Christina and enveloped her into the group hug as well.

Sam continued, "I saw what happened to Isaac. Several of the council members have been isolated out, and to a great extent, our abilities to reason and debate were curtailed. Our activities were documented, so I had to lay low. Outriders began to disappear. I left unnoticed, and since then I haven't heard anything come from Hollywood."

"Where are you staying?" Christina asked Sam.

"I'm in the main house, in an extra bedroom. I am passing word from Keiko-san that we are invited to breakfast." Sam hugged Ari again. "I have been praying for you, and now I thank God you are still with us."

"I just thought the same about you, Sam. Christina, grab one of the canvas bundles so we can show our hosts," Ari said as they left the apartment.

The trio followed Sam down a maze of narrow hallways to a small dining room. The low table easily could accommodate at least ten people. Keiko's preparations began to appear at the table. Small dishes and bowls of various pickled vegetables, cubed tofu, and grilled fish were placed in the center. Their hostess began to spoon out a watery rice porridge into rice bowls and placed them in front of her guests. Christina leaned over to Ari and asked, "What is this?"

"Breakfast," Ari answered. "The rice porridge is called *okayu*. Most Asian cultures have a version of it. They take leftover rice and add a lot of water to it and, in this case, a little salt. I think the Chinese have a version where they use broth instead of water." Keiko placed a bowl in front of Ari. Ari looked up at her Japanese hosts and smiled and spoke weakly, still slurring her words. "*Arigato gozaimasu.*" She bowed her head slightly. "*Itadakimasu . . .*"

"When did you have a chance to learn Japanese?" Silas asked.

"I think I picked it up reading," Ari said. "I only know the pleasantries."

"What did you say?" Christina asked.

"'Thank you,' and then 'excuse me while I go first.' The second phrase doesn't really translate well; it's just a polite way for the guest to say 'the food looks so good I can't wait.'"

Silas poked at the grilled salmon collar, and then looked at Kenji. "Kenji-san—you guys eat fish for breakfast?" Kenji nodded. "Do you have anything that isn't so fishy to eat this early?" Kenji nodded and spoke to Keiko who nodded, bowed, and walked out. A few minutes later she walked back in with a tray with several bowls. Kenji ushered Silas and Sam in to sit in the living/dining room at the table.

Little dishes and bowls were set in front of the two men. Silas thanked their hosts. After blessing their food, Silas looked down at his bowl, puzzled. He picked up his chopsticks and grabbed what appeared to be a bean from a small bowl. He pursed his lips when a string of what appeared to be slimy mucus clung to both ends. He looked up at Sam. "This is a joke, right?"

Sam laughed as he shook his head. "It's called *natto*. It's fermented soy beans. Don't forget that you were the one with the no-fish request." Silas poked at another dish with what appeared to be cubes of ivory-colored cheese with fur. He went to pick one up and the cubes jiggled. He shot Sam another confused and tentative look.

His mentor laughed again. "Tofu with what looks like dried bonito flakes. And by the look of the jiggle-factor, it's soft tofu." Silas turned his attention and the sharper end of one of his chopsticks and poked at slices of neon yellow semicircles of a strong-smelling vegetable. Sam grabbed one with his chopsticks, "*Takuan*. A pickle made from the daikon radish. It's really good with hot rice." He crunched into one and then followed it with a small mouthful of rice.

Silas followed suit. "Weird. Not bad, but weird. But I don't know if I can handle slime this early . . ."

Sam took a scoop of the fermented beans onto his rice and tried to break the enzymatic chain between his chopsticks and the two bowls by waving his chopstick tips in circles. He finally succeeded. "Natto is definitely a refined but acquired taste. Not one of my favorite dishes by any means, but I don't want to insult our hosts. If you swallow it whole and chase it down with rice, it isn't as brutal."

Silas tried to do as Sam instructed, and his face tried to remain polite as he took a huge swallow. "At least with the slime, it goes down easy."

He shook his head vigorously. He repeated the feat, and once again, he shook his head energetically. "Strangely addicting."

Silas shot a glare at the other end of the table, where Christina and Ari giggled at his gastronomic antics. Christina straightened her expression and bragged, "I don't have a problem with fish in the morning." She broke off an oily chunk of the salmon and popped it in her mouth.

Ari shrugged, saying, "I do, but I'm perfectly happy with the pickles and tofu."

After the group finished eating and Keiko began to clear out the dishes, Ari asked Kenji, "Kenji-san, I wondered if there is anyone in your group that can help teach us how to better handle these weapons? We've had to use these on the Nephilim, but I think our chances of survival would improve exponentially if we could refine our hand-to-hand combat." Christina handed Ari the bundle. Ari carefully unwrapped it and laid out the sampling of weapons.

Kenji picked up the longsword. "Lightweight. What metal is this made of?"

"We don't know," Silas answered. "We were hoping that you have a metallurgist or sword maker that might be able to tell us."

"The longsword is handled differently, depending on the design. The very large, heavy ones are made to smash armor and knock the opponent off their feet, where they would be helpless if in full armor. At which point the sword would act like a very crude can opener. Most of its victims would end up bleeding to death inside their armor. For someone that isn't in full armor, life and limbs would definitely be lost."

Kenji continued. "This one, however, is different. This is its more refined offspring. Lighter and easier to maneuver, its primary function is to impale and eviscerate. It's a different type of swordplay than with a samurai sword. Your sword has two sharp edges."

He put the sword down and picked up the dagger. "Very elegant and refined. Slender, with a very sharp tip and edges." He flipped it in the air, caught the tip of it, and then hefted it at a wooden beam. It sunk several inches into the hard wood. "Impressive. Well balanced, just like the sword."

Ari picked up the sai. "I know that this can block a sword, but it seems almost too bulky and awkward." She handed it to Kenji.

The young man handled it expertly. "Oh, no, Ari. This too is as refined as I've seen. Usually these don't have sharp tips like this. This weapon isn't meant to impale. It's meant to have weight to it, which it does. The trident design is meant to be used as a bludgeon. If attacked with a sword or dagger, the person can direct the weapon off to the side and then, with a slight twist, lock or snap the blade off."

Kenji placed the sai down and ran his fingers over the bow. "Wow. Elegant . . ." He picked it up. "Well-balanced." He tried to pull back on the bowstring and managed to only pull it back partially. "Strung for a very strong person, apparently."

Kenji handed Ari the bow and she pulled it all the way back. "Not really. Just someone that has shot a bow and arrow before. You'd be surprised the strength one attains when you run out of options."

"This facility doesn't have much space to practice. I have a house out in the country that will be better suited to your practice sessions. I want to ask a friend who is well versed in swordplay to help teach you how to handle the longsword properly. It may be a few days before he is available. Until then, we will be honored if you stay here." Kenji bowed deeply.

Ari looked at her friends, confused, and then reciprocated the bow. "Kenji-san, we appreciate you, Hide, and Keiko taking us in without any notice. You have been wonderful hosts. We don't deserve the VIP treatment we have received so far."

"It had been prophesied many years ago that three of God's warriors would defeat a great enemy of His people, but that they would need our help in order to achieve that. However, we are confused. The prophesy described two of the warriors having hair the color like the sun, the third with a streak of hair as if touched by God's hand."

The three friends laughed under their breath. "We are sorry for the deception, but we were forced to blend in, in order to stay hidden. My two friends are very much blonde. I think you can see Christina's roots coming in," Ari explained.

"Hey, are they?" Christina sounded horrified as she hid the top of her head.

"And yes, I do have a freakish streak of white hair that I've had ever since grade school," Ari added.

Kenji bowed even deeper. Ari bowed and then spoke to her host. "Kenji, we're just Outriders just like you. No different."

Kenji politely corrected Ari, "Thank you, but you are different. You have been chosen to fight our greatest enemies." He winked. "Excuse, please. We will let you rest now. One of us will come get you for lunch." Kenji bowed and quietly left the room.

The three friends stood staring at each other. Ari shook her head and sighed as she headed back to the apartment. Silas followed her and asked, "What's wrong now?"

"Nothing," Ari said, purposely keeping it short. She turned a corner and continued down another hallway. Christina lagged behind Silas, following Ari.

"Oh, no, you don't. Every time you shake your head and sigh, something or someone set you off," Silas said.

Ari stopped in her tracks and turned on her heels. Her friends stopped in their tracks abruptly so as not to run into her. She held her finger up and said, "It's just that . . ." Ari shook her head again. "Never mind." She turned around and continued down the hallway.

Christina pushed her way past Silas and grabbed Ari's shoulder. "Never mind what?"

Ari stopped again, but this time she didn't face her friends. "You wouldn't understand."

"Try me," Silas said as he crossed his arms. Christina nodded and followed suit.

Ari bit her lip. "You have no idea what it's like hearing stuff like that all the time. It's a total mind freak for me. I mean who can possibly live up to expectations like that all the time? It's like they're setting you up for failure."

"I don't think they mean it that way, Ari." Christina said. "I think they are showing how much they respect you."

"I know, but I'm just tired of being on the pedestal. I just want to be normal for once." Ari opened the apartment door.

Silas laughed. "You have never been normal, Ari. None of us are. We have been set apart. And whether you like it or not, you have come for such a time as this."

Ari stopped in her tracks again. *"What did you say?"*

"Uh, you have never been normal? We have been set apart?" Silas repeated. "Uh . . . Whether you like it or not, you have come for such a time as this?"

"Ari, you look like you just saw a ghost." Christina said as watched her friend's shocked expression.

"I heard that Esther verse recently in a vision," Ari said.

Silas snickered under his breath. "Ari, even your dreams are putting you on a pedestal."

"Some pedestal." Ari plopped down on a pillow, going further into her explanation. "It doesn't end very well. We're being overrun by a sea of Nephilim. We need to get trained up. We'll be able to go on the offensive, attacking small pockets of them. Perhaps it will buy more time until we can get the rest of the Outriders trained."

"Rest? Ari, perhaps you don't remember, but we've all been 'murdered' by our brethren Outriders. I don't think we are very welcome," Silas pointed out.

"Point taken. But eventually, they will have to join the fight," Ari said.

"So I guess now we wait for our teacher?" Christina asked.

Ari leaned back on the pillow. "We wait."

A week later, Ari, Silas, and Christina were quietly gathering their bags. Ari carefully covered the special weapons back in their muslin wrap and carefully secured it with the leather straps. *We need to have scabbards made.*

Kenji knocked before he stuck his head in. "Are you ready?"

"I believe so," Ari answered as she picked up her bag and weapon bundle.

"Kenji, once again we want to thank you for your hospitality," Christina said as she followed Ari and Silas.

"The pleasure was ours," Kenji said as he led them to a van. He loaded their equipment into the back. Sam met them at the van and loaded his duffel as well.

Ari grinned. "Sam, you're coming too?"

Sam winked at Ari. "Someone has to make sure you all stay out of trouble. I thought I could cook for you and tend to your needs so you can focus on your training."

Silas loaded his bag into the back of the van and patted Sam on the shoulder as he passed him. "That's very kind of you, Sam."

"I think he wants to keep an eye on Ari," Christina nudged Ari with her elbow.

They all climbed into the van, and Kenji slid into the driver's side. Ari leaned forward and tapped Kenji on the shoulder. "Hey Kenji, why are we taking a van? Why aren't we self-transporting?"

Kenji pointed at Sam in the passenger seat. "Guilty," Sam spoke up. "You are allowing an old man to travel with dignity. I admit that I do not like to self-transport."

"The house is only a couple of hours from here. One of us will come and check on you a couple of times during the week, and we'll bring out provisions as you need. There is a town about a fifteen-minute walk from the house. We'll pass it as we go out to the property."

Ari used the opportunity to try to get her bearings, taking note of anything that might be useful. As the buildings began to thin out, the terrain became hilly with trees and small patches of land that seemed to be farmed with the occasional subdivision of suburban houses. The terrain soon became even steeper, with the sides covered in cedars and what appeared to be fig.

From the position of the sun and their general direction, Ari knew they were headed west of the metroplex. Soon Kenji turned off, and the van followed a small river, in a valley just wide enough for a few houses and a narrow field next to the river. They climbed up and over one of the hills, and another valley spread out before them. Fields of rice and vegetables lined the river. The van crossed a small bridge and then pulled into a gravel driveway at the far end of the valley. A single-story traditional Japanese house sat surrounded by a thicket of bamboo at the base of one of the hills. A small field stood between the bamboo forest and the back of the house.

As the group got out of the van and stretched their legs, Ari looked around. Typical of an Outrider's safe house, the nearest neighbors lived across the bridge and further up the valley. The dense stand of bamboo made it difficult for anything larger than a rabbit to pass between the stalks, offering itself as a natural defense against an attack from the rear of the house. An additional building almost as big as the house itself resided to the side of the yard. Ari speculated, *Perhaps it has additional guest quarters?*

The group made their way inside the house. As everyone took their shoes off, Ari and the group looked around, impressed with the workmanship. The floors and wood beams and fixtures were hand-planed maple. The warm wood offered a cozy feel to the house despite the sparse furnishings. The three Outriders stood in the middle of a small reception foyer, still holding their bags. Kenji worked his way to the front of them, offering directions. "There eight bedrooms—all are considerably spacious and about the same size. There is a ninth room that is slightly smaller that can be used for prayer or small private meetings. Each pair of bedrooms shares a bathroom. You may want to keep this in mind when you choose your rooms."

"Girls on one side, guys on the other?" Christina suggested.

Ari shrugged. "I don't care. I'm going to the right. You guys can do whatever you want." She proceeded down the hallway on the right side, and turned at the last door on the left.

The bedroom was simple in its design and furnishing. The futon mattress sat rolled up and alone, the only piece other than a small side table against the center of the side wall. Ari opened a door along the inside wall and poked her head inside. She smiled, pleasantly surprised it actually ended up being a shared bathroom. The Jack-and-Jill setup of the bathroom captured the efficiency and space-saving design. Warm blonde wood trimmed virtually everything in the sparsely furnished room. The aroma of the tatami mats played with her mind. The woven straw mats underneath her feet had a slightly sweet, grassy scent, vaguely reminding her of freshly mown hay.

Ari dropped her gear off by the rolled-up futon against the wall. Even before Ari opened the back patio door, she heard birds singing as if happily greeting the new guest. Ari slid the doors open and gazed at the greenery dappled in sun and shade. The breeze felt good to her. The uneven 'clack clack' rhythm echoed as bamboo stalks rubbed against each other when the breeze blew through the grove. The sound was foreign to Ari, but it put her mind at ease.

Silas bent his head into the doorway and said, "I'm bunking in the room next to this one."

"Meaning we'll be sharing a bathroom together? I don't think so," Ari shook her head as she dropped her bag and bundle by the wall.

"Yes, I mean, no. What that means is we have a sliding screen door between the two rooms so I'll be able to come to your aid quickly in case you're attacked."

"If I'm attacked," Ari pointed out, "they will probably take you down at the same time." She unzipped her jacket and laid it neatly on top of her bag. She walked over to the patio door and stepped out onto the wooden patio.

A slight summer breeze tugged at Ari's hair. She inhaled deeply, and the distant scent of wet earth and exotic flowers enticed her to explore her surroundings. Beyond the grass lawn and bamboo forest, Ari could see a tall, forested hill playing peek-a-boo between the waving stalks of bamboo. The sun felt good on her skin. She sat down on the step leading down to the grass and leaned back onto her elbows. *I sure could have used this about a decade ago . . .*

"Ari, would you like to go into town with us?" Kenji asked. "I want to pick up provisions for you and the instructor. He will be here this afternoon."

"Sure," Ari answered as she got to her feet. She closed the patio door and grabbed her jacket.

"You won't need that," Kenji told her. "It will make you stand out."

"Don't you think the holster will make me stand out more?" Ari asked.

"I don't think you will need that either," he answered.

"Just the same, I feel more comfortable. What if I wear this instead of the jacket?" Ari asked as she slipped on a loose-fitting button-down blue linen shirt.

"Perfect. Let's go." Kenji said.

As they passed the common living area, Silas and the others joined them. Sam carried a piece of paper. "Shopping list," he said as he waived the paper.

Once on the road, Ari commented, 'We should pick up a scooter or small car in case we need to get around."

"Can't we just self-transport?" Christina asked.

Ari shrugged "We could, but I think the town is so small, they will notice us without any vehicle. They will begin to wonder how we got here."

Kenji parked the van downtown. Ari was right. The town had only a hundred or so residents, and unusual activity was noticed by the elders. Kenji waved at a group sitting on a bench. "Sam, the market is across the street at the corner. I will meet you there. I want to explain to the mayor you are actors and actresses training on swordplay for an upcoming production."

"Would it help your case if I came with you?" Christina asked.

"Sure."

Ari watched Christina and Kenji bow to the bench of elders before stepping into the small market. Very clean and organized, the store sold all the staples of Japanese country cooking: fresh fish and meats, vegetables, and leafy greens. A few aisles of brightly colored packages made Ari smile at the cute pictures on some of the packages. Sam handed her an empty basket and proceeded to pull vegetables and place them in her basket. She noticed they were watched very closely by the store owner. Ari walked over and bowed deeply saying, "*Konnichiwa*

. . ."

The store owner bowed deeply and reciprocated, "*Konnichiwa.*"

"*Watashi no namae Ari-desu,*" Ari handed the basket to Silas and bowed again. In broken Japanese, she said, "*Kore wa Samu-desu, koreha-shi Silas-desu.*"

The store owner bowed and grinned at Ari. "Your Japanese is not bad."

"You speak English?" she asked.

"I graduated University of Chicago, class of '83. I studied biochemistry. I returned home about five years ago to help my parents with this store."

"We're here for a few weeks to learn swordplay for a production."

"Please let me know if you need something that we don't have. I can usually get it by the next day or sooner."

"Actually, do you know of any leather craftsman in the area? We need to have scabbards made for our swords."

"Scabbards?" the clerk asked.

"Um, sheaths. To protect and carry the swords," Ari said, holding her hand in a cup at her waist and raising the other as if pulling a sword from a scabbard.

"Oh, I see. Old man Tetsuo-san works with leather. He may be able to help you."

Silas handed Ari her basket back and grabbed the basket from Sam. The baskets brimmed with considerably more items than before. Ari laughed. "Sam, who do you plan on feeding, an army?"

"Well, yes, of course! This should last us until the middle of the week," the portly guardian answered. He pulled the items out onto the counter. The clerk totaled up the sale and Sam paid cash.

Ari turned to the store clerk. "I will bring the weapons in the next time we come into town. Thank you." She bowed again and the owner reciprocated.

◆

Later that afternoon, Ari pulled up in a motorcycle. Her heel set the kickstand down then rolled the bike backwards to engage the kickstand. A minute later, Silas pulled up with another motorcycle, and then Kenji pulled up in his van. "Kenji, thanks for negotiating the price on these," Ari said.

The young man bowed quickly. "No problem. I knew he told you the wrong price. I guess he thought Americans wouldn't know the difference."

"Silas, I need to make a quick trip to the organization's headquarters. I keep having visions that they are being attacked, but I can't tell from whom," Ari said.

"Are you crazy? Do you know what they would do to you—to us—if they got to us?" Silas asked. "I would hate if anything happened to you at the hands of your former associates."

"We can bug out if they see us," Ari answered.

"Fine. At the first sign of trouble . . . ."

"I know. We're out of there," Ari said.

"Should we tell anyone?" Silas said.

"Why? We'll be back before we're even missed," Ari said.

"I have a bad feeling about this, Ari."

The two self-transported. The last of the rush hour traffic had cleared the city when Ari and Silas reappeared down the street from the nondescript exterior of the organization's building. The streets and sidewalks were wet from a recent rain. Ari's heart began to race. Silas grabbed hold of her arm, startling the normally steely-nerved Outrider. "Ari, this is insane. If we're found out, you know it isn't going to be pretty. Even if we get away, now that they know we're alive, Amon won't stop looking for us until he knows we're dead."

"They're all eating. We'll be in and out before the Tempest get a whiff of us." Ari strode quickly across the street, with Silas running to catch up.

The front door opened with little resistance. Once inside with the door closed, they were shocked to see the remains of the interior. The interior walls, columns, and even the stairwell were missing huge chunks. The air smelled stale and of death. They checked out several floors of living quarters. Both Ari and Silas covered their mouth and noses with their shirts to repel some of the stench. Several bodies were left in the lower levels.

They picked their way up the stairs to Amon's office. The door to his office hung at an angle from part of a single hinge. Silas shoved the door out of the way with his foot. Careful not to step into the hole in the middle of the room's floor, they walked up to the remains of Amon's desk. Ari glanced at a picture of the overseer wearing an Italian suit and an interesting necklace with a stylized cross hanging from it.

Just then, the two Outriders heard a large crash. Ari looked at her watch. It was late. She grabbed her blade gun. "Amon has something of mine that I want back. I'll meet you back at the house."

"Ari, what about you? I'm not leaving without you," Silas said as another crash happened closer.

Ari frantically searched the corner of a closet. After several agonizingly long minutes, Ari reached deep into the corner of a box and wrapped her fingers around a small metal box. She carefully tucked it inside her jacket and zipped it up. "Let's go." Before Silas could say anything else, Ari ran out the door and almost ran into a Nephilim coming up the stairs. She jumped over the railing, avoiding the creature's swing. Ari landed and tumbled onto foyer's floor. The motion distracted the Nephilim enough to change direction and go after Ari. "I bet you caused all of the mess here!" Ari yelled at the giant.

When the giant cornered Ari, Silas dashed down the stairs and aimed his blade gun at the creature. "Hey, you!" he yelled to make the giant turn around. As it did, Silas shot a blade into one of its eyes. The creature howled, and as it spun back around, Ari threw the golden dagger at its chest. The dagger sliced cleanly through the seemingly impenetrable scales and tough skin and sank in deeply. The creature fell to the ground, lifeless.

Ari cautiously walked up to the body and retrieved her dagger. "Why didn't you throw the dagger earlier?" Silas asked.

"I didn't need to until just now," she answered. The two friends quickly retreated out of the building and back to their temporary home in Japan.

Kenji approached Ari and Silas. "Where did you two disappear to?"

"Uh, I had to retrieve something," Ari said.

The three walked past a pickup truck with a tarp over something in the back. Ari and Silas placed their helmets off to the side near their shoes, and noticed a pair of strange shoes. They stepped into the living room and noticed a strange man with long gray hair sitting at the table with Sam and Christina.

The man stood up as Kenji approached him. "Steve! Great to see you." Kenji vigorously shook the hand of his friend.

"It has been a long time, Kenji-san." Steve hugged his friend.

Kenji wore a grin from ear to ear. "Everyone, this is Steve. He will teach you how to handle the weapons better. He used to teach actors how to handle swords. Now he is learning how to make samurai swords the old-fashioned way."

Sam stood up, saying, "We've already met your friend."

Silas stepped forward. "Hi. I'm Silas Monroe, and this is Ari Sommers."

"Silas . . . Ari . . ." Steve said as he shook both of their hands. Despite his gray hair, Steve looked similar in age as Silas and Ari. Their instructor tied his long hair neatly back into a ponytail. His black Henley shirt and faded jeans reminded Ari of Jim.

"Do you need to rest?" Kenji asked his friend.

"Uh, I think we can start immediately since the first few days will just be used to get familiar with the weapons," Steve answered. "You will all need to dress more comfortably. Shall we meet here with your weapons in half an hour?"

"Where do you want to do this?" Ari asked.

"In the great room," Kenji offered. He walked out on the patio and pointed to the other building. A simple wooden path led from the one building to the other.

"Great room?" Silas asked.

"You will see," Kenji said.

When the Outriders regrouped with their weapon bundles, they walked over to the other building. The panels slid back, opening the entire wall up to the outside. The design of the wooden great room accentuated the simplicity of Japanese design. Wood beams crossed on the outer edges of the soaring ceiling. The entire room was lined with thick tatami mats. Off to one side behind a wall was a corridor with a small kitchenette and a full bath.

Silas and Steve moved a large square low table off to the side against one of the walls. The group spent the next few minutes setting up equipment that they had brought in from his truck. There were some wood mannequins, rope, and targets, as well as several weapons from his practice collection.

"Let's see these weapons," Steve said.

Ari untied her bundle and laid out each weapon for Steve to inspect. "Interesting," he said. "Do all of your bundles have the same weapons?" The two other Outriders nodded. "Hmmmm," Steve vocalized as he thought hard for a minute. He finally spoke to explain. "Usually a fighter will specialize in one or two weapons. They may know how to use the other weapons they have on hand, but by concentrating on one or two weapons, you will be able to master them more quickly. I will teach you how to use all of the weapons. Depending on your comfort level with the weapon and how I think you have handled that piece, I'll determine whether that will be the one that I have you focus on."

Steve strode up the two women. "Of course, all of these weapons require significant upper body strength, something that most women lack." Steve took a thick sisal rope and stepped on one end. He then hefted the rest of it over one of the ancient, heavy beams overhead. He tied off the other end on a wood column, and then looked at Ari. "If you can, I want you to climb to the top and then back down."

"I hate sisal rope," Ari said under her breath. She grabbed the rope above her head, took a couple of deep breaths, and then began to shimmy up the rope. She sandwiched the rope between her legs, crossing her legs in order to gain more friction. She climbed up with little effort, and with the rope still intertwined with her legs, slid down.

Steve gave a surprised look on his face. "Not bad. You climb that better than most guys. Christina, you're next."

Christina rubbed her hands as she approached the rope. Like Ari, she climbed the rope with little effort, and slid down, handling the rope hand under hand so as not to burn her palms.

Once again, Steve looked surprised. "Wow. That was great. How are you at throwing?" He pulled out a bowie knife from his pile and threw it at one of the targets in the corner, a distance of about thirty feet. He hit the target slightly to the right of the bull's-eye.

Christina picked up one of the bowie knives by the hilt. She expertly flipped it in her hand and grabbed the tip by her fingers. In the same smooth and effortless motion, she hefted the knife into the same target, hitting the bull's-eye in the center. The blade of her knife sank in several inches deeper than the instructor's.

Steve didn't show any emotion other than raising an eyebrow. "Silas, why don't you throw one?"

Silas grabbed a knife from the table in a grip as if he were about to stab someone. As he walked toward the group, in one movement he flipped the knife in the air, grabbed the tip, and threw it. He hit the bull's-eye next to Christina's.

"Good," Steve said. He then looked at Ari and motioned with his head she was next. Ari grasped one of the bowie knives, getting a quick feel of his weight and balance. She looked at Steve and asked, "Do you want me to throw with my left or right hand?"

"How about both?"

Ari went back to the table and grabbed another knife. She held each one by the hilt. She stood with her right shoulder facing the target. Like Christina, her practiced throw came from years of Outrider work. In one smooth motion, Ari flipped the blade in her right hand to grab its tip, motioned her arm back across her chest and then across it again backhand, and released the knife. Then, with her body still in motion, she flipped the second knife to its blade in her left hand and used the continuing momentum of her body to throw the knife like a baseball player releasing a pitch. Both knives sank deeply into the target, so close to Christina's and Silas' that everyone could hear metal hit metal.

"Are you serious?" Steve said to the group. "You guys should be teaching me," he said, pointing to himself. "Where did you learn to throw like that?"

"Well, um, knives are part of our acting training. It's the other stuff that we're not as refined in," Ari said. "Silas and I have done some work with shinais, but that sword movement isn't the same as for a longsword, or so I've been told."

"What are your swords made of? If they are brass, they will be too soft to do combat," Steve said, as he held one of the golden swords.

"It's definitely not brass," Silas said. "The metal is pretty hard. We thought you may know since you make swords now."

Steve shook his head. "It's light like titanium, but the color is all wrong. Maybe they've added something to the metal to make it change colors . . . I can send a sample off to have it analyzed if you want."

"That would be great." Silas nodded.

"Until that comes back, and until I know you won't kill yourself or someone else, why don't we use the wooden dowels I brought?" Steve offered a dowel rod to each of the Outriders and grabbed one for himself. They all held a taped end for more grip and comfort.

"Face off with a partner. Now I don't want any movement to get out of hand. We're not here to kill or maim your sparring partner. You are just here to get the movements down, and then you will practice it against a dummy. Christina, why don't you spar with me, and Ari and Silas can partner up."

Silas took a step back and looked to the ground, shaking his head. "Is something wrong?" Ari asked.

"No, nothing is wrong," Silas said.

Ari became upset. "You didn't want to pair up with me, did you?"

"No, that's not it. It's just we used to fight against each other all the time with the shinai. I thought it would be more interesting to fight someone else, but I'm okay with it," Silas said.

"No you aren't," Ari mumbled.

Steve cleared his throat, "Are you two lovebirds done with your private conversation?"

Christina whispered, "Oh, you shouldn't have gone there . . ."

Steve corrected himself quickly. "Sorry. Silas, why don't you switch with Christina. Better? Can we begin?"

Ari and Silas exchanged uneasy glances with each other as he walked to join Steve. Ari shook her head. *This is going to be a long week.*

CHAPTER EIGHTEEN

Weeks went by with their training. On one of their days off from training, Ari lay curled up on her futon. She normally would have gotten up hours ago with the sunrise, but her body screamed for more sleep. In that moment when Ari didn't know if she was dreaming or awake, another vision of the dark street attack hit her. She bolted upright in her bed, her heart pounding as she wiped beads of sweat off her upper lip with her hand.

Just then, Ari felt nauseous. *Ugh. Not again. Lord, You are my Jehovah Rapha. In You, I find my strength.*

Ari finally got up. She padded off to the bathroom and looked at herself in the mirror. "Goodness, your hair!" Her short, wild spikes stood up as if she got electrocuted. Ari patted and combed her hair with her fingers, when a wave of sickness washed over her. She promptly bent over the toilet, unable to keep anything down.

After a few minutes, Ari got up, brushed her teeth, and then took a shower, hoping it would help make her feel better. After drying herself off, she got dressed and headed to the living room. The group had just finished breakfast and was headed out the door, off to town.

"Well hello there, sleepyhead," Sam teased.

"Hey," Ari replied simply. The remnant smell of their breakfast made her feel queasy again.

"Are you hungry?" he asked.

"Not really. I am not feeling too well right now. Thanks anyway."

Christina asked, "Do you want to head into town? We were about to go."

"Thanks, but I think I will pass right now," Ari answered. "Christina?"

"Yes?" her friend answered, holding the door knob.

"Uh, nothing. Never mind. Enjoy your time in town." Ari walked out to the wooden deck and sat down, burying her head in her hands. The morning sun made the dew on the grass glisten like diamonds. She could see the cotton-like tufts throughout the garden where spiderwebs had also picked up the evening moisture. The locusts could be heard in the distance, warming up for their day-long chorus.

Christina looked back at the group as they waited for her by the van. "Hey, guys, I think I'm going to stay back. I'll catch you later." Christina turned and looked at her friend. Even though Ari's body language didn't take much to interpret, Christina knew her friend had something weighing heavily on her mind. She joined her friend on the patio, just sitting next to her, not saying anything. Christina knew that Ari would tell her in her own time.

"Beautiful day, isn't it?" Christina said after several minutes of silence.

"Mmm. You didn't go into town?"

"I decided to hang back. You don't look like you feel well, so I thought I'd make sure you're okay." Christina said as she squeezed her friend and shook her.

"Mmm."

After a few minutes more of silence, Christina got up. "Well, if you need to talk, I'll be inside."

"I screwed up."

Christina stopped and turned around. "Ari, we're all human. No one is perfect."

Ari held the sides of her head with her hands. "No, I mean I *really* screwed up. Silas and I . . . A couple of weeks ago I realized I was late. I didn't think much about it since women tend to miss their cycles when they work out hard like we have been."

"Oh, no. Ari . . ." Christina leaned against the door.

"I felt nauseous earlier this week. The last time in town, I picked up a self-exam pregnancy test." Ari lay back on the deck, covering her eyes with her hands. She didn't want to see her friend's expression. "It was positive."

"How far along are you?"

"From the night of our indiscretion—it's about twenty weeks."

"You barely show, Ari. Have you been seeing a doctor?"

"I've been wearing looser t-shirts to our training, and my pants are just beginning to feel snug. Kenji has been sworn to secrecy, and he has been making sure I'm eating right. He's also keeping an eye on my physical activities."

"Ari, does Silas know?"

"No, not yet."

"What are you going to do?"

"I don't know. I'm definitely going to have it. Depending on Silas' reaction, I may give it up for adoption. I mean I couldn't even be a mother to Alexa, so how am I going to be one to this kid?" Ari's tears welled up as she rubbed her abdomen.

Christina sat next to her friend and hugged her. "Ariana Sommers: you are a wonderful mother. You did the best you could in the worst of situations."

"And now the situation is even worse. I can't go off and fight the Nephilim while I'm pregnant. And how could I justify going off to fight them after I give birth? Who will watch him? It's not like I have the support group of the Old Guard anymore."

"I'm sure Sam or Keiko would love to watch your kid. So when do you plan on telling Silas?"

"I planned on telling him the moment I found out, but I got cold feet. He's been understandably distant to me after I told him I couldn't get into another serious relationship. I'm afraid of his reaction," Ari explained.

"What, that he would hate you more?"

"Yes . . . and no. What if he insists on getting married? What if tells me that this is proof that we were meant to be together? And what about God? If I decide to have the kid and keep him and marry Silas, does that mean I will no longer be under God's blessing? Will He try to curse my new family because I broke the covenant with Him and Jim?"

Christina nudged her friend. "I don't think God is going to curse you. You know that He forgives us and we become new creations in Christ. Our old indiscretions are forgotten and we start again, free of sin and condemnation."

"What do you think I should do?"

The two friends sat there next to each other in silence for a few minutes. Finally, Christina spoke up. "Ari, I don't think God is going to curse you because you made a mistake. He forgives everyone of their sins, if they only admit to it and if they still love His son Jesus as their Lord and Savior. And I imagine that He will help you make that decision and find the right moment and words to say when the time comes to speak to Silas." Christina hugged her friend again and stepped inside.

Ari buried her face in her hands again and cried, asking God for forgiveness.

◆

That evening after dinner, Ari's gaze followed Silas as he returned to his room. She glanced at Christina, who gave a subtle head nod telling Ari of the perfect opportunity. Ari walked down the hallway and into her room. *Please Lord, I need Your strength and wisdom to know what to say to Silas.*

Ari took a deep breath and stepped into the adjoining bathroom. Silas brushed his teeth in front of the sink. Even though he saw Ari in the mirror, he didn't acknowledge her. Ari grabbed her toothbrush, and as she squeezed toothpaste onto it, she spoke up. "I need to talk to you."

Silas finished brushing and rinsed his mouth out. "What about?"

"I don't know how to tell you this."

"Just say it," Silas said. "You've never beat around the bush before."

Ari took a deep breath. "I'm pregnant."

"Are you sure?"

"I did the home pregnancy test a couple of times, and between that result and the symptoms I have had the past couple of weeks, I'm pretty sure. I won't know for sure unless I go to a doctor."

"What do you want to do?" Silas asked as he put his toothbrush in his cup.

Ari shook her head. "Honestly, I don't know. I definitely want to have it, but I don't know if I should keep it or give it up for adoption."

"*Adoption?* You are really considering that?"

Ari nodded, not able to look at Silas while she answered. "I wasn't a very good mother to Alexa. My crazy work schedule had me on assignment all the time, and when I was home, I was too busy or tired to spend quality time with her. And now, exiled from the Old Guard, I don't have the support network to watch a baby while I'm away, or in case something happens to me."

"We could raise our child together. We could take care of him, or her, and I'm sure Sam would help out," Silas offered. "I've only changed a couple of diapers in my life and both with Alexa. I don't know what kind of father I would be, but I am willing to try."

Ari began to cry. "You're not making this easy for me."

Silas gently held Ari's hand. "Ari, let me take care of you. Let me take care of all of us." He gently placed his hand on her stomach.

"I want that. I want to so badly, but . . ."

"But what?" Silas asked. "This is still about Jim and Alexa, isn't it?"

"If you were in my position, wouldn't you still be in love with the family that had been ripped from your arms? It's just been so long and I've felt so miserable and lonely . . ."

"I guess," Silas answered, "but Ari—Jim remarried and restarted his life. This is our chance to start your life over with a new family, just like Jim did. What if you change your mind after you give our kid up for adoption? Or what if you are never able to get back to the Old Guard and reconcile with Jim? Are you willing to waste the opportunity for a new life with me? With us?"

Ari looked down at the counter. Her mind floundered in confusion.

Silas threw his hands up. "So that's it—your love for me isn't strong enough or good enough. And you just want to give up our child for adoption without even trying?"

Ari didn't respond. Tears still flowing, she stood, staring down at the curl of toothpaste on her toothbrush.

"Fine! Do whatever you want. I don't care." Silas' anger boiled over as he stormed out of the bathroom, slamming his door.

For the first time that she could remember, Ari felt damaged and alone. She leaned her back up against the sink and slid down to where she sat on the floor, crying. *"Lord, please forgive me. 'Save me, O God, for the waters have come up to my neck. I sink in the miry depths, where there is no foothold. I have come into the deep waters; the floods engulf me. I am worn out calling for help; my throat is parched. My eyes fail, looking for my God.'"*

Ari took several minutes to gather herself together. During that time she debated with herself what she should do. She picked herself up off the floor, fixed her makeup, and grabbed her leather jacket. Ari stormed into the living room and slid her bike keys off of the hook.

The emotional Outrider had the door handle in her hand when a voice stopped her. "Ari, where are you going?" Christina asked.

"Town. I need to get something. And some air."

Sam ran up to her. "Ari, you shouldn't go into town without anyone."

"Nothing will happen. We're in the middle of nowhere."

Sam grabbed a light jacket, slipped it on, and hurriedly put on his shoes. "Then I'm coming with."

"I'm really not in the mood for any company, Sam." Ari said, protesting.

"I don't care. Besides, I regret not buying those persimmons when I had a chance. Shall we?" Sam said as he held the door. He rolled his eyes to heaven as he closed the door behind them.

About an hour later, Silas came out of his room. He glanced around and saw Christina sitting on a pile of cushions, reading. "Where's Ari? She's not in her room."

"She went to town and begrudgingly dragged Sam along. Why?"

Silas' face became concerned. "We need to find her and get her home to safety."

"Why?" Christina asked.

"I just have this feeling," Silas said. "Let me change and we'll go."

Ari pulled the motorcycle up to the curb of the main street. Even with a small town as the one they were in, the early evening bustled with patrons beginning their long night indulging in one of several izakaya. The smell of grilled fish and meats lingered in the still air; the sound of laughter and cheering surrounded Sam and Ari.

As they passed one such establishment, a pair of eyes watched them walk past the doorway.

Sam looked at his watch. "I'm headed down to the market before they close. Do you want to come with?"

"I'll join you there in a minute. I need to pick up something I wanted to get for a while."

"What is it?" Sam inquired.

Ari tried to smile while she answered. "It's a bracelet for Silas. Except I think I'm going to get it engraved." Sam continued to walk down the main street while Ari turned into a side alley and knocked on a door. A young gentleman opened the door and bowed. Ari bowed and entered.

Two figures stopped at the alley, stalking the couple. One of them continued after Sam, the other patiently waited in the shadows.

A quarter of an hour later, Ari backed out of the doorway, bowing deeply at the jeweler. *"Arigato gozaimasu,"* she said as she slipped the small package into an inside pocket. The jeweler bowed and the door closed. A few seconds later, his lights went out.

Ari took two steps and a shadowy figure stepped in front of her. Ari stopped abruptly and began to step back. "I don't want any trouble," she told the unknown person. Ari realized that in her haste leaving the house, she didn't arm herself. *Lord, I need Your protection. Send Your angels to surround me.*

"When I saw you, I couldn't believe it. I thought you were dead," the vaguely familiar female voice said. Ari strained to see if she could see who spoke, but the streetlights behind the figure kept the person's face hidden. "I actually had to do a double take, didn't I, Josh?"

A hand roughly grabbed Ari's arm, holding her. "Yes, ma'am," the young man said.

"I mean, after all, we came here to eat a few skewers of the best grilled chicken I've ever tasted. I had to come back for more. We should be on an assignment right now, but I think we're going to be delayed a bit longer than I thought. You were the last person I thought I'd ever see again," the voice explained.

Josh muffled Ari's mouth with his gloved hand and dragged her further back into the shadows in the back of the alley. Small businesses lined the alleyway, with metal bars or doors rolled down for the night. The nearest human to hear anything slept over a block away. Josh jerked Ari's head to the side and down.

Ari struggled to get free, her eyes wide in shock and horror. Her longtime mentor and friend Sam lay lifeless in a pool of his own blood. The plastic bag he carried lay a few feet away; persimmons lay strewn on the ground as if a small struggle occurred. Tears welled up in Ari's eyes. Sam was shot in the upper back and then again in the head, through his right temple. His brown eyes stared out, vacant and devoid of life.

"I don't know if you heard, but your now ex-husband Jim married me." The person stepped forward and Ari could now see the voice belonged Sarah. "From the very first day I met you, I wanted to be you. Not just like you . . . I wanted everything you had. And now I've accomplished that. I'm even the top Outrider, just like you were."

"Sarah? I don't understand. You could have been . . ." Ari began to say, but was cut off.

"No! *I am.* There is no 'could have been.' I am the person that sent you crashing off that pedestal. But you still alive poses a real problem: your presence could ruin my perfect life with my perfect marriage." She grabbed Ari and threw her against the brick wall.

Before Ari could recover, she felt a searing pain in her upper abdomen. Her hand instinctively held the spot. Blood began to trickle from between her fingers. Ari's legs began to give out. She slid down the wall to a sitting position; a smear of blood on the brick indicated that the wound went through her.

Ari felt the second blade hit her chest. Her heart pierced; she felt her blood pulse out of the wound with the last few of its beats. Her body slumped to the side and she lay on the pavement, her own puddle of blood growing with each second. Ari tried to reach and grab the blades to pull them out, but her fingers barely twitched.

"I can see why Kane called you a cockroach, Ari," Sarah sneered, "you really do refuse to die, don't you?"

Sarah raised her blade gun, aimed to shoot Ari in her temple. Ari knew a blade inside her skull would not extract cleanly. The barbs would get caught inside the skull cavity, making any chance of survival, let alone recovery, nearly impossible. Sarah pushed the barrel of the gun onto Ari's head. Before the auburn-haired Outrider could squeeze the trigger, she felt the pain and the sound of bone and tendon snapping as a blade hit her right shoulder. Sarah dropped her gun, unable to hold on with the injured arm.

Josh raised his gun at the shadow, only to be shot in his shoulder, and then again in his chest. He collapsed, reaching out for Sarah as if to ask for her help.

Sarah panicked, unable to shoot or continue to fight with her injury. She self-transported out of danger, leaving her cohort Josh to fend for himself.

Silas and Christina stepped out of the shadow and kept their guns out in case Sarah decided to return with help. Christina checked Sam quickly. She closed his eyes and then covered his face with her jacket. She stepped over to Josh, who was shivering and slipping into shock. She pulled the blades out and gently laid him on his back. "Why?" She asked the young man.

"No choice . . ." Josh whispered, "Forgive me." His breath sounded shallow and labored.

"It's not me that you should be asking for forgiveness," Christina told him.

Silas ran up to Ari, pulled the blades out from her back, and checked for a pulse. "C'mon, Ari," he told her. "Not now, not yet. You are an overcomer." He rolled her gently onto her back and unzipped her jacket. A small velvet box fell out of her jacket pocket. Silas quickly picked it up and slid it into his pocket to give to her later. Everywhere around Ari, Silas saw blood. He knew the hit she took to her heart should have killed anyone. *But Ari isn't just anyone.*

Blood ran from the corners of her mouth as she tried to breathe and talk. Tears ran from the corner of her eyes.

"Don't talk. Save your energy," he told her as he gave pressure to her wounds. Ari grimaced, her mouth filled with blood. Silas looked up at Christina. "Get Kenji." Christina nodded and disappeared.

"Please forgive me," Ari whispered and gasped.

Moisture began to build up in the corner of his eyes. Silas winked at his friend. "Forgive you for what?"

Silas turned her head to the side, allowing her to spit out blood that choked her airway. A few large drops fell from the sky, and then a steady heavy rain fell, hiding Silas' tears.

A minute later, Kenji and Christina appeared. Kenji rushed over to Silas and Ari. Silas looked up at Kenji. "I'm sorry to have gotten you out in the rain."

Kenji examined Ari. "Grab the others. Bring them back to Tokyo." Kenji grabbed Ari and self-transported back to Kyrie.

———◆———

The next morning the rain continued. Silas looked at the clock: Kenji and Christina worked on Ari and the others for hours. While he waited, Silas dug in his pocket and retrieved the small box. Ari's dried blood coated the velvet, making it rough and course. He opened the box, wondering if the item became damaged in the attack. Tears welled up in his eyes again. A small blood-stained card inside simply read "Silas, please forgive me." Underneath the card sat a man's platinum ID bracelet. On the top side of the small plaque, Ari had inscribed "SILAS" in a plain, unassuming font. On the flip side she inscribed two scriptural references: "PSA 19:12" and "SoS 8:7."

Silas knew the Bible, but the two verses escaped his memory. He walked down the hall to the common area and searched a small bookshelf for a Bible. *I hope there's one that is in English.* After flipped through a couple, he finally found one. "Psalms 19 . . .12 . . . '*But who can discern their own errors? Forgive my hidden faults.*'" Silas smiled at Ari's quirky apology. "Song of Solomon 8:7 . . . '*Many waters cannot quench love; rivers cannot sweep it away. If one were to give all the wealth of one's house for love, it would be utterly scorned.*'" He placed the Bible back on the shelf and carefully returned the bracelet and card into the stained box. He slipped the box back into his pocket until he could give it back to Ari.

Christina finally came out. Her eyes were red from crying. "We tried to revive Sam, but we couldn't."

"What about Ari and Josh?" Silas asked.

"Josh is rough, but he'll make it. We were able to stabilize Ari. She's alive and breathing on her own."

"What about the baby?"

Christina looked at Silas, surprised. "She talked to you last night?"

Silas rubbed his neck when he answered, "Yeah, and I kind of got angry at her decision to want to give it up for adoption."

"I'm sorry, Silas. Neither Kenji nor I could hear the fetus' heartbeat or feel any movement. The poor little guy probably couldn't handle all the trauma. When Ari is stronger, Kenji will induce labor."

"Labor? Can't he just remove it?"

"Giving birth is less traumatic to Ari's body," Christina answered.

"Yeah, but it's not her body I'm worried about," he said as he pointed to his head.

Christina sighed. "Either way, she will have to come to terms with the death of Sam and her baby. She's a strong gal. We just need to make sure we're here to offer our support and love. She's sedated and resting, if you want to visit her."

Silas perked up. "Thanks." He walked in and saw two gurneys, one with Josh sedated and restrained. On the other, Ari lay motionless. Several bags of intravenous liquids hung on a stand behind her. Her face and body were pale from the lack of blood. Silas slid a folding curtain between the two beds, giving Ari more privacy from one of her attackers.

Kenji returned to her bedside after he washed his hands. He double-checked the bags, then gently rocked a bag of what appeared to be blood before placing it back on its hook. "From the look of her scars, this is probably not the first time she's gone through this."

"Um, I think you're right. Does she know?" Silas asked.

"Partly. She kept asking about Sam and her baby. I told her about Sam, and she became so upset I had to sedate her. She doesn't know about her baby yet."

"Why is Josh restrained?"

"Christina did that. She wanted to make sure he doesn't take off before she can question him," Kenji said. He broke out laughing. "I feel sorry for him already."

Ari stirred. "Sam . . ."

"Ari, how do you feel?" Silas held Ari's hand.

"Silas . . . Sam . . . help him." Ari slurred her words.

Silas looked at Kenji before answering. "Ari, I'm so sorry. Sam didn't make it."

Ari began to sob. "He should have stayed at the house. He only came with me to keep me company. What about the baby?" Ari rubbed her belly.

Silas looked at Kenji again. The physician stepped forward. "Ari, we believe your fetus didn't survive the attack. I haven't been able to register a heartbeat or any movement. I'm sorry."

Ari continued to sob. She covered her face with her hand, the back of her hand covered with tape as it held needles in place. Intravenous tubes trailed down her arm and up to the bags hanging behind her. "He didn't even have a chance at life before he was killed."

Silas gently grasped her other hand. Dried blood still stained her fingers and nails. He didn't speak. He just wanted to offer her someone she could vent her emotions to.

After a few minutes, Ari squeezed Silas' hand. "I appreciate your concern, but I think I just want to be alone for a while."

"Sure, uh, okay. Just call if you need anything," Silas said as he left the room.

For the next couple of hours, Ari tried to grasp what happened. Occasionally she broke out in sobs. Suddenly, Ari grimaced in pain. After a few seconds, she took a deep breath. "I think I felt a contraction," she said as she puffed.

Kenji rushed over and asked, "Are you sure?"

"It kind of felt like it," she answered. Suddenly she groaned, holding her lower abdomen. "I've been feeling them for an hour or so, but I didn't know if the wounds caused the discomfort."

"Ari, you are not strong enough to go through labor right now. It is too much stress for your healing tissue," Kenji warned.

"Kenji-san, I don't really have a say in this. It's just happening." Ari said between breaths.

Kenji examined Ari. "You have already begun to dilate."

"What do I do?" Ari asked.

"Just relax. Don't bear down, not yet. It's too early. Let me get Christina to help." Kenji left the small room and came back with Silas and Christina.

Silas sat next to Ari again and held her hand. He scooped out an ice chip and fed it to Ari.

Ari hadn't realized how parched her mouth was. The ice chip tasted like iron. She realized her mouth still contained her own blood from hours ago. "Thank you," she quietly said to Silas.

"Just call me a chip off the old block," Silas joked.

Ari laughed and then winced. Her chest and abdomen injuries reminded her of their presence. Then her grip tightened around Silas' hand as she felt another powerful contraction.

Christina tried to calm her friend while she checked under one of Ari's bandages. "Ari, try to keep breathing. Don't tense your muscles. You're bleeding from your wounds."

"I would pay a million dollars for either of you to take my place right now," Ari puffed.

"Ari, this may be difficult for you. Your hips haven't fully repositioned to widen the birth canal. The fetus is still pretty small, so I don't think it will be as bad as it could be."

Ari groaned as another contraction overtook her. "Great. As if giving birth is a walk in the park to begin with. Just tell me when, doc."

"You're still not fully dilated. Just hold off for a little while longer, Ari."

For the next hour, Ari clenched her teeth and fists trying to redirect her urge to push at each of the growing contractions. She kept her mind focused on whatever Bible scriptures she could recall at that particular moment. Christina's brow furrowed. She glanced at Kenji. Her eyes led Kenji's eyes to Ari's bandages. Blood soaked through the gauze. Christina added additional bandages on top and pressed at Ari's abdominal wound.

Kenji checked Ari's blood pressure and saw that it had dropped again. He examined Ari. Seeing that she was just barely at the minimum dilation diameter, he took a deep breath. "Okay Ari, this is it. At your next contraction, I want you to push."

Ari was exhausted. She pushed at the next big contraction, but she was barely conscious. She couldn't catch her breath. Christina placed an oxygen mask over Ari's nose and mouth. "Ari, you just have a little longer. It's almost over."

Josh heard Ari's scream before he opened his eyes. Still groggy from the drugs, he tried to get up. He realized he was restrained. He heard several voices talking on the other side of the privacy curtain.

"Ari, stay with us. The head is almost out. You need to keep pushing,"

"Her blood pressure is dropping. Ari—stay with us."

"I'm so tired. No more," Ari pleaded.

"Give me one more big push, Ari. Keep going. Do it now!"

Josh heard Ari scream again.

"You're doing it, Ari. That's it . . ."

Josh heard Ari cry, almost like a wail, and then the room was silent. He never heard a newborn infant cry or the sounds of joy or celebration. Then he heard a man's solemn voice: "I'm sorry, Ari."

Grief and regret filled Josh's heart when he realized he and Sarah may have been responsible for killing Ari's unborn child. He began to cry uncontrollably.

CHAPTER NINETEEN

The breeze that blew into Ari's room felt cool, even with a cloudless, sunny sky. The late summer hinted to the change in seasons. For safety reasons, Kenji moved the Outriders to another home in the northern part of the country, about ten miles south of the city of Mutsu, on the northern most tip of the country's main island of Honshu. Well hidden from the street, thickets of pine and other hearty coastal trees surrounded the house. Ari could hear the waves break from the beach, located several hundred yards from where she sat.

Ari occupied an overstuffed moss-green microfiber chair that Kenji moved to face the opened sliding door panel. He thought her spirits would lift when she viewed the garden and at the thicket of trees beyond. An unassuming small square table occupied the side of the chair. An unopened bottle of water and a box of tissues competed for space against a small arrangement of flowers that Keiko placed to give Ari's room some color.

Ari found little comfort in the serene sight of the trees, or even the gentle rustle of the leaves in the breeze. The oddly shaped ginkgo leaves shook in the wind; the trees looked like they shimmered in the sunlight. Ari stared at the scenery, but her mind drifted elsewhere. Her thoughts and grief distracted her. She could not get beyond the losses she experienced even though a week had passed.

Silas briefly stood at Ari's bedroom door. Worry furrowed in his forehead for his friend. Ari had only spoken a few words since the night of the attack. He knocked on the door jam. "Hey, Ari, we missed you at lunch."

No response or acknowledgement came from Ari. Silas could not tell whether the healing Outrider had even heard him. Ari continued to stare out at the yard.

Silas moved closer. He sat on the step leading out to the garden, on the other side of the small table from Ari. His back leaned up against the sliding panel's frame so he could face toward his distressed friend.

Silas stretched for something to talk to Ari about. "I thought the memorial service you held for Sam and our son Matthew at the cabin yesterday was nice: Short and simple. I liked that. I think Sam would have liked to be buried next to your parents. And I know your parents will watch over Matthew."

He paused before he continued. "I wanted to apologize for the other night if you felt more pressure and confusion because of me. I felt like I caused you to go in to town so you could blow off some steam. I should have gone with you. Perhaps none of this would have happened."

The silence continued, but he knew she heard him. A fresh flow of tears ran down her cheek. He continued to talk to her. "I never quite understood why God seems to allow some to walk with a superficial relationship with Him and appear to go through life blessed and without any misfortune, and others, like you, who are obedient and righteous in His eyes, seem to go through trial after trial like a modern day Job."

Still silent, Ari continued to cry. Silas also continued. "I wish I could help you, Ari. I wish I could make your pain and sadness go away. I wish I could turn back the clock so none of this happened. *'Praise be to the God and Father of our Lord Jesus Christ, the Father of compassion and the God of all comfort who comforts us in all our troubles, so that we can comfort those in any trouble with the comfort we ourselves receive from God. For just as we share abundantly in the sufferings of Christ, so also our comfort abounds through Christ.'* Please say something, Ari. We miss you. I miss you."

Ari still didn't say anything and barely even moved. Her tears and occasional sniffle were the only indications she heard him.

Silas got to his feet and took a step away before he stopped. "I almost forgot: This fell out of your pocket when we were trying to control your bleeding in the alley." He held the soiled velvet box out to her.

Ari's eyes shifted to look at the box, and she closed her eyes briefly, trying to get her emotions under control. "The box is for you, Silas. I was going to give it to you the following morning. I'm sorry it's all stained. You can open it if you want, if you haven't done so already."

"I actually did open it right after you were brought back to Tokyo. I wanted to see if whatever you bought had been broken." He opened the box and held the bracelet up. The sun glistened off the facets on the chain links. He put it on his left wrist and said, "It's beautiful Ari. Thank you."

"I just wish circumstances were different."

"Yeah, me too," Silas agreed. "I will respect your wish, whatever you want or don't want to do."

Ari nodded and returned to viewing the outdoors.

Silas' voice perked up. "We thought of going into the city this afternoon. Kenji thought it might be good for you to get some light exercise."

"Thanks for the offer, Silas, but I just want to sit here."

Silas nodded. "Um, okay. I'll be in the living room if you need anything." He briefly waited for a moment to see if she would say anything before he retreated out of her room.

Five minutes didn't pass before Christina burst in. "Oh, no you don't. I am not going to let my best friend wallow in sorrow and depression, wasting away like some geriatric case in a nursing home. Ari, *you are a child of the Most High.* He loves you so much that He gave His only Son to death so that we may have life. LIFE! Do you think Sam is sad for leaving you? No way. He is up there sitting at the right hand of Jesus, experiencing unspeakable joy without tears or sadness. You should be rejoicing for him."

"How can I rejoice knowing that I caused both him and Matthew to lose their lives?"

Christina looked at Ari, confused. "Ari, what are you talking about?"

"They both would still be alive if hadn't lost my cool and gone into town," Ari explained.

Christina stood behind the chair and hugged Ari from behind. "Don't beat yourself up about the past. You can't change anything that has already happened. If you think you've done something wrong, ask for forgiveness, try not to do it again, and move on with your life. The devil will try to keep you wallowing in sadness and regret until your dying day if he is given the chance. When you can't get over what has happened in the past or keep sinning, you are hanging Jesus back on the cross. I know you love Him, Ari, just like He loves you."

"Does He really?"

Christina looked confused when she answered. "Does He really *what*? Love you?"

Ari's head hung as the tears began to flow again. She spoke softly, "If Jesus loves me so much, why do things like this always happens to me? It's like He doesn't want me to experience love with another person. Every time I do and begin to feel happiness, it all unravels. I feel like I'm cursed."

Christina paused, asking God for the right words to say to her friend. "Well, um, I know God chastens those He loves, like a father to his child. You knew getting into a relationship with Silas was wrong. You felt it in your heart. But you went your own way and decided to be disobedient to what God had placed in your heart. The First Epistle of Peter says "'The stone the builders rejected has become the cornerstone,' and, 'a stone that causes people to stumble and a rock that makes them fall.' They stumble because they disobey the message—which is also what they were destined for. But you are a chosen people, a royal priesthood, a holy nation, God's special possession, that you may declare the praises of* *him who called you out of darkness into his wonderful light."*

Christina looked Ari in the eyes as she continued. "You of all people I know, God has set apart to do His good work. When your Father tells you to do something, it is because He has your best interest in mind."

"So, what? God want me to spend my life as a lonely, single spinster for the rest of my life?" Ari asked.

Christina shook her head. "I don't think so, Ari. Perhaps He is trying to show you the things that you cherish the most? Or maybe He is that jealous God from the Old Testament and wants you to focus on Him and only Him, at least for right now. You need to ask Him why and what you need to do to get right with Him. Now, am I going to have to make you get up and out of that chair? Because you know I will, even if I have to drag you kicking and screaming." Christina stretched her arm out to Ari, offering her hand to her friend.

Ari reached up and grasped Christina's hand. Christina wrapped her arms around her friend as they walked out of the room.

◆

Sarah stood confidently in front of the council. Her husband Jim normally led the inquiries; she hid her bad decisions in the past, and this inquiry felt no different. As she sat down, she held her right arm and winced as if in pain, even though she felt none. She didn't really need the sling to support her arm, but she wore it to sway emotions in her favor. If anything, Sarah knew how to play her audience.

Jim continued to stand as he addressed the room. "For reasons of possible conflict of interest, I remove myself from this particular inquiry. Dave will act as the interim lead council." With those words, Jim stepped around the table and winked at Sarah as he passed her on his way out the door.

"Excuse me, sir, but I noticed that Madam Overseer is not present," Sarah asked.

Dave explained, "Many of us rotate in this role, Sarah. This particular time the roster did not have her listed."

"Mrs. Sommers," Dave said as he moved into Jim's chair, flipping several pieces of paper in a folder, "we've read your report on the incident. Can you please tell us in more detail how you and Josh were attacked?"

"Um, sure." Sarah sat up straight. "We arrived at the coordinate site and didn't realize we were already surrounded."

"Surrounded by what?" asked one of the council members.

"Demons, ma'am."

"How many?"

Sarah shrugged, "Um, I am not sure. At least three or four."

"And how exactly did you end up with a blade gun blade in your shoulder?" asked another council member named Aaron.

"Blade gun blade?" Sarah asked.

Aaron explained, "Yes. The weapon did not have a handle to the blade, and the aerodynamics are such that it would have come from a blade gun. To our knowledge, demons have never used a blade gun."

For the first time ever, Sarah realized her fabricated story may have more holes than she could fill. "I didn't realize that, sir. In the chaos, I knew Josh got hit. Maybe Josh's gun misfired and hit me in the shoulder."

Several members of the council, including Dave, made notes in their files. Dave asked, "Why did you leave Josh? As the lead, you should have brought him back."

"I thought he was with me," Sarah said as she began to cry. "If I could go back and get him, I would."

Dave turned to one of the other council members and whispered something. The council member nodded. Dave looked at Sarah, "Mrs. Sommers, that will be all for now. If we have any questions, we will let you know. Thank you."

Sarah stood up and walked out of the room. Dave paused as he tried to put his head around what he just witnessed.

Aaron spoke up. "As I told you all before, Sarah is not telling us the entire truth. I have brought it up before to Petra and Jim, but they have not taken my grievances seriously."

One of the other council members spoke up. "Are we absolutely sure that the blade extracted from her shoulder came from Silas?"

Dave nodded. "I saw the markings. They were unmistakable. I had commented to him at one time on the beauty of the blades' workmanship and design. Here are the pictures of the blades that Josh used, the ones from the file we had on Silas, and the blade we extracted from Sarah's shoulder." Dave laid the pictures next to each other, and the council examined them. Even though the front half of the blade disintegrated when it hit bone in Sarah's shoulder, the unmistakable elegant curved design embossed within the metal matched Silas' blade.

"So Silas is still alive? Do you think he went back to the Tempest?" asked another council member.

"Even so, why would Sarah lie about that?" Dave answered. "Aaron, did the team finish examining the coordinate area where the attack occurred?"

Aaron handed Dave another folder. "Yes. There were no signs of any attack. Sarah's report mentioned she hit only one demon, but she is missing four of the six of her blades from her clip. We examined the area for the missing blades, and there were none. The weather had been clear between the time of the attack and the investigation, yet we didn't find Josh's body, or for that matter, any blood or trampled foliage. No one had been in that area for weeks."

Dave sighed and sat back in his chair. He rubbed his eyes and forehead. "I don't look forward to the conversation I am about to have with our chief overseer, Petra. She has a special fondness for Sarah, and obviously, so do some of the senior members of the council, including Jim. Be absolutely sure that the information you are giving me is accurate. I don't want to appear that we are picking on their favorite Outrider. Make sure I have your final reports on my desk by this evening. That will be all. Thank you."

◆

The thick fog blanketed the area, adding to the dreary feeling of the day. Josh woke up late that morning, unable to find the internal motivation to get out of bed. After weeks of being threatened and drilled by Christina, his tough-man exterior cracked. Ever since the day Ari led him to the Lord, he had felt a growing subconscious that spoke to him, guiding him in his walk. For the first time in years, he began to feel guilty about questionably ethical actions that before he would never had a second thought about. That dreary morning, he humbly bowed his head and asked for forgiveness from the Lord, and like the week before, he restarted his walk with Jesus. Despite this, he avoided Ari, not knowing what words to say to her. He knew that eventually he would have to talk to her.

Ari also had been avoiding contact with Josh. She still couldn't understand how he could have allowed Sarah to murder Sam and nearly take her life as well. Ari continued to pray for him, to allow God to open his heart and eyes to the truth.

After dressing, Josh grabbed an apple and made his way to the other building where the others were practicing. He stood next to a wood column by the entrance, watching the trio practice mastering their weapons.

Ari faced away from Josh as she took aim with her bow to a straw target in the far corner, fifty yards away on the other side of the room. Steve talked to her. "Ari, the lab results finally came back on the metal. The report was inconclusive. They said that the metal reacted like nothing they had ever seen before. They couldn't get it to break down to analyze its molecular structure. Where did you say you found this?"

"In a cave. We knew the weapons were ancient, from over a thousand years ago." She shot three consecutive arrows; all sank deep within the bull's eye or the innermost circle.

Josh's eyes shifted across the floor to Silas as he swung his golden sword at Christina. Christina blocked his sword's slice with a sai that she had flat against the back of her forearm. Instinctively her head tucked under her arm, freeing her other arm to swipe her dagger at Silas' midrift.

Silas jumped back and swung his sword. Christina redirected his sword blade with her sai to her side and twisted her wrist. His sword now locked, jammed between the tines of sai. Before Christina was able to twist her sai again to free the sword from his grip, Silas stepped forward and kicked Christina back, sending her off balance and tumbling to the floor. Silas went on the offensive, striking hard as Christina continued to tumble clear of the blade. Silas stepped in front of a column and cornered Christina.

"Ready to submit to my superior swordsmanship?" Silas huffed as he pointed his sword at his opponent.

"I would, if it were truly superior," Christina teased.

Silas raised his sword over his head, and Christina took the opportunity to gain the advantage. She threw her dagger, sinking it deep into the sleeve of Silas' jacket and into the column behind him. His right arm was pinned immobile above his head. She used her sai to knock the sword out of his other hand, and then she pressed the length of the sai against his throat.

A couple of claps came from the room; the instructor and Ari walked up to the duo. Ari laughed, "Why, Christina, I do believe that this is the first time I've seen you glowing with perspiration."

Christina flopped onto her back, wiping her brow and upper lip. "Sweat, Ari. I'm glowing with drips of sweat."

Silas finally freed his arm from the wooden pole. He examined the holes in his jacket. "I would hate to see what you would have done to stop me if I decided to go sleeveless."

"Ari," Steve said, "do you think you're strong enough for some swordplay?"

"It depends. Whom will I be sparring against?" Ari asked.

"Me," Steve answered. "I promise to go easy on you. Why don't you put the armor on? It will help support your muscles."

Ari nodded. She walked past Josh to the corner, where a breastplate sat propped against the wall. As Ari adjusted the armor, Josh approached her. "Ma'am," he stuttered.

"Yes?" Ari asked as she pulled on a leather strap.

"I wanted to apologize for the attack. I didn't realize what she planned until it already happened. I should have tried to stop Sarah."

"Don't beat yourself up about it, Josh. As someone reminded me re-

282 | PATRICIA REAMY

cently, you can't change the past. I forgive you. Just be sure not become someone else's pawn."

"I can't believe Sarah left me for dead."

Ari adjusted the plate around her neck then grabbed her sword. Not sure of what he just saw, Josh tilted his head as he saw the breastplate adjust to Ari's petite figure. "In times of stress, you will find out who will be at your side and who will leave you for an easier path," Ari said as she walked past.

Ari approached Steve. Steve raised his sword and gave Ari last minute instructions. "Ari, if you need to stop, just give the word." Ari nodded. They both raised their longswords out in front. Ari stared at Steve from behind her blade. Steve was about to make his move when, suddenly, Ari stumbled backwards and dropped her sword to the floor.

Ari felt a wave of shock and sadness as the vision revealed itself. Her eyes jerked from side to side as saw her former colleagues fight for their lives against the Nephilim. The weapons they used were ineffective, and one by one, she saw her friends cut down by the creatures' swords and arrows. A familiar, more mature face of her daughter falls lifeless to the ground, her heart pierced by a dagger. "No, Lord. Not Hollywood. Not Alexa . . ."

"What's wrong?" Christina asked. "What happened?"

"It's Hollywood. They're going to be attacked by the Nephilim."

"How many?" Silas asked.

"Hard to say, but I estimate at least a dozen or so," Ari said as she got up.

"A dozen? Ari, we barely were able to handle one." Silas winced.

"Yes, but now we are armed with something I know can defeat them. The question is, is our training enough?"

The three Outriders looked at Steve as he spoke, looking at the group skeptically. "I suspect you are not actors, are you?"

Ari shook her head. "Would you believe us if I told you that we are warriors of God, fighting against demons?"

"With your stamina and abilities, it doesn't surprise me at all," Steve admitted.

Ari said, "Steve, we need to ask a favor. Our work requires a certain amount of anonymity. . ."

Steve held his hand up. "Say no more. I work with celebrities all the time. Mum's the word. I think my work here is done anyway. Kenji knows how to get ahold of me if you need a refresher." He approached his students and shook their hands. "It has been a pleasure working with all of you." He reached out to shake Ari's hand. Ari reciprocated, except she pulled him in for a hug. Steve held Ari tight. "Don't you dare let anything happen to any of you or else I'll come back." The Outriders helped load the truck and watched their instructor drive away.

Ari stared at the long winding driveway as the dust settled. Christina stepped to her side and asked, "What now?"

Ari shook her head. "Honestly, I don't know. We need to help them, or at the very least, warn them."

"You realize that you face an inquiry and more time on the security block," Silas told Ari. "You essentially broke out."

"But without our help, you know they don't stand a chance," Christina pointed out as she packed the weapons up.

"Yeah, I seriously weighed the possibility of spending the rest of my life down in the security block against helping the very people that put me there to begin with," Ari said.

"Perhaps we need to step back and assess our options," Silas said. "The only way to get a two-year-old kid to stop a temper tantrum is either by punishing him or giving him what he wants, or at least dangle the candy in front of him."

"I'm not quite following this train of thought," Ari said.

Silas leaned forward. "We approach the Old Guard, tell them about the attack and that we know how to defeat them and will help, but in return we want amnesty: a full and irrevocable pardon."

"And if they don't bite?" Ari asked.

"We tell them they have some housecleaning to do." Silas unwrapped a small bundle. Inside were two used blades with dark stains. "I pulled these out of you, Ari." I have another bundle with those that were extracted from Sam."

Josh shook his head. "I don't know if that would be too wise. Sarah has become a favorite of the council as well as the chief overseer."

"Who, Isaac?" Silas asked.

Josh shook his head. "Petra. And she and Sarah seem to hang out a lot with each other," Josh replied. "I think Petra mentored her or something."

"What happened to Isaac?" Ari asked.

"After they found out you were missing, they interrogated Isaac. Before they killed him, Petra forced him to support her for his position. At first he didn't agree, but then he gave in."

"And how is it that you know all of this?" Ari asked.

"I hang with Sarah. She can't keep a secret about anything."

Ari shook her head. "I don't know . . ."

"If what you told me about what happened to the organization is true, then Hollywood is the last stronghold of Outriders. Love them or hate them, *they are our family*, Ari. We have an obligation to do what we can for them," Josh pleaded.

"Josh—do you think you can get us in without anyone getting hurt or killed?" Silas asked.

"Hmmm . . . I think so, but the timing has to be perfect."

"And what time would that be?" Ari asked.

Josh didn't answer. He just grinned from ear to ear.

CHAPTER TWENTY

The low clouds and rain of late fall settled on Hollywood. The bottom of the clouds hid the ridgelines. Occasionally, the whiteness tried to spill further down the hills but vaporized a dozen yards, down as if they hit a hidden barrier. The cool winter temperatures were unusual for so early in the year.

Alexa yawned as she plodded into the kitchen. The 18-year-old headed straight for the fridge and a caffeinated soda. Fresh out of Outrider training, the young lady loosely French braided her straight brown hair and tied it back with a bandana. Her fitted gray t-shirt was partially hidden under a black hoodie. Faded jeans and black jazz shoes finished her wardrobe. The young lady rolled her eyes when she saw Sarah approach her father and hang her arms over his shoulders, hugging him from behind.

"That's my greeting to my dad," Alexa growled.

Her friend Trina quickly caught her reaction. The ebony-skinned young Outrider also wore a bandana in her hair. Trina gave Alexa a nudge, and the two giggled. Sarah glared at her stepdaughter before camouflaging it with a pasty smile.

The minutes passed as more Outriders and overseers entered the common area for the meeting. Dave and Aaron took their seats next to Jim. Aaron nudged Dave and whispered, "She's late again."

Dave whispered back, "She does that on purpose. She is showing her power and domination over everyone by making us wait for her. She'll make a grand entrance down the staircase. Just watch."

As if on cue, Petra took her time, as if taking each step of the stair with care and thought. She smiled at the group as she made her way through the waiting crowd. She stood at the head of the table. "Good morning, everyone."

Eyes shifted from their chief overseer to the four mysterious figures who had just self-transported to the back lawn and began to approach the house. All of them wore hooded capes, hiding their identities and vulnerabilities. A couple of the Outriders stood up with their hands on their blade guns.

Through the lightweight waterproof fabric of the hood, Ari could see the tense reaction of the group inside. Josh and Silas led the group, with Ari behind them and Christina taking up the rear. They all wore their armor and weapons with the newly made scabbards and belts. Ari felt like something from the medieval times, in the middle of a crusade.

Still on the other side of the pool, the trio stopped as Josh continued. He unveiled his head, laying the hood down neatly onto his back. The interior mounted a cheer and greeted their lost friend and colleague. Josh approached Petra. "Good morning, Madam."

"Josh, it's great to see you. We thought you were . . ." Petra said, not quite sure what she saw.

"Dead, Madam?" Josh finished her sentence.

"Yes, yes. We're so glad you are okay," Petra said. "Who are those people?"

"They are the ones that saved me, Madam. They are not here to harm us. However, there is a great enemy that is on the way to destroy Hollywood and all that live here."

"Who, The tempest?" someone offered. The group broke out laughing.

"Actually, no. The Tempest is dead. Most have been killed and the few remaining have been dispersed to the corners of the earth," Josh explained. "The ones who destroyed the organization are now on their way to destroy you."

The room became eerily silent. Josh continued, "The organization's building was destroyed not too long ago."

"When is this attack supposed to happen?" Jim asked.

"We are unsure, sir, but we do know that it will happen in the next few weeks. Madam, these warriors have agreed to help train us to destroy this enemy. All they ask for is food, shelter, and amnesty from us."

"Amnesty? That is an odd thing to ask for," Petra said aloud. "Agreed, provided they don't intend on killing us along with the enemy."

"Oh, no, ma'am." Josh grinned as he rushed to the door and waved to the trio.

As Silas, Ari, and Christina walked inside, they removed the hoods from their heads. Ari felt the tenseness in the room. Silas scanned the faces to see how everyone reacted. The newer Outriders questioned each other as to who they were. The older Outriders and overseers stood in silence, shocked.

Sarah couldn't believe her eyes. "How is this possible? You're all dead."

"With man this is impossible, but not with God; all things are possible with God," Christina said.

Petra laughed. "You're kidding, right? I can't agree to anything. Ari escaped from the security block. She can't be trusted." With a nod of her head, several Outriders began to encroach on the exiles. Silas and Christina moved in front of Ari to protect her.

Josh stepped in between the two groups and held his hand up. "Wait. No one is taking anyone into custody, not yet. Madam Overseer, you have to believe me when I say they are your only hope in surviving an attack from the Nephilim."

"Why do you say that?" Petra asked.

Josh answered, "They possess weapons that are effective against them. And they have been trained to use them."

"Show us," Petra demanded. The trio exposed their golden weapons. Petra scoffed, "These medieval utensils? How do you know that these weapons will defeat the Nephilim?"

"Madam, we have been fighting them off and on for the past several years," Ari answered. "Up to now the attacks have only involved one or two individuals. The attack that will happen here will involve several dozen Nephilim."

"Three of you won't be able to defend us," Sarah said.

"True," Ari said, "but we can train you how to use these. You won't be experts in a couple of weeks, but you will be proficient enough to do some damage to the enemy."

"How are we supposed to come up with these weapons on such short notice?" Sarah asked.

"We know where there is a stockpile, as if they are waiting for us to use them against God's enemies," Silas said.

"Interesting," Petra said under her breath. She nodded again, her Outrider moved against the exiles, holding them by their arms.

"Hey! What are you doing?" Josh asked as he struggled to free himself.

"I'm sure we will be able to handle the Nephilim just fine without your help," Petra said.

Josh and the exiles were disarmed and escorted to the security block. Ari and the others were stripped of their street clothes and handed a cotton hospital gown and matching bottoms. After Ari dressed, she noticed movement in one of the cells. She ran up to it. "Isaac?"

"Ari? What are you doing here?" the elderly man asked.

Ari noticed a frailness in his voice she never heard before. "Have they mistreated you here? So help me God if they did," she said as the guards grabbed her. They beat her with a billy club until Ari fell to her knees. They dragged her into the isolation cell at the end of the block and locked the metal door.

The others were pushed into cells and their doors locked. Christina cried out, "What did I ever do? What did any of us do to deserve this?" The guards left, leaving the prisoners alone.

Silas pressed his head against the heavy steel mesh, trying to see the isolation cell's door. "Ari, are you okay?"

He heard a muffled groan come from behind the heavy steel door. Ari had curled up into a fetal position. Her ribs and back hurt, and as a last shot, she had taken a hit across her right jaw. Darkness ruled the isolation cell. Ari floundered around the cold cement floor of her cell with her hands. She tried to find a blanket or something to help ward off the chill. With the exception of a toilet in the far corner and her body, the cell was empty. She huddled in a corner, her knees up against her chest, her arms holding them close.

Ari began to pray, focusing on the positive. *I thank You, Lord, that Your mercy has kept us alive and that You have reunited us with Isaac. I know we are here as part of Your plan. I just have to learn patience.* She heard her name called again. "I'm fine. Cold, but I'm fine."

"Do you have a blanket?" Christina asked.

"No. There isn't anything in here," Ari answered. "I'll be fine. I survived this room for seven years. I just have to do it again. I'll just close my eyes and imagine I'm outside in the warm summer sun."

Dave and Aaron stepped off the elevator and stepped up to Christina. Dave poked his fingers through the steel grating. Christina covered her hands around them. Tears flowed down his face as he spoke. "They told me you were dead."

"I was," Christina said, a tear falling onto her cheek. "Ari revived me."

"We don't have much time. Is what you say true? The Nephilim are going to attack here?" Aaron asked.

"Yes, if they continue to follow the pattern of attacks," Silas said from a couple of cells away from Christina's.

"What can we do?" Dave asked.

Silas laughed. "Pray. Hard. And keep running."

"We should be able to fight them," Dave said.

"The blades are pretty much useless against them. Unless you can hit their eyes to blind them . . . but there are only a handful of us that have shooting skills that good," Silas said. "And three of your sharpshooters are locked down here."

"How bad is this going to be?" Aaron asked, walking over to Silas' cell.

Silas looked the overseer in the eyes. "They will continue to come back every night until they are absolutely sure they have destroyed all of you. And for those of you who escape: They will hunt you down, no matter where you hide on this earth. And once they have destroyed the Outriders, there will be nothing left that has the strength to stop them from destroying the rest of God's people."

Silence overtook the security block as the weight of the words sunk in.

"So, what, this epic battle will happen here in metropolitan Los Angeles?" Aaron asked.

"The battle will begin here, but the war won't end here." Isaac's voice wavered. The two overseers were shocked to see Isaac. Dave ran back to the elevator receiving area to see if an extra set of keys could be found. "Don't waste your time, Dave. Petra broke the key inside the lock."

"Sir, we were told . . ." Dave began.

"I'm sure Petra and those who serve her have told you many lies. What she has become is a shame, really. She is a very bright and talented woman. Apparently, sometime in the past, she stopped listening to the Holy Spirit and chose to follow her head instead of her heart." Isaac shook his head as he talked.

"We need to go before they find out where we are," Aaron said.

"Dave . . ." Ari's voice wavered from behind the heavy steel door.

"Ari?" Dave approached the end of the block and put his ear close to the crack of the door. The others could hear Ari talk to him, but her voice was too soft for anyone to hear what she said. After a few seconds, Dave nodded, "I will, Ari. I promise." He walked up to Aaron and patted him on the shoulder. "We better get going." Dave pressed his hand against Christina's cell, allowing her to mirror her hand to his before the two men stepped back into the elevator.

◆

Once again, time seemed irrelevant to Ari. She knew approximately how much time had passed from the daily meal they were fed. A small slit opened, flooding light into the dark chamber Ari lived in. Temporarily blinded, she saw a bread roll and a bottle of water on her metal tray. The slit closed as Ari asked, "Please, sir. May I have a blanket?" She asked that every day and never received a response until today.

"You should have one with your mattress," a male voice answered.

"There is no mattress and no blanket. Just the gown on my back."

Ari could hear steps walking away before they approached again. The tiny slit opened and a blanket was shoved through the small opening.

Ari grabbed the blanket and wrapped herself in it. "Thank you, sir. May God bless you for your kindness and mercy."

Christina gave a short blessing over their meals before the prisoners ate in silence. Ari could smell the meal the others were given. Slowly cooked onions and meat perfumed the entire floor. Ari tore into her bread. Even though it was stale and hard to chew, she savored every bite. She had read that prisoners in some of the famous castle prisons were given nothing but bread and water not only to break their spirits but also because the meal barely sustained the prisoners. Without energy or willpower, the prisoners had neither the physical nor psychological strength to mount an uprising.

Ari scooted over to a far corner and felt the wall for scratch marks. Carefully counting each, she scraped the hard cement with the tip of a metal spoon she had. "Nineteen."

"Nineteen what, Ari?" Christina asked.

"Days. It's been nineteen days since we got here."

"Shouldn't we have been attacked by now?" Silas asked.

"They're coming. My visions are more detailed every night," Ari said.

"Are we safe down here?" Christina asked.

"The only way they can get in here is from the elevator shaft, and it's too narrow for them to climb down," Silas answered.

Christina voiced concern. "What if no one is left to feed us or even let us out?"

Ari laughed. "If that happens, we will all wish the Nephilim were able to get to us."

Silas lay on top of his bed and stared at the ceiling. "If this is the way we're going to die, this really stinks. I always thought I'd go out in a blaze of glory."

"Yeah," Ari chimed in, "I never liked the idea of dying locked in a dark, cold hole."

"So what are you going to do about it?" Isaac asked.

Ari didn't even have to give his question a second thought. "Nothing. Absolutely nothing. God wants us here for a reason. Perhaps we are here to find you, Isaac. I wait for Him to tell us what our next move will be."

That evening, Ari and the others woke up by the sound of the elevator and footsteps. They came directly to Ari's cell door. Despite her being curled into a tight ball on the far side, the guard dragged Ari out by her foot. The bright lights blinded Ari; her eyes didn't have any time to adjust after weeks of darkness. She was forced to her feet.

Jim felt sickened and repulsed by Ari's physical appearance. Ari tried to wrap herself in the blanket, but the guard removed it from her possession. Her cotton gown was soiled and stained, her short hair matted and overgrown. By the look and odor coming from her, she had not been given a chance to shower or bathe in quite a long time, possibly since arriving. She had also lost considerable amount of weight. She held herself and shivered; her eyes watered from the lights. Her senses were being assaulted from the sudden change.

Jim gave her a few seconds to adjust. He looked at the others and noticed they were in much better shape than his former wife.

"Ari," Jim began, "can you get ahold of more of these weapons? And can you and the others teach us how to use them?"

Ari cried. "Why would I want to save you or anyone else here after what you just put me through? We came here to help you, and this is how you treat us?"

"I'm sorry, Ari. I never thought they would treat anyone like this. Please forgive us," Jim said.

"I want to hear that apology from Petra," Ari said. Christina and Silas voiced their support on her comment.

"That might be kind of hard right now," Dave said.

"Why?" Josh asked.

"She and several other overseers were in what is left of the east wing of the second floor. That side of the house collapsed and we can't get to them. We don't know if they are alive or not, but since we haven't heard any noises or voices, we assumed they were killed."

"The attack has begun, and you're right—we can barely slow them down let alone stop them," Dave said. "They made it inside the house and to the second floor and first basement levels. They suddenly gave up and left."

"They leave before sunrise. I think they are sensitive to sunlight," Ari mentioned. "Up until recently they have only attacked near dense forests where they are near the shade. They will return after sundown."

Silas shook his head and said, "If the attack has started, it's too late. There is no way we can teach you how to handle these weapons in a few hours. It takes weeks of intensive training."

"Then it's too late for us?" Aaron asked.

"How many were there and how many were you able to kill?" Ari asked.

"Dozens. We were able to kill two," Jim said.

"And how many Outriders did they take out?" Silas asked.

"About twenty of us. We had no idea," Jim answered.

Christina did a quick calculation in her head. "At that rate, they will have eliminated all of you before the weekend."

"We need your help," Jim made a plead to the prisoners.

Ari grabbed the blanket back from the guard and wrapped herself in it. Christina and Silas looked at her for an answer and prayed. "I'm going to regret this," Ari mumbled. "We will help you with the following conditions: we all get amnesty from anything in the past or future; after all, God is the final judge."

"Agreed," Jim said.

"I'm not done with my conditions," Ari interrupted.

"By all means," Jim said.

"We want a full investigation into the reasons why Isaac and I were

294 | PATRICIA REAMY

imprisoned and attacked."

"I have no idea what you are talking about, but agreed," Jim said again.

"We want full control of the war room decisions, and we want to be in charge of this and any future Nephilim battle and its preparation."

"I don't think I can give you that much authority," Jim said.

Ari replied, almost cutting Jim off. "It is crucial that we be able to control who and where they are in order to best optimize our strengths against their weaknesses."

Jim rubbed the back of his neck. "Ari, I don't think the remaining leadership here is going to fly with our organization being led by a former Outrider with a questionable past."

"Then the deal is off," Silas said.

Christina crossed her arms. "Yeah, I'm not picking up a single weapon to fight your battle without Ari in charge."

"You trust her that much?" Dave asked his wife.

"I trust her with my life," Christina said.

Jim glanced at Dave and Aaron to see if they agreed with him. Dave bobbed his head to the side, signaling he agreed with Ari. Jim rolled his eyes. "Fine, I agree to those terms, provided you allow us to assume control again after the battle is done."

"Agreed, provided the leadership will support us in our decisions during the battles," Ari said, and Jim nodded in agreement. "Um, one more request . . ."

"What now?" Jim asked.

"We need quarters—a place to sleep and clean up and get some food."

"We had to shift some folks around, but you can stay in one of the training-level bunk rooms. There should be linen and towels as well as basic toiletries. As far as food—you are welcome to anything we have."

Ari asked, "I'd like to get cleaned up. Where are our belongings?"

Dave and Aaron grabbed bags from the receiving area and handed them to their owners.

"Our weapons. We'll need them eventually as well," Ari said.

"We'll make sure you get them when you are done cleaning up and dressing," Jim said.

"What time is it?" Ari asked.

"Eight-thirty in the morning," Jim answered.

Ari continued, "Have anyone that is able-bodied meet us in the common area in one hour. Dave—I need for you to assess everyone to find the best sharpshooters. These Outriders will have to be able to shoot a three-inch moving target at fifty feet. If there are other Outriders that can throw a hand blade accurately—keep those in mind as well."

Dave nodded. Ari continued her instructions. "Aaron, if you can please escort Isaac to Jesse." Aaron nodded as Ari spoke to her mentor. "Isaac, sir? I would appreciate if you stayed with Jesse. I think that would be the safest place for you right now."

Ari followed everyone to the elevator and to the training level. The Old Guard was between classes, so the exiles had the entire floor to themselves.

Ari looked at Christina, "Chrissy, you should be with your husband."

"Dave and I agreed I need to focus on the work at hand," the blonde Outrider said, biting her lip.

"Christina," Ari corrected her friend, "after the meeting, spend a few hours with your husband. It may be the last time you will be able to. Just report back to me before dinner."

Silas checked out one of the bunk rooms. "Do you want the guys in one room and the girls in the other?"

"Why don't we all stay in one room? If we need to get going quickly, we'll be able to do it more efficiently if we're all in one location. I'll sleep toward the back of the room, if you don't mind," Ari suggested.

"Uh, sure. Josh and I will bunk in the first couple of bunks by the door. Why don't you and Christina shower first?"

Ari and Christina disappeared behind the door at the back side of the bunk room. The girls dropped their street clothing on benches in the dressing area and grabbed towels from a rack before stepping in the communal shower area. The water instantly warmed up, and Ari lingered under the hot water. Almost done with her shower, Christina glanced over to her friend and noticed her huddled on the floor under the water. Ari hadn't even lathered yet. She just stood under the water as she inhaled the scent of the shampoo. "Ari, are you okay?"

"I just spent weeks in isolation without a shower or bath. This is the first time since then that I felt warm. And I miss the smell of soap."

Christina saw tears in Ari's eyes as Ari held herself and slid down the tiled wall. Christina knew that every person had a breaking point. Jim and Alexa showed no emotion to Ari about her return; no doubt it added to her friend's stress. "Ari, don't fall apart now. We need you."

"I'll be fine. I just need a few minutes," Ari said, getting up to lather her hair.

Christina dried off and moved into the dressing area. By the time she put her shoes on, Ari had dried off and dressed herself. For the first time since she worked under Jesse, Christina saw the extent of the injuries Ari had received over the years. Even though Ari's scars had faded and were barely noticeable, Christina's trained eye followed some of the more serious-looking wounds. Ari's back and shoulders bore the most marks, many of them crisscrossed and overlapping on her skin.

Ari looked in a mirror. She looked pale, and her overgrown hair covered her eyes. Her clothes hung on her from her weight loss.

The two girls walked out, and Silas and Josh walked past them into the bathroom. Ari and Christina spent the rest of the time before the meeting, praying.

CHAPTER TWENTY-ONE

The common area began to fill up. Someone had swept the floor, clearing it of broken glass and debris. Incredibly, the dining room table remained unscathed. Some of the chairs and furniture around it were broken or missing. When the coast was clear, Conrad returned to the kitchen. He had evacuated to one of the lower levels along with Jesse when the Nephilim broke inside. He fixed the group a simple breakfast of oatmeal, bacon, and scrambled eggs, setting up the pots and pans like a buffet.

Ari scooped a spoonful of oatmeal into a bowl and added a sprinkle of brown sugar and raisins. She knew the richer foods would make her sick if she didn't slowly work back to them. She scooped a small spoonful of scrambled eggs into the side of her bowl. Ari looked up from the buffet. Her longtime friend Conrad greeted and hugged her. "I thought I would never see your face again, girl."

Ari continued to hug her friend. "I know, I'm glad to see you too."

The foursome moved to sit down when several Outriders next to them got up and moved to another section of the dining room table.

The group ignored the cold-shoulder treatment as they blessed their food and ate. When they had finished eating, the trio moved towards the front of the table, where Jim and Dave talked. Jim quieted everyone down and handed the floor to Ari.

Ari stepped up to the front and looked out to the faces. Most looked at her with indifference. *I can do all things through Christ who strengthens me.* "Good morning. For those that don't know me, my name is Ari. To my right are Silas and Christina, who have been travelling with me for the past few years. We have been in several battles with the Nephilim, and as you can see, so far we are still alive. They are near to impossible to kill without the proper weapons."

Ari continued. "Unfortunately, your previous leaders didn't think you needed to be trained before you engaged the Nephilim, and you saw the results last night. We don't have time to train you with these weapons, but we can take advantage of your current strengths and use them to our advantage."

Ari continued, "In a moment, Dave will break up the group according to those who can sharpshoot and those who can handle hand blades. The first group will be part of the front line. Our job will be to take out as many Nephilim eyes as we can. The blade won't kill them, but they can't kill what they can't see. After the meeting, we will need to build a series of barricades on the back lawn."

"The Nephilim have weapons too—longswords, bows and arrows, and spears, and they can shoot and throw them a surprising distance. The barriers will not only protect you from their onslaught but also will slow them down should we have to retreat."

Ari turned her gaze at Silas as she continued with her plan. "The second group will accompany Silas to where we found a large stockpile of these weapons. You will bring back as many of the weapons as you can carry. Make sure to bring back as many of the daggers and quivers of arrows as you can. During the battle, if the first group retreats, your job will be to stop the giants with these," Ari said as she flipped her dagger, making it stick in the wooden table.

Ari then looked at the back of the room. "Jesse, Conrad, and Isaac—I will leave you in charge of the logistics inside—you need to set up a safehouse somewhere on the training floor or in the security block levels. Have the overseers and those that don't feel comfortable in the first two groups help you move supplies down there. These floors are only accessible by their elevator shafts and are too narrow for the Nephilim to make their way down. These floors will be our fallback position should things go terribly bad. Make sure to have enough medical supplies and provisions to last everyone for several days. Have a few of the Outriders help you fashion ladders or climbing ropes for the elevator shafts."

Ari pointed to herself, Silas, and Christina. "The three of us will be mingled among the first two groups, fighting alongside all of you to keep the Nephilim off you. If you see me aim an arrow at you, duck. That means there's a giant about to clobber you. Any questions?"

"Do you think we really have a chance against these things?" one of the younger Outriders asked.

"Yes, I do. If our God is for us, who can be against? Everyone meet back here for dinner at 4:00. We'll give further instructions at that point. May God bless you and all that you put your hands to."

The group congregated around Dave for their assignments. Ari walked over to Silas, slipped the ring of Halcyon off, and handed it to him. "I hope this works without my finger. When you get back, I need you and your team to help make the barriers on the lawn. Both the outer and inner perimeters will have staggered walls allowing our people to be able to slip through easily. Also, we probably need to have another wall of sandbags against where the windows were located, to protect those that are inside the house."

Sarah stormed up to Ari. "Why did you pull the men off digging for survivors on the east wing?"

"If we don't prepare for their next attack a few hours from now, there won't be any survivors to dig out anyone," Ari said as she pointed at someone and flagged them to come to her.

"That's ridiculous," Sarah said, "I'm digging them out myself."

"Sarah, I need for you to be part of the team. Your hand blade skills are better than most," Ari explained.

Sarah appealed to Jim. "Jim, please send help to dig out the overseers." Tears began to flow down her cheeks. "My mother is one of those who is trapped."

Jim looked confused. "Mother? You never told me your mother was a member of the Old Guard. Who is it?"

"Petra. My mom is Petra." Sarah sobbed. "Please . . ."

"Ari," Jim said, "we may be able to utilize some of the overseers who are not in the battle lines, at least until the med ward requires our assistance."

Ari's face wore an expression of hurt and humiliation. *All this time . . . the pieces are falling together and this all makes sense now.* Ari subtly nodded, then walked away. She shook her head to clear her mind of the distraction as she turned to talk to Josh. "I prayed about this, and at first I questioned God whether you were the right choice."

Josh looked confused. "Right choice for what?"

Ari put her arm around Josh's shoulder. "It is a personal favor. I had an opportunity to look over the group assignments before the meeting, and I noticed both you and Alexa are in the group of sharpshooters. I'm going to be all over the place, trying to make sure everyone is where they should be and not about to be killed. I can't be worrying about Alexa; I have to keep focused on everything else. If you can please . . ."

Josh held a hand up. "Say no more, Ari, ma'am. I have her back. I promise nothing will hurt her."

"I don't know if you should make a promise like that. Just watch her back, and hands off," Ari said.

"Are you kidding? I've seen what you can do with a dagger and arrow. I wouldn't dream of it." Josh chuckled nervously.

"Thanks."

Ari looked over to Dave, who had just finished giving out the assignments. Ari snuck up on Christina and bumped her friend with her shoulder. Christina looked at Ari, confused. Ari nudged her head towards Dave, then bumped her shoulder into Christina again. Christina smiled, tears welling up in her eyes. She hugged Ari before tapping her husband on the shoulder then holding his hand.

Dave looked at Ari, as if to ask for permission. Ari smiled and nudged her head toward their sleeping quarters. She nodded to make sure he knew all was well. Christina held Dave's hand tight, leading him through the crowded floor. Passing Ari, Dave threw her the clipboard with the assignments. His head disappeared downstairs, his waving hand the last thing that Ari saw before he turned the corner.

Late that afternoon, the group gathered again. Dressed in a black leather jacket, Ari stood on a chair to get everyone's attention when the last of the Outriders had finished eating. Dave whistled through his fingers and the room's eyes fell on Ari. "Everyone has been paired off. Be very aware of your buddy, and also be aware of the person to the other side of you. Both people should always be in your peripheral vision. If you get injured, your partner is responsible for getting you to the secondary line and to help. No one, and I mean no one, gets forgotten, is that clear?

"During battle, things are going to feel like they are chaotic. Just remember that God isn't causing the chaos and confusion. Ask God for guidance if you don't know where or what you should do next. If you see glow sticks shot over your head, retreat to the next rear position. Never have your back against the enemy, even when retreating. If you have retreated into the house, don't talk unless you have to. Listen for instructions as to what to do next. Sharpshooters—make sure to grab a gear bag from Silas and one from each pile on the right. Group two, grab a gear bag from Christina and two from each pile. We will try our best to keep you supplied."

"The Bible says, *'Today you are going into battle against your enemies. Do not be fainthearted or afraid; do not panic or be terrified by them. For the LORD your God is the one who goes with you to fight for you against your enemies to give you victory.'*

Jim stepped forward. "Everyone, let's pray." Every head in the room bowed; some of the younger men removed their baseball caps. "Dear Lord, we ask that Your mighty hand be with us tonight as we fight Your people's enemy. Give us the strength, might, and wisdom to defeat them. Have Your angels surround us and guide us, keeping us safe from harm. We give You all the honor and glory in Your Holy name, amen."

Ari hopped off the chair, retreated to the corner of the room by the fireplace, and stashed her armaments. As Silas and Christina gave her last-minute status reports, she suited up into the breastplate and matching back plate, cinching the leather straps on the sides. As she did so, the metal began to transform its shape to Ari's. The plate appeared to be made from the same metal as the ancient weapons, only she noticed that the plate was more flexible, allowing her to bend over and twist.

Christina and Silas were already suited up in the special armor. Ari continued by slipping the strap of two quivers of arrows over her head, and then a special sheath that held five of the daggers on her right thigh, allowing her to throw the weapons with little effort. Her left thigh held a sai. She finished her look with a black baseball cap she had borrowed. Ari turned it around backwards, preventing her hair from blowing in her face.

Silas was dressed similarly, also wearing a breastplate but he donned a longsword and its sheath strapped to his back. He also carried daggers on his left thigh and a blade gun and extra clips under his arm and around his belt. Christina also carried a bow and two quivers of arrows, along with the daggers and sais.

Ari admired the shape of Christina's breastplate. "Christina, did anyone tell you that you're shaped like a model?"

The tall blonde blushed. "Really? I thought the shiny gold color made me look fat."

"Just remember, guys—this armor won't protect you from everything. Just like our arrows and spears, their arrows and spears can still pierce the metal, given the force is great enough. Take one of these," Ari said as she handed each a rectangular shield made of the same metal. "Since we are going to do a lot of moving between the lines, these might come in handy. We have twenty-eight Outriders in the front line and fourteen in the secondary line. Dave and several other overseers will be assisting between the lines."

There was still a half hour before the sun would set. Ari and her friends walked the front lines, offering last minute encouragement. Silas told jokes to ease the tension. Staggered sandbag walls lay about ten feet from the edges of the ravine, and the secondary line was laid immediately behind the pool in the center of the yard.

Ari and Christina climbed ladders and out onto the roofline of the house. A small sandbag barrier was laid out directly above the entrance to the house. Extra quivers propped up against the sandbags. From their vantage point, they could get any Nephilim that came up from the ravine to the first line of barriers. Ari looked at Christina. "Now all we have to do is wait."

The moment the sun set behind the ridgeline, Ari sensed movement even though there was still light in the sky. "Get ready! They're on the move, everyone!

As the twilight grew darker, the first attack that evening engaged everyone in Hollywood. A volley of arrows flew up from the ravine. Ari yelled, "Incoming arrows overhead!" The Outriders huddled under shields as the dozens of arrows arched down onto the lawn. A second volley of arrows followed. Shortly after a third volley, the first of the Nephilim appeared at the edge of the lawn, crawling out of the ravine.

Ari and Christina purposely aimed for the closest threats. Their arrows pierced the seemingly impenetrable scales on the Nephilim. The first group of Outriders began to shoot their blades. One by one the Nephilim fell back into the ravine, only to be replaced by others. After only fifteen minutes, the assault stopped. The lines of Outriders on the lawn looked up at Ari. "Keep looking forward. Stay in your positions. They are planning a different line of attack."

No sooner than Ari commanded everyone to hold their ground, the second wave of the attack began. This time, the attack concentrated just off center, directly aligned with the back door's position. As this position was out of range for many of the Outriders, some began to move closer to help. "Keep your position!" Ari yelled. She and Christina did their best to kill as many as they could. The giants were literally climbing over each other to get to higher ground. At any given time there were at least six Nephilim all attacking the same forward position.

Ari yelled, "Dan and Katy—fall back!" The two positions closest to the assault were soon overwhelmed. Silas ran forward and engaged the Nephilim at the next most vulnerable position, and several overseers supported the other side. The Nephilim had effectively broken through the first line of defense, and Ari knew that they would then try to split their forward line in half, spreading their attacking wedge of fighters out as they continued to try to advance.

Several Nephilim broke through and made a run for the house. Ari and Christina were able to stop them. As more slipped through, the second line effectively stopped them before they could make it to the pool. As more Nephilim got footing on the lawn, Ari and Christina's position was assaulted by spears and arrows. As the fighting intensified, Ari could hear screams of pain—not only the otherworldly sounding Nephilim but also human screams.

The two friends huddled behind the sandbags. "Now what?" Christina asked. "We're cornered."

"We need to be able to take out their shooters," Ari said. Ari readied her bow. She popped up over the barrier and took out one of the marksman. She hid behind the sandbags again to string another arrow. Ari and Christina did this several times before Ari realized she needed to have the first line retreat.

Breaking a couple of glow sticks, Ari shook them vigorously and then tied them to an arrow. She shot the arrow into the air, followed by another. The first line began their retreat as Ari and Christina and the second line offered fire cover as best as they could.

Suddenly Ari heard a muffled cry. She gasped as she saw Christina tumble over the edge of the barrier and roof to the ground below. "CHRISTINA!" Ari strapped the remaining quivers and a shield to her back and jumped down. She could hear the shield repel arrows and spears as she bent over her friend. Ari quickly removed an arrow from the side of Christina's throat and applied pressure. The projectile had missed her trachea and artery. *Thank you Jesus. Your mercy and grace amaze me.*

An overseer ran out and carried Christina inside while Ari fended off arrows and spears with her shield. She turned around and fired arrows into the assaulting Nephilim with renewed resolve. When she crept close enough, Ari grabbed a longsword and ran to the front line to help Silas. *Lord, according to Acts and Ephesians, we already have Your supernatural dunamis power. Let Your power and glory reign here on earth as it does in heaven. Show these Nephilim who is victorious!* Ari's sword slashed, cutting the coils that threatened to trap Silas.

She raised her sword as it clashed with another giant's sword. Sparks flew. As strong as Ari was, she was no match for the Nephilim's size and muscle. The giant bore his sword down toward Ari. Ari kicked her assailant back and swung. The golden swords clashed again. Ari's sword grew brighter with each contact, glowing as if being heated in a furnace. Her sword met the creature's one last time. Ari's sword burst into flames; the impact of the contact sent a brilliant shockwave out into the ravine.

The Nephilim closest to Ari and her sword vaporized. Further into the ravine, Silas could hear otherworldly wails and cries. The battle was over. Ari moved to the edge of the lawn and looked into the ravine. Silas walked up behind her.

"How in the . . . Ari, how did your sword do that?" Silas asked.

Ari shook her head. "I don't know. I declared dunamis power over our Outriders."

A small celebratory cheer began, but Ari held her hand up, quieting everyone. "Silas, grab a couple of strong guys and follow me." Ari handed her sword to one of the men and strung her bow again. "Take care of any Nephilim on the lawn right now. At first light, we'll need to crawl down into the ravine. For now, quietly bring the injured Outriders inside the house. We'll triage the injured in the hallway. We need to gather our dead and lay them out respectfully and make sure they are covered." Silas nodded and pointed to two men.

Before climbing back onto the roof, Ari scanned the surviving Outriders for her daughter. She saw her talking with Josh, apparently retelling the story of the one that almost got them. Once up on the roof, Ari held her bow with an arrow at the ready, pointed down as she scanned the battleground for any threatening activity. As the sky grew lighter, Ari knelt and bowed her head. *"Thank you, Jesus. I give You all the honor and glory. This victory would not have been possible without You."* She jumped down, joining Silas. She addressed the fighters. "If you're injured, please report to Jesse. Otherwise, you're dismissed. Get some rest. You deserve it. Well done, everyone."

Ari joined Silas as he finished decapitating the injured Nephilim on the lawn. He and Ari made their way into the ravine, joined by two Outriders. The scrub made their progress slow. Ari could see at least a couple of dozen Nephilim in various states of injury, all abandoned by their counterparts as they retreated. The trio ended the Nephilim's suffering by offering clean sword strikes to their necks.

Unknown to Ari and the men, Alexa gave Josh the slip, losing him in the mass entry back into Hollywood. She followed the small group into the ravine. Several dozen yards behind them, she stumbled across what appeared to be a nearly dead Nephilim. The creature had somehow removed a dagger or arrow from its chest and lay barely breathing and apparently unconscious. Alexa removed one of her daggers from its sheath and bent over to slice its throat open. Alexa raised the edge to the giant's throat. Still holding the dagger in his hand, the injured Nephilim plunged his dagger deep into Alexa's chest.

Ari and the team heard a short cry from behind them and moved quickly up the slope. Ari reached the scene first, shooting the Nephilim between its eyes, killing it instantly. Ari could see blood and something slender protruding out of Alexa's back. She ran up to Alexa as she collapsed to the ground. Ari quickly pulled the dagger out and applied pressure to both wounds. Alexa's precious blood continued to flow between Ari's fingers. "Silas! Over here!"

Silas turned to one of the men. "Go get help, quickly!" The young man scrambled up the hill. "Here," Silas offered as he pulled out two bandages from the pockets in his jacket. He ripped the packaging off one and handed it to Ari.

Ari pressed it against Alexa's chest wound, and the young lady groaned. Blood trickled from the corner of her mouth. Silas applied the second bandage to her back. "Alexa, stay awake. Focus on this strange-looking man to my left," Ari told her daughter as she pointed to Silas.

Silas contorted his features into a funny face, making Alexa smile. She tried to laugh, but coughed blood up instead. Alexa focused on her mom's face for the first time in years. Her eyes watered before she stopped breathing, still staring at Ari for help.

"No, I refuse to believe that you are dead, Alexa." Ari said, tears staining her cheeks. "God breathed life into you. I am not going to allow the enemy to steal what God has given you. You are still alive, do you hear me?" Ari held her limp hand. "You are just sleeping, but it's time to wake up right now. *TALITHA KOUM!* Little girl, I say to you, *get up!*"

Refusing to believe the daughter she had not seen for over fourteen years died in her arms, Ari repeated this several times. Suddenly Alexa grabbed Ari's hand and sat straight up. She coughed out a black mass of blood and began to breathe. The young Outrider looked at Ari and Silas before grasping her chest. Ari removed the bandages. Other than a bloody hole in the shirt, there was no sign of trauma to Alexa.

"What did you do? How?" Alexa asked.

Silas stumbled and sat on a large rock. "That's twice now that I've seen you do that, Ari."

A group of Outriders scrambled down the hill. Ari waved them off. "She's fine now, guys. She may need a bit of assistance up the hill, but she's fine."

Dave reached out to Alexa to help her up. He then reached out to Ari, but she waved him off. "I don't think I can stand, not yet. Besides, we have to finish our job down here. We'll be up in less than an hour." Ari looked at her hands. They were stained up to her elbows in Alexa's blood. Fresh tears flowed from her eyes as she closed them. She thanked God and gave Him praise that she could never come close to matching in the mercy He just gave her. After a few minutes, Ari got up and joined the men.

◆

Later that morning, Ari checked on her friend and daughter in the med ward area. A dozen Outriders lay in the hallway leading to the med ward. Christina was sitting up, holding Dave's hand. Their foreheads touched as they quietly talked to each other. Ari turned and saw Alexa on a gurney in the med ward. She was alert and trying to talk Jesse out of keeping her there overnight for observation.

Jim looked up from the bedside and walked over to Ari. "Thanks."

"No problem. After all, she's my daughter too."

"Technically, no," a voice told her from the doorway. Sarah had her arms crossed. "After your supposed death and Jim and I married, I adopted her. You have no legal rights to her. Jim and I have a request for you to keep your distance from my family. It is signed and approved by the council." Sarah tossed an envelope at Ari. "If you come any closer than ten feet to any one of us, I can have you thrown into the security block."

Ari gritted her teeth and walked out. She turned, addressing her comment to Jim. "I have a meeting with the war room leadership at three this afternoon. But since we can't even be in the same room with each other, I will have Dave relay to you what we discussed."

Ari turned and walked briskly down the hall. As she passed Dave, she said, "I'll see you for a war room meeting at three."

I can't have emotions cloud my judgment. Not right now. Ari sat down next to Silas at the dining room table. She began to unhook the leather straps holding her breastplate and back plates in place. Slipping out of her armor, she unzipped her jacket and plopped down into a chair. "What's the damage?" she asked Silas.

"Thirty-one in all. We lost twenty in the chaos from the first night, not including the five overseers who were killed in the collapsed wing of the house. Today six were killed: four from the front line and two from the secondary line. We have fourteen with injuries; all but three are serious enough they will be out of action for the next couple of days."

Ari looked at Silas and said, "Eventually we will have to face the entire Nephilim nation. There are hundreds. They will be pouring over the land like water over a waterfall. For now, we're okay. It will take them months or years to regroup. In the meantime we will have to consider evacuating. We need to find a suitable location that is remote enough where people won't end up being a side casualty. We'll discuss all of this at the war room meeting at three. Right now, I need to ask a favor . . ."

Ari grabbed her gear and knocked on the door of her old bedroom suite. Jim answered the door. "Yes? Can't this wait until later?"

"Silas, Christina, and I feel that it can't, sir. We ask that you call the council together so that there isn't any conflict of interest, sir," Ari told her former husband.

"Uh, okay. Give me a half hour and we'll meet you in the council chamber."

Ari and Christina sat patiently on a bench just outside of the council chamber. Silas and Josh stood, leaning up against the wall. The council filed past them, entering the room. Jim held his arm out, allowing the four exiles into the room, before he stepped in and closed the door behind him.

An hour later, Sarah strode into the chamber and stood in front of Jim. "What is the meaning of all this?"

"Please have a seat, Sarah," Aaron told the Outrider. The faces of the council were solemn. As Sarah made her way back to the chair, she noticed the four exiles casually lined up against the side wall.

Aaron stepped from behind the table and approached Sarah. "First off, we all would like to give you our condolences on the death of your mother, Petra. Our prayers are with you and your family."

"Thank you, sir." Sarah's eyes teared up as she rubbed her mom's cross pendant in her fingers.

"Now for the reason why we called you here, Sarah. We have positively identified the following blades as coming from your gun."

Sarah shifted in her seat. "Yes, I'm sure there are a lot of blades that have come from my gun."

"We also have a witness who has testified you coerced him to join you in skipping out on your Outrider assignment this past September

5. This despite your assignment's record, which stated the assignment as completed with injury to yourself and the death of Josh from a demonic attack. Your evening of hooky took place in the Japanese town where you literally ran into Ariana and Sam. After cornering Sam, you tried to coerce Josh to kill him. For no known reason, you wished to kill an outstanding member of our organization and one of our overseers, Sam Williams. When Josh refused, you carried out the deed, despite alleged pleas from the victim," Aaron continued.

Sarah glared at Josh, but didn't say a word in response.

"Shortly thereafter, you cornered Ariana, where you shot her once in the abdomen. The shot did not kill her, so you could tell her about everything that she lost."

Sarah remained silent, her jaw clenched as her internal anger began to rise.

"These blades were pulled from Sam's body and from Ariana," Aaron continued. He sat on the edge of the table and threw his glasses onto the surface.

"Sarah Sommers, you are charged with one count of murder, one count of attempted murder, falsifying your assignment documents, lying to the council, and one count of conspiring with the Tempest. You are an embarrassment to our organization and to those who hold our duty to serve God very seriously."

"Conspiring with the Tempest? How did you come up with that charge? Even if it were true, you would never be able to prove it." Sarah sat back confidently in her chair and grinned.

"Not completely true, Sarah," Ari said, speaking up. "I don't know if you thought I was dead or just dense, but you clearly laughed at me and said, and I quote: *I can see why Kane calls you a cockroach.* The only people who knew that nickname for me are all Tempest associates of his." You obviously have hung around enough with him to know this because you were not even part of the Old Guard when I had my last encounter with him. I never noticed until that fateful night, but the cross you wear around your neck matches not only your mother's but also your father Amon's."

Sarah bolted from her seat and attempted to pull her blade gun out to shoot Ari and, if given the chance, Josh. Her gun barely made it out of its holster before several blades struck her shoulder. Her gun fell to the ground, and Sarah cried out in pain,unable to move her arm.

The only person who didn't have her weapon drawn was Ari. She wanted to make sure that the council knew she didn't harm Sarah.

Silas asked, "How did you know about the connection between the necklaces?

"I saw Petra with one and a picture of Amon with a cross. The cross looked familiar, but I couldn't place it until that night in the alley."

Jim sat in his chair, apparently shell-shocked at the accusations. Ari approached him from the other side of the table. "I'm sorry, sir." Ari turned and removed both the cross from around Sarah's neck and the one she held from Petra.

"Come with me," Ari said as she passed Silas. The two transported to a seaside village on the French Mediterranean coast, Villefranche-sur-Mer. Ari approached a portly man sitting alone as he sipped his wine. She sat down opposite of him, making the man almost choke on his drink.

"I like the remodeling you've done at the organization's headquarters. I think you've invented a new fashion style: Post-Nephilim."

Amon began to reach for something, and Ari stopped him. "I wouldn't, at least not in this crowded café. Too many witnesses. And I have someone with their gun trained on you, should anything happen to me."

"Why, Ariana, you look like a piece of refuse at a garbage dump, literally," Amon scoffed as he eyed Ari from head to toe. Still wearing the bloodied and soiled clothing from the battle, Ari's appearance fit his description. "What a surprise. How did you find me?"

"I guessed. I knew this was one of your favorite restaurants. I take it several of you survived the Nephilim attack?"

"Is that what they're called? How did you know?"

"We just fought them, at least in this one battle."

"Is that what happened to you?"

Ari sipped his water. "Actually, yes, but we were somewhat prepared. Unfortunately, not all of us made it." Ari threw the bloodied necklaces on the table.

Amon's smile vanished. "What have you done with them?"

"Me? Nothing. During the initial attack by those giants, part of our building collapsed on Petra and several others, killing them almost instantly. Your daughter Sarah has been taken into custody for murder, attempted murder, and falsifying documents and testimony. It will be years, if ever, before she sees the sun again. But having a mole inside the Old Guard is the least of your worries right now."

"Why do you say that?" Amon asked.

"I found out quite by accident that the Nephilim don't like to leave their destruction incomplete. I'm here to warn you: They know several of you have survived and they will hunt you down, no matter where you are in this world."

Fear filled the eyes of her adversary. Ari got up. "I pray that your heart and ears be opened to Jesus and that you repent and make your life right before they find you." A loud crash of a tray startled Amon. He turned to see what caused the commotion. When he turned back, his adversary had vanished.

Ari finally made her way down to the bunk room. Several Outriders talked to Isaac, Christina, and Dave. "Christina, shouldn't you be in the med ward?" Ari asked.

"He released me," she said. Why don't you join us, Ari?" Christina asked.

"Maybe for a little bit, but in a few minutes. I want to get cleaned up." Ari grabbed her duffle and made her way to the shower. The hot water reinvigorated the tired Outrider. Ari sniffed the soap and shampoo as she lathered. She watched as trails of dirt and blood washed down the drain.

After getting dressed, she joined the growing group in the bunk room. Ari looked at the faces of her friends as she sat down on one of the bunks facing the others. The group retold each other what happened in the past night. For the first time in a long time, Ari began to relax. *Perhaps our lives can return to normal for a little while.*

Christina turned to Ari, still laughing. "Ari, remember what Steve did when he pinned Silas against the wall with the daggers?" The room erupted in laughter as Christina attempted to look like a scarecrow with her good arm hanging from the elbow.

Suddenly Christina's smile vaporized, as did the laughter in the room. Ari turned around to see where the attention focused behind her. Jim stood at the doorway of the bunk room. He gave a sheepish wave to everyone. "Hi. May I join you?"

Eyes suddenly shifted to Ari. She reached into her duffle and pulled something out. "Sure. You can have my seat." She abruptly got up and left the bunk room.

"You don't have to," Jim told her.

"As long as your family has that paper telling me I have to keep my distance, I do," Ari said.

"Nobody will do anything," Jim argued.

"Sir, with all due respect," Ari cut him off. "You will not be the one who has the pleasure of a return trip to the security block because someone violated this order." Ari abruptly turned and left the room.

She moved to the end of the hall by the elevators and sat at one of the tables. Ari unraveled her earbuds and tried to turn her personal music player on. After an attempt of tapping the side of it and pressing a few buttons to get it to work, she slammed it onto the tabletop, frustrated. She buried her hands into her damp hair, not knowing what else to do.

"Ari," the familiar voice of Jim spoke to her from the other side of the hallway. He respected the distance he needed to keep in order to not to get her into any possible trouble. "I will have the restraining order against you dropped."

"Thanks," Ari replied.

"We never had a chance to talk since you came back. We thought you were dead. If I had known you were alive, I would have never remarried."

"I know," Ari replied again.

"Why didn't you come back sooner? Or try to get hold of us?" Jim asked.

"The situation was too dangerous. Isaac knew at least one mole existed. They were systematically eliminating his supporters from the Old Guard."

"Ari, you are one of the best Outriders. No one would have messed with you."

"That may have been true, but you and Alexa could have been targets because of your association with me." Ari paused for a moment. *Holy Spirit, please guide my words.* "Jim, I know what I put you through seemed terribly unfair. And now you've been dealt a blow with Sarah's deception. You have been through a lot of heart-wrenching events in the past day. I would be lying if I told you I didn't want you and Alexa back. But for me to take advantage of your situation would be to take advantage of you while you were vulnerable. I feel I need to give you a chance to decide what is best for you and Alexa. I will keep my distance from both you and Alexa until you can sort out what you want to do."

"So if I tell you that I don't want to get back together, you would be good with that?" he asked.

"I would honor that as best as I could," Ari admitted.

"And if I told you that I missed you and want us to be a couple again, but need to approach our reunion slowly?"

Ari swallowed to hide her enthusiasm of the prospective of getting back together with Jim. "I would honor that too, to the best of my ability."

Jim nodded. "Give me until tomorrow morning to pray about this." He began to walk away and stopped. "I'm glad you're okay, Ari. It's good to see you." He continued down the hall back into the bunk room.

For a moment longer, Ari sat on the bench and stared at the wall that Jim had just vacated. *And therefore I have hope.*

Exhausted, Ari pattered back to the bunk room. She passed the group and headed to her bunk in the far corner. Ari flopped down face first into her pillow. *Thank you, Jesus.* Despite the people and the noise in the room, she closed her eyes. Before she could finish another thought, God reached out and touched Ari. For the first time in a long time, Ari felt great peace settle into her heart. She fell asleep quickly, confident and secure, knowing God was still in control.

A SPECIAL NOTE FROM THE AUTHOR

I would be remiss in my calling as a Holy Spirit-filled Christian if I didn't at least talk to you about this. Has anyone ever told you God loves you, and He has a wonderful plan for your life? I have an important question to ask you, and all I ask is for you to be honest with yourself. If you were to die this very second, do you know for sure, beyond a shadow of a doubt, whether you would go to heaven?

The Holy Bible reads: *"For the wages of sin is death, but the gift of God is eternal life through Christ Jesus our Lord."* The Bible also says, *"Everyone who calls on the name of the LORD will be saved."* No one is excluded from this invitation, and everyone, including you, is always welcome to join.

I pray the Lord will bless you and your family with long and healthy lives. Jesus, make Yourself real to whomever reads this, and do a quick work in their heart. If they have not received Jesus Christ as their Lord and Savior, I pray they will do so now.

Dear Lord Jesus, I ask You come into their heart. Forgive us of our sins. Wash us and cleanse us. Set us free. Jesus, we thank You, for You're coming back again for us. Fill us with the Holy Spirit. Give us a passion for the lost, a hunger for the things of God, and a holy boldness to preach the gospel of Jesus Christ. We're saved, we're born again, and we're forgiven. We will never be the same again.

If you've accepted Jesus Christ as your Lord and Savior, all of your sins are forgiven. I ask you continue your walk by attending a Bible-based church in your area. Remember, He loves you and has a great plan for your life!

CPSIA information can be obtained at www.ICGtesting.com
Printed in the USA
LVOW04s1238220715

447173LV00003B/3/P